# Moon Over Tokyo

## SIRI L. MITCHELL

HARVEST HOUSE PUBLISHERS

EUGENE, OREGON

Published in association with the literary agency of Alive Communications, Inc., 7680 Goddard Street, Ste #200, Colorado Springs, CO 80920. www.alivecommunications.com.

Cover photos © iStockphoto

Cover by Garborg Design Works, Savage, Minnesota

**MOON OVER TOKYO**
Copyright © 2007 by Siri L. Mitchell
Published by Harvest House Publishers
Eugene, Oregon 97402
www.harvesthousepublishers.com

Library of Congress Cataloging-in-Publication Data
Mitchell, Siri L., 1969-
  Moon over Tokyo / Siri L. Mitchell.
    p. cm.
  ISBN-13: 978-0-7369-1759-9
  ISBN-10: 0-7369-1759-4
  1. Women journalists—Fiction. 2. Americans—Japan—Fiction. 3. Friendship—Fiction. 4. Tokyo (Japan)—Fiction. I. Title.
  PS3613.I866M66 2007
  813'.6—dc22
                                                                        2007002497

**Printed in the United States of America**

07  08  09  10  11  12  13  14  15  / LB-SK /  12  11  10  9  8  7  6  5  4  3  2  1

*To all those who find themselves in foreign places,*
*holding on to familiar dreams.*

# ACKNOWLEDGMENTS

To Carolyn McCready and Terry Glaspey, for your excitement about this project. To Beth Jusino, for wise advice. To Kim Moore, for polishing my words and sharing a fascination for Japan. To Lanna Dickinson, for challenging me to write just a little bit deeper. To Narelle Mollet, for correcting my Australian. To my friends at New Hope International Fellowship Tokyo. To Juliana Gittler of *Stars and Stripes* Pacific. And, as always, to Tony. Without you, I would have missed out on Japan.

*It is obscured, blocked.*
*Still, I know there must be a*
*moon over Tokyo.*

1

*Melancholia.*
*Summer's drifting clouds pass by.*
*I drift home again.*

HOW MANY OF US NOTICE THE INSTANT OUR LIVES CHANGE? The moment
we step out of "what has been" and into "what is to come"? I didn't.
But looking back, unraveling all that had happened before and everything that happened after, I think I can pinpoint the exact moment.
Surprisingly, it had nothing to do with Eric's coming and nothing to do
with Gina's leaving.

It had everything to do with me.

I remember folding my six-foot frame into a chair and nibbling on
a cookie I was pretty sure hadn't gone bad while I'd been on vacation.
I knew I'd probably live to regret it. But after a ten-hour plane ride, a
three-hour commute into Tokyo, and sixteen hours of jet lag, my stomach
wasn't listening to me anymore.

I'd gone home for vacation to celebrate my birthday and attend my
sister's wedding. My little sister's wedding. After having celebrated both
another birthday and the happiest day of my sister's life, my thoughts
were anything but joyous. They were waspish thoughts buzzing around
the question, what about me?

Both literally and figuratively.

My sister had embarked on a life I would soon have no claim to…

although I fully intended to insert myself into it from time to time. Being sad for me and happy for her was making a seesaw of my emotions. Facing my return to life as a journalist in Tokyo hadn't made it any easier. And the fact that I'd have to deal with Neil had made it even worse.

I never should have started dating Neil. I worked with him. He was a nice-looking guy. And I had total respect for him as a writer. I thought he was the best one at the paper. Several months before, I had come to the point in my life where I just wanted to be with someone, and he was the one who seemed like the most obvious candidate. But every time we'd gone out, our dates had degenerated into bull sessions about work or about our careers in general. It was like talking to a brother.

And then one night, we'd kissed.

I'd wanted to, so it wasn't as if he ambushed me or anything. It was inevitable. We'd been going out for two months, and it was time. But it was all wrong. Everything was out of sync. Our heads, our lips, our noses. It felt like kissing a really good friend. Which is what he was…and I hoped still would be.

*I hoped, I hoped.*

I liked kissing. Kissing could be one of the best things in the world. Or it could not. To me, it revealed the character of the relationship. I'd dated three really great kissers. But even then, something had always been lacking. And I had known it from the first kiss but stayed around too long just to figure out what it was.

None of them turned out to be worth the time or effort…and that's not counting all the average kissers I'd dated.

I just wished there were some other way for me to figure out where my relationships were going. Some other way than kissing. It was like baring the soul. I'll show you mine, you show me yours, and…oh, gee, sorry, never should have done that, can I take it back? Even I think it's rude. But when you know things aren't headed anywhere, it's always best to make a clean break.

After Neil, I'd decided not to kiss anyone anymore. At least not for an entire calendar year. It was too disappointing, and it had ruined too many good friendships. It was the first time I'd ever made a promise like that to myself, and I fully intended on keeping it.

So far, so good.

Besides, I'd been living by myself for a long time and someone else would have messed up my routines. I knew exactly what it took to get along with me: A pint of chocolate ice cream in the freezer, a steady supply of bananas, and a good book. Life didn't get any better than that. I just hoped Neil would understand.

I bit into another cookie, but it didn't feel right. They were supposed to be chocolate chip with extra crunch, but it sagged when I bit into it.

*Why am I here? What am I doing? Why can't my life be easy?*

Why? Because I was Allie O'Connor, and for some reason known only to God, I insisted on doing things the hard way.

I possessed one computer, one bilingual TV, a DVD player, a beat-up old car, and three suitcases into which I could fit everything else I owned. I lived in Tokyo, Japan, the most foreign city on earth, according to National Geographic's *Traveler Magazine*. I lived there because I was a reporter with the *Stars and Stripes* military newspaper.

What was I doing? Killing time until I was brave enough to stop talking about writing a book and actually do it. Writing a book was not just a before-I-turn-forty dream for me. It was a burden. A responsibility.

Why couldn't my life have been easy? Why couldn't I just have lived in the States where I could drive to the grocery store instead of walk, where I could speak the native language, and where I could drive on the right side of the road?

I had no idea.

Yes, I did.

I'd come to Japan because I'd felt guilty about writing everything else besides my book. So I'd decided to take the idea of book-writing seriously. If I were really supposed to write a book, I had decided I needed inspiration. With a capital "I."

At least I was practical about it. I knew I needed to live in a country where I could get by in English. I might have tried Australia, but it didn't seem quite exotic enough. I needed a literary culture. Something that would spark my creativity. Something unexpected. That's why I had decided on Japan.

The problem was that after I had found my job with *Stars and Stripes*, after I had sold most of what I owned and moved to Tokyo, after I'd settled into a hotel-like room at the U.S. military's Hardy Barracks, I realized what I was really looking for was the expected. I was looking for the Japan of my daydreams. The one decorated with bold strokes of red, white, and black. I wanted tea ceremonies, beautiful simplicity, and people who were polite to a fault. Houses that were gossamer constructions of rice paper, tile roofs, and thick logs. Kimonos and order and cleanliness. But by the time I arrived, the Japan of my daydreams had almost disappeared. I was about thirty years too late.

I contemplated the cruel realities of life as I ate two more cookies. When they were gone, my time for feeling sorry for myself was up. That was the rule. To steer myself away from depression, I started a mental list of things I could look forward to. As soon as I could scrape myself off the chair, I would call Gina. She'd probably come right over with her Australian accent and drag me out on some adventure. We'd take a trip to Hakone sometime that fall. Gina had made me promise to go with her before she left Tokyo and returned to Australia. For good.

And there was church. I loved my church. And I'd go the next afternoon. After service, I would catch up with my English-speaking friends. We were an odd mix of English teachers, college students, spouses of Japanese nationals, and working professionals who lived scattered across the Tokyo region. Living so far from each other and being so busy in our jobs, we were rarely able to meet outside of church, and therefore had few chances to build community. But on Sundays, I never felt like I'd connected until I'd talked to everyone.

And thinking about those church friends started me thinking about the impending gap in my social life, the one that would be a gaping hole once Gina left. I would need an all-the-time friend. A combination of my church friends and Gina. A friend who shared my faith and who I could talk to more often than just on Sundays. Someone I could share life with…and someone I wouldn't be tempted to start kissing.

So right there, sitting in the chair, I prayed for a friend.

I thought maybe I needed to be a little more specific so I prayed for a luxury: a friend who would live nearby and speak English. A friend who would make the coming year more fun than the previous one had been.

Did you catch that? That prayer? It wasn't very long and it wasn't really very thoughtful, but right there, that's when everything began to change.

## 2

*Cicadas' chatter,*
*screeching through the night,*
*keeps me company.*

THE NEXT MORNING, SUNDAY, I SLEPT IN UNTIL TEN. Thankfully, church didn't start until two. I got up and ransacked the communal kitchen's cupboards for something to eat. I'd left an opened box of cereal in the cabinets while I was on vacation, and it had already started growing fuzz. I threw it away and opened a new one. I crossed my fingers hoping the ultrahigh-temperature sterilized milk I'd bought before vacation would still be good.

It was.

I took the bowl back to my room and surfed the Internet while I ate. Then I got up and took a notebook from my messenger bag. I sat back down and took a new rollerball pen from a drawer. I always fiddled with plots for a novel in my notebook before committing them to a computer chip's memory. I worked in a loose outline form.

I put the pen to the paper and began to write.

*There was a girl.*

*There was a guy.*

I drew flowers along the margin of the notebook. Filled in the white spaces with swirls. Did there have to be a guy? Maybe there wasn't a guy. Maybe there was just a girl.

I picked up the pen and struck out *There was a guy.*

So now there was just a girl.

What was this girl's name?

Nothing makes me close a novel faster than a heroine with a pretentious name. Or a tricked-out name. Or a name with too much symbolism. I think ordinary people have a lot to offer, so I stick with ordinary names. Ann was a personal favorite. So was Meg.

On the paper I made a subpoint. Wrote *Ann*.

So what happened to Ann? What did Ann do? Maybe ordinary Ann had an extraordinary day. Maybe Ann woke up and decided to…move to Japan.

I put the pen down and sighed. All I could seem to write about was myself. And that wasn't a good sign. It reminded me of high school when I wrote to figure things out. Figure myself out. Writing had been an extension of my introspection.

I didn't want my novel to be a coming-of-age story, and I didn't want it to be veiled autobiography, either. I wanted it to be stylish and vivid. A stunning debut that probably would never get published because the chances of a first novel being picked up were miniscule. And even if it had a chance of getting picked up, I'd probably have to write a second one before a publisher would take me seriously. Even though I'd written hundreds, maybe even more than a thousand newspaper articles, books were different. And if I ever did manage to sell a book to a publisher, I'd still probably have to keep writing for a newspaper. Only one percent of writers make a living only by writing. And the simple, most terrifying truth was that most people who start writing a book never complete it.

Me included.

Usually, about 30,000 words in, I'd reread my manuscript, review what I knew about getting published, and decide the current project would never be able to defy the odds. And it didn't look as though I was going to do it that morning, either.

I put the pen down, closed the notebook, and decided to call Gina. She was always good at raising my spirits. I woke her up, but she accepted my apology on the condition that I take her out to lunch before church, fill her in on the wedding, and cough up my latest excuse for not writing.

"How did you know I'd been having trouble?"

"Well, you called me, didn't you? And I don't want a flimsy excuse like last time. It'll take you forty-five minutes to get here. A real writer would be able to think of something extraordinary, something really nutty. So get to work!" She hung up the phone before I could answer.

I showered and then rifled through my closet for something cool to wear to church. As in cucumber. I needed to be as close to naked as I could get without being indecent.

At least everything in my closet matched. An intrepid reporter needed clothes she could depend on. Clothes that would make her presentable to both a sergeant and a general. Everything was black, white, or clover-leaf green. And stylish.

I wasn't fashionable. I couldn't afford to be. Not in Japan.

To be fashionable in Tokyo was not to fight a single decisive battle in which one finally gained ownership of the perfect pair of jeans or designer purse. To be fashionable in Tokyo was to commit to a war of escalation. To not only invest in having the right clothes for the year, but also for the season and the month. I just didn't have the budget for it. One good thing about Japan: It made you figure out how to be comfortable with who you were because you couldn't afford to be anyone else.

If the lines of my wardrobe were simple, they were also sleek.

At least I liked to think so.

Being tall was part of my identity, so I tried to use it to my advantage. I was striving for long and lean. Trying to minimize my gawkiness and emphasize my gracefulness.

I hoped that one day I would succeed.

As long as I wasn't in motion, displaying my innate clumsiness, I could pretend to be anything I wanted. I knew I was lying to myself. Just because I was tall didn't mean I knew what I was doing or what I wanted or where I was going. Height was a curse. It made people look up to me. In more ways than one. But deep down I knew the truth. Inside me a short person was crying to be let out.

I gave up looking for something cool to wear and went into the bathroom to point a blow-dryer at my long auburn hair. Applied just enough heat to stop it from dripping. Then I ran a comb through its length and gathered it into a pony tail, twisting it into a bun at the nape of my neck.

I held my glasses up to the light to see how dirty they were.

Very.

I cleaned them and put them back on my nose. They were skinny black rectangular frames. I hadn't picked them because they were trendy. I'd bought them right after I'd returned from a deployment to Iraq because they were sturdy. I had a rimless pair when I'd been there and had grown tired of trying to coax the lenses back into the frames...un-frames... wires...every time they popped out.

I returned to my closet and pulled a green-and-white flowered skirt from its hanger. Found a skinny white polo shirt to go on top. It had the smallest of cap sleeves, which made it the coolest clean and ironed shirt I owned. By that time I was late.

My church was only about four miles from my apartment, but it had no parking—at least not any that could be had legally—so I took the subway. It was a thirty-minute trip each way with a five-minute walk at either end. And adding Gina to my route would add an extra fifteen minutes.

I looped my messenger bag around my neck as I left the building at a run. After skidding around the chain link fence by the gatehouse, I ran up the street to Nogizaka Station and waited at the corner for the light to turn. If the traffic had been less heavy, and there hadn't been a policeman standing right there, I would have taken my chances and jaywalked. As it was, I nearly got hit by a taxi when the lights were with me. I dove down into the station, bought a ticket, and fed it to the machine. It snatched the ticket from my fingers and then spit it out on the other side of the turnstile. By the time I reached the platform, I was sweating.

If I'd thought about it, I would have dropped a fan into my bag before leaving the house. I had at least a dozen at home. Instead of hawking magnets or pencils to advertise their services, Tokyo businesses were smart. They handed out fans in the summer and packets of tissue during other times of the year.

I closed my eyes and thought cool thoughts. Thoughts of the Northwest. Mount Hood with snow on top. Puget Sound with fog. The Olympic National Rainforest. I could almost feel the breeze. Did feel the breeze. Opened my eyes to find it was the train on the opposite side of the tracks pulling into the station.

When my train came, I rode it to Otemachi, where I switched lines and headed out past Ochanomizu to the end of the line at Ikebukuro.

I left the train and let the turnstile devour my ticket. Above ground, as I walked through the neighborhood, I could hear the relentless screeching and clicking of cicadas. The first time I heard them when I'd arrived in Tokyo, I thought someone was broadcasting an Internet dial-up over a sound system. As if that weren't loud enough, a backup group composed of a hundred other insects scratched, rubbed, grated, and talked. I'd never actually seen any of the bugs making those sounds. If I did, if

I ever saw them all together at the same time, I knew I'd go insane. I tried—daily—not to think about it.

I walked several minutes and turned several corners before arriving at Gina's building. I went inside and buzzed her. She clicked me in without interrogation. I slipped through the door and waited for the elevator. It was as stuffy and humid inside as it was outside. The unique scent of Japan coated the walls: smells of yeasty miso soup, fish, and fried food.

Gina opened her door when I knocked and then stood aside to let me enter. Her apartment was tiny, both long and narrow. A small kitchen area had been carved out of the space by the door, a bed sat at the other end of the room, and the rest of her life had been arranged in between. I sat on her bed while she changed from her boxer shorts. I saw a cockroach climbing the wall, shielding its ascent behind the room's only chair.

"Cockroach. Over there on the wall." I pointed.

"Nasty buggers!" She took a rubber band from the kitchen counter. Looped it around her left pointer finger and drew it back along her forearm. Closed an eye. Took aim. Stopped. Opened the eye and turned her head to look at me. "Are you going to help or not?"

I sighed. Then I slid off the bed, removed one of my shoes, and crept toward the chair.

Gina resighted along the rubber band, drew it back to her elbow, and then let it fly. It hit the cockroach square on the back.

Stunned, the roach fell to the floor.

I hit it with my shoe, left the shoe on the floor and jumped on top of it for good measure. I hate cockroaches. They are an atheist's only irrefutable theological argument. If there really was a loving God, then why would he create such a nasty insect?

We ate at the neighborhood Tully's as I told her about the wedding.

"And how were the parents?"

I shrugged.

"Civil?"

"They tried to be." My parents had filed for divorce the summer I graduated from high school. It hadn't been a huge surprise. They'd always had politics in common, but they didn't have anything else...except my sister and me. And in the end, we hadn't been enough. When I got married, if I ever got married, I'd long ago decided to give my marriage the best odds possible. I planned to have politics and everything else in common with my husband.

"Why can't people just be happy? I can have a ton of fun with my mom, with my dad, and with my sister, but we don't have any fun anymore when we're all together. It's really hard to go home. They want me to move to Oregon, but then my heart would be divided in two."

"Well, when you need a shoulder to cry on, don't come to me. At least you have a sister." Gina was an only child who was sure she'd missed out on half of life because she never had a sibling. She figured her life would have been perfect if she'd had a sister, so she didn't like hearing the truth. "Ask me how teaching was while you were gone."

I asked and she filled me in on her most recent teaching mishaps. I managed to avoid talking to her about my writing, but only because I had to dash off to church. "Sure you don't want to come?"

"To church? Me?"

"God loves everybody."

"Yeah. And that's one of my biggest complaints. How can he love murderers and rapists and fraudsters? And if he does, then why should I care that he loves me?"

"See, this is what comes from being an only child. You want all the love for yourself. Don't want to share with anybody."

"I'm serious."

"No, you're not. You're just grumpy because I woke you up. Call me this week. Bye."

I hopped back on the subway, got off at Ochanomizu, and ran up the stairs into daylight. My pace slowed as I crossed the bridge squatting over the river. I'd only been out of town two weekends, but it had seemed like two years. I noted nothing had changed in my absence except the plants underneath the bridge, loitering along the river.

They were bigger. Greener. Meaner.

Tokyo was in the sub-tropics, but you wouldn't know it until summer. It was almost menacing how green everything became. How fast plants grew. How things that looked dead during the winter suddenly sprang to life and tendrilled out to consume the world.

Once over the river, I passed the Japanese Rail station. A jackbooted nationalist political party was still broadcasting their messages in front of the entrance. The throngs on the sidewalks were still accessorizing with

Starbucks cups. This time of year, succumbing to Frappuccino mania, the cups were see-through plastic, spiked with green straws.

I waited at the intersection for the light to change.

At major intersections in Tokyo, instead of having to cross twice in perpendicular directions, the lights stopped traffic in all directions so pedestrians could cross at any angle they wished.

I went diagonal.

Half a block down the street, I turned into the Ochanomizu Christian Center. I rode the elevator to the eighth floor, got off, and stepped right into Hawaii.

At least it felt that way.

The Japanese love Hawaii. When they think of paradise, they don't think of clouds, angels, and harps. They think of palm trees, hula dancers, and ukuleles.

My church was a branch of a parent church in Oahu, so the Hawaiian theme was overt. And fun. The greeters wore flowery shirts and leis. Church information cards were stored in a hollow coconut shell, and resource tables were draped with Hawaiian fabrics. As I walked away from the elevator, a greeter—my favorite one—smiled at me. She wrote my name tag, dotting my *i* with a smiley face, and then gave it to me. I stuck it on my shirt, pulled open the door to the auditorium, and slid inside.

People were already on their feet singing. I hoped I hadn't missed much because the music was one of my favorite parts. The band was excellent; most of the members were professional musicians. We sang three songs, alternating between English and Japanese, before the sermon began. The pastor spoke in English, and his wife provided the Japanese translation. It made for a long service, but you would never have caught me complaining. The church was eighty percent Japanese, so they were doing me a huge favor.

Afterward, it was my friend Julie who pointed out the new guy. New guys—or girls—were rare in July. Most expatriates stayed as far away from Japan as they could in the summer. They either took vacation or flew back to their native countries on home leave. New people usually started appearing at the end of August.

"Which one?" It was hard to see in the auditorium because the lights were so dim.

"The tall handsome one. The one talking to Yoshi-san. Said he just started working at the embassy."

I felt my eyebrows lift. Our church wasn't the social church in Tokyo. There were about five English-speaking churches in the city, and they all fulfilled different purposes. We didn't have any members from any of the embassies that I knew of. And in a church of two hundred, I would have known. "Has he been here before?"

"No. This is his first Sunday."

"I guess he speaks Japanese…" Only a Japanese speaker could have gotten Yoshi-san to laugh and then begin talking so fast his head looked as if it were going to nod right off his body. "I'll go over and say hi." I always tried to meet the new people. Mostly because I knew how lonely it could be to live in a foreign country. And I always hoped one of them would end up living near me, in Roppongi or Hiroo.

You can take the girl out of the suburb, but you can't take the suburb out of the girl.

I went over and stood behind the newcomer, waiting for a break in the conversation. The new guy was tall. As tall as I was. He had thick blond hair, but he felt Japanese. Maybe because he was wearing dark, skinny pants, and a snug knit shirt? No…it was something in the way he was standing. Seeing him nod and hearing him say, *"So, so, so desu"* only strengthened the impression.

Yoshi-san must have been telling a joke because he kept talking and talking, all the while his eyes twinkling. Then he paused for a moment and began to laugh.

The new guy did too. And as he did, he turned slightly. He must have picked me up in his peripheral vision because he turned fully toward me.

I gasped.

He stopped laughing.

"Eric?"

"Allie?"

## 3

*Chance encounters drop*
*me in unknown places like*
*the wind twirling straw.*

PICTURE YOUR NEMESIS FROM HIGH SCHOOL. Remember all the feelings seeing that person used to evoke. Now think about what you'd do if you ever ran into that person again.

You probably wouldn't.

Because I didn't.

I ran into Eric Larsen in the middle of Tokyo, and I didn't punch his lights out, I didn't lecture him on the irresponsibility of the machinations of capitalism, and I didn't run the entire contents of his briefcase through the nearest shredder.

I smiled.

And then I started to laugh.

What else was there to do? I could have thought of dozens of people I would have liked to have seen at my church in Tokyo, and at the very bottom of the list, Eric's name still would not have been there. "How are you?"

He was laughing too. But his laugh sounded delighted, as if I was some sort of serendipity. "This is great! Allie O'Connor. How are you?"

"Fine."

"Great to see you! Fabulous. Wow. What are the chances?"

Slim to none.

At that point, Yoshi-san was wondering what was going on, so we filled him in. He excused himself and left us to catch up on old times.

"So what you doing here?" Of course, I already knew why he was in town, but I was hoping that what Julie had told me was a mistake. I was hoping he was just passing through.

"Working. At the embassy."

So she hadn't been mistaken. "For very long?"

"Three years. Normal assignment."

"Terrific."

"What are you doing here?"

"Working. For a paper. The *Stars and Stripes*."

"That's great. Good for you."

I smiled at him.

He smiled at me.

"Um…" Not thinking about Eric Larsen for years, having forgotten about him entirely, left very little to talk about. "Where are you living?"

"Hiroo."

"Hiroo?" Hiroo was right down the street from Hardy Barracks. Hiroo was where the military hotel was. It was where I took refuge, where I did my local shopping, and sipped my Starbucks.

*Not funny, God. Can you see me? I'm not laughing. Didn't you hear my prayer? I'd said* girlfriend, *hadn't I?*

I looked into Eric's cornflower blue eyes, took in his square face, and the thick blond hair standing up from his forehead with such precision. He'd always looked Dutch to me. Still looked Dutch to me. Something about him had always proclaimed Solid Citizen.

As I stood there, I remembered all the reasons I had never liked him. It wasn't that we had run in the same crowd in high school, had mutual friends, or even the same classes. It was that we had been opposites.

Everything he had believed in had been everything I had hated.

Eric had been a Young Republican, the captain of the debate team, and one of the only high school drinkers of espresso. That was in the early nineties before Starbucks had begun its insidious creep across the continent. I had been a liberal Democrat, editor of the school's literary magazine, and one of the only high school drinkers of green tea. I hadn't known him enough to personally hate him. I had disliked him on principle. On instinct.

But as I stood there, I realized I couldn't avoid him. Especially not if he was inhabiting my part of the city. "That's where I live too."

"Great! Did you take the subway? We could ride home together."

We could indeed. We both had to go to Ochanomizu Station to start our trip home, but we didn't have to end it at the same station.

We walked back the way I'd come. It was marginally cooler, the sun already shining from an oblique angle. Summer nights in Tokyo didn't last very long. As a consequence of not participating in daylight savings time, the sun rose in the summer at four thirty and set by seven.

We ambled down the steps into the station, bought tickets, went through the turnstiles, and waited for the train to come.

"Allie O'Connor. I can't believe it's you. I started to think I'd never run into you again."

Well, he was one up on me because I hadn't thought about him at all. But he had just moved from…somewhere…to Tokyo, and he was probably just as homesick as anyone who moves to a foreign country. The least I could do was be polite. "So what happened to you after graduation? Where did you go after high school?"

"Harvard."

Of course he had. He was exactly the type. "And you've been with the State Department ever since?"

"After I got my master's at Georgetown. How about you? What are you writing?"

"Articles mostly. For the paper."

"No poetry? Or books?"

I shrugged. I was writing poetry. I had journals filled with poems. And I was trying to write a book. Had a notebook filled with assorted plots and a computer folder crammed with a dozen works in progress. Nothing had ever gone past one hundred pages.

"I always loved your writing."

"My articles?" He'd been reading my newspaper articles?

"No, your high school stuff. It was beautiful. I always wished I could write that way. It made me see emotions." He pushed away from the pillar he'd been leaning on. "I thought you'd have been a published author by now."

*Me too.*

It looked as though Eric had become the person he'd set out to be.

And it looked as though I had not. I reminded myself we were no longer in high school, and I no longer had to live up to anyone's expectations but my own. And how many people can say they've lived in Tokyo? Or been a journalist? Or written three hundred haiku poems?

The train came. We stepped into the car and sat down side by side, facing the interior aisle. I turned my head the tiniest bit in his direction and snuck a peek.

He had been driven in high school. Ambitious with a confidence placing him far above the rest of us lesser mortals who were mired in clique rivalries as we slogged through midterm exams. He had thought jocks were irrelevant and cheerleaders were just wasting energy. He had never said it in those words, of course, but I could tell that's what he'd been thinking. If he'd taken a seat on the other side of the political fence, I would have admired him for that disdain, but he'd opted out of the whole high school social scene without being a geek or an outcast. "Are you still a Republican?"

He grinned. "Are you still a Democrat?"

*Touché.*

"Politic-neutral, officially. I push the president's policies."

"Must have been really hard for you, working under Clinton."

He shrugged. "Are you still a tree hugger?"

"I never actually hugged that tree. I chained myself to it."

"My mistake. How long was that for again?"

"Forty-eight hours." Forty-eight of the longest hours in my life. When nighttime falls in the forests of the Pacific Northwest, everything creepy and freaky comes out. Trees are nice and trees are important, but after that episode of insanity, I had stepped aside to let others champion the cause.

"That's right, forty-eight hours. I lost a bet because of you. You lasted longer than I thought you would."

And that reminded me. "Whatever happened to Paige?"

"Paige? I have no idea."

He didn't know? Paige had been his high school sweetheart. They'd been perfect for each other. She had also been a blue-eyed blonde. She wore button-down shirts, crewneck sweaters, and headbands to hold back her stick-straight hair.

He laughed, flashing even teeth. "I haven't thought about her for years."

"Well, thanks a lot. I owe my friend Joanna twenty bucks then."

"Joanna Palmer? Why?"

"Because I was sure you'd end up marrying Paige and have two kids and a cat. She always thought you'd wind up with someone else."

"Who?"

"I have no idea. She never said. But she was sure it wouldn't be Paige."

"Why?"

"She thought you were too much alike."

"She was right. We were. So how *is* Joanna?"

"Haven't heard from her in years."

4

*Scented wind blows up*
*from the bay. I smell salted*
*memories of fish.*

WE RODE THE SUBWAY IN SILENCE AFTER THAT. I counted the number of designer purses in our car: six. The number of pairs of stiletto sandals: ten. The number of people dozing: fifteen.

As we neared Otemachi Station, I stood up.

Eric stayed in his seat, watching me, brows raised.

"This is where I get off."

"Oh. Before you get off, is there anywhere to buy food in Hiroo? Other than National Azabu or Meidi-ya?" National Azabu and Meidi-ya were the two highest-priced grocery stores in Tokyo.

"There's a small wholesale market. It's over by the New Sanno. The military hotel. You'll be able to access the hotel with your State Department ID." We were gliding into the station. I was holding onto my subway ticket by the edges, between my finger and my thumb, making it arch back and forth by flicking it with my finger.

The doors opened.

"Where exactly?"

"Along that main street, Meiji-dori. It's a little hard to see, but if you're watching for it..." I flicked the ticket once more and then made a move toward the door.

Eric raised his hand. "Bye. Thanks. Glad I ran into you."

I held up my hand.

"I'm sure I can find it."

He might. Or he might walk right past it. And then he'd have to shop at National Azabu and spend twelve dollars for a package of tortillas or thirty dollars for a turkey breast. Tokyo was always easier if someone took the time to show you the way. I didn't know much about Japan, but I did know where to buy a banana for twenty cents. And wasn't that hard-gained knowledge worth sharing? I shoved my ticket into my bag. "Know what? Why don't I show you where it is?"

Two stops later, I rose once again from the seat.

And once again, Eric stayed seated. "Here? Are you sure? I changed at Kasumigasecki on the way in."

"Ginza's faster. The lines are closer together." And there were escalators in both directions, a miracle in a subway system reached mostly by stairs. Countless numbers of stairs. I didn't know how people in wheelchairs or with walkers navigated through Tokyo. They didn't have the option of doing it by subway.

Eric got up and followed me off the train.

I moderated my gait to the speed of the crowd and was herded toward the escalator. I realized, halfway up, that I was standing on the wrong side. My brain had been reprogrammed during my vacation in the States. I stepped to the left. Immediately a stream of people passed me by as they marched toward the top. I waited for Eric. He was the last one off.

The trick to getting anywhere in the city was to stay with the crowd. Chances were you'd planned on going the same direction anyway, and once you were part of the group, you just got swept along with everyone else. It was like moving on automatic pilot. You might not walk as fast as you would on your own, but you ended up getting there with a lot less hassle and a lot less wasted energy.

We did a quick U-turn through the station and rode a different escalator down. We arrived as the train did. Stood aside for the people getting off, and then stepped in as the alarm rang. The door hissed shut behind us.

And then I felt it: People looking at me. Men looking at me, checking me out.

I made a quick sweep of the car with my eyes without turning my head, but I didn't see anyone. Never, in fact, saw anyone—any male—actually doing any looking. But I felt it just the same.

Two seats were available, but they were at opposite ends of the car.

Eric gestured to the one nearest us.

I started to shake my head but then thought better of it. Why not? Whatever else I'd thought of him, he'd always been a perfect gentleman. It was one of the things which had added especial vigor to my animosity. If he'd been a jerk, it would have lent a glaze of rationality to my feelings. Taken them past the realm of politics and instinct and into an area of social etiquette anyone could have understood.

I sat down and he stood in front of me, holding onto a ring dangling from the ceiling.

Three stops later, we got off.

He headed toward the nearest exit.

I stopped him. "Where exactly do you live?"

"In Verdun." He smiled. Relented. "Between the French and German embassies."

I gestured farther down the tracks. "That exit will get you closer."

"Thanks for the tip."

It felt good to be able to show Eric around. Nice to be the confident one in Tokyo for a change.

We fed our tickets into the stiles, walked up the switchback stairs, went outside, turned the corner, and kept walking. We passed an Italian restaurant perched on top of a McDonald's. I'd forgotten how vertically organized Tokyo was; how retail shops were stacked four and five stories high. Farther on we passed a small discreet five-star hotel. I pointed out the Soup Stock restaurant next to it. "This one's great. They only serve soup…and curry…but you can have it with bread or rice. The red pepper soup is terrific."

"Still a vegetarian?"

I shook my head. "It's not very practical when you're a traveling journalist."

We walked past the corner tire store, a tiny drive-in garage barely wide enough for a small car, filled with tires. Drifted by two clothing stores, one atop the other, and then waited for the light to change just past Segafredo Espresso. "There's a Starbucks just down the street in the other direction, past the subway station."

"Where do you live?"

"Not far. About a mile. Back toward Roppongi."

"I thought you said you lived here."

"It's as close to Hiroo as anything." And if I had a choice, Hiroo was where I'd choose to live. As it was, single contractors at the *Stars and Stripes* were required to live in the barracks. It was too expensive to house us in the city.

"Sorry to take you out of your way."

"It's not a problem." Just as long as he didn't think I'd done him any favors or that he owed me anything.

The light changed and we walked across, dodging kids carrying cups of shaved ice and mothers wheeling strollers.

"I could show you how to get there—to the store—from here, but is this the way you'd be coming? Where's your place?"

"Up the hill." Up the hill. Of course it was up the hill. Everything in the area seemed like it was up a hill. "But you could just tell me. I've already taken you out of your way. I don't want to make you walk even farther."

"Oh. Well…" Telling him was complicated. "You could—" There were lots of ways to get to the store, but there weren't any square blocks in that part of the neighborhood and none of the streets, except the major ones, were named. And to explain, I'd have to tell him about landmarks so normal to me that they had almost become invisible.

He was watching my face. Waiting.

"Why don't I just walk you there? It would be easier to show you. So take me to your place, and we'll start from there."

Eric's apartment complex was at the top of Hiroo's tallest, steepest hill. He pointed it out as we passed. The complex was attractively land-scaped in the Japanese style with miniature pine trees and stone lanterns. It had a circular drive, and was wrapped by a Japanese-style tile-topped stucco wall.

At the end of his block, we dove down a narrow street, following its zigs and zags to the bottom of a hill.

It made me wonder who had named those hills, because they all had names. At the bottoms, lacquered stakes had been driven into the ground with the hill's name spelled in both English and in Japanese. Why were there multiple names for what I considered to be one large hill? Did the streets follow ancient paths up the slope? I tried to imagine the Japan of the past. Tried to fill the street I walked with traditional houses. Tried to replace the vending machines with trees and the cars with carts.

I couldn't do it.

I had no idea what Tokyo looked like before the 1940s. Before allied forces carpet bombed eighty-five percent of the city, before the remainder had been bulldozed and rebuilt in the 1950s...and every fifteen years thereafter.

Tokyo was a city without a past, leaning far forward into the future. It was a mishmash of buildings, architecture, and styles. Of ideas and trends and fashions competing for attention. Still strung together with electric and phone wires, it reeked of sewer fumes during certain times of the year. It was a city of a thousand things so foreign to Western eyes that we soon stopped noticing them. Sitting on the edge of the sea, Tokyo was so densely built that she had forgotten her origins.

And yet, when the wind blew just right, the air was perfumed with the smell of the ocean.

Tokyo was a city with buildings so high they made their own weather patterns; so spiked with skyscrapers that typhoons, confronted with the sight, lost confidence, dropped their rain, and moved on past. The city was an incongruity, so full of contradictions that it had almost ceased to be itself. And I had almost ceased trying to understand it. Just hoped, at that point, to be able to survive it.

I hoped Eric would find some way to survive it too.

We ducked into a canyon formed by apartment buildings and then turned along the main street—Meiji-dori—and up the steps into the Hanamasa wholesale store. Tucked into the block at an oblique angle, you might walk right past if you weren't paying attention. I took a basket, handed it to Eric, and then took one for myself.

Then I gave him a tour.

Wholesale in Japan was a completely different experience than whole-sale in the U.S., unless you shopped at the Costco in Machida. Then it was exactly the same. But Hanamasa sold bags of nine apples instead of just five. Seven-pound packages of meat instead of two. Occasionally, I saw chefs shopping for their restaurants, selecting fruits and meat, or buying chopsticks by the hundred pairs and soy sauce by the family-sized bottle. Hanamasa crammed all that bounty into a T-shaped store the size of a 7-Eleven. The way they did it was with teeny-weeny aisles.

We started out, at the base of the T, in the vegetable section because it was the only place you could start. I passed by the mysterious Asian vegetables because I'd never discovered what they were or how to cook them. I did pick up a ten-pound bunch of bananas for four hundred yen. Which roughly equated to four dollars. Bananas at Hanamasa were always a good deal.

We both picked up heads of iceberg lettuce.

I threw a box of cherry tomatoes into my basket.

Eric threw a package of snow peas into his.

We walked past a section of deli meats and frankfurters, turned the corner to the left and walked by the chicken case. I stopped to pick up a package of yakitori shish kebab-style meat. I'd heat them up for the next two nights for dinner.

Eric walked a little further and selected a package of chicken breasts.

We followed the aisle around as it switched from chicken to pork. Then completed the U as we turned into the beef section.

Eric went down a few of the shorter aisles and rejoined me, his basket filled with packages of noodles and bottles of sauces. I'd always been tempted to do the same, but I couldn't read Japanese and wouldn't have known what to do with them once I got back to the barracks.

We passed the fresh fish and the frozen fish and came to the deli section, which featured giant bags of pickled vegetables and assorted salads. Eric spent some time looking at the pickles. He finally picked up two bags and put them in his basket.

Then we turned back toward the base of the T and headed toward the front door, passing the dairy case on our left and the frozen fruits and vegetables on our right. I threw a bag of shelled peas into my basket.

Eric picked out a kilo bag of rice crackers. It featured pictures of fish on the front.

I knew fish was a big deal in Japan, but I had this rule about junk food: If I was going to eat it, then I wanted it to taste like junk food. I wanted artificial cheese flavorings and salty greasy fingertips when I was done. I didn't want fish seasonings or bait breath.

But Eric was making a big deal out of it. "This is great! A whole kilo."

He took out a credit card to pay for it, but both the cashier and I saw it and tried to stop him. I'm sure she was saying what I was saying, "Cash only." The number of cash-only stores in such an ultramodern society was puzzling. And by cash, I meant the green kind. You couldn't buy a checkbook from a bank if you wanted to. And if you couldn't pay cash, then sometimes the only other option was to do a wire transfer. That's the way Gina paid her rent and the way I tithed.

I took out my wallet and gave Eric a five-thousand-yen bill.

"Thanks. I'll pay you back later."

We walked to Eric's a different way so he could place the store in relation to the military hotel. We cut behind the military's New Sanno Hotel.

"Have you been inside yet?"

"Where?"

"There. The New Sanno. You can get in with your State Department ID."

"_That's_ the New Sanno?"

"That's the New Sanno."

"They were still building it when my family moved back to the States."

"From where?"

"From here."

"You lived in Tokyo? When?"

"For about four years. Before we moved to DC…and then to Oregon."

"So this is like coming home for you."

"It feels familiar, but different. We didn't live in Hiroo, and all my memories are from a boy's perspective…"

"Do you like Japan?"

"I love it."

"But you must have learned the language in school."

"A little. I don't remember much. I studied it at university too, but it's been a while."

"But you understand the culture."

"Not really. I know it—some of it—and I accept it, but I haven't ever really tried to understand it."

"And you still love it?"

He flashed me a smile. "I still love it."

Dang it. There went that theory. The one that told me I was having a hard time in Tokyo because I didn't understand the culture and I didn't know the language. I'd have to think up another explanation.

We walked up an alley by the French Embassy, all the while climbing a different hill with a different name.

At his apartment building, he asked me to come inside.

I shrugged. Why not? At least I'd get a chance to see how a Westerner with a good housing allowance lived. I was already well-acquainted with the other side of expatriate life, Gina's side.

I followed him into the compound through automatic sliding doors. He shifted his bags. Pulled his wallet from his pocket and held it up to a card reader.

A door clicked.

"Could you—" Eric gestured at the door while he juggled his bags.

I shoved the door handle down with my elbow, pushed and held the door open with my foot while he passed through.

We rode the elevator up four floors and got out. There were only two apartments visible on the landing. He set his bags down in front of one of them. Held his wallet up to another card reader. Opened the door. Ushered me through it and into the life I wished I had.

A grown-up's life. An adult life.

## 5

*Morning's glory, dead
by evening. Hope dawns in your
face with daybreak's sun.*

ERIC'S HALLWAYS WERE LINED WITH WAIST-HIGH BOOKSHELVES. From the picture rails, metal tracks built into the ceilings, hung art. Not posters or prints, but actual pieces of art. They dangled from wires the way art did in museums. He had framed textiles. Masks. Weapons I wasn't quite sure were legal to possess or move across international borders.

I think he saw me straining to look into his living room.

"Take off your shoes." He gestured at the tiled section of flooring just inside the front door. "Stay awhile."

In accordance with Japanese custom, I slipped my shoes off and lined them up beside Eric's, pointing in the direction of the door. Then I crept into the living room while he disappeared into the kitchen with his bags.

His heating system was set into a cabinet running the width of the living room. Three spotlights shone down on the top of the cabinet, each one highlighting a celadon green ceramic vase.

He came in while I had stooped to look at them.

"They're from Thailand."

"When were you in Thailand?"

"Before I came here."

"For how long?"

"Two years."

"I covered a military exercise in Thailand last year. Cobra Gold."

"Where?"

"Sattahip."

"Near Pattaya?"

"Right."

"It's not what it used to be."

I had no idea what it used to be, but the previous year, Pattaya was home of an infamous red-light district, cheap restaurants, and beautiful beaches…if you didn't mind your water polluted.

"Did you get into Bangkok while you were there?"

"For a day trip."

"I wish I'd known. I could have shown you around."

As I turned away from the vases, I caught a glimpse of the dining room table over his shoulder.

"Is that…teak?" I aspired to teak. It was so sleek.

"It is. From Singapore."

"You were in Singapore too?"

"My first assignment for the State Department."

Lucky dog. Singapore was known by some in the expat community as Asia-lite. All of the exotic sights, tastes, and sounds of Asia, and none of the health problems or language difficulties.

Luxurious by Tokyo standards, Eric's apartment had three bedrooms, both a living room and a dining room, two and a half bathrooms…even a small patio. But it wasn't the size of his apartment that impressed me.

If looking around the rooms was the same as looking into his life, then I could tell he lived on purpose. He knew who he was and what he liked. He was living exactly the kind of life *I* wanted. The kind of life I'd been hoping to have.

How was that possible?

He was a Republican!

I too was collecting souvenirs from the places I visited. Sort of. Nothing on purpose really, but something from every deployment. Something from every assignment. And someday, when I had the perfect place, I was planning to take everything out and put it on display.

As I looked around, it felt as if, somehow, Eric had already arrived at the perfect place. Already lived in the magical land of Someday.

Once I'd finished the tour, I slouched into the corner of his black leather-and-chrome couch while he went to get me a glass of water.

He returned with two glasses and the bag of rice crackers he'd bought at Hanamasa. He arranged everything on the glass-topped coffee table in front of us.

"I like your place."

"Thanks. The Realtor worked hard to find it for me. Lots of space for the money."

"I meant your…things. Collections."

"Oh. Well, thanks for that too." He reached for his glass, took a drink, set it back down, and then looked at me. "I had to do something while I waited."

What could he possibly have been waiting for?

He opened the bag and took a handful of crackers. And I got the surprise of my life. The reason the packaging had pictures of fish on it was because they *were* fish. Dozens, hundreds of dead, dried, one-inch fish.

I watched in fascinated horror while he shook a handful into his palm and then popped them into his mouth.

I could hear them crunch.

He swallowed and shook another couple into his hand. He held them out toward me. "Want some?"

"You didn't eat those in high school, did you?" Because if he had, he wouldn't have been Mr. Too Motivated for High School. He would have been a cast-out: The Guy Who Ate Little Dried Fish.

"No." He laughed. "In high school, I just tried to fit in."

"By being the loudest, most obnoxious Republican in school?"

His eyebrows shrugged. "We all had our roles to play, Miss Bleeding Heart."

"Is that who you think I am?"

"That's who I thought you were."

"Really?"

"I always thought of you as the leader of the left. Just think: If we could have allied ourselves, we might have ruled the school."

"Such as it was. Why were you like that?"

"Like what?"

"Everything had to be organized and analyzed. And judged."

"I didn't judge you."

"You judged everyone."

"No, I didn't."

"It felt like it."

"Why?"

"It's pretty hard to measure up to class valedictorian, president of the Young Republicans, and captain of the debate team."

"Well, what about you?"

"What about me?"

"What about the self-righteous scorn you heaped on me?"

"I never *heaped* anything on you. I never even talked to you!"

"Maybe not verbally, but what about the literary magazine?"

"You were not the sole recipient."

"Who else would have been the intended audience of *Farewell to a Tree?*"

"That was not about you."

"There was no symbolism in the elephant yanking it out of the ground?"

"It was set in *Asia*."

"Or the debate with the donkey about the fate of the tree?"

"A nod to *Aesop's Fables*. You know…talking animals."

"Come on, Allie. An elephant and a donkey? Debating? About the fate of a tree?"

"It was not about you." At least not entirely.

"But it was about politics."

"Yes." Exactly.

"And why would I not—as a Republican—have felt judged?"

"I would prefer the term 'convicted.'"

He laughed. "I'm sure you would. Never mind. It's not important anymore."

"Convictions are always important."

"I meant what happened in high school ought to stay in high school. We weren't friends then, but that doesn't mean we can't be friends now." He reached into the bag and grabbed another handful of fish. "Sure you don't want some?"

I held up a hand. "No. Thanks." I pushed away from the couch. "I should be going."

"If I had a car, I'd drive you."

"No big deal." And it wasn't. I only had two bags. True, one of them had ten pounds of bananas, but I'd grown used to being a packhorse since I'd arrived in Tokyo.

I went to bed that evening in discomfort. It seemed to have to do with Eric, but I didn't know why. True, I'd prayed for a new friend that lived in Hiroo, but Eric wasn't the person I'd had in mind. He wasn't the type or the gender or anything at all I had been thinking of. I supposed I could let the past stay in the past, but more than most people care to admit, high school left a deep imprint on the soul.

Eric was everything I hoped never to become.

But he had everything I ever wanted.

And he'd been in Bangkok the same day I had been. Had I seen him? At a distance, maybe, without knowing?

Probably not.

Why would he have been touring the grand palace or the temples? Taking a ride on a long-tail boat or buying a length of Thai silk? But still. The possibility had been there. I might have run into him. In Bangkok, of all places. And then what might have happened?

*That* was a good premise for a story. What might have happened? Not that anything would have happened between Eric and me, but something could happen between fictional characters.

*Thai Dreams.* No. Too boring.

*Thai Temptation.* No. Veering off into red-light districts.

*My Thai?* Cute. But then the guy would have to be Thai, and it sounded just a little…patronizing. A bit too colonial.

*One Day in Bangkok.*

Maybe.

*24 Hours in Bangkok?* Too spy-thriller.

*One Night in Bangkok?* Yes. Besides being the title to a catchy song, it could be the catchy title to a novel.

*One Night in Bangkok.*

I rolled out of bed. Wrote the title down in my notebook. That could be an idea worth writing. Of course the male protagonist would have to be short, dark, and handsome.

As I slipped back into bed, my thoughts turned once more to Eric. Maybe I could just hope I wouldn't run into him. Maybe his job at the embassy would keep him chained to his desk. There probably wasn't any good reason to ever have to hang out with him.

By the time my eyelids grew heavy, I'd convinced myself that the encounter with Eric was just one of those funny things Tokyo liked to toss in your direction just to see how you'd react. Well, I'd reacted. I'd also been polite, and I'd helped him out. I'd done my duty to humanity. I'd been a model citizen.

I'd never have to speak to him again if I didn't want to.

## 6

*Whine, Mosquito. Do
not think I will not swat you
if you drink my blood.*

If only I could have said the same thing about Samantha.

Isn't there always someone at work who seems to do the same thing
you do, only they get just a little more attention, a little more praise, and
a little more recognition? That person, for me, was Samantha. We always
competed for assignments.

We both had dark hair, but that's where the similarity ended. She
was short and curvy. A real knockout. Frankly, she was beautiful. And I
didn't hate her because she was beautiful. That was the fortunate result
of genetics. I hated her because she smart, polished, *and* beautiful.

She was one of those.

But that morning I was given an unexpected gift of the most useful
kind: information.

"Hey, Allie." Samantha didn't talk, she purred. The volume of her
voice registered somewhere between a whisper and a sigh.

I'd only sat down next to her so I wouldn't have to sit next to Neil. I
didn't mind saying hi to him from a distance. "Hi, Neil."

He glanced up at me and sort of smiled. Then he went back to reading
his copy of the *Asahi Shimbun.* So things weren't bad, but they weren't
back to normal yet either, dang it.

For that day, at least, it appeared Samantha was the lesser of two evils.
I swung my attention back to her. "Hi, Samantha."

"So, did you have a good vacation? Tell me all about it."

38

For some reason I had done nothing to perpetuate, she thought we were best buds. Until assignments were doled out at staff meetings. Then it was every girl for herself.

"It was great."

"Well, while you were gone, I made a decision." Her cat's lips curled up at the sides. "I'm going to take the State Department exam."

She looked at me as if she were expecting something. Some reaction. But then Rob, our bureau chief, came in and the meeting started. There were all the usual assignments: routine events at the Naval Air Facility in Atsugi, Yokosuka Naval Base, Camp Zama, and the Air Base at Yokota. But there were also several more interesting, in-depth stories. One of which I wanted.

And Samantha did too. "The murder case at Yokota? I was just talking to the Office of Special Investigations the other day. Should I call back and set up a formal interview?"

"Yeah. Great. Thanks."

Yeah, great, thanks? Had I missed the discussion about who could cover the story better? Me. About who normally covered the extremely rare crime stories? Me. About who knew the phone number of OSI by heart? Me.

"Um…" Rob shuffled through some papers. "Atsugi's replacing some of their sewer system and dug up something of historical interest. Anyone volunteer?"

Like anyone *would* volunteer. Historical interest was synonymous with years of paperwork and tedious investigation…and that's before they would announce what, exactly, they'd found.

"Allie?"

I looked up. "Yes?"

"Great. Thanks."

Samantha got a murder. I got sewers. When life laughed at you, most of the time I didn't find it very funny.

We all pushed away from the table and trickled away from the conference room. Samantha dogged my heels on the way back to our desks in the cubicle farm.

I stopped in the middle of the hall.

She ran right into me and spilled her coffee all over *my* shirt. "What!"

She frowned. "Sorry."

"Did you want something?"

"Yes. In fact…you should really try to blot that coffee before it soaks into your shirt." She grabbed my forearm and pulled me toward my desk. "Sit." She shoved me into my chair, pulled some Kleenex from my box, and handed them to me as if she were doing me a favor. Then she sat on the corner of my desk and watched me.

"Was there something you needed?"

"Yes. You and I both know you're the one with the best contacts at OSI."

"The Office of Special Investigations? The office you called just the other day?"

"Yes. And there's no need to be snippy. I just wondered if you'd give them a call and let them know I've been assigned to this case. That way they won't have divided loyalties. They won't save up information, thinking they'll be talking to you too."

"You mean ask them to be nice to you? No. It wouldn't be doing you any favors. Those OSI guys are tough. The minute they smell fear… well…"

I saw her eyes narrow, but then she dug deep inside and somehow managed to turn her frown upside down. "You're always the one who gets the criminal investigations. Look at it this way. We both get to broaden our résumés a little. And sewers can be fascinating. I'm sure you'll find a way to put your unique spin on things."

The only thing I truly hated about my job was Samantha.

But as I tried to think of some snappy retort, what she'd told me earlier began to register in my brain. "What did you say, again? Before the meeting?"

"What? About the State Department test? I've decided to take it."

And if she took the State Department test…and passed…she couldn't torment me anymore because she wouldn't be around. She'd be G-O-N-E. But it wasn't quite so easy. She had to pass it first, and the test was hard. What Samantha needed was a tutor. If he were handsome, so much the better.

I immediately thought of Eric.

Perfect.

I walked home in a celebratory mood. If I could divert Samantha's and Eric's attention to each other, then maybe I'd be able to neutralize the former and sideline the latter. I'd have taken care of two problems at the same time.

I had always been good at multitasking.

That evening, as I opened the fridge, I realized I'd forgotten to buy groceries. But hadn't there been some *yakitori* left from the night before? I was sure that...

I bent down and looked through all the shelves. I couldn't identify one piece of meat belonging to me. So I could have a salad or a banana. Or both.

I let the door swing shut and stood for a moment, trying to decide what to do. I was hungry. Starving. Famished. And I couldn't call takeout because I couldn't speak Japanese. And I couldn't go to the compound's hilltop store up by the helicopter pad because it was closed.

McDonald's was the only option. But then, sometimes only fries would do. And they sold some good things at McDonald's in Japan. Things like chicken McNuggets and Filet-O-Fish sandwiches.

As I walked back through the parking lot, I swatted mosquitoes. I knew I couldn't kill them all, knew when I got to the restaurant that I'd have welts rising all over my arms. But that would teach me to forget to buy enough groceries, wouldn't it?

I cruised Gaien-nishi-dori looking for an empty parking spot. I made it all the way to the intersection past Hiroo without finding one. But that was okay. I had never gained full confidence in my ability to parallel park. Parallel parking on the wrong side of the street from the wrong side of the car was always hit-and-miss. I usually just hoped I'd miss hitting another car.

I decided to park at the New Sanno, run down the street to McDonald's, and then shop at Hanamasa—again—before going home. I squeezed the car into a too-small space in the underground garage, jogged up the ramp to ground level, and waved at the guards as I walked off the hotel grounds. Then I rounded the corner and walked down the small street that dead-ended right in front of McDonald's.

I waited for the light to change, still slapping at myself, then half ran up to McDonald's, pushed a button on the door, and slipped inside as soon as the door slid open. I ordered fries and McNugget-os. Added a "banilla" shake for good measure. It was hot; I was thirsty. Why not?

It was faster to pronounce food offerings in Japan the way the Japanese did. They don't have a *v* sound and, except for the letter *n,* they don't pronounce consonants by themselves. To speak foreign words ending in a consonant, the Japanese had to add a vowel. I'd never figured out the rules for which vowel, but after McNuggets, I knew they added an *o.* After hamburger, it was an *a.*

As I chain-ate fries, the doors slid open and Eric walked in. He was wearing a suit and tie. I suppose I shouldn't have been surprised to see him. We lived within a mile of each other and frequented a commerce area only two blocks wide. I froze, hoping he wouldn't see me.

He didn't. He was too focused on getting to the counter.

I watched him order. It sounded as though he did it in Japanese, but I couldn't tell for sure. He had to wait a few minutes for whatever it was he ordered, but he didn't fiddle with the tray. Didn't jingle coins around in his pocket. Didn't shift his weight from foot to foot. Didn't do anything but stand there and wait. When his food finally came, he took the tray, bowed his head at the cashier, and turned around.

I was still staring at him, so when he turned, he happened to be looking straight at me.

I waved. What else could I do? It was too late to pretend I didn't recognize him. "Hey."

"Hi." He set his tray down next to mine, slid into the booth next to me, and popped a French fry into his mouth.

"Working late?"

He swallowed and then looked at his watch. "Actually, I left early. It's Sunday in DC."

"What time do you normally leave?"

He shrugged. "Nine."

"And when do you start?"

"Nine."

"You work twelve-hour days?"

"Most of the time."

"It's that busy?"

"Washington likes to think everyone's awake when they are. Just about the time I'm ready to shut down my computer, message traffic usually comes in that makes me stay."

"You're not required to be there, are you?"

"No."

"So you stay just for fun?"

His eyes met mine. "To get ahead, you have to stay ahead."

"You look really tired."

His lips lifted in a half smile. "I am really tired. I thought I'd been smart finding my apartment so fast. It just meant I had to jump into work that much more quickly."

"Did you take any vacation this summer before you moved?"

"I took some leave at the end of June. Went to Oregon."

"How are your parents?"

He shrugged. "My dad and Judy are fine."

Judy? "Your parents got divorced?"

"A long time ago. Back before we even moved to Japan."

"Then...in high school..." Eric's parents had been The Parents when we were in high school. His mom...stepmom...had been the president for the local chapter of MADD. They'd chaperoned our prom. They'd cochaired the committee for the parent-sponsored graduation party.

"That was Judy."

"So...what about your mom?"

"She lives in Medford with my grandparents. Helps them with their flower shop. She was never meant to be a diplomatic wife. When we were in the Philippines she got sick. At least that's what Dad told us. She went home to Medford for a visit and never came back. I think she had a nervous breakdown."

"You don't know?"

"We don't talk much in my family beyond politics. Especially after the divorce."

"And Judy?"

"Judy was great. Is great. She was a foreign service officer when she and Dad met, so she was perfect. She knew how everything worked. Knew how to cope, knew what was expected. She loved other cultures, loved traveling..."

It didn't seem quite the right time to mention Samantha, but I didn't want to miss the chance to ask. "Hey. Speaking of traveling and the State Department, I have this...friend...at *Stripes* who wants to take the State Department test. I know you're really busy, and she doesn't know I'm telling you this. When things at work settle down, maybe you can talk to her about the test. I've heard it's hard, and I know she'd appreciate it."

"Sure." He slipped a hand inside his suit jacket and pulled out his wallet. He took out a business card and gave it to me. "What's her name?"

"Samantha."

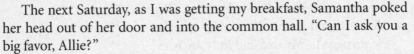

The next Saturday, as I was getting my breakfast, Samantha poked her head out of her door and into the common hall. "Can I ask you a big favor, Allie?"

A big favor. Samantha's big favors usually turned out to be major inconveniences. Like picking up something heavy from the grocery store. Or finding some obscure food item at the Atsugi commissary.

"Please?"

It was the weekend. If it had to do with work, I wasn't going to do it. "What?"

"I'm supposed to meet your friend today. Could you go with me?"

Go with her to meet Eric? I could do that for her. Sort of complete the handoff. Make sure they got off to a good start. Say, "*Sayonara.*" Why not? "Where?"

"At Segafredo's in Hiroo. He's supposed to be at one of the tables outside."

I glanced at my watch. "When?"

"At ten."

"Then you're late."

"What!"

"It's nine forty-five. It'll take you at least twenty minutes to get there."

"Don't scare me like that. I'm taking a taxi." She pulled her head back inside her room and shut the door.

I put the lid back on my bottle of milk and put it in the fridge. Then I went into my room and stood in front of the closet.

*What to wear? What to wear?*

I decided on a green split neck shirt with short sleeves and black skirt. Pulled on some black yoga shoes with a strap across the mid-step. Not, of course, that I had ever actually twisted myself into a pretzel. Because I was tall and slender, people assumed I was also limber...so why work at it? The yoga shoes were comfortable. And simple. I went into the bathroom and pulled my hair back into a pony tail.

I threw my journal into my messenger bag. Tossed a paperback book in beside it.

And I still waited another three minutes for Samantha.

## 7

*Magpie, do you spread
your wings this night so lovers'
hearts can finally meet?*

SHE SWEPT OUT OF HER ROOM ON TWO-INCH HEELS, a bag slung across her shoulder, classically and impeccably dressed. "Ready? I called the taxi. Thanks for coming."

I hurried to keep up with her, following along behind, feeling more like her secretary than her colleague. We left the barracks and crossed the street in front of the antique store to wait for the taxi. Enticing containers had been placed on the lawn in front of the store; they were filled with old plates and teacups. I meant to go in there one day. Someday. When I had the time.

The taxi dropped us by the bakery near National Azabu, across the street from Segafredo. We dodged cars on our way across the intersection.

Samantha jabbed me in the side with an elbow. "Which one is he?"

"The one reading the newspaper."

"That's not helpful."

"What—? Oh." There were at least three men sitting at tables by themselves. They were all reading newspapers.

"The blond."

She looked up at me with a smile frozen on her face and talked to me between her teeth. "They're all blond."

Hmm. Funny. So they were.

Eric glanced up, saw me, and stood up. "The one standing up."

"Okay. Thanks. Bye now." She walked away from me, hand extended toward him.

Bye now? *Bye now?* No, no, no, no, no. Not so fast, *chica!* "Hey, Eric. Great to see you. How's your week been?"

Eric's eyes zoomed right over Samantha's head and locked on mine. "Okay. Thanks for asking." By that point he had navigated between shiny round zinc tables and had come out onto the sidewalk to stand between Samantha and me.

Her eyes were throwing daggers at me even as her lips were smiling. I smiled back at her.

Eric smiled at me.

We were all smiling.

And then a bicycle bell dinged.

Eric was standing, his back to a table, while Samantha and I were filling the sidewalk. One of us was going to have to move.

The bell dinged again.

It wasn't going to be me.

The woman on top of the bicycle was old, and she wasn't about to be blocked by a gaijin. The bicycle wheel just about had to make a track up Samantha's white slacks before she finally decided to yield the sidewalk.

I grabbed Eric's arm and pulled him inside to stand in line with me. If I hadn't had any plans, one had suddenly materialized. Leave Samantha by herself with Eric?

Not a chance.

I didn't mind Eric tutoring Samantha. I didn't mind him helping her out. I did mind Samantha helping herself to him. I'd seen the way she flirted with men. It was so sophisticated, so seductive, that they were lulled into submission before they even knew what was going on.

But Eric, apparently, wasn't with my game plan.

Because when Samantha came through the door, he immediately ushered her ahead of him so she could stand next to me.

And she didn't waste any time trying to get rid of me. "Thanks so much, Allie, for taking the time to walk down here with me. I don't want to keep you from your plans. I know how much you have to do this morning." Amazing how loudly Samantha could talk when she wasn't purring.

I looked over my shoulder at her. "Not a problem. I've decided to save all those errands until this afternoon. We can walk back together. Or take a taxi if it's too hot for you." Hey, if she wanted to pretend we were friends, then why not play along?

I glanced over at Eric, remembering the tiredness that had lined his face earlier in the week. It was gone now. I smiled at him.

He smiled at me. "What can I get you?"

"A cappuccino."

"Coffee? Allie O'Connor drinks coffee? Since when?"

"Since I started working for a living." I chalked it up to an accumulation of nights in the press room. I'd been polluting my body for years.

Leaving them unchaperoned, I sat down at the table outside, dropped my messenger bag to the floor, and waited. Eric came along a few minutes later with Samantha. He set a tray down in the middle of the table. Samantha took a cup of coffee, I took my cappuccino, and that left the green tea for Eric.

He'd ordered tea. Green tea.

"Weren't you the one who single-handedly started the espresso craze in the state of Oregon?"

He looked at me from over the rim of his cup.

"So...you only drink coffee at work? Or...?"

"I don't drink coffee at all."

"Since when?"

"Since I realized I didn't need any more stimulants coursing through my veins. I get enough of an adrenaline pump at work to last me through the weekend. And on the weekends, I'm supposed to try and relax." His phone purred. It was sitting in the middle of the table, and it was on vibrate. He scowled and picked it up. Talked for a minute and then hung up. "There's been some message traffic from Washington."

"And?"

"And so I have to go in later. It's still Friday in DC, and I'm duty officer this weekend." He didn't look as though he was in much of a hurry, sitting there, hands circling his tea cup.

"Is it ever someone else's job?"

"To do what?"

"To do everything that needs to be done."

A corner of his mouth lifted. "Occasionally."

"So, Eric? What do you do at the embassy?"

He blinked. Dropped his eyes from me to Samantha.

"I work in the political section. Bilateral and Policy Unit with a focus on external affairs."

"State Department" was a language that looked like English and sounded like English, but wasn't really the same thing at all.

"Really. Sounds fascinating."

I noticed a shade of a smile on his lips. "It can be."

"What does a typical day look like for you?"

He shrugged. "There's no typical day, per se. I stay in contact with my counterpart at the Ministry of Foreign Affairs to keep a handle on Japan's take on regional affairs. We'll pass messages and talking points back and forth. I arrange official visits for senior politicians. Draft letters for the ambassador. Take care of taskings from Washington. On any given day, I might do all of the above or none of the above."

"I've heard the test is rather challenging."

"I'd agree. When are you taking it?"

"April."

"Then you have lots of time. Have you ordered a study guide?"

"Just last week. It hasn't arrived yet."

"Which career track are you registering for?"

"I haven't decided. What would you suggest?"

"I'd think with your background you'd be a good fit for public diplomacy."

"My thoughts were leaning in that direction too."

"The first thing you really need to do is get the study guide. Then decide what career track you want to pursue. Once you register, it's hard to change your mind. The exam is multiple choice and essay questions. You're lucky. Most people hate the essay part, but for you, it'll be easy."

I sipped my cappuccino and listened while Eric talked about the test.

"I'd also get all the books on the suggested reading list."

"I was going to ask about that."

"When I took the exam, it seemed like there were forty or fifty books, but I was glad I'd read them. I'm sure they're listed on State's website." He looked at his watch and then pushed away from the table. "I wish I could stay longer, but duty calls. Nice to meet you, Samantha. Good to see you again, Allie."

Samantha and I didn't stay much longer, either. We decided to walk back to the barracks.

"Thanks for introducing me to him, Allie. It'll be nice to have a contact while I study. In fact, maybe I could talk him into weekly study sessions. It wouldn't hurt my chances…and it sure wouldn't hurt my eyes, either. He's really good-looking."

What had I done? I'd hooked Eric up with Samantha Barracuda for no good reason. They never would have met if it hadn't been for me. Nice going, Allie. "You aren't…are you a Republican?"

Samantha smiled at me. "As Republican as Ronald Reagan. My parents knew him. Did I ever tell you that?"

Well, that clinched it. I'd just identified Eric's dream woman. Samantha was smart, she was classy, she'd make a perfect diplomat's wife. *And* she was a Republican.

Maybe he'd give me a finder's fee.

The next week, every time I saw Samantha I thought of Eric. And every time I thought of Eric, I thought of what a stupid thing I'd done.

By Friday, if I'd owned a whip, I might have become a flagellant. Something was seriously wrong with me. Something to do with why I cared so much about Samantha and Eric.

Who cared?

*Me.*

Why should I care?

*I shouldn't. I should not care.*

But I couldn't stop. Not even when I caught myself staring at my digital alarm clock, trying to catch the exact moment when those red LED lights blinked from 10:36 to 10:37. And from 10:37 to 10:38. From 10:38 to 10:39…I finally shut my eyes, but the image of all those light formations had blazed an imprint behind my eyelids. An imprint looking disturbingly like Eric's right ear. Which was slightly higher and just a tiny bit larger than his left ear.

How did I know things like that?

I got up, threw open my door, and stalked into the kitchen. I grabbed my carton of milk from the refrigerator and took a long swallow. And another. Noticed that Samantha's door was open.

I put the milk carton back and then stuck my head inside her room. "Hey."

She looked up from her desk. Her elbow was propped on a stack of books. Another pile waited on the floor beside her. She was wearing her rimless glasses and holding a highlighter. "Hey."

"What are you doing?"

"Studying."

"For what?"

"The State Department exam."

"Why?"

"Because I'm meeting with Eric again tomorrow. And I have no intention of wasting his time."

"That's...nice of you."

She turned all the way around in her chair to look at me. "You're not interested, are you?"

"In what?"

"Eric."

"Eric? Why?"

"Because he's your friend."

"Pfft. No."

"You knew him first."

Yeah, maybe I had, but Samantha had said it first. In high school we used to call those dibs.

"Well, thanks. For being a friend."

A friend?

*Nice try, God.*

Samantha and Eric met the next Saturday at the same place and the same time. I went along out of morbid curiosity. I was pretty sure Eric wouldn't fall into Samantha's lap, but I wanted to make sure. And we were all friends, right?

I had promised myself I would actually do some writing.

Or reading.

Put the time to good use.

And I might have, except Samantha kept asking Eric questions and answering his own. Impressively. And underneath her professional demeanor I saw her smile at him once or twice as if he were the only eligible bachelor in Japan.

And he didn't look overly upset at the attention. He was laughing. Frequently. And every time I decided to pick up my book and shove my nose into it, he'd laugh again.

What did he see in her? Beyond the beauty, the intelligence, and the compatible politics? Didn't he want something more in a relationship?

But wasn't Eric and Samantha what I'd wanted?

Wasn't that what I'd planned?

And hadn't my mother once told me to be careful what I wished for? How old did you have to be in order to actually take your mother seriously?

8

*Pushing up from slime,*
*Lotus, swim up through water,*
*journey toward the sun.*

ONE THURSDAY AFTERNOON SEVERAL WEEKS LATER, Samantha stopped by and sat on the corner of my desk. She fished a paper clip out of my magnetic paper clip holder and picked at it with a fingernail, bending it straight. "Can I talk to you? As a friend? I'm not quite sure what to do about Eric, and I was hoping you could give me some advice."

I pushed at her leg and simultaneously tried to pull my notebook out from under her with the other hand. "Do you mind?"

"Hmm?" She looked up from her paper clip...*my* paper clip. "Oh. Sorry." She shifted her weight to release the notebook and then settled back into place.

"What is it you want to do with him?"

"I want him to take me seriously before I deploy to Iraq in January."

"You mean help you study? He already is."

"But I want him to ask me out. Take me to dinner. Take me back to his place."

"He's not that kind of guy." At least I didn't think he was. I really, really hoped he wasn't. Please, God, take *me* seriously. Give Eric the gift of celibacy. Now.

"Not the kind of guy to take a girl out to dinner? You mean he's...is he..." her voice dropped to a whisper, "...gay?"

"No. I mean he's not the kind of guy to...you know...hop into bed."

She raised an eyebrow. "That's not quite what I had in mind. At least not yet. I'd just like to deepen the relationship. You know him. What more can I do? When I'm studying with him, I can talk to him about the test and politics, but he's so...hot...that when I try to just talk to him, I can't think of anything to say."

I'd never had that problem with Eric. My biggest problem was trying not to yell at him.

"Talk to him like you'd talk to anyone."

"He's not just anyone. And, frankly, my long-term plans don't involve a lot of talking."

That was Samantha, a Liberated Woman on the prowl. If she'd been a bubblehead, I wouldn't have worried. But she was the total package. Brains and beauty. "He's not a toy, he's a *person!* And how long do you think a relationship can last if you can't find anything to talk about?"

"Well, he's a man and I'm a woman. I'm sure we'll eventually find something to discuss. Thanks anyway." She flashed me a smile, dropped my paper clip back into the holder, and left.

I fished it out and tossed it into the garbage can.

That night, Eric called.

I wanted to warn him about Samantha, but I couldn't figure out how to say it. And if he knew what she was really like, then what would he think about me? Especially since I'd introduced them?

"Allie? Are you there?"

"What? Yes. Sorry. What were you saying?"

"The Azabu-Juban Festival. Do you want to go? On Saturday?"

"Um..." He'd asked *me*. He hadn't asked Samantha. Or maybe he had. But if he had, then I would have heard Samantha gloating about it. So he'd asked me first. Ha. Take that, Samantha! "Sure." But just because—

"Great. I was thinking maybe we could head down the hill in the late afternoon. Four o'clock?"

"Four o'clock. Fine. I'll meet you at your place."

After Eric had hung up the phone, I continued the conversation I was having with myself. Just because I didn't want Samantha to sink her greedy little claws into Eric didn't mean I wanted him for myself. Just because I was happy he'd asked me first didn't mean...well, it didn't mean anything at all.

Usually, I stayed away from events in Tokyo. I didn't know the traditions being celebrated, I didn't know what was being said, and there were always far too many people.

In fact, we had only just passed Arisugawa Park and started down the hill by Nishi-Machi International School that Saturday when I began to notice the pedestrian traffic.

There were young men and women wearing *yukata*, traditional cotton summer *kimono*. Somehow, they made the women look fresh and dainty, while the men looked sexy, as if they'd just rolled out of bed and pulled on a bathrobe.

As we walked down the hill, the density of the crowds increased. Once we got into the center of the Azabu-Juban shopping district, it was hard to breathe, let alone walk. It didn't take long for me to become separated from Eric. He still hadn't learned how to navigate the crowds. I threw a glance over my shoulder and saw him stuck in the middle of the street, fifty yards behind me. I waved a hand over my head, gesturing toward the sidewalk in front of the Daimaru Peacock grocery store. Ten minutes later, he made it.

"You have to stay up with me!"

"I would if you didn't move so fast."

"Just keep shuffling your feet. Try not to stop."

I merged back into the crowd, Eric beside me. For about three steps. And then he slid behind me. I didn't realize it until I felt his hand on my waist.

It wasn't an unpleasant sensation, and it had the added benefit of keeping us together. We shuffled past groups of giggling girls and groups of Western teenagers dressed in *yukata*. We drifted by people handing out fans. I took one and turned it so the Berlitz English School advertisement faced me. I adjusted the angle of my fanning so Eric could capitalize on the resulting breeze too.

We passed a food vendor selling octopus-on-a-stick. I'd never tried octopus before. In principle, I didn't have anything against trying it. And it might have tasted good, but why should I have to try it for the first time shoved onto a stick and all of its tentacles hanging out?

The octopus vendor distracted me, and then I had to dodge a couple pushing a stroller the wrong way, against the crowd.

I felt Eric's hand slip off my waist. A sudden, unexpected coolness.

Glancing around, I discovered him standing behind me, not ten yards away. I had no idea how he could just stand there without being swept along in the current of humanity, but he was doing it. The couple with the stroller had been swallowed up by the crowd, and with them, the protective wake I might have used to reach Eric.

We stood there, both of us, impervious to the crowd, yet separated by it.

He lifted an eyebrow and inclined his head. Could I reach him?

I shook my head.

And then he moved. Let the crowd take him forward. He cast out an arm as he went by, and I lunged for his hand.

Smoke from a brazier grill entwined with the scent of incense and wafted through the street. My stomach thought about growling, but it was too hot and the humidity too savage to seriously consider eating.

I passed the back of my hand across my eyebrows to wipe away the sweat. I started to wipe it across my tank top, but then I realized it was as damp as my forehead.

A nice big cup of shaved ice. *That's* what I needed.

I elbowed Eric and gestured toward a shaved ice vendor on the side-walk. We sidestepped through the crowd and then stood in line for five minutes. We watched the vendor hand-crank his machine and deposit piles of ice shavings into cups. Then he dipped a ladle into a tub of syrup and spilled its bounty over the top.

I loved shaved ice. It wasn't crunchy, like a Slurpee. It was crispy, and it provided the best antidote to humidity I'd found since I'd been in Japan. When my turn came, I stepped up and chose a flavor and a size. "*Gokiburi*. Big one. Me-ron." That was as good as my Japanese got.

Apparently it wasn't very good, because the vendor and Eric started laughing. Guffawing. Eventually, when he was left gasping for breath and wiping his eyes, the vendor bowed. Several times. He probably thought he'd offended me.

He had.

Eric finally stopped laughing long enough to explain. "*Kakigoori* is shaved ice. *Gokiburi* is cockroach."

The vendor snickered as he heard Eric explain.

"You just ordered a big, melon-flavored cockroach."

Yeah. I'd kind of already figured that out. If I hadn't been me, I might have laughed too. But it was super humid, I was hot, and I just wanted to buy a shaved ice.

The vendor, all apologies, cranked my ice out, poured the syrup, and then handed me the cup.

"*Domo arigatoo.*" I turned to Eric. "Since you're so smart, you can order your own."

He stepped up to the counter and had a complete conversation with the vendor in Japanese. I pretended not to notice when they shared a laugh.

We stepped away from the street and ate our ices on the sidewalk behind the shaved ice stand. "You know Japanese pretty well, don't you? Better than you said you did."

"I guess…maybe. It's starting to come back. And I'm taking lessons at the embassy."

I'd studied Japanese too, before I'd moved to Tokyo. And I went to some Japanese classes once I'd arrived. But then I'd reached the lesson about counting and decided I was done. I didn't mind the three different systems of writing. What I couldn't overcome were all the different systems of counting. Completely different systems. At least six of them. If you tried to buy three pencils at a Japanese store, you'd use a different word than if you were buying three tomatoes. I just couldn't get past that.

There were other things about the culture I enjoyed. I enjoyed the literature. Loved Murakami. I enjoyed the poetry. Loved haiku. Loved that it could evoke such a vivid image in just seventeen syllables. Loved that it always referred to natural themes. Both beauty and discipline came together in the span of those few syllables to create something which neither alone might have done. Haiku was exactly the sort of influence I'd wanted for my writing, except it seemed to have backfired. I'd become so minimal with my words that I didn't know if I were capable of writing a novel. Japanese literature I could admire. Their numbers I couldn't even begin to understand.

"So how's your cockroach? Crunchy?"

"It's excellent, thank you."

The corner of Eric's mouth turned up.

I gave him the eyeball.

He wisely returned to eating his ice.

Should I mention Samantha? I snuck a glance at him. He was just so…innocent. So, so…nice.

"About Samantha…"

I blinked. I hadn't been thinking out loud, had I? I was pretty sure I hadn't felt my lips move.

"Allie?"

Relief. It had been Eric. He's the one who'd brought up Samantha. "Yeah. What about her?"

"How good of friends are you?"

I caught myself before I snorted. "Did you ever have people ask to see your notes from class in high school because you were so smart and they wanted to make sure they didn't miss anything?"

"All the time. I told them they could take their own notes."

"Exactly. So how good of friends did you consider them to be?"

His eyebrows knit together for a moment, then his brow went smooth and his blue eyes looked into mine. "I see."

I hoped so. He didn't have to do any favors for Samantha on my behalf.

"I hope you know I consider you a good enough friend that you don't have to ask for my notes. I would gladly share them with you."

"Thanks. You're a pal."

"No, really. I mean it. You could miss an entire class, the whole year's worth, and I'd tell you everything word for word."

I licked my spoon as I considered his words. "What, exactly, are you trying to tell me?"

"I'm telling you not to worry. I'm happy to help Samantha out with studying."

I felt my face drain of blood. But then it all came back in one gigantic wave. He liked Samantha? Was that what he was telling me? "You're asking me to stay away?"

"No. I'm just telling you there's no real reason for you to have to be there."

Of course not. Two's company, three's a crowd, right? But then, it didn't matter, did it? Because I wasn't interested in Eric anyway.

It's just that I hated seeing men fall all over themselves whenever a person like Samantha smiled. And, really, I'd thought Eric was different. Maybe that's what had caused the ice in my stomach to turn into a bowling ball.

I'd been wrong.

*O Cricket, cease your*
*noisy bombast! Don't you know*
*Love comes in silence?*

THE NEXT FRIDAY, ABOVE THE MUTED SOUND OF MY COWORKERS' TYPING, I heard the familiar wop-wop-wop of a helicopter flying overhead. The Hardy Barracks complex housed not only the barracks where I lived, not only the *Stars and Stripes* building where I worked, but also a helicopter pad and—next to it—the hilltop convenience store/movie rental/gas station/rental car outlet. I could have lived in Tokyo indefinitely without ever having to leave the compound. Not that I had ever contemplated it, at least not seriously, but it was nice to be able to rent a movie or pick up a pint of ice cream on a whim. The helicopters, however, I could do without.

Was it mine or Eric's? Someone from the Department of Defense or the Department of State? A general or the ambassador? At least it had come during daylight hours. Sometimes they landed on the compound's helipad at night…right after waking me up from a sound sleep.

I tried to ignore the noise and concentrate instead on writing my article. The who, what, where, why, and how of the Air Force's new uniform changes.

I'd just gotten back into it when I heard Yuka-san, the *Stripes* translator, say my name. To someone else.

I turned and found myself looking at the back side of Eric. So I took a moment to admire the sight.

Most of the men I'd dated had been tall and lean to the point of being gaunt. They had looked as if they survived on the heady ideas of philosophy alone. Or altruism. Or protest, demonstration, and resistance. During my senior year in college, I'd even dated a union representative who was trying to organize migrant workers in the orchards of the Northwest. But Eric was exactly the opposite. Not, of course, that I was thinking of dating him. He was tall, but he wasn't gaunt. He was…solid. Not overweight by any means. Just sturdy. A real hunk.

Hunk?

Good grief.

No. He was…staunch. A typical staunch Republican.

Which didn't at all explain why looking at him gave me so much pleasure. Or why, when he turned in my direction, I smiled at him.

*I wonder what he'd be like to kiss?*

I stared at his lips as he walked toward me. And that hair. That stiff, unbending hair. I wanted to rake my fingers through it. I wanted to own it. Have the right to touch it whenever I chose. And that scared me. Because those were the kind of thoughts that led to kissing. And I'd already decided I wasn't doing that anymore. I was on sabbatical, and I wanted to stay that way. I wasn't coming off until July. Eleven more months. And I certainly wasn't coming off for Eric.

But…

What would it be like to be embraced and not be impaled by a bony rib? To sit on someone's lap without being pierced by a jutting knee?

I imagined it might be kind of cozy.

But then that's what all Republicans wanted you to believe. *Come join our cozy club! Come be part of our old boys' network. Try us, you'll like us! We'll tax you into the poorhouse.*

Ha.

Not likely.

"Allie, hey. I was wondering…do you know if Samantha's in?"

Samantha. I blinked. The weird sort of hunky illusion I'd cast over Eric shimmered for one last moment and then dissolved.

Thank goodness.

"Maybe. I have no idea."

"Oh. Well…"

"Eric?"

He stepped closer.

"About Samantha…just be careful."

He shifted his attaché case from one hand to the other. "I always am."

I thought about how much time he appeared to put into the study sessions with her. About the outlines he prepared. "I'm not talking about studying."

"Neither am I."

"Oh."

"Allie?"

"What?"

"Are you okay?"

No. Clearly, I wasn't. "Yeah. I'm fine. And I'm sorry."

"For what?"

"Introducing you to Samantha."

"There's nothing to apologize for. You haven't done anything wrong. And neither have I. So...Samantha's desk?"

I pointed him in the right direction and then walked down the hall to the vending machines. It seemed like a good time for a break.

My cell phone rang that evening just as I was logging off my computer at work.

"So are you on for Roppongi tonight?"

It was Gina. She's the only person I knew who started a conversation as if she was already well into it.

"Roppongi?" I felt my nose scrunch. "Really?"

"Why? Did I say Shibuya? Because I meant to say Roppongi."

I sighed. "Okay. What time?"

"Nine o'clock. Your place."

She hung up before I could answer. Because she knew what I would have said.

I would have said, "No. Can't we just go out to dinner like grown-ups?" Because it wasn't possible to be a grown-up in Roppongi. At least not at night.

Roppongi at night was one of the strangest experiences known to man. An interesting mix of East and West. Of people in the know and the totally clueless. There were discreet members-only clubs on the back side of Roppongi-dori. And there were neon-ringed bars with thirty-dollar cover charges filled with foreigners lining the avenue. It was a meeting of East and West fueled by the hope of the perfect one-night stand.

You could get high on drugs so new the FDA didn't even know about them. You could watch the different tribes of Japanese practice dancing on the street. In unison. It was like walking through consecutive music videos. The surfers all had bleached blond hair and unnaturally dark skin. The eighties tribes had punked out hair and deconstructed silhouettes. The punks had Mohawks. The rockers wore skintight jeans. The Elvis impersonators had their hair combed into perfect pompadours.

Roppongi was an experience you didn't want to have too often.

Gina liked to barhop. And she didn't like to pay cover charges. A combination that stressed me out because when I was with her I had a fifty percent chance of being escorted out of every establishment we visited. Especially after a few drinks had loosened Gina's inhibitions—not that she had very many to start with—and she began dancing tables.

So why did I feel the need to go?

Because Gina needed some kind of guardian angel. And a place to crash afterward. Besides, she had a way of meeting people. Interesting people. People I might enjoy talking to when they weren't drunk.

I went home and ate dinner. I surfed the Internet for a while and then decided to change. I pulled on a pair of low-waisted loose fitting black linen pants, stretched a black tank top over my head, and slipped into some cheap black rhinestone-studded flip-flops. You never knew when you were going to get a beer spilled on you in Roppongi, so black was my color of choice. It hid the stains. Then I twisted my hair up on top of my head and secured it in the long beak of a hinged clip.

The gate guard phoned me at eight thirty. No surprise there. Gina was always early when it was time to have fun.

I went out to meet her. She was wearing an Indian-looking halter top with small mirrors and sequins embroidered into the fabric. Giant hoops swayed in her ears. She had worn her hair in a way that offered no hope of it staying perched on top of her head. Even then, it was slowly sliding backward.

"You're early."

"And if it weren't for me, you'd be late. Or not show up at all."

"Let's just go." And get it over with.

We started out toward Roppongi Hills, the landmark tower for my part of the city. If all else failed when I was driving around town, if I could make it to that monstrous tower, I knew I would be able to find my way home.

We walked up the hill beside the elevated expressway. It was too hot a night to hurry. We shuffled along, our flip-flops marking the cadence, and waited at the top of the hill for the light to change. We passed the Roppongi Hills-everything complex. The pride of its builder, the tower complex was the ultimate in vertical living. Subway lines, shops, restaurants, offices, and residences collected and organized into seven hundred and eighty-one vertical feet of space. It was the adult version of the area we were heading toward. Roppongi Hills was also open late at night, but there, people were much more likely to be sipping wine, watching a movie, or reading foreign newspapers than exchanging sloppy kisses with strangers.

The closer we got to the entertainment district, the brighter the neon signs became, the younger the people, the louder the music. Bars were stacked on top of each other like towers built from Legos. Gina bopped into a bar, patting the bouncer on the cheek as she passed. We climbed the stairs to the second floor and settled into a couple of chairs. But it wasn't crowded enough to be entertaining, so in thirty minutes we were back out on the sidewalk, staring down the street at a bouquet of neon signs.

"We need a beer…and some boys who would like to buy them for us. Let's go…" Gina glanced up and down the street before deciding to cross to the other side. "Let's go over there!"

Our stay "over there" was more profitable. We netted a beer apiece and some pleasant conversation with two Brits. But after an hour and a half, although we'd danced, they still hadn't loosened their ties, and the conversation had plunged into the technical details of their jobs.

Over and over again.

Gina pointedly turned her wrist over and looked at her watch. Then she vaulted from her chair. "We have to go!" She grabbed my hand, yanking me from my chair and leaving me to apologize while she bored into the crowd.

I tried to shrug. Waved with my free hand. "I'm sorry! Thanks! Nice to meet you! Good luck!"

Once we were screened by the crowd, she stopped. "You're the tall one! Would it hurt you to do some pushing and shoving for a change?"

We traded places.

Gina held onto my forearm as I bulldozed toward the door.

Once on the sidewalk, we both sighed. Then we took greedy gulps of air.

I took the clip from my hair, shook it out, and then refastened it.

Gina's hair was dangling, in a small bun, at the nape of her neck.

"Do you want me to fix this?"

"Would you?"

I pulled the pin from it, wound it on top of her head, and pushed the pin back in.

"Thanks. Well, we had one beer. Let's go find another. Let's go…"

"Could we just go home?"

"Home? It's only eleven!"

I sighed and turned around, meaning to find a low-key alternative to what I knew would be Gina's high-energy suggestion. But I found myself looking instead at Eric Larsen, who was walking down the street toward me.

# 10

*Do not slip away,*
*Turtle, into muddy pond.*
*I want to feed you.*

"ALLIE?"

"Eric! What are you doing here?" If ever there were a model Roppongi Hills person, Eric was it.

"I came with someone from work. Told him I'd see him on Monday. I've had enough."

*Me too, me too.*

I turned from Eric toward Gina. She was staring at him. "Gina? This is my friend Eric. He's headed home to Hiroo. Let's walk with him."

"Have you cloned yourself? It's only eleven! Listen, I just want to knock one back. One more bar, one more beer, and then we'll go. Promise."

I looked at Eric. Willed him to be man enough to drag me away.

Gina must have seen my look because she attached herself to Eric's arm. "Come on. Eric wants to go, don't you, Eric?" Not waiting for his answer, she patted his arm. "He said yes. And we need you to come so you can introduce us."

"Gina..."

"Come on, come on, come on. Stop being cranky." She was already walking down the street, talking to Eric and ignoring me. If there's anything worse than barhopping in Roppongi, it's barhopping by yourself in Roppongi.

Gina led the way into the next bar.

Eric, God bless him, paid the cover charge for all of us and made us legal. Gina towed us around groups of people until she found an alcove holding a vacant couch. Then she sat down, patting the seats beside her for Eric and me.

We sat down. One on each side of her.

Gina took one hand from each of us. Gave them both a squeeze and then pressed them into her lap. Looked at Eric. Looked at me. "So where did you two meet?"

"Gina, it's not like that. We went to the same high school."

"High school? So this is like some sort of reunion!"

"And we go to the same church."

"Perfect. Perfect. And what do you do?" She was looking at Eric.

"I work at the embassy."

"A dip-lo-mat! A Polly!" She cocked her head. Stared at him for a long moment. "But you're okay. I think I like you. You know Allie's a bit stuffy, don't you?"

"I—"

Gina turned to me. "I'm not talking to you, Stickybeak. I'm talking to him." She turned back toward Eric. "Now. Where was I?"

"Allie."

"Right. She's a bit stuffy. A little rigid. A bit too earnest. Thinks a bit too long before dipping her toe in. But she's a good sort. So if you're a decent soul and you promise to try to loosen her up a bit, I'll let you have her."

"But—"

"Still talking to him." She lowered her head, looked up at him for a long moment beneath her brow. Then her face cleared. "Oh! I see how it is." She swiveled her head back toward me for a moment and then leaned in toward him. Whispered something. Then laughed. Kissed him on the cheek.

"Time for a beer." She slipped away from the couch. Releasing our hands, she turned around, took them back up, and joined them together. "Well. Time for you to get reacquainted." She winked and then left, leaving Eric and me holding hands.

Sitting on a couch.

The only two sober people in all of Roppongi.

"She seems like a nice friend."

"I have to watch out for her." I withdrew my hand from Eric's but realized he wasn't paying any attention to me. His eyes were trailing Gina.

I followed his gaze and saw her talking to someone. Saw him reach out and caress her on her rear. She jabbed him—hard—with an elbow and stalked away.

"I think she does a pretty good job watching out for herself."

I couldn't help myself from laughing. "And me. We met at a bar, here in Roppongi. It was my first weekend in town and someone at work told me I just had to visit." Someone? It had been Neil. And he'd meant it as a joke, but I hadn't known him well enough then to decipher his dry humor.

"So you just ran into each other?"

"She saw me being pestered by an obnoxious drunk and pretended she knew me. Gave me an excuse to get away."

"Nice."

"It was."

We all walked out of the bar around midnight.

Gina took Eric's hand between both of hers as he turned to leave us. Shook it. "I like you. I really do."

He gave her a half hug. "I like you too. I really do." He looked over at me. "Bye, Allie."

"Bye."

He headed off in a direction taking him deeper into Roppongi, but he had to go through all of it in order to go home.

My own plan was to get out of Roppongi as quickly as possible. We walked home the way we'd come in relative silence. At least on my part.

Gina whistled. Hummed. Broke into song now and then.

She flashed her passport at the gate guard while I signed her into the barracks. We went up to my room. Got ready for bed.

"Do you have a T-shirt or tank top? Something I could borrow?"

"Just don't ask if you can use my toothbrush."

"I have mine right here." She pulled one out of her purse, looking proud of herself. "But could I beg some toothpaste?"

Once she finished brushing her teeth, she pulled one of my T-shirts on, crawled into bed, and fell asleep before I'd finished in the bathroom.

But she was wide awake at ten the next morning.

"So, tell me about that Eric person."

I rolled away from her and pulled my pillow over my head.

"Seriously. I want to know."

I lifted the pillow just a tiny bit. "What about him?"

"Everything."

Maybe if I told her something—one thing—she'd leave me alone. "He went to my high school."

"So you said. And were you friendly then?"

"Friendly? Not really. I hated him."

"Why?"

I knew I would never win this battle. I pulled the pillow off my head, sat up, and joined her as she leaned back against the wall. "There's not much to tell. We're polar opposites."

"Opposites attract."

"He's a Republican. I'm a Democrat."

"You Yanks have such a fixation with your own politics. As near as I can tell, both your political parties sit just shy of center."

"How can you say that? They're completely different!"

"Not when you're from a country running Greenies and Communists in elections."

"Greenies?"

"Environmentalists. Wacky tree huggers."

"*I'm* a tree hugger."

"No, you're not. You just think you are."

"No, I am. I actually chained myself to a tree once."

"Good onya. So if you're a tree chainer, then what is he?"

"A Republican. Big business. Power. Money."

"Are you sure you're giving him a fair go? He didn't seem like one of those to me."

"Well…" He didn't, in fact. "You should have seen him in high school."

There was a knock on the door.

I went to answer it.

Gina called out behind me. "Why?"

I opened the door. It was Samantha.

"Wasn't he as handsome back then?"

Samantha came into the room, trying to look over my shoulder. "Who is that?"

"Gina."

"Oh." Samantha didn't approve of Gina. I think it had something to do with detecting a rival.

I would have closed the door, but I didn't want Samantha to think I wanted her to stay.

"So was he or wasn't he then?"

"No! He wasn't…isn't…he's not hot."

"Isn't he?"

"Who?" Samantha walked further into the room and said hi to Gina. "Who's hot? Or not?"

"Eric."

"Larsen?" She was looking at me with raised brows.

I nodded.

"Yes, he is. He's the definition of hot."

"And how do you know Eric?" Gina looked as if she couldn't decide who to throw a dart at, Samantha or me.

"Allie. She set us up."

"You set *Samantha* up with Eric?" She'd decided. The dart had been hurled at me.

"Yes. No. Not really. Eric's helping her study for the State Department test."

"And *you're* the one who introduced them."

I shrugged.

"She did." Samantha smiled in my direction as she curled up on the bed next to Gina. "And he's delectable. So nice and manly, you know?"

Yes. We all knew. There was something solid and strong about Eric. Even I knew that.

"Thanks, Allie." Samantha might as well have started licking her whiskers.

"Did you need something, Samantha?"

"Hmm?"

"Can I get you something?"

"Oh. I'm hungry. Do you have any cereal hiding in here?"

I got a box of Grape-Nuts from the cupboard, handed it to her, and shoved her out the door.

"Don't you have anything else?"

"No."

I kicked the door shut behind her. Turned and walked right into the heel of Gina's hand.

"Ow!" I put a hand up to my forehead. "Why'd you do that?"

"Well now, maybe you'll remember!"

"Remember what?"

"Remember that the next time you decide to just give some guy away for free to call me first. Okay?"

"What do you mean?"

"Samantha? What were you thinking! He's perfect for *you*."

"No, he's not."

"Yes, he is."

"He's a Republican!"

"He could be a social Democrat for all that matters. I'm not talking about politics; I'm talking about a person. A person who is really something special."

Gina took a shower, put her clothes back on, and had a glass of milk. All the while not talking to me. She was in a mood. But she turned away from the front door, just after she'd pulled it open. She paused, held one finger up, and stabbed at her temple. "Think."

I did.

## 11

*O Crane, in languid*
*pose, rest there a while so I*
*might enjoy your grace.*

I DIDN'T HEAR FROM GINA FOR FOUR DAYS. Not unheard of, but considering the way she'd left my room, it was a bit ominous in terms of our friendship. Then, finally, she called.

"So I invited Eric over to your place on Friday night. Is nine okay?"

"For what?"

"For whatever. I'll meet you there."

She hung up before I could reply.

I spent half an hour getting dressed that Friday evening. Nothing seemed quite right. I got frustrated with myself for being frustrated with my clothes. For caring so inordinately much about what to wear. I stepped back from the pile of discarded black, white, and green clothing on my bed and took a deep breath. Then I deliberately put all my skirts and dresses back into the closet and chose something casual. A pair of green-and-white plaid Bermuda shorts. At least, they were shorts for *me*. I think they were probably intended as capris for a normal-sized woman. I pulled a green skinny polo shirt on over it.

Left my feet bare.

Left my hair down.

Eric showed up first. It felt awkward for me, and it seemed as if he felt the same. It had to feel odd showing up at someone else's place when the person who invited you wasn't even there yet.

We smiled at each other. I offered him a Coke. Got myself one. Drinking Cokes took about ten minutes with polite conversation about work interspersed between swallows.

I was sitting at the chair by my desk.

Eric was sitting in the other one.

I jiggled the computer mouse with my elbow just enough to clear the screen saver. I glanced at the computer clock when I set my empty Coke can down.

Gina was late. I didn't know how to interpret that.

At least when she came, fifteen minutes later, she brought the party with her. She threw her purse onto the bed and plopped down beside it. "I was thinking games. Do you have any? Maybe…Scrabble?"

"No. Absolutely not. Anything but Scrabble. I'll even play cards."

She blinked. "You're a writer. It's not like you don't know any words."

"I know lots of words. It's just that I know them all in order."

I saw Gina and Eric exchange a glance.

"Should I tell her, or do you want to tell her?" Gina was pretending to whisper.

"Maybe neither of us should tell her. Maybe she needs to figure it out herself."

"In America we're taught it's rude to talk about people."

"In Australia too. But here's the thing…we're in Japan! There are no rules. At least not the normal ones."

"I am not—"

"Normal people have closets full of clothes in three colors? And three colors only?" She glanced at Eric. "Did you know that? Did she do that in high school?"

"It's called *style*. It's called being efficient."

"What is it about her? Do you know? Because I haven't been able to figure it out. Why do we love our Allie so much?"

"She's idealistic, independent, and abnormally earnest in the pursuit of her goals."

Me, abnormally earnest in the pursuit of my goals? That sounded positively Republican!

Gina was nodding. "Well. That's about what I'd say. Except that part about pursuing her goals. Did you know she's a writer and she hasn't even written a book?" She looked at me. "Did you want to play a game or not?"

"I don't have any games."

"You don't have any games? None?"

"I have a pack of cards. Maybe. Somewhere."

"Never mind. We'll play the dictionary game. Aussie slang. I'll give you a word and you two make up the definition and then I'll see who comes closest."

"That's not a game!"

"Fine. Then you think of one. Some hostess you are. I'll think I'll leave."

I watched, astonished, as Gina pushed away from the bed, slung her purse over a shoulder, and marched toward the door. "Aren't you going to open the door for me?"

I got up from my chair and went over to the door. "You don't have to—"

"Shh!" She winked at me. "You can thank me later." She slipped out the door and was gone.

I stood there for a long moment before I shut it. Stood longer still before I turned around to face Eric.

"Would you like to…" What? What was I supposed to do with him?

"We could go for a walk."

"Let's go for a walk."

I slid my feet into some white driving moccasins.

We left in a hurry. I grabbed my ID card, but forgot my purse. And then, once we were outside, I had no idea where to go.

But Eric did. "There's a great restaurant down toward Hiroo. We wouldn't have to eat dinner. We could just have something to drink. Or dessert."

Relief. "Great. Fine. Sounds good."

We turned and walked down Gaien-nishi-dori. Heard the bugs buzzing, chirping, humming. I swatted at mosquitoes. Bumped into Eric during a particularly vehement swat at the back of my arm.

He gave me a quizzical glance.

"Sorry. Mosquitoes love me. If this were a hundred years ago, I'd be long dead of malaria."

He smiled. "That would have been a shame."

I would do anything to avoid the welts I get from mosquito bites. And usually I did. Usually I didn't wear perfume in the tropical heat. I wore mosquito repellent. *Eau de DEET.*

But thinking I would be staying inside that night, and thinking Eric was coming over…well…"You're probably one of those people who never gets bit."

He shrugged. Didn't deny it.

"I wish there were some way you could grant me immunity."

"How about this?" He slid closer to me and wrapped an arm around my waist, drawing me to his side. "At least one side of you will be protected."

I put an arm around his waist. Drew him still closer. An automatic reaction for someone who enjoyed a kiss. Used to enjoy a kiss. Was on probation from kissing. Is that why it felt so nice? Because I was having such infrequent contact with people of the opposite sex? Whatever it was, it didn't feel flirty. It felt like something else.

Sooner or later, I would have to get my words back or I'd be out of a job.

The restaurant turned out to be halfway between Eric's house and the barracks. It had a Mediterranean feel. Clay tiles on the floor. A relaxed atmosphere. A perfect ambience for putting puzzling thoughts out of my head.

"How'd you know about this place?"

"Samantha told me."

"She would know. She's been around." In more ways than one.

"She said the plum wine is good."

It probably was.

"Do you want anything? To eat?"

I looked at the menu again. It all sounded good. The tapas. The main courses. I promised myself I'd come for dinner sometime. I flipped to the desserts. They looked good too. But heavy. I flipped back to the tapas. Couldn't get past the idea of dates wrapped in bacon, served over a slab of parmesan cheese. A combination of sweet and salty that was peculiarly attractive at ten in the evening.

The waitress came to take our order.

That's when I realized I'd forgotten my purse.

I shut the menu.

Found Eric looking at me.

"You okay? Aren't you having anything?"

"Um…I forgot my purse. No money."

"My treat. What would you like?"

I'd forgotten that about him. He was most definitely a "ladies first" kind of guy. I wavered. Made up my mind. "The dates in bacon."

He glanced at the waitress. "Make that two."

Really. "I could order something else. We could share."

"Order what you want. Why shouldn't we both? Especially when it happens to be the same thing."

When Eric ordered a glass of Australian red, I did the same. Why not? We'd done everything else the same.

Soon, we were sipping wine and talking about my job. About his job. In earnest this time. Kept talking through the dates and bacon, which were really good.

Eventually we began to discern the bottom of our wine glasses.

The waitress brought the check. Eric drew it toward his side of the table.

"Sorry about the purse."

He smiled at me. "I'm not."

I smiled back. "Thanks."

I felt a strange reluctance to leave the restaurant. Somehow, sitting there, I could imagine myself to be the person I hoped I'd one day be. I could imagine myself to be sophisticated. Urbane. Funny, because in high school, I'd hated people who looked like me. Mostly because they looked like everyone else. People like Eric. Back then, I'd been all about broomstick skirts and tie-dye.

The things we do to be taken seriously.

Finally, when I couldn't delay any longer, had nothing left to swish around the bottom of my wine glass, I rose to my feet.

Eric quickly did the same. Stood beside me for a moment. Then pressed a hand to my back. Ushering me, shepherding me, forward. Out into the night.

In front of us, suspended in the sky, was something I had not seen for a long while. Not since I'd moved to Tokyo. "The moon."

My words made Eric stop. Step nearer. "The moon?"

"I haven't seen it in…forever."

I heard amusement in his voice. "It's there nearly every night."

But I wasn't. I'd forgotten about the moon. I wasn't usually out at night. And when I was, there were so many buildings, so much activity between myself and the sky, that I was never able to see it.

How beautiful, the moon.

My face was uplifted, tipped up toward its glow, when I realized Eric was watching me. I turned toward him, face still uplifted.

He leaned forward. Just a little. Looked into my eyes. Blinked. Then took a deliberate step backward.

Had he been…? He *had* been. He had been on the verge of kissing me. But he hadn't.

Why not?

Why was I suddenly so unkissable? It wasn't as if I'd been unwilling. I'd quite forgotten, in fact, that I was not supposed to be kissing anyone at all. Good thing I didn't *want* to be kissing anyone. Didn't want to be kissing *him*.

Eric smiled, grabbed my hand, and tugged me across the street. "There's a park over here."

It didn't look like it. But maybe he was a private sort of person. Maybe he didn't like to do his kissing in front of the moon and everyone else. Not, of course, that there would *be* any kissing taking place.

"Come on."

We walked up half a block alongside a tall stucco wall. And then we turned into the block and it opened up, as Eric had said, into a park. The ground was covered with sand and encircled by the spreading arms of trees.

There were tiny playhouses for small children. A menagerie of animals poised on fat coils of springs. Swing sets. A huge climbing structure built from logs, connected with a web of netting and metal slides, for older children. And, best of all, a disc hooked onto a cable running from the top of the log structure down to the opposite side of the park.

I dropped Eric's hand and started climbing.

By the time I reached the top, he had grabbed the disc from its lowest point and walked it back up the cable toward me. Pushed it up to me. "Do you need—"

Before he could finish his sentence, I had hopped onto the disc, wrapped my legs around the cable, and whizzed right by him. Closed my eyes. Went streaking through the moonlight, the motion making riffles in my hair.

When I reached the platform, I got off the disc and sat down. Then I pulled my shoes off and set them beside me. I stepped down and stood right there in the sand. Dug my toes in, luxuriating in the grittiness. I'd always loved the beach.

Eric sat down in the sand at my feet, one leg bent in front of him, the other pulled up toward his chest. "Been a long time? Since you were at the beach?"

I shrugged. "I went this summer when I was home." It had been strictly a sisters' escape—a day trip away from the madness of the wedding.

"Seaside?"

"Cannon Beach."

"We used to go to Newport."

I smiled. "To Mo's?" To an Oregonian, Newport was synonymous with Mo's. The restaurant was an Oregon tradition. They served the best clam chowder I'd ever eaten. The best clam chowder most people had ever eaten.

"To Mo's."

I sat down beside him. "They don't have Mo's here."

"Have you been to a beach here?"

"No."

"Why not?"

I shrugged. "It probably wouldn't be the same."

"How could it be much different? It's the other side of the Pacific. There'd be sand. Waves. Everything that's good in a beach."

"Except Mo's."

"How long have you been here?"

"Two years."

"And you've *never* been to a beach?"

I shook my head.

"Well, that's sad. There's hardly any city in Japan more than a hundred miles from the water. Next Saturday afternoon, we're going to Kamakura."

"Can't. I'm going to Hakone with Gina. It's her last weekend in town. From our trip she goes straight to the airport." I leaned toward him and gave him a friendly jab with an elbow. "But thanks just the same. You didn't have to plan that just for me."

He leaned back onto his elbows. "Maybe I did it for both of us."

Looking down toward the sand, I felt suddenly shy. "Well, thanks."

"Didn't you write some poem about sand? In high school?"

"I wrote poems about lots of things in high school." Still wrote poems about lots of things. Only they were shorter.

"But that one was really good. I could almost feel it." He scooped up a handful of sand and let it drain away between his fingers.

I lay back in the sand, experimentally. It felt good. I wiggled around to make a hollow for my body and then looked up, right into the moon.

Closing my eyes, I cupped cool palmfuls of sand and imagined I could be anywhere in the world. But I opened my eyes to find Eric stretched out beside me, gazing up at the moon. Felt his warm hand cup my own.

We lay there for a long while without speaking. Two foreigners, washed up on a beach in the middle of Tokyo.

# SEPTEMBER *Nagatsuki*
## *Autumn Long Month*

12

*This season that I
love must pass before the next
one I love can come.*

SOMEHOW GINA HAD GOT IT STUCK IN HER HEAD that the only way she'd experience the quintessential Japan was to stay at the Fujiya Hotel in Hakone. And somehow Gina was able to figure out how to get combination passes to the mountain area that were good for a round-trip train ride to Hakone and then all the buses, trams, boats, and cable cars we wanted to use once we were up there. It was supposed to be a good deal.

*If* we could figure out the schedules.

*If* we could figure out where to catch the train.

*If,* in fact, the train we were on was going to Hakone and not Hakodate or Hirosake.

"Relax."

"I'll relax when we get there."

"You're supposed to be the intrepid globe-trotting reporter."

"I only trot in English."

"You know you're a paradox, right?"

"Don't you mean icon?"

"No. I mean paradox. At least I think I do. An irony or absurdity, right?"

"Absurdity?"

She flashed a grin that said she was proud of herself. "Yes. I'm quite certain of it."

"I think I liked being a paradox better."

"I'd love to call you one, but you're really quite absurd. You're a reporter, right? You're supposed to be curious about everything, and you haven't investigated Japan since you've been here."

"I have too."

"Really."

"Yes! I've been to Yokota."

"Is that the navy base or the air force one?"

"Air force."

"And?"

"And what?"

"And where else have you been?"

"I have a job. A real one. I can't just go traipsing around Japan anytime I feel like it."

"I work too. Worked too."

"I know. I'm sorry. It's just that I like—"

"You like being in control, and Japan terrifies you."

"It doesn't terrify me."

"It makes you uncomfortable."

"It doesn't...maybe..."

She gave me the eyeball.

"It's hard to buy a train ticket when you don't speak the language."

"There are tourist agents in town."

"Words are how I speak."

She nodded her head emphatically. Pointed to her chest and held up two fingers. "Yes. Me too." She gave me a shove that knocked my head against the window. "Idiot."

"Ow!"

"I'm serious."

"I am too. That hurt!"

"Well then, I'm sorry. For that. But not for the other."

"Words are what I'm good at, Gina, and I don't have any here."

"Then you're turning your strength into a weakness. Is it not possible for you to start from a place of complete ignorance? To pretend you know nothing? To learn about the world all over again?"

"I'm a journalist. My job is to know things."

"But not everything. Maybe the things you assume about life just aren't valid here."

"How could they not be? They've worked everywhere else."

"But this isn't everywhere else. Stop placing expectations on Japan, and it just might surprise you. You might even fall in love with it."

"I tried learning Japanese. It didn't work. I didn't get it."

"I'm not talking about learning the language. I'm talking about living life. Stop being and start doing."

"I can't."

"Sometimes you have to give something up to get something."

"Like what?"

"Control. Sometimes you have to go completely off your head, go crazy and…hop a train to Hakone and get lost in one of the world's most civilized nations before you can see what you're missing."

"Are you saying I'm boring?"

"No. You're one of the most interesting people I know."

"Are you saying I'm a coward?"

"No. You moved to Japan, didn't you? And you volunteered to go and cover the war in Iraq last year, right?"

"Yeah. And that was crazy, see?"

"No, it wasn't. It makes perfect sense for you."

"But Iraq's a foreign country."

"Iraq was about work. And you went to an American base."

"There were coalition forces."

"Yes. Coalition forces, speaking English, in the middle of an army base. And you were filing stories, right?"

"Exactly!"

"And how did you feel about that?"

"I loved it!"

"Exactly!"

"Exactly what?"

"Of course you loved it. You were in a foreign country, so you could pretend you were the person you'd like to be. Only you were in a controlled environment, doing your job about eighteen hours a day. Right?"

"I wasn't there on vacation."

"Did you ever set foot outside the base?"

"It wasn't allowed."

"Aren't you seeing a pattern here?"

"Are you trying to analyze me?"

"No, I'm trying to help you. Sometimes you have to give up a little control in order to get some. See?"

No. I didn't see. I didn't want to see that my best friend was leaving me all alone in a foreign country. "Now you're the one being paradoxical."

"I don't mean to hurt your feelings, but I had to say it before I left because nobody else will." She was right, in a sense. Because who was left? "Well, here's the diagnosis: I should think before I act and you should act before you think. Where's your writer's intuition? Why do you always give away everything in your life that could be good?"

"Like what?"

"Eric. Writing."

"I write all the time."

"But not what you want."

"It's just not working out. I don't have any inspiration. So maybe it's just not what God wants me to do right now."

"What utter rubbish."

"You don't even believe in God. How would you know what he wants me to do? Or not?"

"If I did believe in God, I wouldn't create some deity who gives people talents and doesn't require that they be used. You haven't even tried."

"I try nearly every day."

"Do you?"

"Yes."

"Then you're not putting your heart into it."

"How would you know?"

"Because if you had, you'd have a book by now."

"I can't just order up a book. That's not how it works."

"Why not?"

"I just...can't. It's not the right time. I'm still building my résumé."

"How many articles do you really have to write to build a résumé? And how many haiku poems do you have to create in order to feel that you've mastered the art form?"

"For a person who doesn't believe in God, you sound a lot like him."

"That's because we both read the same book. It's entitled *We Love Allie*. But it's tough love, mind you. Listen. You cannot give up yet. Especially if you haven't even tried."

"You are. You're leaving."

"I'm not giving up. I'm going home. There's a difference. I don't have to prove anything to anyone anymore. It's okay for me to be a normal Aussie living a normal Aussie life. I've figured out what I want. And it's not here. It's there."

"Then why can't I do that?"

"Because you haven't figured out what you want yet, have you? And if you leave here, you'll still have the same question following you around like a phantom. Leaving doesn't do anything for you, but it does everything for me."

"So I just get to stay here?"

"No. You just get to live here. *Live.* That's the key."

"I've been living here for the past two years."

"You've been breathing here for the past two years. There's a difference. Don't mess this up. Promise me. Japan is a gift waiting to be unwrapped. Don't leave without opening it."

"I don't even know what it is."

"Yeah. Well, those sorts of presents usually turn out to be the best kind, don't they?"

I sighed. "So...what are you going to do once you get home?" Home. Everyone in Japan talked about going home. Not going back. Because going back implied somehow that in your current life you had gone forward. But being in Japan wasn't like being anywhere else on earth. Being in Japan was a sojourn. And sojourners always returned home.

The Fujiya turned out to be a grande dame of a hotel that had been built in the 1890s. Its rambling, sprawling evolution was clearly evident from the outside. A complex of five buildings accumulated from 1891 through 1960 dotted the hilltop before us in a fantasyland of the different eras of Japanese architectural style. With names like Comfy Lodge and Flower Palace, we might have expected to run into either Teddy Roosevelt or Madame Butterfly. The peeling paint we saw on our approach hid an aura of privilege and prestige on the inside.

We climbed the dragon-draped staircase leading to the lobby, checked in with an English-speaking concierge, and were given keys. Then we walked past the reception area, passing a substantial stairway that disappeared into the upper level of the building. That part of the hotel looked and felt like a lodge. Dark wood dissected white walls, and red carpets ran across the floors. Water radiators accordioned, silently, from the walls. An out-of-era circuit box still projected from the wall, and near it, a wooden-pegged coatrack. The hotel didn't look grand, but I had the feeling it was supposed to. New carpeting had been laid over wood floors that still creaked. Fresh paint had been applied to unevenly plastered walls. The hotel's rollicking, frolicking days were over, but it still welcomed guests with dignity. If the Fujiya wasn't trying hard, it was because it didn't have to. It was already part of Hakone lore.

We eventually found our room. It was on the fifth floor of a new building, located conveniently near an abandoned concierge desk, a forgotten outpost in a fading empire under attack by the bourgeoisie.

The room was nice. And spacious. Gina would have given her life for an apartment of a similar size. It was furnished with blond wood furniture, a small refrigerator, and an electric kettle for making green tea. At the far end was a sitting area with a table placed between two armchairs. There were rice paper shoji-screens covering the windows. I walked over to them and slid one aside. Our room looked out into trees that stretched up a long hill. At the top I could see the railroad we'd come in on.

It was soon time for dinner, and since we had our travel passes, we decided to use them. We took another train up the railway line and got off in a town called Gora. As the train ascended into the mountains, it tunneled into an early evening mist that dampened my spirits even as it restricted my sight. The second we left the train station, I wished we hadn't. "There's nothing here."

"There might be. We haven't seen everything yet." Gina dragged me off the platform, out past the gates of the station, and into the town. "Where's your great American spirit of adventure?"

We stepped into the street. Gina looked left and then right before heading out in the direction of the tourist shops.

There were, to be exact, five shops huddled around the train station. As with all good Japanese souvenir stores, they sold a mix of local culinary specialties and local crafts. We saw woodwork decorating everything from wallets and purses to pens and toothpick holders. There were piles of cellophane bags filled with loops of noodles and tidy stacks of boxes packed with colorful candies. But nothing really fit the requirements for dinner. At the last shop, Gina finally just asked the owner for a restaurant suggestion. Had we walked a few steps more, we might have found it ourselves.

We rounded the corner and ran into restaurants. Several of them.

"Ta-da!"

"But—"

She didn't wait to hear what else I was going to say. She pushed a button to activate the automatic door opener and then stepped behind me and literally pushed me through it.

After a surprisingly good dinner we left the restaurant and debated whether to return to the hotel or walk around Gora. And then Gina saw a billboard advertisement for some gardens. The arrow at the bottom of the sign pointed up a large hill.

"Let's go!"

"But it's foggy and it's getting dark."

"Just think how mystical it will all look."

"But haven't you seen a Japanese garden before?"

"Loads."

"Then why do we have to see this particular one?"

"Because it's here. And what if it's world famous, and I had the chance of seeing it on the eve of departing Japan, and I didn't? Can you imagine how that would feel? You could always come see it again…"

And she, of course, couldn't.

So we climbed the hill, passing three other restaurants along the way. The town seemed to get livelier the further we moved from the train station. At the top of the hill, the road came to a T and we paused, hanging on to a stop sign to catch our breath. Then we turned left, following more signs, until we arrived at the gates of the garden, which happened to be closed.

"Closed?"

"That's what it says."

"How can it be closed?"

"Um…because the gates are locked? It doesn't look like a Japanese garden anyway. You probably have lots of these in Australia, right? It's an arboretum or botanical garden."

"But botany is my favorite thing."

"I thought kangaroos were your favorite thing."

She snorted. "Kangaroos? Why do you Yanks think they're so cute? They're overgrown rodents. Aussies are the only people on earth who will run over their national mascot and leave it to die on the side of the road."

The Kangaroo Speech. I'd known it would stop her from pouting. I took her arm and turned her away from the gate. We began walking down the street.

"Did you know kangaroos are constantly pregnant? A joey outside the pouch, a joey inside the pouch, and one in suspended animation. Did you know they could do that? Suspended animation? It's like freezing an embryo or something. It's freaky."

She talked all the way down the street, to the top of the hill. Then paused. "Let's not go back the same way. Let's see something different."

So we continued walking the ridge of the hill, calculated when we had passed the train station, and then turned down a side street and began our descent. The whole time we'd been in Gora, I'd had the impression of being in mountains, of course, but it felt as if the town were located in a broad valley. As we descended the hill though, the mist began to thin, drilling peek holes into the mountains. And they were close! I could see them in glimpses. A snatched glance, a swirl in the mist and then the view would close and another would open somewhere else. It was enchanting. Fantastical. Amazing.

# 13

*Sun, shine for me while*
*there is still time, for Winter*
*will come much too soon.*

AS WE WERE WALKING BACK TO THE HOTEL FROM THE STATION, Gina tried to talk me into an *onsen*.

"You mean the hot springs? Where you sit around naked in a huge hot tub with people you don't know?"

"They're gender separate, you goon."

"No."

"Why not?"

"Because."

"Well, I'm going to. I'm not going to let your cultural peculiarities keep me from enjoying the quintessential Japanese experience."

"Cultural peculiarities? You're going to use my nationality against me?"

"Why shouldn't I? Everyone else does."

"No."

"You're not afraid to be seen naked, are you? You don't have a weird birthmark or three...um...breasts, do you?"

"No!"

"So you're just going to nod out on my only real Japanese experience? And you've the gall to call yourself my friend?"

My heart sank. I could deal with cultural superiority. I could handle questions of pride. But I wouldn't be able to sleep with guilt.

Twenty minutes later we were sneaking through the halls of the hotel on a mission to find the *onsen*. At least we were still wearing our street clothes. Yuka-san had warned me that normally you had to wear hotel-provided cotton *yukata* robes and slippers to *onsen*. And that's all you were supposed to wear. That seemed just a little indecent to me. Apparently the Fujiya management thought so too because there had been a politely worded note on top of our *yukata* telling us not to wear them around the halls.

"So how does this work again?" I figured if Gina were so set on going to the *onsen*, then she must have done it before.

"We'll figure it out when we get there."

"You don't know?"

"No. I've never done this before. First and last time, remember?"

"But what if we do it wrong?"

"We'll just watch and see how everyone else does it."

"I am *not* going to stare at other naked women just to figure out what they're doing. You do it." We both snorted with laughter. It diffused the tension until we reached the *onsen*.

I let Gina step in first.

She slid open a battered, rattly wood door that framed squares of opaque glass and then she parted a short *noren* cloth curtain that hung from the top of the door frame and ducked through.

I did the same and bumped right into her on the other side.

We both stood there staring. A sunken area lined with small cubbies suggested we take off our shoes and store them. And after that, there was a step up to tatami mats. The room seemed small. But maybe it was because the space was tight. A metal cage filled with towels, a long stretch of counter and mirror, showers, and deep shelves lined with baskets were all crammed into the space of an average-sized dorm room.

"There's no one here."

"That's right. Because they're all in there." Gina nodded toward a door at the far end of the room. At that moment, it slid open, revealing a dimly lit space, a brown-tiled floor, and what looked like a huge hot tub filled with women. The sound of laughter bubbled out.

"So what do we do?"

"Erm...we'll start here." She took off her shoes and slid them into a cubby.

I did the same.

"What next?"

"Well...we'll just step around to this side. And...take one of these."
She shoved a basket at me. Took one for herself.

All along the shelves, the baskets were filled with clothing. So I was
guessing the idea was to strip. I took my watch off. "Are you sure you
want to do this?"

"Of course."

The outer door slid open. A group of three women came in. Sleek,
chic, young women. We stood aside so they could...do their thing.

They stripped and then walked over toward the showers, chatting the
whole time. Once they'd rinsed off, they went into the onsen room and
slid the door shut behind them.

"There. See? That's what you do." Gina was nodding as if they'd just
confirmed all of her suspicions.

"Then you do it."

"You first."

"Are you chickening out on me?"

The outer door slid open again. A middle-aged woman entered.

Then the inner *onsen* door opened and a group of naked older women
came out.

We were trapped, pressed against the wall, trying to avoid the woman
who was in the process of getting undressed and the group of naked
women who were trying to put their clothes on.

After they all left, we sighed. In unison.

"All right. I admit it." Gina was sounding kind of defensive. "I'm just
not a get-naked kind of girl. Especially around other girls."

"It just...seemed like everyone was having so much fun in there. I
wouldn't want to ruin their good time. I mean, we're obviously foreigners."

"We'd probably make them feel uncomfortable."

"Exactly."

"Yeah."

"Yeah."

"We're big wusses."

I took my watch from the basket and pulled it back on. "No. You're
the big weenie. You thought you would do it. I was a coward all along."

"What? And for that you deserve a yellow badge of courage?"

We grabbed our shoes, shoved our feet into them, and scampered
out the door.

It was too early to go to bed, so we wandered the halls. The air of shabby elegance grew even stronger on closer inspection. We'd come almost abreast of the Tea Lounge. But instead of walking further and entering the lobby, we turned and entered the Magical Room. At least that's what the sign over the door frame called it. I would have dubbed it Grandma's Attic.

Kitschy pictures of a nude in a garden and an internally illuminated picture of Lake Ashi and Mount Fuji decorated what was intended to be a clubby lounge. We slumped into a pair of deep-seated velvet chairs upholstered in powder blue and gold. They sat on top of a sea foam green Chinese-style carved carpet. Architectural details proved the age of the hotel. The tall ceilings were plastered and cambered with exposed beam decoration in a style that was distinctly Arts and Crafts. Mosaic tile decorated the brazier chimney that sat in the middle of the room.

I turned toward Gina and noticed her staring out darkened windows. When a group of noisy women came and settled themselves into a grouping of chairs, she nudged me and then got up.

I followed her out of the room, past the lobby to a sun porch riddled with pre-air-conditioning techniques of sliding doors and transom windows. I must have walked through the room earlier, but I hadn't paid it any attention. Although it was clean and kept, it had an air of abandonment, as if it had been scorned for the relative comfort and luxury of the Magical Room. Rows of bent cane wood chairs, reminiscent of old-time cruise ships, looked out upon the misty night.

We pulled two chairs out of line, pushed them together and sat down, staring into the void of night created by the glare of artificial light.

"I'll miss you."

It was difficult to tell who had said it first.

The next morning we got up just after the sun rose and checked out of the hotel. The traditional way to tour the Hakone/Mount Fuji region was to partake in a circuit that included seven forms of transportation: the narrow gauge rail (which we took to Gora—again), the funicular, the cable car, the ropeway, a boat, a short hike, and then a bus. Gina wanted to do all seven, but we also had to make it to Tokyo in time for her to fly back to Australia. Our intention was to catch the first train up to Gora so we could catch the first cable car to the summit of the mountain and the first ropeway to the volcano.

By the time we disembarked from the boat, there was no time left for a hike. But Gina still insisted on looking for a souvenir from the trip. For both of us. I followed her in and out of shops with mounting anxiety.

It's not that I wanted to hurry along my last day with my best friend, but I also didn't want her to miss her plane. I didn't know what I was going to do without her. She could be opinionated, pushy, and blatantly rude, but she knew me. She was the only person in Tokyo who really knew me. And loved me. She pulled me out of my protective gaijin shell and, on occasion, made me think.

And maybe she was right. Maybe I did need to let go of my fears.

Fears?

She hadn't talked about fears. She'd talked about control.

I wasn't afraid of anything, was I?

We walked up the steps to another shop.

Gina stopped. Stood looking at all the objects covered in wood mosaic. "This is it. I'm getting something here. Last chance."

"What are you getting?"

"I don't know. I haven't decided yet. But let's get the same thing. Then we'll have a souvenir from Japan in common."

Gina and I looked at combs and mirrors and a selection of small boxes. Mostly because we couldn't afford the really big ones. Gina rounded the corner of a display and a minute later, I heard her voice from the other side. "I found them."

"Found what?"

"The things we're going to get. Come look."

I walked around to the other side and joined her. She handed me a box identical to the one she was holding. I turned it over. The bottom had the same style of pattern the top did. Or...wait. Maybe the top was the bottom. And the bottom the top. I searched for the lid. Couldn't find it.

"How do you open it?"

Gina's eyes were sparkling. "I don't know. It's a puzzle."

I looked at it more closely. Pressed at the top to see where the pieces were joined.

"Not that kind of puzzle. Not a jigsaw. The puzzle is in how to open it."

I looked at the sides. Nothing indicated to me that it was meant to be opened. All the surfaces were smooth. The solid wood along the edges was unbroken. "How do you open it? Because I'm not buying a box I can't open."

"I don't know. Here." She thrust a piece of paper at me.

The paper contained numbered instructions. Instructions I didn't understand. It had a diagram of the box. Lots of arrows pointing in different directions.

"You try." I handed the paper back to her.

"She can tell us." Gina gestured to a clerk who walked over. "*Sumimasen.* Could you show us how this works, please?"

Bowing, the woman placed her hands on the sides of the box and then used her thumbs to slide the sides back and forth. Each end was actually constructed of three narrow horizontal pieces. The sides slid, as a whole, up and down. And magically, the center of the box was revealed.

"And how do you...?" Gina mimed putting the box together.

The woman took the sheet of paper from me and turned it over. "Begin here." She pointed at the last instruction. Then she flipped the paper over again. "End here." She pointed at the first instruction. She used her thumbs once more, sliding the wood together, turning the box, and then sliding some more.

We bought two. And then we hopped a bus to the trian station, arriving just in time.

We boarded the train and took our assigned seats. But in between Hakone-Yumoto and Tokyo when the train seemed less crowded, we walked to the back and sat down in the very last seats of the very last car. As the train rocked down the tracks we stared out a huge picture window at the scenery retreating from us as if someone were winding it up into the mountains for storage. As if the Magical Room really was. As if our time in Hakone had been a kind of Japanese Brigadoon that, thereafter, would exist only in our imaginations.

We reached Shinjuku Station with an hour to spare. As we walked through the station, I found myself stopping in front of a food vendor, gazing longingly at fruit salad sandwiches.

Don't ask me why.

We decided to complete Gina's quintessential Japanese experience by taking one last visit to the Takashimaya department store. Specifically, the food department in the basement.

I trailed Gina to the cantaloupes.

"Look at this: ten thousand yen. For one!"

"Did you see these?" I pointed to a fruit basket containing exactly eight pieces of assorted fruit, cushioned in foam and cradled in paper. "It could also be yours for the bargain price of ten thousand yen. One hundred dollars..."

"Well, there's a guava among the bunch, isn't there?"

"And an apple!"

After a while we got tired of goggling over nine-dollar apples and two-dollar cherries, and followed our noses to the bakery area. We picked up samples of croissants and French bread, and then took a moment to buy some foccacia-style open-faced sandwiches for later.

I glanced at my watch. Elbowed Gina. "You only have fifteen more minutes."

"Okay, okay. I just want to see the bean curd guy one more time."

The bean curd guy worked in a glass-enclosed booth making what I could only describe as bean curd popovers.

We stood in front of the glass as he dipped a ladle into batter and slowly filled metal molds. Into the center of each, he placed a bit of chocolate-colored bean curd. Then he slid the tray into an oven.

"I love the way those smell!" Gina smiled, tapped on the glass, and waved the two-handed, spread-fingered wave peculiar to Japan.

The baker smiled and waved back.

"However, I truly hate the way they taste." She sighed and turn around. Started walking.

Ten minutes later, we'd returned to the train station and found the lockers where Gina had deposited all of her worldly possessions while we'd been in the mountains. She swiped a credit card to open the lockers and then wrestled the suitcases out and onto the floor.

I took one and set it upright onto its wheels, pulling out the handle for her.

"Thanks. Well...Hey! I have something for you."

"The puzzle box, right? We already exchanged them."

"No. Something else. Just wait..." She unzipped one of the suitcases, felt around inside, and then pulled something out. "Here it is. For you!"

I took the object from her. It was a red doll. A round red doll with one black eye and one empty space meant for an eye. Maybe she'd gotten it at a discount. "Thanks. Um...what is it?"

"It's a *daruma* doll. So you don't have one, then? I didn't think you did. And you can only have one at a time."

"Thanks. He's...cute."

She laughed. Took it, held it up to her face, and wiggled it at me. "Idiot. Don't you know what it's for?"

"No."

"It's for wishing. You make a wish and when it comes true then you draw in the other eye."

"I wish you could stay."

She sighed and then pulled me close in a fierce hug, squishing the *daruma* doll between us. "I can't."

## 14

*Whimper, Dog. Sometimes
the wound will not heal until
the heart's tears are cried.*

THE NEXT WEEK I FELT AS IF I WERE A WOUNDED DOG. I was prone to whimper at the most inopportune moments. I was subject to teary eyes and melancholy thoughts. I felt abandoned. Deserted. And most of all, I wanted my mother. It didn't help that I was working on an article about adoptions by military couples of Asian children.

One afternoon as I was working on the story, Eric called.

"How are you doing?"

I sighed. Slumped further into my chair. "Fine."

"How's Gina? Did she make it back okay?"

"I assume. She hasn't e-mailed. Probably been too busy being a normal Aussie living a normal Aussie life."

There was a long pause. "Are you sure you're okay?"

"I will be. Did you need something?"

"I almost hate to ask you this, but I'm stuck. I need a word."

Well, I had plenty. Normally. "Fire away."

"What's another word for 'wonderful'?"

"Super. Fabulous. Terrific."

"No. Something...a little less than wonderful. I'm trying to say someone had a wonderful time even though they didn't."

"As in, 'a wonderful evening'? Something like that?"

"Yes."

"So they didn't have a wonderful time, they hated it, but they have to be polite. Is that it?"

"Exactly."

"Maybe...um...pleasant. Could they have had a *pleasant* evening? The same way some people have a pleasant colonoscopy?"

"Pleasant—perfect! Thanks."

The weekend loomed before me. Even though I hadn't done something *every* weekend with Gina, Saturday was a gaping hole in my schedule needing to be filled. And I didn't want to spend it hanging around with Samantha and Eric. What I needed was a trip to Yokota. I'd do some grocery shopping, look around the BX department store, eat at the Mexican restaurant on base, and maybe even take in a movie if I felt like it.

I diddled around on Saturday morning. Spent some time surfing the Internet. Outlined a new story idea. Wrote several new haiku poems. Ate lunch, and then finally headed out the door.

Before I started the drive to Yokota, I swung by the New Sanno Hotel to drop off some dry cleaning. Since my return from vacation to the U.S., I'd had to remind myself to turn close on left turns and to turn wide on right turns. I'd also caught myself holding my breath on Tokyo's narrow streets, pulling my shoulders together in an attempt to squeeze the car through cars parked on both sides of the streets.

It should have been a quick trip. Park in the underground garage, turn the dry cleaning in at the concessionaire's in the basement, turn around, and drive away. But it was never as quick to park there as I expected because the parking spaces were sized for extra-petite cars. And then, after I'd dropped off my dry cleaning, I decided to run up to the café on the first floor to get a latte for the road.

That's when I ran into Eric.

He was sitting on a chair in the lobby looking like part of the décor.

He smiled when he saw me.

"I'd offer to buy you coffee, but you don't drink. Aren't you supposed to be studying with Samantha?"

"It was a quick session."

"So you're just...?"

"I'm taking the bus to Yokota. Decided it was better to wait inside with the air-conditioning."

Yokota. He was going to Yokota too. That figured. On any given Saturday, half the people at the embassy and *Stars and Stripes* went to Yokota. The following Saturday, it was the other half.

Looked as if Eric was on my rotation.

There was no point in hiding my own plans for the afternoon. There weren't that many places where off-base people went when they were on base. They tended to visit the BX and the commissary, a grocery store. And at Yokota, they both shared the same building. It would look extremely rude if I ran into him there. And besides, I figured I could use the company.

"I'm headed that way too. Want a ride?"

"You're driving?"

"Just give me two minutes to get some coffee and then we can go."

"Wonderful."

Just wonderful. When I had prayed for a friend to replace Gina, had I given God the impression that I wanted it to be Eric? Because that's the way it seemed to be turning out.

I got my coffee and we took the elevator down to the basement. I backed the car out so he could get in the passenger's seat. Otherwise he would have had to climb on top of the car parked next to us to have room to open the door.

I pulled out onto Meiji-dori and waited for the light to change. "Are you planning on getting a car?"

"I haven't decided. I take the subway to work, so I don't really need one. Do you use yours often?"

"Often enough." The light changed, and I pressed the accelerator to the floor. Even then, it took several seconds for the gears to catch and the car to move. I pulled onto the expressway lane and headed up the ramp to pay the toll.

"How much did you have to pay for it?"

"Five dollars. I figured I'd never find one cheaper. Couldn't pass it up."

"Five dollars? For a car?"

"One of the secretaries at work was moving when I came in. She begged me to take it. It was too old to take to a used car dealer. The only other option was to junk it, but that would have been a hassle. If I'd held out another day, she might have paid me to take it."

"It's not a bad car."

I laughed. It wasn't good, either. "I'll drive it until it falls apart or the JCI expires…Japan's Compulsory Insurance. Whichever happens first. Then I'll have to get something new. Newer." As it was, driving my car felt like driving a shoebox. The materials were just as thin. The noise of the road infiltrated the vehicle as if the windows were made of rice paper. And it was a completely stripped down version: a Saturday Special from some weekend a decade and a half ago. It didn't even have cup holders, which was inconvenient when you were trying to drive, hold a latte, and pay a toll at the same time. "Could you hold this for me?" I held my coffee out toward him.

He took it from me.

I slowed to a stop and held a thousand-yen bill out to the toll-taker. He gave me change. It cost about 1500 yen to get to Yokota and 1500 yen to get back.

Eric had noticed the map on the floor of the passenger's side and picked it up. He flipped through. "Where is Yokota?"

"Fussa-shi. Straight west of Tokyo. It's marked on the map."

He did some flipping back and forth for a while. "You could probably get there without taking the expressways. We should try it coming back."

Easy for him to say.

It *could* be done. I had even heard people talk about it. I'd just never tried it because I hadn't wanted to get lost. Driving in Tokyo is unlike driving anywhere else. The streets have no names. Literally. They also meander in a variety of directions and are made even more hazardous to navigate by the proliferation of one-way streets. And sometimes by two-way streets that turn into one-way streets during certain hours of the day. Expressways were titled "express" for a reason. They got you where you wanted to go—in or out of Tokyo—in a hurry.

We drove above a never-ending city through a maze of sound barrier walls hiding all but the sky and skyscrapers. It was two lanes in both directions—a laughable example of underplanning if it hadn't been so tragic. A simple fender-bender could clog traffic for miles. A three- or four-car accident, for hours. The traffic wasn't usually very thick on

Saturdays. Still, it took about ten miles for it to clear enough for my car to begin to beep.

Five-dollar cars came with adorable little quirks. Mine had several: a self-fogging windshield and an automatic speed alarm. Unfortunately, it was the only automatic gadget in the entire car. When I reached the speed of ninety kilometers an hour, it activated. Because, really, if there were a law like, say, a speed limit, why would you intentionally want to break it? And wouldn't you want to be notified if you did? So at ninety kilometers an hour, roughly the equivalent of fifty-five miles an hour, the car began to sing a cute melody; a delicate but insistent pling-pling-pling as we barreled down the expressway.

I usually turned on the radio and used the English-language Armed Forces Network to drown it out.

But then Eric wasn't usually with me.

We started over the Tama River. It was low and the river was gurgling mud. "If it were winter, you'd be able to see Mount Fuji." Had it only been a week since I'd been up to Hakone?

"I climbed Fuji as a kid with the Boy Scouts. They say you're a fool if you've never climbed it…but you're twice the fool if you climb it more than once. It's not a paved path or anything, but it's crowded. There were people—old guys even—passing us on the way up. We all bought walking sticks and had them stamped at the stations."

"How long did it take?"

"To walk up? Six, seven hours? It's not that hard, but the descent is easier. You slide all the way down on cinders. Or you hop a bus, drive halfway up, and start from there."

"You can drive?"

"Sure. Tour buses go up there all the time."

"Then why would you want to walk?"

I saw him turn to stare at me. "Why would you want to ride? Aren't you supposed to be the Democrat? Commune with nature? Hug a tree? All that whoo-whoo stuff?"

"I'm just saying—"

"I know. Sorry. I'm being insensitive. But seriously, it used to be an act of worship to climb Fuji. So how can you worship without making some kind of sacrifice?"

## 15

*Blushing Red Apple,*
*shall I pluck you now or shall*
*I leave you for Frost?*

JUST AFTER WE CROSSED THE BRIDGE, someone pulled out right in front of me from a tiny side street. I pressed my hand to the horn.

Honking was not done in Japan. No one did it. Ever. Except for me. Here's what I expected when I moved to Japan: I expected that everyone would be polite. And that the national character of politeness would be transferred to their roads because I knew everyone had to take a very expensive driver's education course before they could get a license. And I just figured...well...it was Japan!

I had a hard time believing I'd been wrong.

I'd run into the same lack of common courtesy in other aspects of life and had grown to suspect that the Japanese were changing, that their youth were less considerate, less kind. *I* was the one on the subway who gave up my seat for a pregnant woman or an elderly man. *I* was the one who stopped my car in the middle of the street for someone to cross. Me—a gaijin.

Eric cleared his throat.

I glanced over and saw him clenching the door handle.

"Is it possible people entering the road have the right-of-way?"

Huh. I'd never considered that possibility before. "Maybe." But it still seemed insane to me to pull out in front of someone without even looking. And it happened every time I got behind the wheel.

But in the interest of not generalizing and in an effort not to be an ignorant barbarian, I had to admit there *were* some things the Japanese did well when it came to traffic. At construction sites, or even at the possibility of one, someone stood in the road with a flashlight waving people around the obstacle. And when they didn't, they had a stand-in. A life-sized automated sandwich-board man dressed in the proper uniform with a moving arm that held a blinking light to swing you through.

And if the construction coincided with a sidewalk on a small street, they went one better. They laid a plastic walkway down with arrows pointing you in the correct direction. And they stationed men on both sides of the street. One to usher you across and ask your forgiveness for the inconvenience, and the other to help you on your way once you reached the other side.

We made it to the base, thirty miles away, in just over an hour. Nearly record time. We'd flown down the expressway, but when we got off and started through town, the traffic lights snarled things up. It never ceased to amaze me that in the most technologically advanced nation on earth, the traffic lights were never synchronized.

We flashed our ID cards to get on base. "Have you been here yet?"

"It's been awhile. Seventh grade. We'd come for sports tournaments and eat at Burger King after."

"You're in luck, then. It's still here." I pointed it out as we drove past, and then I parked the car and looked at my watch. We agreed to meet at the entrance to the building at four o'clock, two hours later.

I gestured toward the escalator. "The BX is on top, along with Cinnabon, Baskin-Robbins, the Hundred Yen store…souvenir shops. The commissary's over there." I gestured to the other end of the lobby area.

"Thanks. Well, see you later."

"Bye. See ya."

Then we both stepped out in the same direction, heading for the escalator.

We went through a whole Laurel and Hardy episode, each trying to let the other step onto the escalator first. We finally both stepped back and eyed each other.

"It shouldn't be this hard."

"It shouldn't." Then I had an inspiration. "Rock, paper, scissors. Go!"

We flashed our signals and stared at the results.

"Ha! Paper covers rock." I slammed Eric's rock with my hand.

He grabbed it to help me step up onto the escalator. It made me feel feminine, God bless him, which is harder than one would think when you're six feet tall.

I browsed through the women's clothing, looked at shoes and selected a pair, and ended up in the book section, right next to Eric. He was flipping through the latest issue of *Foreign Affairs*. I grabbed a copy of something with "Vast Right-Wing Conspiracy" in the title before I realized the words "How to Protect Yourself from the Loony Left" were also part of the title.

I dropped the book to the shelf and decided my energies were better devoted to grocery shopping, so I went to buy the shoes.

Several minutes later, Eric joined the line behind me.

I bought a minibon while I waited for him. I stood when I saw him coming and shrugged when he looked at me with questioning eyes. "We might as well shop at the same time. We've done everything else together today."

Once in the commissary, we wheeled our carts down the aisles side by side. He stocked up on vegetables while I stocked up on fruit.

When we came to the personal hygiene products, I dallied where it was safe—in the toothbrushes. Mostly because I didn't really want to know what kind of shampoo or soap Eric used. Because then what was left? Deodorant? He was a good guy and everything, but I just didn't want to know.

We met up in the cereal aisle.

I threw a box of Grape-Nuts into my cart.

"I didn't know anybody ate those anymore."

"What do you eat?" I leaned over and looked into his cart. "Cocoa Puffs? I didn't know anybody past the age of seven ate those anymore. Are you low in energy? Lacking concentration? Do you ever feel lethargic? Sluggish and indifferent? Maybe you're eating too much processed sugar!" I plucked the box out, returned it to the shelf, grabbed the end of his cart and pulled it down the aisle ten yards. "I give you…granola! Crunchy, munchy…"

"You left out chocolaty."

"Your stepmom actually *let* you eat Cocoa Puffs when you were little?"

"Yours didn't?"

"No." We ate eggs back when they weren't bad for you. And multigrain hot cereal on special days. Bleh. "Well…" Things were getting just a little too maudlin for the cereal aisle.

We ended up staying on base for dinner, eating shameful amounts of tortilla chips, and drinking too many refills of Diet Coke—with ice cubes!—to count. And by that time, a movie was due to start at the theater, so we stayed for that too.

It was a psychological thriller. Exactly the kind of movie I hate myself for sitting through when I wake up soaked in sweat with my heart pounding in the middle of the night. I grabbed Eric's forearm and leaned over to whisper in his ear. "If I suddenly become an insomniac, I'm blaming you for it."

"Just close your eyes during the scary parts."

I shook my head. The scary parts didn't bother me. It was the voices in my head that lingered long after those sorts of films were over.

And that one was extra creepy. Midway through the movie, I found my head buried in Eric's shoulder. I can report that his deodorant, whatever brand it was, worked. And it smelled rather nice too.

He jiggled his shoulder. "Hey. We could leave."

"No, we can't."

"Why not?"

I ventured a peek. Dove back into his shoulder when I saw the scene hadn't changed. "Because we paid for the tickets. It's like getting on a roller coaster. Once it starts, you're committed. For better or worse. You know you'll survive; it's just a matter of how painful it is to get through."

"Want me to tell you when it's safe?"

I nodded.

We survived the movie. Eric loved it. I just hoped I wouldn't be psychologically scarred for the remainder of my life.

The drive home went quickly until we reached the outskirts of Tokyo. In advance of expressway intersections, large signs were posted to warn of traffic congestion. The first sign we saw was lit with red, signaling blockages at all major arterials.

"Get off and we'll take the back roads. It'll be faster."

"You mean…follow the expressway underneath?" That could be done. Because for every elevated expressway, there was usually a road underneath following the same path.

"No. The back way."

"There is no back way." At least, not one I had been brave enough to try.

"In a region of thirty-five million people, there's a back way to everywhere."

"If we get lost, then you're the one who has to ask directions."

"We won't get lost."

I looked at him.

"We won't. Trust me."

We left the expressway at the first possible exit and wound through areas of Tokyo I'd never seen and would never be able to find again if I'd wanted to try. Eventually, we wound up in the luminous glow of Shibuya, waiting as lights stopped traffic so people could cross in front of us in at least six directions.

Shibuya was a modern Wonder of the World. Every two minutes the sidewalks crowded with people, gathering, waiting, anticipating the change of lights. And then the lights changed. They stepped off the sidewalk and the intersection became a street party for one brief minute, looking as if it could not contain even one more person. But then the people crossed, thinned out, and wandered away, leaving you to wonder how they could become nearly invisible when they were the largest group of people you'd seen in one place just short seconds before. But by the time the light changed once more, another group had amassed, filled with entirely different people, just as large as the one before it. Where did all those people come from? Where were they all going? And how did the city contain enough people to pass through Shibuya at the same rate all day long?

Ten minutes later, I was turning into the driveway at Eric's apartment. I got out to open the trunk and helped him cart everything into the lobby. "So how did you do that?"

"Do what?"

"Get us back here."

"It wasn't difficult. Tama River on one side. Expressway Number Three on the other. And Roppongi Hills once we got near enough."

"Well, thanks. For the day. For navigating."

"Thanks for taking me with you. And dropping me off."

I waved his thanks aside and turned to leave.

"Allie?"

"What?"

"Call me if you get scared."

"The movie wasn't *that* scary."

Unfortunately, at two the next morning, I found out that yes, indeed, it had been.

# OCTOBER
*Kannazuki*
*Month of No Gods*

16

*Stay, you who do not
hear. Among eight million gods,
who will miss your luck?*

I TURNED THE PAGE OF MY CALENDAR TO OCTOBER and then blinked as I tried to interpret the English translation of the Japanese word.

*Month of no gods?*

In a country practicing both the Shinto and Buddhist faiths, that didn't sound right. I blinked again, but the phrase didn't change.

"Hey, Yuka-san?"

"*Hai*, Allie-san."

"What does *Kannazuki* mean?"

"This is old name for October: Month of no god. In this month, all the eight million god go to Izumo Shrine. So in Izumi Province this month is *Kamiarizuki*, month with god." She smiled as if it all made perfect sense.

"So they all...just...go on vacation?"

"Vacation? Not so much. More like...meeting."

"Convention?"

"*Hai*."

A convention of the gods. All eight million of them.

"Hey, Allie, it's Eric. I'm taking Saturday off."

I clamped the phone between my shoulder and my ear as I kept typing on my keyboard at work. "You mean the whole thing?" In my limited experience, after his meetings with Samantha, he always had some reason to check in at the embassy.

"The whole thing."

"Good for you." It was about time he learned the definition of "weekend."

"So let's go somewhere."

"What, after you meet with Samantha?"

"We're not meeting this week."

Really. That couldn't have been Samantha's decision, so he was showing signs of independence. He wasn't going to surrender to her without a fight. Well then... "Sure. Let's meet at Segafredo."

"No. Somewhere outside the city."

"Yokota? Atsugi?"

"Kamakura or Nikko."

"Um..."

"Your choice. Which is your favorite?"

"N/A. Not applicable."

"You haven't been?"

"Nope." Mostly because I could never figure out how to ask someone to help me buy a train ticket.

"Ever?"

"Never."

"Then let's do Kamakura."

"Sure. Fine. As long as you promise to bring a guidebook." Most guidebooks included a list of handy phrases in Japanese like *Help, I don't feel well* and *I can't speak Japanese.* I didn't own any guidebooks because I preferred my guides to be actual people instead of inanimate books.

"Are you listening to me?"

I was trying to figure out how to close the story I was writing. "What?"

"I'll be at your place at six."

I deleted a sentence. "Six? Um...in the morning? On Saturday?"

"I'll call on Friday if I need to be there earlier."

I started typing a new sentence and then realized he'd stopped talking. "Wait. What?" He'd already hung up the phone.

I wasn't able to get ahold of him the rest of the week. He never answered his phone when I called his apartment, and he didn't have an answering machine.

Neither did I, so I couldn't complain.

But at least I carried a cell phone. And it had voice mail.

He didn't call on Friday, but I couldn't remember by then what not calling was supposed to mean. So I set my alarm for early Saturday morning.

Not early enough.

He knocked at six. I was still in the shower. I jumped out, shrugged into my silk kimono, and tore down the hall to answer it.

Eric was wearing a pair of slim black pants and a polo shirt. A backpack was slung over his shoulder. He stopped dead when he turned and saw me standing there.

Something about the way he was looking at me made me drop my eyes and try to figure out what was so interesting. It didn't take me long. In the future I decided to remember it's best not to put a thin silk kimono on over wet skin.

Definitely not a good idea.

I stood aside to let him in. "Sorry. I'm not ready yet. I'm still—" I gestured to the bathroom, clutching my bathrobe to my chest.

"No problem."

I moved to walk around him at the same time that he moved in the same direction to let me pass. We did an increasingly embarrassing shuffle for a few steps before I paused.

"If I could just...I have to...closet...clothes."

*Inarticulate moron!*

"Oh. Sorry." He flattened himself against the wall so I could pass by.

I pulled a blouse and a pair of pants from a hanger. And the beauty of my clothing system was that, hey, they both matched! I rifled through my dresser drawer for some unmentionables that I hoped against hope would also be unseeables. By the time I passed Eric on my way to the bathroom, he was looking at a light switch as if it were the most fascinating invention since the lightbulb.

*Hurry. Hurry. Hurry, hurry, hurry.*

I directed the blow-dryer at my head with one hand while I tried to climb into my pants with the other.

It didn't work.

In fact, several long strands of hair got sucked into the engine and wrapped themselves around the fan. "Ow!" I turned the blow-dryer off.

Eric's voice pierced the sudden silence. "Are you okay?"

"Um…" No. "Yes. I'm fine." Somewhere in my bathroom was a manicure kit leftover from the days when I'd vowed to become a professional-looking journalist and keep my fingernails polished. (Okay, fine. From the days when I'd decided to go to war against Samantha. On her terms. Obviously, it hadn't worked out for me.) But inside the kit I was hoping to find a pair of tiny scissors.

I threw open the cabinet under the sink and bent down to look inside. Succeeded only in conking the blow-dryer against the sink, adding immeasurably to the level of my pain which was peaking at about nine on a scale of ten.

I pulled open a cabinet drawer, found the manicure set, and opened it to find nothing but a tiny pair of fingernail clippers. I had to let go of the hair dryer in order to pull them from the pouch.

Ow. Pain.

I bent down again and rested the blow-dryer on the counter.

Relief.

I soon discovered that by propping the blow-dryer against the mirror, I could hold onto the hair with one hand and the clippers with the other. But I still couldn't actually see the hair in the mirror, because of the obscure angle of my pose.

Only one thing left to do.

I dropped the clippers and the hair, gritted my teeth and got dressed.

*Ow. Ow. Ow.*

And then I called out to Eric. "Could you come here? And if I ask you to do me a favor, would you promise not to laugh?"

"I would never laugh at you."

I opened the door.

"At least not in front of you."

Twenty minutes later, when we walked out of the barracks, I was sporting a short lock of hair that looked like a braided lanyard. Or, as Eric helpfully pointed out, an extraslim dreadlock.

We got on the subway at Nogizaka Station, transferred once, and then surfaced at Tokyo Station. Eric stood in line to buy our tickets, and then we raced to the platform to wait for our train.

We had just settled into our seats when Eric seized his backpack, unzipped it, and starting pawing through it. He looked up, shoulders slumped. "I forgot the guidebook."

We looked despairingly to the subway platform as we pulled away. "It's fine. No big deal. We'll be okay without it."

We would be. We'd have to be.

We were.

An information booth sat inside the station in Kamakura. It didn't have much historical information about the city or its sights, but it did have a good walking map, with bus and tram stations marked, and that was all we really needed.

The minute we left the station, I felt something I hadn't felt in a long time: an unrestrained breeze, fresh from the ocean. I closed my eyes and turned my face toward it. Breathed deeply. It made me feel buoyant. Lighthearted. Happy I'd chosen to go there with Eric.

Even though he *had* forgotten the guidebook.

The main draw in Kamakura, according to Eric, was the Great Buddha, so that's what—who—we decided to visit first. As we walked up the street, I noted shops I wanted to stop at on the way back down: shops filled with comfortable fisherman-style cotton clothing. Boxy silk-screen printed dresses. Loose pants with matching tunics. Other shops were selling paper kites and souvenirs. I liked the town. It had the carefree beach feel I loved with the intriguing addition of a Japanese motif.

As we approached the end of the street, we saw a wall enclosing what looked like a garden. There were lots of trees inside. A low building on the right sprouted a tendril of a ticket line. Above the wall we could see the upper half of the Great Buddha. Apparently he was sitting out in the open, enjoying the same breeze I was. It was a welcome relief. Usually Buddhas were enshrined in incense-scented temples, enveloped in dim light and haloed by flickering candles.

Eric offered to stand in line, so I handed him my money and sat on a bench, enjoying the serenity of the gardenlike grounds.

Once Eric had purchased the tickets, we walked through a roofed gate and followed a stone path around a corner. We came out into a long vista that led to a series of stairs and then up to the Great Buddha himself.

He didn't look like I had expected.

No jolly bald head. No bowl-full-of-jelly belly. The Great Buddha looked...half-Indian. No doubt about it. From the dot in the middle of his forehead to the earrings in his ears and the suggestion of an arch in his eyebrows. His thumbs were pressed tip to tip in a *mudra* gesture, an upside down "okay" sign.

Maybe he was a closet Hindu?

I stopped midstride and then stood for a long time, just staring at the statue.

Something was wrong with it.

I couldn't figure out what it was. Even seated in the lotus position, the Great Buddha seemed to loom over the people standing and kneeling in front of him.

Something was not quite right. But I didn't know what.

Its eyes were closed, but it was inviting. Patient. Serene.

The closer I walked the more intimate the statue became. And soon, I was standing right in front of it.

Beside me, people were praying, heads bowed, hands clasped to their foreheads. But I stood there, looking up. And at once the statue seemed both larger and smaller. More intimate and more immense.

And whatever had seemed wrong had been righted.

Eric walked up beside me. "Want to go inside?"

I drew my eyes from the statue and turned to see if he was joking. "The Buddha? Are we allowed?" That seemed a little indiscreet. Like poking around someone's bowels.

Eric gestured with his head toward the side of the statue.

Sure enough, a line had formed behind a sign. And a man was collecting money. The equivalent of twenty cents.

We went down some steps and entered into the hollowed bronze cave of Buddha's interior, a rough inverse of the outside. It was clearly constructed by hand. And clearly the work of men. It didn't feel powerful. It felt claustrophobic.

We took a few minutes to tour the inside of the temple before leaving. As we left, I turned around and looked at Buddha one last time. And the feeling, whatever it was, returned: Something was wrong with him.

As we drifted back down the street, I looked in the clothing stores. The styles were deconstructed. Reminiscent of the clothes I wore in high school. I loved those kinds of clothes, all asymmetric angles and natural fibers. But I left without buying anything because who wants to be caught dead in the clothes you wore in high school?

Eric looked at his map. Looked back the way we had come and then down the street. "It looks like Hase-dera Temple is close. Want to go?"

We backtracked a bit and then waited in line, paid our admission, and were ushered into a world of water: Ponds, fountains, and water gardens were animated by bright-colored koi diffracting reflections with their lazy turns.

We hiked up the hill in the direction of the temple. Up, up, and up some more. If we'd had a guidebook, I might have known to pass on that temple. Too much work.

At the top, we rested on a veranda beside a snack bar and gazed out at the ocean. To have a panoramic view of something other than buildings was exotic. And stimulating. After I revived I began to look around at the outbuildings surrounding us. We meandered over to one and walked up the steps. It housed what looked like a miniature columned temple set on top of a large wooden base.

A little boy had grabbed one of the protruding wooden spokes and was spinning it around, solemn-faced.

I waited until after he left and gave it a good push.

Then I wondered what I'd done. Wondered if I should stop it mid-rotation.

Eric glanced up from the temple brochure. "Congratulations. You've rotated the sutra."

I assumed a shocked expression. "I am *not* that kind of woman!"

He went pink around the ears. "Not the *Kama Sutra*. Sutra. Books of Buddhist theology."

"I know. I'm just kidding."

"It says rotating them is the equivalent of reading them."

"Really. Well, that's much more efficient than reading through the Bible in a year. It was kind of fun. I think I'll do it again. Maybe I'll even convert." I reached out to give it another spin but stopped as I saw some Japanese tourists climb the steps.

Instead, I turned my attention toward the texts displayed in glass cases along the walls.

We visited the other outbuildings and toured the temple. As we descended the hill, we decided to detour into a cave. We had to duck to go inside, but it was worth it. A network of narrow tunnels provided access to larger rooms. Inside the rooms, the floors were lined with tiny statues; larger ones had been carved into the walls. The whole was lit by dozens of candles; it reminded me of Catholic shrines I'd visited in Europe.

After the cave, further on, was a table set up in front of some trees. Behind it sat a man.

A priest?

Maybe.

He was selling small wooden plaques with scenes painted on the front. A rope was attached to the top of them for hanging.

"Those are for...what? Do you know?"

"Prayers. You write your prayer or wish on the back and then hang them over there." He pointed to a spot where a rack held at least fifty wooden plaques. The breeze had caught them by the corners and clattered them against each other. "The winds carry the prayers to heaven."

I closed my eyes. I felt the wind on my face, the wind carrying prayers to heaven. What a lovely thought. I imagined the wind carrying my own prayer to the ear of God. I'd asked him for a friend to replace Gina. I was still waiting for his answer.

## 17

*Chrysanthemum, King,
Emperor of Autumn, who
will rule while you sleep?*

AFTER HASE-DERA, WE TOOK OFF OUR SHOES AND SOCKS and walked along the beach for a while. Octobers on the Kanto Plain, which stretched away from Tokyo toward the mountains, were glorious. If you could survive a Tokyo summer, then your reward was a Tokyo autumn. Shirtsleeve weather lasted through the end of November.

For a weekend, the beach was surprisingly deserted, though a few forlorn beach clubs were still propping their doors open for tourists, like us, who had strayed from the temple circuit.

I plopped down on the sand and drew my knees up toward my chin. Then I set about burying my feet. "You'd think there'd be more people here."

"Beach season is over at the end of August."

"But that's exactly when I'd start coming. It's not quite as hot, not quite as humid. That makes no sense."

Eric shrugged. "It's when school starts again for Japanese kids."

"So school starts, beach ends? Doesn't that seem rather arbitrary?"

"It's just the way it is."

I leaned back and peered up at him. "Why don't you sit down? Or are you thinking of bolting for the office?"

"What? No, not at all."

"You're a really bad liar."

"I wasn't lying."

"Yes, you were."

"I wasn't."

"When you lie, you start to go all pink at the back of your neck. And then, when you're embarrassed, you go pink around your ears."

"Allie, stop."

"And then you start to get annoyed. Are you really that important? No offense, but they can't require you to work twenty-four/seven, can they?"

"Require? No. Expect? Yes."

"But it's only because you *do*. If you *didn't*, they wouldn't expect you to. Would you sit down? You're making me nervous."

He sat down, looking as if he didn't want to get sand on his clothes.

"Here. Stick your feet out." I pointed to a spot near my hip.

He pivoted in the sand so he was facing me.

"Not like that. Like mine."

He drew his knees up toward his chest.

"Perfect." I bulldozed sand up to his feet with both hands and then started packing it firm on top.

He started wiggling his toes. "Stop—"

I grabbed his ankle. "Relax. You are the most uptight of uptight Republicans I've ever met. I mean, you're nice and warm and charming, and you can be so persuasive when you want to be. Look at you. Have you ever *not* had life figured out? Have you ever *not* known where you're going?"

"Yes! Especially lately."

"Really."

"Yes. I have no idea what I'm doing here. I've never felt more inept in my life."

I left off packing sand and patted him on the knee. "It's Japan. We all feel that way."

"It's not *Japan*, Allie, it's—"

"Hey, I know. We need to get your mind off work."

"It's not—"

"Let's play twenty questions."

"Allie, would you listen to me for a minute?" He pulled his feet away, crumbling all my hard work, and leaned toward me.

"You ruined it!"

He looked at me as if he were trying to figure something out. Then he gave up and started laughing. "I guess I did. So...twenty questions. I hate that game."

"Then just ask me anything. Anything you want to know."

He opened his mouth. Shut it. Opened it again and then sighed.

"Anything at all. Like...favorite food."

"Okay. Fine. On a hotdog: mustard or ketchup?"

"I don't eat hotdogs. Do you know what they put into hotdogs? All the gross stuff a real dog wouldn't even eat." I looked up at him. He looked bemused. "But I do put ketchup on hamburgers. Try a 'best.' They're easier to think of."

"Um, best..."

"It can be anything."

"Best...Bible story."

Bible story? Okay. "Best Bible story: Ehud, the left-handed man. Did you ever read that one? The guy with a 'secret message' for the king from God? And when everyone leaves the room, he stabs the king in the gut."

"Nice story, Allie. But pretty ruthless. Couldn't the king have been rehabilitated? Maybe he was just misunderstood. Or maybe...his *environment* had corrupted him."

I ignored his digs at my political party. "It's a great story. Classic cloak-and-dagger. Richly told in just twelve short verses."

"Okay. *Worst* Bible story."

"Jonah. What a ding-dong. Who's stupid enough to run away from God? And then try to hide from him once he's found you?" Even atheists know the basics about God, omniscience being one of his high points. Omnipresence, another.

"Most of us."

"Us who? That is *such* a Republican thing to say. You try to define yourself as Everyman when you clearly think you're superior."

"I *am* superior. I've never tried to hide it."

I felt my mouth fall open and then I realized he was only kidding. "You are such a...a...a *fink!*"

Eric pretended to gasp. "A fink! My innocent ears are burning." He looked at me as if he were disappointed in me. "Can't you think of something better than that?"

"You're just too...too..."

"Boring?"

"No."

"Stuffy?"

"No."

"Handsome?"

"Yes!" I clapped my hand over my mouth.

"Really?"

I thought for a moment. Took my hand away from my mouth. "It's not just me. Everybody says so." As my words replayed in my head, I winced. I'd just made everything worse. So I did the only thing I could do. I jumped up and started running down the beach.

*Stupid, stupid, stupid.*

I'd always been flirty. I'd always liked guys. Big deal.

But Eric wasn't a *guy.* Not in the Allie, kiss-and-get-to-know-you sense. Eric was…gaining on me!

I shrieked.

And that's when he put on a burst of speed and grabbed me in a bear hug.

"Let go!"

"Not until you say God bless the GOP."

"Not a chance."

"Or you could just say what you said before."

"Which is?"

"Just tell me I'm handsome. I kind of liked that."

I kicked him in the shin.

"Ow!" He let go.

I jogged away a few steps.

"That's right, I'd forgotten. Democrats are all about playing fair until they actually start to play."

"You're a big boy. You can take care of yourself. Isn't that the GOP motto?"

"Kick away, donkey. Your time will come."

I made a pair of ears above my head with two fingers. "Hee-haw."

We found a noodle restaurant in the center of Kamakura for lunch. We removed our shoes, stepped up onto a tatami-covered platform, and sat on cushions. Eric ordered thick *udon* noodles served with curry sauce. I ordered a bowl of ramen.

I cast quick glances at him, trying to figure out what had possessed me to blurt out that he was handsome.

It had to have been peer pressure.

But the more I looked, the more I realized he was. His face was just very…nicely molded. His eyes were a piercing blue, the color of a robin's egg. And his lips had a nice kissable indent at the top. Not that I was thinking about kissing them. It's just that I knew, from experience, that those were my favorite *kind* of lips to kiss.

Our bowls of noodles came. Eric lifted his bowl in one hand and with an easy motion, scooped a noodle into his mouth with his chopsticks.

I had a little more trouble with mine than he did. I could handle chopsticks…about one time out of two. Apparently, it was not going to be one of my graceful, competent days. Of course it wasn't. Because Mr. GOP had it all figured out. And the way he was using his chopsticks was downright sexy. There was no other way to describe it. In the right hands, chopsticks were sexy. They just were.

The Japanese have perfected the art of eating gracefully. They're the world's most fastidious, tidy eaters who rarely use napkins, even when they're wearing thousand-dollar dresses or carrying ten-thousand-dollar purses. They can eat entire meals using only two long, slender sticks which require nothing more than precision and perfect balance, and the knowledge of exactly how tight to pinch them together. When to grip hard—on a noodle—or when to loosen up—a cherry tomato. Knowing all the while that if you were wrong, your food would slide away from you in a moment.

"You have to slurp more."

I blinked. "Excuse me?"

"To eat noodles in the proper Japanese way, you have to slurp."

Slurp? Well, that was something I could do.

Before we left the restaurant, we conferred about what to see next. Temples, obviously—the walking map was dotted with them—but where to start?

Eric remembered reading about a temple in the neighboring town of Kita Kamakura. It was supposed to be the prototype for Buddhist temples. We decided to trust our afternoon to his memory and hopped on a train.

Too bad we didn't have a guidebook. It might have shown us exactly where to go. And maybe even explained Buddhism and its hundreds of sects. Speaking of which, "What *is* Buddhism?"

"World Religion 101 says, 'It's a way of discovering the true nature of reality.'"

"So it's not a religion?"

"Buddhists don't really believe in any kind of God, at least not a personal, knowable one. Buddhism is more of an exercise in ethics and personal responsibility. A kind of, 'change the world one person at a time' philosophy."

"Sounds admirable. So what's the goal?"

"The end of suffering."

"You mean heaven?"

"Not really. It's not a place; it's a state of being. Nirvana. Eternal bliss through an absence of pleasure or pain."

"So how do you get saved from suffering?"

"By achieving mastery over the things you do and the things you think. By becoming wise. Buddhists are very moral. And they try to provide a solution to pain and suffering."

"So what is the solution?"

"Figuring out why people suffer and then figuring out a way to stop it."

"Have they?"

"They have. Buddhism says all suffering is a result of desire."

"How do they figure?"

"You suffer because you're selfish. You crave things. And when you get what you crave, you cling to it because you're afraid you'll lose it, which creates a different kind of suffering. And, being human, as soon as we've satisfied one craving, we come up with another."

"So to get rid of suffering...?"

"You have to get rid of desire."

That sounded familiar, reminiscent of something I'd heard in church. "Death to self, right? Sounds reasonable. So you do that by..."

"Achieving mastery over the things you do and the things you think. By becoming wise."

"So if suffering is self-imposed and you can program yourself not to crave, then you can eliminate desire."

"Exactly."

"You do the right things and think the right things, then what happens? And how do you know if you're doing it right? I mean...what if you mess up once? Or twice? What if...you hurt someone? Or tell a lie? Or what if you just have a bad year? Does that ruin all your chances?"

Eric shrugged. "I don't think anybody really knows. You just do the best you can and become the best person you're able to be."

"So it's all up to you?"

"Basically. It's interesting. Most Buddhists I know are much more self-controlled, much more into spiritual disciplines than most Christians I know."

"I wonder why."

"Because it all depends on them? Think about it. Success or failure rides on every action."

"That's a lot of pressure."

"Or a lot of motivation, depending on how you look at it."

"They're nice people."

"Very nice people."

"I'm a nice person."

He grinned. "Most of the time."

"But even I know I don't have it in me. I can't...I mean...I'd screw it up!"

"You'd just have to try hard. Try harder."

"But that's what I'm saying. I don't think I could ever try hard enough. It must be scary, don't you think, to look back on your life and wonder if you'd tried hard enough? If you'd done everything you could? If you'd left something undone? I mean, saving yourself is a huge burden. I don't know if it can be done. And if it can, I know I'm not one who could do it. If I can't keep one New Year's resolution, then how am I going to do the right things and think the right things and figure out how to be wise with any sort of consistency?"

"That's basically what I came up with too."

"So what if you do everything right? And you reach Nirvana. Then what happens to you?"

"You're freed from yourself. You as Allie, an individual, cease to exist."

"I just melt into nothingness?"

"You melt into everythingness."

"You just die?"

"If you're dead, at least you aren't suffering."

"But you aren't feeling any pleasure either. You're feeling nothing at all. It would be like...being in a sensory deprivation tank."

"That feeling of nothing, to a Buddhist, would be peace."

Peace. I'd always thought of peace as an absence of adversity. I'd never thought of it as an absence of everything I'd ever known.

We got off the train and followed signs to Engaku-ji Temple. It was both nearer and farther away than we had imagined. A short walk from the train tracks, it literally clung to a hilltop for survival. The hike up the top was so steep that we paused midway.

"And this is worth it because...?"

"Open your eyes, Enviro-Girl. There's beauty all around you. Isn't this the kind of thing you went around hugging trees for?"

"Yes. So *other* people could enjoy it. I've lived in the Northwest. I'm good. Don't need to see any more trees."

"Right there! *That's* the problem I have with Democrats. You think you know what's best for everybody. And you don't care if they want what you think they need or not, you just—"

"*You* just hurt my feelings. I'm calling a truce."

"Terms?"

"No more politics."

"Until?"

"Midnight."

"When?"

"Tonight. Deal?" I stuck out my hand.

"Deal."

We shook on it.

Our deal might have gotten us away from needling each other, but it didn't stop me from thinking about Eric. Or his lips. At least when he was insulting me, his lips were in motion and that nice little indentation wasn't as noticeable.

For the rest of the afternoon, I tried to keep my distance. Because I was not going to be tempted into kissing those lips.

Seriously.

At least not for another year...ten months.

Something like that.

## 18

*Tie-dyed Leaf, with shades*
*of red, green, yellow—Nature's*
*Rastafarian.*

I THRASHED AROUND THAT NIGHT, DREAMING OF LIPS—Eric's, who else's?—and a gigantic Buddha. Actually, Eric's lips belonged to the Buddha. I kept asking him what was wrong with him, and he kept telling me I would understand if I would just come a little closer.

I kept saying, *But I don't want to kiss you.*

And he kept saying, *It's the distance that keeps you from seeing rightly.*

After coaxing me closer, he suddenly stood up from his platform and stomped on me with a giant elephant foot.

It didn't take a degree in psychology to figure out the symbolism. But one thing still bothered me: Something was wrong with the Buddha at Kamakura.

And I *would* figure it out.

My week was going pretty well. My story on the USS *Kitty Hawk*'s impending deployment was basically writing itself. And then Eric called.

"What if you had to write an evaluation for someone that had to sound good even though they weren't doing a good job?"

"Go to Google. Type in 'definition' and the word 'lie' and then press 'Enter.' "

"I can't."

"How do you get yourself into these situations?"

"Don't ask. I can't tell."

"Um…how about, 'It was almost a pleasure to watch over his shoulder while he worked'?"

"Not bad, but I know you can do better."

"Am I being paid to do your job?"

"No. It's pro bono. You feel sorry for me."

I gave up trying to edit my story and talk at the same time. " 'His meticulous work habits should result in perfect work'? We are talking about a 'he,' aren't we?"

"I really can't say. But that's pretty good. It's implying the current result isn't perfect work. Nice."

"Only if it isn't."

"It isn't. Can you think of anything else?"

"It would help if I knew what this guy's problem was."

"Sloppy work, procrastination, inattention to detail."

" 'Never has a subordinate kept me so busy'? This feels like *Jeopardy*, Eric."

"You're doing great. Try Subordinate Evaluations for 500 this time."

"I'd be ashamed of myself if I were you, letting other people do all your hard work."

"It's called delegation. And you're better at it than I am."

"If that's supposed to be flattery, you're going to have to do some practicing."

"Come on. Help me out."

"Okay. One more…um…" I chewed on the end of a pencil. "What about this: 'Devotes attention to so many tasks, it's amazing any of them get accomplished.' "

"Thanks. I knew you could do it! You're the best." He hung up.

The best? Then why did I feel as though I were using my special powers for evil?

That Saturday morning I was restless. Eric-Buddha had haunted my dreams again, and I needed to clear my head. I started off to Segafredo ahead of what I assumed would be Samantha and Eric's meeting. Not that I was checking up on them or wanted to interfere. I just needed caffeine! And for some reason, Segafredo sounded better than Starbucks. And, okay, fine! I just wanted to see how Eric was reacting to Miss Perfect Diplomatic Wife.

I ordered a cappuccino and then claimed a table outside, hoping the fresh air would help me wake up.

I had just opened my journal and started writing when Eric arrived.

"Allie. Hey. Didn't expect to see you here. Mind if I sit with you while I wait for Sam?"

Sam? "You mean Samantha?" Sam? He called her Sam now? She'd cast her spell over him. He'd officially gone over to the dark side.

"Something wrong?"

"No. Why?"

"You just looked a little...green."

Green. How appropriate. That's how I felt. A vivid mix of green and blue. Just color me teal. "I'm fine." Or I would be once a) Samantha took the State Department test and passed, b) Eric moved on to his next post, or c) I decided to quit my job and move home. Any option would do.

"What are you working on? Anything interesting?"

Interesting? Not even remotely. Not if you could call Ann/Meg getting out of bed and figuring what she was going to eat for breakfast interesting. It was banal. Mind-numbingly boring. Truly terrible. Quit my job? Maybe I should. It was the only possibility of the three I could control at that moment. Not, of course, that I was going to do it, but still, it would be nice to the say the words "I quit."

I quit.

That was a good title for a book. In fact, it was a good first line for a book.

*I quit.*

From there, anything could happen. Anything at all.

I liked it.

It was good. It was very good. The best two words I'd written all morning.

All year.

Eric started saying something, but I wasn't interested. I needed to pursue the *I Quit* idea.

"Just…" I held up one hand while I turned several pages in my journal. A thought like that one needed wide open space to develop. I wrote the title. Wrote the first line.

*I quit.*

Good, good.

Now…who said it? Was saying it? Who was the person that just quit? What did she quit?

She?

She. It was a she. It was a…an…Ann. So Ann quit…what? What did she quit?

Her job. She quit her job. Just said the words and walked on out. Left everything.

And then I'd got it. The germ of the idea. The best idea I'd ever had. She walked out of her job, out of her life, and took a huge do-over. And she did it by doing the opposite of the first ideas that came into her head. She didn't trust herself to be able to make the right decisions, so she did everything the opposite.

It was genius.

It was edgy.

It was surprisingly good.

I could see the book, the whole thing in one flash of searing insight.

The book would cover one…week? Month? One month in the life of a woman who walked out of one life—one she hated—and started a new one. Based entirely on doing the opposite of everything she'd ever done.

That was it.

That was The Book. My book.

Color me…the color of euphoria. Vivid fuchsia pink with orange polka dots.

I put my pen to the page and started writing. I didn't stop until later.

Much later.

In fact, it was only on my way home at twilight that I realized I didn't know what had happened to Eric. Or Samantha.

I thought of calling him when I got home, but then I sat down at the computer and transferred my words from the journal to a Word document. Took the story from there and kept writing. Didn't pause for a bathroom break until eleven that evening.

By then it was too late to call.

I woke up at three to go to the bathroom, and she started talking to me. Ann did. And she wouldn't stop.

So I felt around for my glasses, shoved them on my nose, and then padded to the desk and jiggled the mouse to activate the computer.

I sat down and wrote for an hour. And then she was satisfied. And so was I.

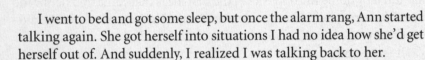

I went to bed and got some sleep, but once the alarm rang, Ann started talking again. She got herself into situations I had no idea how she'd get herself out of. And suddenly, I realized I was talking back to her.

*Okay, Ann, what are you going to do?*

*Are you sure you want to do that? Is that smart enough for you? Because you're pretty smart. Why would you do something like that?*

*Help me out here.*

And then I came to a standstill. Ann had met a guy. A guy she *never* would have dated in her former life. And that presented a problem. The attraction was there. I could feel it, but they couldn't get together right away. There had to be something pushing them apart…or was it pulling them apart?

Push or pull?

Which would it be? What made sense?

I studied the problem while I crunched through a bowl of Grape-Nuts. I looked at it from different angles while I took a shower. I even tried to diagram the situation while I took the subway to church.

There had to be something. There *was* something. I just had to figure out what it was.

I remembered seeing Eric as I walked into church, but I was in a strange sort of trance. Everything the pastor said evoked some sort of

Ann-scene in my head. I used the blank spaces in the bulletin to note my thoughts, but soon turned it over and wrote in the margins until I filled them up. I was staring at that last millimeter of white space when a new bulletin came sliding onto my lap.

I looked up.

Eric.

I smiled. Took it. Kept writing.

The story just would not stop. It was all I could do to be friendly to people after the service. What I really wanted to do was snatch everyone's bulletins and keep taking notes. Where I really wanted to be was hunched over my keyboard, pouring the story into my Word document.

Someone suggested going out to dinner.

No. Absolutely not. I waved goodbye and punched the button for the elevator. Stood there, arms crossed in front of me, shifting from foot to foot. I pushed the button again.

"Once is usually enough."

I looked up to see Eric. "Have to get home."

"Are you feeling well?"

"Fine. I'm fine." I needed another bulletin. Quick. I leaned a little to the right, to look over Eric's shoulder at the welcome table.

He pivoted, followed my gaze. "You need another one?"

I nodded. "Yes." Even to my ears, it sounded like a plaintive whine.

"Just a second." He walked to the table, took a handful, and came back. "Here."

I grabbed them. Fumbled through my purse to find my pen. Found it and started writing.

At some point I felt Eric's hand at my waist, propelling me into the elevator. And later, I felt that same hand at my waist, guiding me out.

We must have walked out of the building. Must have crossed the bridge, crossed the street, walked down the steps, and into the subway station. We must have because I glanced up for a moment and discovered us to be on the platform, waiting for our train.

I smiled at Eric.

He returned the smile and then opened his mouth to say something.

The story came back. I put the bulletin to my knee and bent to write. Then I realized I'd been rude and straightened. "Sorry. What?"

His lips quirked.

I bent down. Wrote until the train came. Sunk into a seat and wrote some more.

What seemed like several minutes later, I felt Eric pulling at my elbow.

"What?"

"It's our stop."

I raised my head. Glanced around.

The train had stopped. The doors were open.

I darted underneath his arm and out the door just as the warning sounded.

"Thanks. I'm hopeless."

"You're priceless."

Yeah. Whatever. Would it have been too antisocial just to have sat down on one of the seats lining the wall of the station and write for a while? I only had one bulletin left. "Just—"

"Did you eat yesterday?"

"What?"

"Eat. Food. Did you have any?"

"Food? Yes." Hadn't I? Wait… "Breakfast."

"Did you eat today?"

"Eat…?" Why was it so hard to think and talk and want to write at the same time?

"We're getting something to eat before you go."

His mouth was moving and I was hearing words, but they didn't make any sense. I blinked. Tried to focus on his face.

"We're going to…" He looked into my eyes. Sighed. Then he grabbed my hand and threaded it through his arm.

"You're not leaving until you order something."

We were standing in line at McDonald's. I didn't want a hamburger or chicken nuggets or fries. I just wanted to go home and write.

"Do you want me to order for you?"

"What?"

"Allie, pay attention!"

I *was* paying attention. I had just noticed that the trays at McDonald's had tray liners. Tray liners that were probably blank on the back side. And people were just throwing them away! "What?"

"Food. What do you want? Because you're not leaving here—"

"Fine. Okay. Get me...some kind of combo meal. Do you mind if I just wait for you over there?" I gestured toward the trash cans. There were lots of little kids looking as though they might be finished soon. If I could just grab one of their trays, then I could take one of those tray liners and I could start writing again.

It didn't work.

The kids just kept lollygagging, dipping every single one of their French fries into ketchup and taking about twelve bites to eat each chicken nugget. I was trying to figure out how I could take their trays away from them nicely when Eric appeared with our food.

"Wonderful!" I took the tray from him, slid all the food onto the table, grabbed the liner, and turned it over. It was blank! I could have cried. I lifted my purse to my lap and took out my pen. But before I could make contact with the paper, Eric took it from me.

Just grabbed it right out of my hand!

"Listen here, you...big..."

"Fink? Sticks and stones, Allie. I'm not giving this to you until you finish your food."

I ate a hamburger, some sort of double-decker something. I balked at the fries. "I'm done."

"Great. But I'm not giving you your pen until you finish everything."

"I'll take the fries home. Save them for later."

He gave me the eyeball. "Right."

So I ate them, every single one. And all the while, the tray liner called to me. "Done. Can I have my pen back?"

Eric handed it to me. "With my compliments."

He was just being gentlemanly. It was a Bic.

Some time later, after having consumed all the blank space on the back of the tray liner, I looked up to find Eric watching me. The tray was gone and so was all our trash. Eric had his hands wrapped around what I assumed was a cup of green tea.

"How long have we been sitting here?"

"About two hours."

That didn't seem right. I'd been writing like a crazy woman and the tray liner wasn't *that* big.

Eric bent down to pull something out of my purse: a stack of tray liners. He smoothed them out on the tabletop.

I counted them. Ten.

Wow.

Something was seriously wrong with me.

"Ready to go?"

"Um...just..." I glanced up at him. He was slouched in his chair, weariness evident in his eyes. I didn't see any reason to keep him hanging around when I could write at home just as well. "Yeah. Let's go."

Eric led the way outside and then headed down the sidewalk with me when I turned in the direction of the barracks.

"There's no need to walk me back. This is Tokyo."

"If I let you go by yourself, do you promise you won't start writing on the way?"

"Yes."

"And you'll call me when you get there?"

"Yes."

"And you'll get some sleep tonight?"

"Yes. I'll be good. I'll be fine. I promise."

I lied.

I stopped at an intersection and let four...five...okay, about twelve green lights go in order to take some notes about a scene. I would have called Eric, but when I remembered, it was much too late. I might also have gone to bed if the sun hadn't already risen by the time I thought of it.

## 19

*Why bloom, Cherry, in*
*a season when there are none*
*to bloom beside you?*

MY PRODUCTIVITY LEVEL THE NEXT WEEK WAS ABYSMAL. I had four stories to write. I turned all four in late. And when I got them back from Rob, I found out they were all mixed up. Somehow, I had inserted some paragraphs about new facilities at Atsugi into an article about the history of Yokosuka. And the new Japanese quarantine rules for pets were all mixed up with an article about checking guests into the New Sanno Hotel.

By Friday, I could barely keep my eyes open, so I went home sick. I changed into my pajamas and stayed up all night writing. I wrote all day Saturday and all day Sunday. I remembered thinking I should go to church, but by the time I thought about it again, it was too late. Eric called that evening. I brushed him off.

When Monday rolled around again, I had a little talk with Ann about the appropriate relationship between author and character.

It didn't work.

I hated myself for it, but I called in sick Wednesday, Thursday, and Friday.

But on Saturday evening at ten o'clock, I'd done it. I'd typed the last word.

It was finished.

I hit "Save," closed my file, and then groped for my bed. I fell into it and started to close my eyes, but I remembered something. I picked up the phone and dialed Eric's number.

"It's done."

"You finished?"

"I did it."

"Congratulations, Allie!"

I slept in on Sunday until three.

The next day was fine. The rest of the week, even.

But then doubt assailed me. Assaulted me. Beat my confidence to a pulp.

What had I been thinking? A novel about a woman who quits her life? Who would want to buy a story about that? It wasn't life changing. It wasn't brilliant. In fact, it was kind of…un-brilliant. It was…well, it was quirky. And I didn't think quirky was good. Quirky didn't sell books. Quirky didn't sell anything at all.

Except for Big Mouth Billy Bass, the singing fish.

I meant to let the book sit, let myself rest for a month, and then start editing. But at that point, I was afraid to read what I'd written. Afraid the book I'd finally got around to writing wasn't good. Afraid it wasn't smart. Afraid it was just silly. Most of all, I was afraid my best efforts hadn't been very good at all. That my best was so close to the industry worst that my dream had no chance of coming true.

Maybe I was supposed to be a journalist.

Maybe that's who I was.

Maybe it would have to be enough.

Eric was waiting for me at church that Sunday.

"So…?"

"So."

"When can I read it?"

"I haven't decided yet."

"Decided what?"

"What I'm even going to do with it."

"As in who you're going to send it to?"

"As in if I'm going to send it out at all."

"You aren't going to send it out?"

"I didn't say that. I said I wasn't *sure* if I'm going to send it out."

"Why not?"

I shrugged.

"You're not afraid, are you? The Allie O'Connor I know isn't afraid of anything."

"Then you must know a different Allie O'Connor because this one is."

"What are you afraid of? Letting people know you've written a book?"

"Finding out I've written a bad book. I'd rather have written no book at all."

"You're an author whether you send it out or not. No one can ever take that away from you. Not many people have the determination to sit down and write a whole book."

"I know. And of the few who do, very, very few actually write a book worth publishing."

"So you'd rather not know whether it's good?"

"I'd rather not know it's bad."

"Do you think it's bad?"

"I don't know."

"So you're not going to send it out?"

"I...don't...know. Just leave it alone."

"I can't. I can't watch you give up on your dream. I won't do it."

"Only one percent of writers make it."

"So you're going to give up before you find out if you're in the one percent?"

I nodded.

"Really? Because that doesn't sound like you."

I'd had it with Eric and all his memories of high school. "The me that you remember doesn't exist and never has. So don't bring me—her—up again!"

For the first time since he had started attending my church, I didn't take the subway home with Eric. I told him I had an errand to run. I hated lying, so I made one up. I decided to go to Omotesando and get a head start on Christmas shopping.

Omotesando is the Champs-Elysées of Tokyo, a broad tree-lined avenue boasting stores of all of the major fashion designers. It ended at Harajuku Station, capital of Japanese teen street fashion and birthplace of everything strange, bizarre, and odd in clothing. It was a good place to hang out. Just as soon as you started feeling sorry for yourself for not being able to spend thousands of dollars on your wardrobe, you'd run into a Harajuku-bound teen and realize that, really, your clothes weren't so bad after all.

The district was also home to three very important places: Shakey's Pizza, Kiddyland, and the Oriental Bazaar. Shakey's actually had an American-style buffet. They had strange things on their pizza, like corn niblets and pickled ginger, but you could eat all you wanted. Kiddyland had the best collection of toys in Tokyo. It was especially great for Japanese cartoon character paraphernalia. And the Oriental Bazaar? Four floors of every kind of souvenir imaginable, from washi rice paper to tea sets.

I set out for Shakey's and got an unexpected surprise.

It was closed.

So I crossed Omotesando and dived into the youth culture of Takeshita-dori. I was looking for Gina's favorite food: a Harajuku crepe. Preferably one rolled around a piece of cheesecake. I'd worked long and hard for two weeks, so I figured I deserved it.

I found what I was looking for and devoured it on my way back to Omotesando. Armed with a sugar high, I passed through the hallowed doors of Kiddyland. I had hoped to find something for my niece and nephew, my older sister's kids. I walked out with a gift for Gina as well. A weird stuffed animal named *Totoro*. He was grey with an owl-like body, rabbit ears, and cat's whiskers. That would give her something to think about.

The kid gifts behind me, I went to the Oriental Bazaar and wandered through, trying to decide what to get the rest of my family. I'd done summer-weight kimonos the previous year. I could give silk-screen prints, but I hated choosing art for other people. Pottery was too heavy. Traditional silk kimonos were too expensive. *Noren* door hangings were possible, but would they know what to do with them? And more importantly, would they do it?

When I ended up in the antique section, looking at old cooking implements and carved wooden screens, I decided to save decision making for another day. I could have taken the subway to the barracks, but the sun was shining and the temperature was perfect for walking. A slight chill in the air warned of winter weather to come.

I walked past a dozen high fashion boutiques and then segued into a more residential area of apartment buildings and ribbon-thin townhomes. One had a garage at street level angling beneath the ground at nearly forty-five degrees. It had a roof so low the car nearly touched it. And I couldn't imagine how the driver got in or out with only about three inches of clearance on either side. I stood there for a minute pondering the possibilities before I just gave up and continued on.

I walked into Aoyama Cemetery, enjoying the sudden plunge into relative silence. It sprawled through the heart of Tokyo, encompassing several hills. At its center was a major intersection where cherry trees stretched arm in arm in all directions. As I waited for the light to change, I gazed at the trees. Their leaves were on the verge of turning colors, the memory of their blossoms long discarded. They were trees a person would normally view as a background. As a serene backdrop.

Except for one.

Too late, one cherry tree had decided to bloom. One lone tree amidst the hundreds resident in the cemetery glowed with pale color. But at a time of year when gingko leaves were touched with blazing yellow and creeping vines were starting to blush red, the delicate pink flowers of the cherry tree looked all the more ethereal. All the more poignant because it was too late.

When the light changed, I followed the road down the hill through a tunnel of cherry trees. At the bottom I waited at the corner for another light, standing in front of a ramshackle ramen restaurant. It was practically famous and very good, but it looked like a shed both outside and inside. One day, a typhoon would come and blow it away. But that afternoon, it was still standing. The garbage cans in front were filled with chicken carcasses that had been picked clean by the stealthy neighborhood gang of cats.

Only one car was on the street. It was a black convertible with a tan leather interior. A Ferrari. The driver was suave in a way only the Japanese can be, from his shaved head, to his shades, to his simple but stylish clothes. But it wasn't the man that interested me. It was his companion. For sitting in the passenger's seat, as if it had every right to be there, was a large dog—a sheepdog—of equal height with the man.

They sat there together, accessorizing both each other and the car.

The dog's posture was perfect. Its head held at a dignified angle, staring straight ahead. As I looked at it though, the dog turned its head to look at me. Seemed to ask what I thought I was staring at. And then the light changed. The man shifted gears, the sheepdog returned its gaze to the windshield, and man and beast roared off down the street.

There had to be a story there somewhere, some sort of sleek allegory. A comment on modern Japan. But even if there were, I didn't know enough about Japan to write it. And I didn't want to write another book.

The first one had almost killed me. I wasn't about to start another.

# NOVEMBER | *Shimotsuki* *Month of Frost*

## 20

*Stretch out your red hands,*
*Maple Tree, and touch the sky.*
*Winter's clasp will come.*

I WENT TO WORK ON MONDAY WITH ONE QUESTION IN MY MIND, and I wanted to ask it of Yuka-san. "Have you ever seen a cherry tree blossom in the fall?"

"*Hai.* Yes."

"Are they a different kind?"

"No."

"Then why do they bloom so late?"

"Some might say it bloom too early. If you stand outside and close your eyes, is it spring or fall?"

I shrugged.

"It can be both, yes?"

"Why do they do that?"

"This kind of tree, it bloom on its own cycle. And is it not more beautiful when it finally bloom alone?"

As I worked on my article that morning, the image of a single cherry tree in bloom was never far from my thoughts.

Around lunchtime a voice broke into my thoughts. I stopped writing and lifted my head to listen. Slow-moving trucks or vans with attached speaker systems were commonplace throughout the city. Usually the cadence of the speaker reminded me of a public service announcement or a political advertisement. But this voice was different. It rose and fell in a familiar chant. It was the *yakiimo* man. The sweet potato seller.

I went into the conference room and pressed my face against the window.

The *yakiimo* man drove a vehicle resembling a pickup truck, but it had a roof on top of the bed. Inside were several covered metal drums filled with roasted sweet potatoes. To serve one, he'd put on heavy gloves, lift the lid, and pull one out. I loved the smell of those *yakiimo*-mobiles: wood smoke and embers. It conjured memories of smoking piles of leaves at home in the fall.

I loved sweet potatoes too, but I'd never bought one from the *yakiimo* man. I didn't know how to ask for one. And I didn't know how much they cost.

The next day Eric made one of what I was beginning to believe were weekly phone calls.

"Is there a way to say 'I was happy to see you again' if you really weren't?"

"Are you trying to tell me something? Listen, I know I kind of yelled at you on Sunday, but I was sleep deprived, so I'm sorry."

"What? No! I'm trying to write a thank-you note for someone else's signature. And they want the phrase without the sentiment."

"You know how I love writing in code."

"Please. Consider it mental calisthenics."

I sighed. Then I held the phone away from my ear and made an ugly face at it before speaking again. "Okay. What was the phrase? I was happy to see you again? But they weren't happy."

"No."

"You do know that everyone realizes politicians lie, right?"

"I don't."

"Could you just do it for me? This once? As a favor?"

"No."

I sighed again. "Okay. Let me think. Maybe…'I hadn't expected to see you again' or 'I never thought we'd encounter each other in Tokyo…or wherever.' Or maybe, 'What an unexpected encounter'? If you put an exclamation point at the end, it could be construed as good. Misconstrued. You have to acknowledge the meeting without assigning it an emotion. Does that work for you?"

"Um…"

"Let me rephrase that. Make it work for you."

"Is that the best you can do?"

"Best? That was like pulling an elephant out of a hat! If I do many more of these, I'm going to start asking for a byline."

"Okay. Thanks."

Thanks? *Thanks* was all the thanks I got?

That night Eric-Buddha was back. I tried to reason with myself, tried to tell myself that it was just a dream. But it didn't work. We went through the whole thing again.

I told him I didn't want to kiss him, that I didn't even like him.

He told me I couldn't like him until I understood him, and that to understand him, I had to come closer.

I told him I wasn't going to let him stomp me with his big elephant foot.

And then he said I had to step away from what I thought I knew and step closer to what I didn't.

When I told him I couldn't, he blew me a kiss that turned into a cherry blossom.

The next week, after work one chilly night, I came home, cranked up the heat, and changed into some green Thai fisherman's pants and a white tank. Hungry for something hot, as opposed to cereal or a bagel, I whipped up a Japanese-style bowl o' soup I'd bought at the hilltop store. They translated the instructions into English up there, typed them onto address labels, and affixed them to the package. All the great Japanese taste without any translation difficulties.

I surfed the Internet as I ate and experimented with slurping. Slurping worked, just like Eric had said. Slurping and surfing did not. After I'd wiped up my mess, I opened my desk drawer and took out my manuscript for the first time since I'd finished it.

How bad could it actually have been?

An hour later, just after I'd used up all the ink in my red pen, I heard the wop-wop-wop of a helicopter. I threw the pen in the trash can. I glanced at my watch and saw that it was eight thirty. I grabbed a pen with blue ink and started back to work.

But then I heard a knock on my door. I decided it was Neil. And if it was, it probably meant he was hungry.

"No. You cannot have one of my Ding Dongs. Go away."

There was silence for a long moment. And then somebody said, "What if I don't want one of your Ding Dongs? Can I stay?"

It wasn't Neil.

Who was it?

I went to the door and opened it. "Eric. Hi." He was looking spiffy in a suit and tie.

"Hi."

"I thought you were Neil."

"And that I liked Ding Dongs?" He flashed a smile. "They're not my favorites."

"Then you should try them frozen. They're better that way."

He raised his eyebrows and nodded.

I opened the door wider. "Come in?"

"Thanks."

"Did you come in on the helicopter?"

"No. Drove out with the ambassador. Am I interrupting you?"

"No. I was just…working." I walked to the desk and tidied my manuscript. Not that he would have read anything. Because what was there *to* read? It was a mess.

He looked around the room and then walked toward my dresser. He took the puzzle box from it, walked to a chair, and sat down, all the while turning the puzzle box over in his hands. "I used to have one of these." He fiddled with it. Turned it over and fiddled some more. And then the sides began to slide out and slide up and down. And then it was open.

"How did you figure that out? I never know where to start."

He shrugged. "It's a pattern. If you remember the pattern, then it's not so hard to figure out where to start."

He reached inside and pulled out a piece of paper. "These aren't the instructions, are they?"

"No. I'm not that much of an idiot, thank you very much. But…what is it?"

He handed it to me.

It was a note from Gina.

*I miss you. Come visit me. Don't be an idiot.*

I smiled.

"Love note?"

"Hmm?" I refolded it and then looked over at him. "No. Just a note from Gina. She's the one who gave it to me."

"How is she?"

"She's doing well. She hasn't found a job yet, but she's looking…and it's summer down there…"

"So how's the writing going?"

"Fine."

"Any thoughts about sending it out?"

"None." Especially not after what I'd just been reading.

"Are you sure? You spent so much time on it…"

As if I didn't remember! I got up, stalked to my desk, and grabbed the manuscript. Stalked over to him and dropped it on his lap. "Here. You read it. If you think it's worth anything, then you can send it out."

I waited all week for Eric to tell me what he thought about my book. He didn't say a word about it or anything else. He didn't even call and ask me to do his work for him.

He smiled at me on Sunday, but as closely as I looked, I couldn't discern anything from his smile.

I finally stopped holding my breath whenever he called. Stopped trying to read his face whenever I saw him. I came to the conclusion that he must have been too busy to read it. Or too embarrassed to tell me what I already knew. It was bad. Terrible.

I interpreted the peculiar letdown I felt as relief.

The next Saturday I happened to be at Segafredo when Eric and Samantha had their study session. It was just a little too cold to sit outside, and I had already staked out a table on the second floor, so they ended up joining me. It was kind of cozy. Or it would have been without Samantha. I noticed something interesting. In between a discussion on the cause and effects of violent crime and the benefits and drawbacks of outsourcing basic manufacturing jobs overseas, Eric skillfully dodged Samantha's invitation to go to lunch. Several times. She said she was meeting some friends who worked at the Dutch Embassy and promised stimulating discussion over great beer at some new restaurant.

Eric demurred. Said he had planned to meet up with his own friends. Identity and location unspecified.

It was enough to make me look up from my novel.

Trouble in Lover's Paradise?

During that tense moment I figured one of them would have to admit to lying. Probably not Eric, since I knew he "didn't lie."

Samantha's move. She couldn't hang around indefinitely because she'd just said she had to meet her friends. I happened to know that she didn't really have many friends. She was one of those hyper-motivated people who spent so much time doing her job well that she had no time left for socializing. She was scary. If I'd thought I would be a journalist for the rest of my life, I might have been more intimidated by her. As it was, I still held out some small, rapidly diminishing hope that I'd one day break into publishing in a big way...which was looking smaller all the time.

Samantha sat it out a minute longer and then made a point of looking at her watch and shrugging. "Maybe next time."

Maybe. Maybe not.

She threw her books and notes into her bag, pulled on her jacket, and left.

Leaving Eric and me staring at each other.

"So...*friend*."

I felt my eyes narrow. "*I'm* your friend?"

"Aren't you? How would you like to go to Roppongi Hills for lunch?"

Roppongi Hills was the latest and greatest in a series of shopping areas springing up around Tokyo. From a sphere of a building in the middle to a giant statue of a spider, it had an eclectic harmony. The sheen of a fountain cascaded over an entire wall in the plaza and a park, looking lonely down below, had been created to wander through. But there were several problems with Utopia. The long alleys between the buildings and its location at the top of a hill had created a series of unintentional wind tunnels. And a cluster of cylindrical shopping areas had created my own personal vertigo.

I knew, for instance, that there were two Starbucks somewhere inside and a third just across the street. I knew, for instance, that one of the lowest levels contained a food court. I knew one shop sold nothing but umbrellas and another, nothing but stationery; Gina had showed them both to me before she'd skipped town. We had spent several Saturdays hanging out at Roppongi Hills, but I had never actually been able to find any of those places again, even with the help of a map.

Somehow I became effectively trapped between the same two buildings, the same line of shops, the same barren sidewalks, the same elevator circling between Kate Spade and the shops above. The only up side I could see to the whole complex were the bathrooms which had heated seats, musical toilets, and mood lighting.

So when Eric asked if I wanted to go, my reply wasn't negative; it was plaintive. "I can never find anything there."

"What are you looking for?"

"I don't know." Everything I wasn't seeing but knew I was missing.

I agreed to go on the promise of lunch and the pledge that Eric would mark up a Roppongi Hills map for me with all the important locations: entrance, paper shop, umbrella shop, food court.

"Do you think there's more of a chance of running into Samantha if we walk or if we take the subway?"

"Prefer not to be seen sneaking around, Lover Boy?"

"Would rather not make her feel bad knowing I preferred other company."

I was preferred company? Then I must be moving up!

Or she was moving down.

We decided to walk. We cut through Arisugawa Park, passing the pond at the lower end.

It was ringed by a dozen old men, throwing their fishing lines into the water. They sat on metal-framed stools, passing their days in hopes of catching fish they would never eat. At least, considering the green slime congealing around the edges of the pond, I hoped they wouldn't. They sat in clumps, clustered along the shoreline, rarely speaking, rarely looking at each other. One day soon, I knew, they would disappear, as they hibernated for the winter. But once spring returned, they would too.

We exited the park at the opposite corner, right next to the stand for the neighborhood's friendly policeman. The police force in Tokyo didn't carry firearms, and they didn't do much hunting down of criminals, but they were more than happy to answer questions. Their *koban* police boxes were always equipped with maps of the neighborhood. I'd heard rumors they had also been equipped with convenient automated information kiosks too, just in case you happened to visit when the cop was on patrol.

Talk about service!

We angled toward Roppongi Hills, approaching from the back side. At one of the convenience stores along the way, Eric paused, nodding toward the door. "Do you mind? I have to pay a bill."

Convenience stores in Tokyo were convenient in more ways than one. You could grab a Coke, an *onigiri* rice ball, or a newspaper, and you could pay your phone bill too. I'd accompanied Gina on a similar errand several times.

Eric paid his bill, collected the receipt, and we were on our way.

When we stepped into the shadow of Mori Tower, I tugged on his arm.

"This is the point at which I always enter the Twilight Zone. So here's what's going to happen. We'll go inside, find the Information Booth, and bag a map. And then you'll show me how to get out of there. Got it?"

"Yeah, no problem. I've got you covered, Calamity Jane."

## 21

*Mikan Tree, you look*
*so lovely without your clothes,*
*baring hidden fruit.*

"IT'S JUST A BIG CIRCLE, SEE?" Eric was holding a map of the Roppongi Hills complex, pointing to the building he swore to me we were standing in.

"That's the problem. I don't do circular reasoning. It's like promising to balance the budget by cutting taxes. It doesn't make any sense. It's not linear."

"I'm pretty sure you can do this. Just think of it this way: You enter a prison, you see too many people. You think, *It's overcrowded; we have to have more space!* You loosen the rules, you let people out, but guess what? They start committing crimes again, and you've ended up exactly where you started. Get it?"

I gave him a shove. "Don't forget it's people like me who pay you to live in style in downtown Tokyo. What is your rent, anyway?"

"About eight thousand dollars a month."

"Eight *thousand*? Eight thousand *dollars*?"

"Give or take according to the exchange rate."

I shook my head. "One thing at a time." I handed him a pen. "How did we get here?"

"You mean what door did we come in?"

"I mean what street, what cross street, what door, what escalator. Everything."

Eric sighed and drew an *X* at the very edge of the map. "This is Hiroo."

"Okay. So…if I'm standing here, right beside you…" I shifted so I stood right beside him, "…then Hiroo is to the left."

Eric turned the map upside down. "It's actually to the right."

"But now I can't read it."

He sighed again, took me by the arm, and then shuffled me around 180 degrees. "Better?"

"Okay."

"So, we came in here." He drew a circle around an entrance on the map.

"Could you just…I need you to draw a line from the X to the circle."

Eric's lips pressed together, but he drew the line for me.

"And where are we now?"

"Right here." He placed a dot inside one of the buildings.

"Could you just—"

He drew a line from the circle to the dot.

"Thanks."

"Now. Where would you like to go?"

"Let's go to lunch. I know there's a food court around here somewhere. And you're still buying, right?"

We found the food court, several stories below ground. I convinced Eric to label it (1), and then we—actually me—started a legend on the side of the map.

"Do you think you can find your way out?"

"Yes."

"Great. Let's go."

"Can I have the map?"

Eric handed it to me. I followed the line to a bank of elevators. We took it up several floors and walked out at exactly the same place we'd entered. Things were definitely looking up. And then I saw the Zara clothing store, and I started getting the shakes.

"This is what always happens! I thought this time was going to be different! What did we do wrong?"

"What are you talking about?"

I shook the map in the direction of the store. "Zara!"

"So?"

"So this is what always happens! I go in the door by Zara, and the mall suddenly shrinks from multiple, multistoried buildings down to one single hall."

"Show me what you do."

"I go in *that door!*" Was he stupid? Hadn't I just said that?

"Calm down. Just…here…" He grabbed my hand. "Just show me what you do."

I didn't really want to. Didn't see how that visit to Roppongi Hills could be any different than my last visit, but he kept holding on to my hand. I shoved the map against his chest with my other hand and started toward the door.

We walked into the mall and down a long curving hall. When we came to the end, right before having to exit the building, I pointed off to the right. "If we took that escalator, we'd end up passing Kate Spade. And there's no way through there to any other part of the mall. I've tried."

Right was also the direction one would go to find the bathrooms, so I excused myself. I spent about five minutes in a relaxed-lighting stall playing with the buttons on the control consul of the toilet.

I kid you not.

At least when you're in a bathroom in Japan, you're by yourself. You might as well stay for a while and enjoy the experience.

I adjusted the heat for the seat until I got it just right. And then I explored the other buttons. A push on one button made the sound of a toilet flushing. I played with the volume control so it wasn't quite as loud. A push on another made the sound of a mountain stream. The third one…Yikes!

*So that's what a bidet is all about.*

The fourth one…whee! A blow-dryer.

That sent me scurrying out the door.

Eric was lounging against the far wall. He pushed off when he saw me. "You okay?"

"Fine."

He was looking at me strangely.

I was trying not to look at him at all. I was also trying not to laugh. "I'm fine. Really."

"Fine. So…what was the problem again?"

"The problem is I know there are more than fifteen stores in this place, but I don't know how to get to any of them. This is what I do. I wander between Zara and Kate Spade about three times and then I just end up going home."

"What store in particular are you looking for?"

"There's supposed to be an umbrella shop."

He looked at the map, turned it over, looked at it for a long minute, and then turned it back. "Hanway?"

"Maybe. I've only seen it once."

"It's on the fourth floor."

"Of what?"

"This. This building."

"It's here?"

He glanced up above our heads. "There."

"So how do we get *there*?" I glanced up above our heads.

"There's this newfangled invention called an elevator. Would you like to try one?"

Five minutes later, we stepped into an elevator and pushed a button for the fourth floor. "If they hadn't hidden it so well, I might have realized this was here."

"Yeah. It's pretty hard to see. Especially when they put those elevator signs all over."

"An outline of a box is not an 'elevator sign.'"

Eric consulted the map, turning it sideways. "Well...doesn't it qualify as one if it's marked on the map?"

"Let me see that." I took the map from him and looked at it. Sure enough, on the legend, in little tiny print, was an outline of a box...and beside it, the word "Elevator."

We found the umbrella shop. We also found the paper shop along with a shoe store, a convenience store, a bookstore, and other specialty boutiques. I couldn't really afford to buy anything, especially not a custom-designed umbrella at the Hanway store, but I enjoyed looking.

After descending to ground level, Eric showed me another part of Roppongi Hills that I hadn't known existed. There were several tiers of shops hanging off the back side of the complex, which looked out on the garden below.

We capped the day off by browsing through a Tsutaya store at the bottom of Roppongi Hills' footprint. It had an impressive collection of foreign-language books, CDs, and movies. It also had a Starbucks. Eric and I browsed separately but eventually met up at the same table. He with a copy of the latest *Financial Times* and a cup of tea. Me with a copy of the latest *Washington Post* and a cup of coffee.

"Oh my word."

Eric looked up from his paper. "What?"

"Have you heard about the latest senate scandal?"

"Which one?"

"The one your guy started."

"I've heard. And I don't want to hear anymore."

"But they just found out—"

"No, thanks. Don't want to know. He should be tossed in jail, and they should throw away the key."

"But he's been in the senate for decades. How will Republicans get anything done without him?"

"We'll find a way. We're better off without him."

Harsh words for someone who had been talked about as a presidential candidate. "What about party loyalty? Innocent until proven guilty?"

"What about integrity?"

Well, that sure struck a sore nerve.

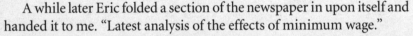

A while later Eric folded a section of the newspaper in upon itself and handed it to me. "Latest analysis of the effects of minimum wage."

I took the page, looked at the graphs. They were filled with arrows and lines pointing in dismal directions.

I handed it to him. "This probably surprises you, but I know that raising the minimum wage doesn't necessarily raise the standard of living.

I know that if employers have to pay more, then they can't afford to hire as many people. You're the ones who talk about putting people to work to get them off welfare. But why should we ask them to find jobs if we can't pay them a decent wage? There's no motivation. It's not the best solution, I admit. But nobody's proposed anything better. Have you ever thought of anything better?"

"Honestly? No."

We sat reading until we'd drained our drinks. And then we stayed a while longer. Reading was one of my favorite things to do, and it was a luxury to do it in the presence of another person.

We walked out of the store into twilight and walked up the hill together.

"I guess...the shortest way back for me is up there." I nodded toward busy Roppongi-dori.

"Thanks for coming. For spending the day with me."

I surprised myself by saying, "I enjoyed it." And then I remembered something else. "Thanks for showing me around."

He smiled. "Wait. Here." He pulled the map from his bag. "All marked up, just like I promised."

"Thanks. But you keep it." I pressed it to his chest. "I think I prefer a guide." What was I doing? I was flirting! With Eric!

"Anytime." He wasn't quite flirting back, but then, I wasn't sure he even knew how to flirt.

"Okay, then. Thanks."

"Bye."

"Bye."

We both took several steps backward.

Waved.

Turned around.

Turned back.

Waved.

How embarrassing.

I stole one last peek over my shoulder, but Eric had already blended into the crowd.

It took me several days to recover my social equilibrium. Obviously, church was slightly awkward. But by midweek I had recovered, just in time for Eric's phone call.

"I need to ask you a favor."

"You're *asking* this time? *And* calling it a favor? Usually you just demand a linguistic miracle. And last time the only thanks I got was thanks."

"Which technically qualifies as a thank-you. What were you hoping for?"

"I don't know. Maybe an 'I promise I'll never, ever ask you to do this again.'"

"Okay. If you help me out with this, I'll never, ever ask you to do it again. I promise."

"Do you swear?"

"I try not to. Especially around women."

He was such a good citizen. "Lay it on me. What is it? An evaluation? Another thank-you note?"

"I need you to come with me to Tsukiji."

"Tsukiji Fish Market? Why?"

"I just do."

## 22

*Air chills. How does it
feel to lose all your warmth, to
be cursed and not loved?*

WAY TOO EARLY THE NEXT SATURDAY MORNING, I found myself seated next to Eric in a subway car. "So explain this to me again. Specifically, why I'm sitting in a deserted subway car before six in the morning on a Saturday. Because normal people sleep in on Saturdays."

"There's a CODEL coming to town."

"A CODEL. What's a CODEL?"

"Congressional delegation."

"Right. Which is important to me because…?"

"Because the wife of one of the congressmen said she wants to visit Tsukiji."

"And why did that require waking me up so early?"

"Because I have to figure out how to tell her no. Legally, we can support her visit as long as it coincides with her husband's, but there's no way I can justify siphoning off an employee of the State Department just to show her around town."

"You can't or don't want to?"

"It's a large delegation, and this congressman doesn't have any seniority. I'm already using volunteers to take care of the other wives. I have no cars, no resources…"

"So this poor woman is left to fend for herself because you don't want to have to trot her around town this early in the morning?"

"I can't. I'm already scheduled. I'm the control officer. I'm in charge of the whole thing. So I really need your help to figure out how to say no."

"Okay. But you have to concentrate. Ready?" I pushed the tip of my tongue against the roof of my mouth. "Nnnn…" and then I pursed my lips into a circle, "oooo. No. Think you can say that?"

"Help me out here, Allie."

"It's a simple word, Eric. And it only has one syllable."

"I need some reasons."

"You're starting to disillusion me. I thought you were this great big nasty Republican who said no to everything just on principle. You know, who's afraid of the big bad tax…"

"Seriously. We just can't make up a separate itinerary for her."

"And let me guess, you can't actually tell the congressman that. I think I've figured it out. You people don't ever actually really say anything, do you? You spend so much time trying to figure out what not to say that by the time you actually say something, it's turned into nothing."

"No—"

"See! I knew you could say it!"

His neck was turning red. "I need you to help me figure out how to give her information that would lead her to make the decision herself."

"That was a sentence with about ten too many words." But I was intrigued. "What kind of information?"

"I don't know. That's why you're here."

"So for whatever silly reason, you can't say no—"

"Nobody says no to a congressman…or a senator."

"Why not?"

"Congressmen sit on committees and senators confirm the appointment of every ambassador."

"Oh. Now I get it. It's all politics."

"It usually is."

"So what do we have to do again?"

"Figure out a way to get the congressman's wife to tell us she doesn't want to go to Tsukiji."

"You have too many principles. You're in the wrong business—"

He opened his mouth to say something.

"—*however,* since I believe in integrity in government, I will help."

"Thank you."

"In fact, here's a freebie. You can start by telling her she'll have to catch a subway no later than six o'clock. Let her do the math."

Tsukiji Fish Market, one of the largest in the world, was a city within a city. Gina had tried to rope me into visiting it once, when the famous tuna auctions were still open to the public. I'd never visited, but I had researched Tsukiji for a tourism-related article. The fish market operated on its own schedule, by its own rules. Something close to fifteen thousand people worked in more than one thousand wholesale shops or related organizations. The peak of activity was from five to eight in the morning.

We reached the market about quarter after six. The floors of the auction houses were being cleared. Tuna so large they looked like the bodies of headless seals were being loaded onto hand-pulled dollies and towed down a covered alley in between warehouses.

We followed behind, trailing a dolly as it was pulled into another smaller garagelike structure. We stood and watched as the tuna was hefted onto a stainless steel table. The squealing blade of an oversized table saw sliced through its frozen flesh as if it were a block of wood.

The pieces were placed onto a wheelbarrow and pushed out into the alley once more. We followed it, dodging motorized carts and mini trucks, right into a huge hangar-sized warehouse.

I had officially entered Tsukiji Market.

Stalls without walls stretched the length of several football fields. They were delineated by the subtle, and not so subtle, differences in display. In one stand, all kinds of small fish were stored in plastic tubs. In another, shellfish were fanned upon ice in an exotic arrangement. In still another, narrow tanks held lobster and crabs, eels and rays.

As we passed, a man plunged his hand into the tank and brought out a writhing eel. He placed it on a long plank and drove a stake into its head.

The writhing stopped.

Using the stake as an anchor, he sliced into the eel, cleaned out the guts, and carved it into fillets with a long curved knife. I could appreciate the deftness of his hands and the skill with which he handled his knife, but I could not bring myself to appreciate the spilling of anything's guts. Not before seven in the morning.

We slipped through the aisles, dodging the vehicles. And when the aisles became too narrow, we turned sideways and slid through them.

"I'd never be here in the States. OSHA wouldn't let me." Thank the Lord for government oversight agencies.

"No kidding. Which is another problem. If a congressman's wife got run over by one of those trucks on my watch…"

His face had visibly paled, so I tried to distract him. "I never knew there were so many fish in the ocean."

He smiled. Tried to smile. "And this happens every single day."

"How can there be anything left?"

We passed dozens, hundreds of stalls, and all of a sudden it was too much. Too much noise. Too much smell. Too many fish. Too many lights. My head began to whirl.

I grabbed for Eric's arm. "Stop."

"Are you okay?"

"I need…something."

"What?"

I shook my head. Tried to stop my eyes from twirling.

He looked into my face. "Did you eat breakfast?"

At 5:15 in the morning? "No."

"Can you make it over there?"

I looked past him at a convenience store. Low blood sugar can do funny things to your head. So I blinked, certain I was imagining it. I wasn't. A convenience store held court in the middle of Tsukiji's largest warehouse.

"Yes. If I can…"

"I'll hold your hand. Just a second." He looked both ways for traffic before starting across the alley. If I had to jump out of the way of one more cart, I was going to run from the market screaming.

We made it to the store.

"What do you want?"

I was too hungry to care and too overwhelmed to answer. I could only sit down on the railing separating the store from the market's major thoroughfare. At that point, I would have settled for eating one of the newspapers sitting in the racks out in front.

Huh. They had the *Daily Yomiyuri*, the *Japan Times,* and the *Asahi Shimbun*. The three biggest English-language newspapers in Japan. But who, in there, would buy them?

As I puzzled over that question, Eric joined me. He had bought two packages of sweet buns and handed me one.

Through the wrapper I could see a small dark hole in the side of the bun that foretold of a filling. A dark-colored filling, which could have been chocolate...or bean paste. Frankly, at that point, I didn't care which one it was. I tore off the cellophane and bit into it. I didn't catch any flavor until I'd swallowed the first bite.

Chocolate.

I could have kissed Eric, but I didn't. I gave him a smile instead.

When I could focus my eyes again we crossed back into the market heading diagonally away from the store in a direction we hadn't yet visited. There, the scenery changed. We had left the fruit of the sea and wandered into the fruit of the earth. We'd made it to the fruit and vegetable wholesale market. The stalls there were made from stacks of boxes and pallets. There were vendors selling apples and pears, and vendors selling tomatoes and carrots. Some vendors were devoted to mushrooms, and others to potatoes. One vendor was selling nothing but flowers: delicate lilies in long cellophane-wrapped boxes.

We drifted through the aisles for a while and then moved out into the sun, touring the long outdoor alleyways. From both sides, awnings of all shapes, colors, and sizes stretched from the open doors of the stalls, nearly meeting above in the middle of the street. And over them were slung electrical wires from building to utility pole.

Outside the warehouse the vendors sold tools the fish market dealers needed to run their businesses. One store sold nothing but knives. Another, nothing but packing materials. We took a random turn into an area that felt apart. Different. It provided a quiet respite from the noise. The stalls didn't sell much. Mostly ledger books, calculating equipment, and scales. But one had a few souvenirs displayed outside. Sushi magnets among them. They were smaller than those normally found in Tokyo. But they were much cheaper. And the magnets were extra strong. At least that's what the package said.

A bargain!

Clutching the magnets, I went into the shop, parting the *noren*, and walked right into a family drinking tea. I bowed, excusing myself, and was able to indicate I wanted to buy them.

Afterward we continued the length of the alley and then turned to join a larger street. Eric stopped toward the end of it in front of a sushi shop. "We have to eat here."

I stood away from the store and looked at the sign. Sushizanmai. "Here? Why?"

"One of the foreign nationals at work said this one's the best."

And so I soon found myself perched on a lattice-backed stool, watching the sushi chefs prepare our...well...it was only nine o'clock in the morning, but I was pretending to have lunch. It made the idea of sushi more palatable.

"What kind do you like?"

In all honesty, I didn't really like sushi. I tried to avoid it as much as possible. "Something un-chewy."

"Eel?"

"No thanks. Actually, Eric, I have a hard time with sushi. It's raw."

"Then close your eyes when you eat it."

I laughed.

"Seriously." Eric said something in Japanese to the chef.

The chef nodded, went to work, and, several minutes later, placed two plates in front of us.

I looked at mine. "I'm only doing this if you promise not to let me eat *that* by accident." I pointed to a piece looking as if it had red ball bearings sitting on top of it. Only they were transparent. "I might be able to eat it if I didn't know what it was, but those are fish eggs, aren't they?"

Our eyes met.

"They are."

"And the other ones have raw fish on top, right?"

"Right."

"There's just something about raw food I can't get over."

"Why? Because of the way it looks or the way it tastes?"

That was a good probing question. I'd never tasted raw fish before. "Because of the way it looks."

"Then close your eyes. Really. I'll hand you a piece. Sometimes the less seen the better."

And because it was Eric's eyes I was looking into, because he seemed so confident, and because I knew he never lied, I did it. I tried one with a burgundy-colored piece of fish. At least I hoped it was and I guessed I did. It was no longer there when I opened my eyes.

It was good.

In fact, most of the pieces were good.

One piece was chewy, but it was also sweet. So...I decided not to think about what it might have been. And I gave my stomach a pep talk after I'd swallowed it.

"Which one did you like the best?"

"The last one was kind of sweet…"

"Scallop."

"And the first one was…it was good. Some kind of fish? I might eat it more often if they had it in the States."

"They do. It was *maguro*. But in English it's spelled t-u-n-a."

"No."

"Yes."

We hopped on the subway about ten. We sat side by side facing the center aisle.

"So."

"So."

"Are you doing anything for Thanksgiving?" I wasn't, and it had just occurred to me that we might as well celebrate together.

Eric's eyes dodged toward his feet, and then they bounced back to look into mine. "Samantha invited me to go to the Tokyo American Club with her and her friends. They're having some big…thing."

I was sure they were. The Tokyo American Club was a members-only club to which all the big expat businessmen belonged and, more importantly, many Japanese businessmen with important influence. I wondered how Samantha had pulled off that invitation because I assumed she couldn't afford the twenty-thousand-dollar entrance fee.

"Maybe…I could ask Samantha if you can join the crowd."

"Oh. No." I could give Eric a turkey and—possibly—a pumpkin pie, but Samantha? She could give him his career on a platter. Decorated with sprigs of parsley. Why wouldn't he choose to spend the day with the perfect candidate for diplomatic wife? "No need. I have plans." Or I would by the time Thursday rolled around. "Just wanted to make sure you weren't going to be sitting home alone."

"No."

Several minutes passed in silence before Eric cleared his throat. "So… about the CODEL."

The CODEL. What would be Eric's most convincing argument? Not, of course, that he was arguing with the congressman's wife or even trying to keep her from doing something she wanted.

Good grief. I was starting to think like Eric!

So what could he use? The possibility of death by automated cart? "Tell her she has to be at a subway station no later than six o'clock. Tell her she'll have to have footwear she won't mind getting slimy. And tell her it smells like fish."

# DECEMBER | *Shiwasu*
*Month of Running Priests*

23

*Camellia, Empress
of Winter, ever green while
fainter flowers sleep.*

I WAS COUNTING ON DECEMBER to give me one of the best Christmas presents I'd ever received: Samantha's deployment to a war zone.

I couldn't wait!

She tried to squeeze more study sessions out of Eric as the date approached. He didn't comply. Blaming it on the CODEL, he even canceled a meeting when the group actually came into town, but he seemed apologetic about it. As if he really would have preferred to have been helping Samantha study.

Men.

Samantha couldn't leave town fast enough in my opinion. Knowing I would be assigned twice as much work gave me nothing but pleasure. She had unofficially stopped working the first week in December, anyway. She said it was so she could get all her paperwork together, get her shots, update her will. She had one up on me there. When I'd deployed, I'd actually had to create one.

She also planned a party her last Saturday night in town before going home for Christmas prior to her deployment. After eating at some chic Thai restaurant in Shibuya for dinner, she planned on going to a karaoke bar after. I got roped into going against my better judgment. It had turned into an office function plus Eric. Someone suggested getting her a group gift. Guess who was chosen to select it?

Me.

Guess who was the sole contributor?

Also me.

Somewhere up in heaven, I'm sure God was busting a gut laughing.

I found a cheesy "We'll Miss You!" card for everyone to sign. I had a harder time with the gift. You don't want to get too sentimental when you're sending someone off to a war zone. You don't want to make them realize they might not come back. I decided on a gag gift.

I bought a big funnel from the Auto Supply shop at Yokota and put it inside a glass display case. I printed instructions onto a label, which I affixed to the front of the glass, and then I placed the glass case into a cardboard box, fastening it with a bungee cord.

"What's this?" Samantha shook the box and then began to unwrap it. "You guys really shouldn't have." She smiled. And then she tore the paper off to reveal an innocuous-looking brown box. Turned it around and then saw the inscription. "Mortar Catcher Kit?"

"Open it up!" That was Neil. I'd showed him my masterpiece before I wrapped it.

She undid the bungee, keeping the lid closed, and then she lifted the glass case out, holding it up for everyone else to see. "Mortar Catcher Kit. To be used to direct mortars to unoccupied areas. Number one: In case of mortar attack, lift glass."

Neil lifted the case.

"Number two: Remove funnel."

Samantha picked up the funnel.

"Number three: Hold funnel on top of head."

Neil took the funnel from Samantha and held it above her head.

"Number four: Yell, 'Here, mortar, mortar, mortar. Here, mortar, mortar, mortar.'"

Everyone burst out laughing.

Except for Samantha. Her eyes narrowed. "Unoccupied areas. Very funny."

I thought it was hilarious.

The food was great, the party fun, but I checked out when the group left the restaurant and headed toward the karaoke bar. Samantha had been hanging on Eric's arm practically the entire evening. If she could get any closer, they'd be Siamese twins.

Hmm

Had there ever been Siamese twins of opposite genders? Could be an interesting story. Not that I was thinking of writing another book. But if I ever did…I googled "Siamese twins" on my cell phone as I walked toward the subway station.

Oops. "*Cojoined* Twins" were the new "Siamese Twins" and…nope. They started out as identical twins.

Well, like I said, I wasn't thinking of writing another book.

I heard Samantha stumble into the hall early the next morning.

She knocked on my door. "Allie?" She might have thought she was whispering, but she wasn't. "Allie!"

I rolled out of bed and flung open my door. "What!"

"Shh! You'll wake someone up."

"Where have you been?"

"Wouldn't *you* like to know?" She collapsed against my door in a fit of giggles. Giggles? Samantha wasn't a giggler. "It was amazing. *Totally dreamy*."

"What was?"

She yawned. Put up a hand to cover her mouth. "I'm tired. Have to leave early, early tomorrow. I'm going to the desert. But first—" She stuck up one finger in the air. Swayed with the effort. "First, I'm going to bed. Again." She staggered away from my door and down to her own. She unlocked it and pushed it open. "Good night." Her door started to shut. Then swung open. "Oh. One thing. Just remembered."

"What?"

"He said to say hi."

"What? Who?" The door shut before she could answer me. But only one response would have made sense.

Eric.

Samantha was long gone by the time I crawled out of bed around lunchtime. I kept examining her words. Rearranging them. Trying to turn them into something else. Form them into a different picture. But the only face that could match her words was Eric's.

I didn't go to church. It's not that I was running away from God. I was trying to avoid Eric. Dang it! If men like him couldn't be trusted, then who could? What line had she used on him? That's what I wanted to know. What exactly had been the magic words? What did he see in her?

And what had stopped him from seeing me?

My phone rang early that evening. "Allie?"

"Hi, Eric."

"Are you sick?"

"Maybe."

"Anything I can do?"

"I don't think so. Did you go to the karaoke bar last night with Samantha?"

"I did. I expected to see you there."

"You know what they say about three."

"What?"

"Two's company. Three's a crowd."

"There were a lot more than three in our crowd."

Until it evaporated into two. "Out late?"

"Not especially."

"Samantha came back around two."

"Was she okay?"

"Fine. Drunk, but raving about what a great time you two had."

"I guess it was. If you like that sort of thing."

*That* sort of thing? "What did you do, just go along with it because you were too much of a gentleman to decline? I have to go, Eric."

"Allie—"

I couldn't bear to hear anymore. I hung up the phone.

He'd told me he knew about Samantha, hadn't he? He'd told me he was being careful, hadn't he? Then what had happened? And why was I having so much trouble breathing?

I had to get out of my room. Walk, run, drive, do something. Pulling on a coat, I yanked my door open, and almost ran right into Neil. "Hey, Neil. Sorry."

"Hi."

I was about to walk right past him, but something about his posture stopped me. "What's wrong?"

He looked at me. I read misery in his eyes. "Um…"

"Spill it."

"Well…" He shrugged. "You know."

"No. I don't."

"It's just…"

"For a writer, you're being particularly ineloquent. Do you need a dictionary?"

He shook his head.

"Thesaurus?"

"No."

"Then start with the basics. Who, what, when, where, why, and how."

"Samantha. Um…you know." He started to blush. "Anyway, last night." He took a quick peek at my face. "My room. I have absolutely no idea. Um…yeah."

"Are you telling me you slept with *Samantha* last night?"

"Shh!"

"Right before she deployed?"

"I did."

I reached over and patted him on the cheeks. "I could just…kiss you!"

He flinched. "No. Please don't."

I looked at him.

"Not, of course, that you aren't good at kissing. Other people."

One thing still bothered me. "Did you tell her to say 'hi' to me for you?"

The red in his cheeks started to spread toward his ears.

"Never mind. Don't answer."

I returned to my room, sat down at the desk, and picked up the phone. I started to dial Eric's number but then hung up instead. Because what, exactly, would I say to him? "I'm sorry I thought you'd slept with Samantha?"

He didn't know what I'd been thinking. Unless he'd guessed somehow. Which I'd hoped he hadn't. He hadn't, had he?

*Please, God, may something turn out right in my life for once.*

I picked up a pencil and began tapping on the desk with it. Something else bothered me. Something about my reaction. The part when I was having trouble breathing. If it had been about Samantha, I should have been mad. Angry. But it hadn't been about Samantha, had it? And I hadn't been enraged, had I? I'd been heartbroken.

My reaction had been all about me.

I'd taken the whole thing personally, hadn't I? Much too personally for a casual friendship. I tossed the pencil back in the drawer. Then I leaned down and conked my head on the desktop, just to make sure I still had a brain up there somewhere.

Okay, so I wanted to kiss him. It shouldn't have been a big deal. But it was. Why?

*Why, why, why?*

Because he was my friend. God had answered my prayer. Maybe not the way I'd expected, but he had. I'd have to draw the other eye on my wishing doll. He'd given me Eric as a friend. Which was the whole problem. I couldn't kiss a friend. And I couldn't kiss a Republican. I wouldn't. Why should I? Politics had been the only thing holding my parents together. And why would Eric be interested in a cultural failure like me? Besides, it would ruin everything the way it always had. And if I lost Eric's friendship, then I wouldn't be able to survive Tokyo.

I'd have to be insane to give up everything for a single kiss…and everyone who knew me knew I was a total lunatic. What was I going to do? I had seven months and two weeks.

That should have been enough time to figure it out.

# 24

*One hundred and eight
gongs and Moon shines bright. I have
no desire but this.*

I'D ALWAYS BEEN A HANDS-ON, MECHANICALLY-INCLINED PERSON. So when I was assigned an article on Japanese New Year traditions, I took the research seriously. I headed straight for Yuka-san's desk and made copious notes while I grilled her about Japan's New Year's festivities. Which information I, of course, was planning to confirm by research later.

"This is most important holiday in Japan. Business close from first to third. And people spend this with family. We clean all clothes and house. We replace tatami floor mat and put new paper in shoji screen. We finish all task before new year begin. When I go home from work on December 31, I have nothing undone. I finish everything because in new year we start everything new again. The old year is now behind, new year has started."

"Do you have any traditions? Things you do only for New Year's?"

"We make special decoration of pine, maybe bamboo and plum tree branch. We put these on both side of entrance. This bring good luck to house. We also put *shimenawa* above entrance."

"What is *shimenawa?*"

"This is rope of straw with strip of paper. Cut like…" She moved her finger through the air in front of her in a zigzag pattern.

"Lightning?"

"*Hai*. Like lightning. This keep bad luck from house. We offer food to household god."

"What kind of food do they like?"

"We give them *mochi,* chestnut, sardine, black pea, *mikan.* On the evening before New Year Day, we eat *toshikoshi.* This is *soba.* We eat this for long life. We wait for midnight for *joya-no-kane,* the temple bell."

"All the temples ring bells?"

"All temple, one hundred eight time."

"One hundred and eight? Why?"

"Man has one hundred eight desire. If you hear the bell one hundred eight time, all desire are taken away. We give each other New Year greeting, and we give *o-toshidama.* Parent give children money. And when you visit friend or relative, you must take *o-toshidama.* And we send *nangajo,* New Year card. The postman keep these and collect for each house and then on New Year Day deliver all at same time."

"And what do you do on New Year's Day?"

"This is very auspicious day. It represent rest of year. So it is good to see the first sunrise of new year. We do no work because everything is clean. We have much joy. No anger. We make visit to shrine."

"Which one?"

"In Tokyo, Meiji Shrine is very popular. Starting at midnight, we make resolution and pray for good luck. On the second day of new year, the store put away new thing. And in Tokyo you may go to Imperial Palace for New Year greeting."

"To greet...?"

"The emperor and imperial family."

"They actually let you go inside the palace?"

"The palace? No. But you may walk onto the ground."

"The emperor does this every year?"

"*Hai.* Every second day of January. Many people come from all over Japan."

Too bad the article was due before then.

"But you may also go to Imperial Palace on emperor birthday."

"When is it?"

"December twenty-third."

"Of *this* month?"

"*Hai.*"

"And it's the same thing as the New Year's greeting?"

"No. Not so much. There are more member of imperial family present at New Year greeting. And at birthday, guest may sign the birthday greeting book."

"But is the ceremony the same?"

"*Hai*. You walk to Imperial Palace and you wait for emperor and he greet you and you wave and say, '*Banzai!*'"

"*Banzai?* I thought that was a war cry."

"It mean ten thousand year. We say, May emperor live ten thousand year."

"Long live the king?"

"*Hai*."

To call or not to call? But it wasn't really a tough question because I didn't spend all that long deliberating. I hadn't seen Eric since I'd figured out something strange and demented inside me actually wanted to kiss him. When I made a surprising discovery like that about myself, the journalist inside me just had to try to make some sort of sense out of it.

I called him at work.

"Eric Larsen."

"Allie O'Connor."

"Allie. Hi."

"Hey. I have to do some research for an article this Saturday, and I figure you owe me one for the Tsukiji CODEL junket."

"Ah, yes. You know, I hate to tell you this, but the congressman's wife decided not to go to Tsukiji after all."

"Really. That's a shame. So about my research?"

"I'd love to go."

*I'd love to go…?* I sensed a "but" somewhere in close proximity. "Did you just say yes, or were you using State Department jargon for 'but I'd rather die than be seen with you in public'?"

"Yes."

"Yes, you want to go, or yes, you'd rather die?"

"Allie, somehow I think you may have formed the wrong impression about me. Let's start over. Yes, Allie O'Connor, I would love to go with you to…where *are* we going?"

I told Eric to meet me at the barracks at nine. The subway stop for the Imperial Palace was on my line. I felt as if I were turning over a new leaf: I was showered and fully clothed when he arrived.

I noticed Eric was wearing a wool overcoat, gloves, and a scarf. "What's the weather like?"

"Cold."

I sighed. But it *was* December. We'd had unseasonably warm weather for far too long. I burrowed into my closet, looking for my coat, and pulled it out by the hem. It was a long down-filled quilted "puffy" coat. In black.

I wasn't brave enough to buy a white winter coat.

My gloves were playing hide-and-seek. I yelled, "Ollie, Ollie, oxen free," but they didn't appear. Too bad. I'd buy some new ones. That would teach them!

And me.

The great thing about a puffy coat—with big pockets—is that you can put anything you want inside of it.

I shoved my journal, a pen, my camera, subway guide, wallet, and stocking cap inside before they started to fill up.

"Do you have a wrench?"

I turned away from my desk to look at Eric. "Why?"

"I could figure out how to disconnect the kitchen sink for you."

The thing about Eric was that he had this dry, deadpan humor. You had to listen for it or you were likely to miss it. So maybe I was attracted to him because—*was I truly, honestly attracted to him?*—I snuck a peek at him in profile.

Dang it! I was!

When had *that* happened?

We took the subway straight to Nijubashimae and joined the crowds of people ascending from the station to the street. I had hoped we'd be early. But as we walked across the street toward the palace grounds, we could see a crowd of people walking across the bridge that spanned the moat. The good thing was that we'd be among the first in the new line that was just then being formed.

We followed the people in front of us and stood in a line indicated by ropes strung in parallel. We slowly approached a series of folding tables that had been set up underneath an open-sided tent. I surrendered the entire contents of my pockets to a guard as Eric did the same. Once approved, we walked out of the tent and joined a growing line. Lines. Three identical lines were forming side by side by side. It wouldn't have been problematic except that the entrance gate was the width of one line, not three.

Which line would be first? Or would it be a giant free-for-all?

A sense of expectancy buoyed the crowd, but it had none of the boisterous restless energy of Times Square at midnight. Everyone was quite reserved.

The line behind us grew as my reserve of patience shrunk. I began to wonder what the Japanese must think of Eric and me. Was it proper to treat the Imperial Palace as a tourist site? To turn the emperor into a trophy photo? Was there someone, some Japanese person, who ultimately would not get to see the emperor today because I had taken their place instead? Or maybe they thought I was doing them an honor by participating in a ceremony that had a long and ancient tradition.

Eric bumped my arm.

I turned my head toward his.

"Look."

I looked up beyond the bridge, saw a wave of people descending, spilling over the bridge and out the gate on the other side. So it wouldn't be long.

People were carrying flags. There were men, flaglike themselves, in white *yukata* with a red spot on the back, carrying long, tall banners with the symbol of the royal chrysanthemum on top. One man was carrying an emblem of the rising sun.

"Wasn't that outlawed after World War II?"

"For a while. Then the Japanese navy brought it back."

I took notes on the sights and sounds for a few minutes. Tried to think of some sort of advice for military tourists who wanted to do this. "Come early" would most definitely be at the top.

Fifteen minutes later, the guard at the front of the line ushered us all forward, and the lines surged. He motioned us through the gate. What I had assumed would be a bottleneck of nightmare proportions disintegrated before it could form. No one pushed. No one shoved. No one vied to be first. No one was in any kind of hurry.

It was all very dignified. And very crowded.

But I still took pictures. I took them before, during, and after we went over the bridge because the bridge we crossed was The Bridge. The one you could see from the sidewalk if you stood at one end of Ginza. The bridge that spanned the enormous moat in one graceful arch and then disappeared inside a wooden gate. It was the bridge leading to the cloistered world of the imperial family. The one you knew you'd never be allowed to cross.

But we were! And we did!

And after we crossed it, I turned around and walked backward so I could capture a rare view of Tokyo from the inside looking out.

Inside, I saw what I'd been looking for. The remainder of the white buildings with winged metal roofs you could see from the outside. But we went further in, following a path through a series of gardens, until we finally came to a vast space several soccer fields in length—a courtyard covered with pea gravel—and in front of us, I assumed, the Imperial Palace.

It didn't look very imperial.

I looked distinctly Northwestern. It was long, low, and geometric in profile, composed of exposed wood and patio-to-ceiling windows. But I could tell we were only seeing the back of an enormous building. It was capped off by a glassed-in outer hall. And a glass projection in the middle looked like a giant-sized bay window.

We filed into the courtyard with everyone else, filling up the space. Guards stood at regimented increments between the crowd and the building. Hardly anyone was talking. Hardly anyone was moving. Everyone was just…waiting.

And then the family appeared. The men were dressed in cutaway morning coats. The women in suits, topped by hats.

The emperor made a short speech.

Hundreds of miniature Japanese flags suddenly appeared, waving in the wan sun, and the crowd began to chant, "*Banzai, banzai, banzai.*"

The emperor waved.

And it was over.

We filed out in the opposite direction from which we'd come.

Still subdued, there was more talking among the crowd at this point. Some quiet laughter.

"Not the way I'd choose to spend my birthday."

"But then, you're not the emperor. They come to honor him. So he honors them."

Honor. It was a nice old-fashioned sentiment completely unsuited to modern life. Nobody talked about honor anymore.

Nobody except Eric.

## 25

*Year grows old, hunching
under Memory's weight, bowed
with discarded dreams.*

IT WAS CHRISTMAS EVE, AND TOKYO HAD HARDLY BATTED AN EYE. I'd been to an evening service at church, but for all intents and purposes it had seemed like almost every other day in the year. And now I was sitting in a subway car somewhere in the tangle of tunnels beneath Tokyo.

"It was a nice service." Eric sounded as though he was making a valiant effort to come up with something good to say about Christmas in Japan.

"Christmas always feels strange here. But it was. A nice service." I hadn't been to one before. My last two Christmases in Tokyo had been on weekdays. I'd had the day off, but I'd worked anyway—what else was there to do? "Where did you spend Christmas last year?"

"In Singapore. I was duty officer. If an emergency came up, I had to handle it."

"Any emergencies?"

"Couple lost passports. Nothing from Washington."

"Who'd have thought we'd be spending Christmas Eve together?"

"Without clubbing each other to death?"

I laughed. Now that I knew Eric, I understood he was a nice guy underneath all of his Republican pretension. He'd always been the poster boy for the uptight conservative look: buttoned-up shirts, button-down collars. Now he was the picture of urban sophistication. When had Eric become stylish? And where had he picked up his style?

And he actually looked good. Handsome.

He ran a hand through his hair.

I remembered when all I'd wanted to do was mess it up. Ruin the perfect symmetry of his features. I noticed my fingers itching. They still wanted to do it, but for an entirely different reason.

Eric's eyes swung in my direction. Fixed on my own. "I always wondered why you disliked me so much. In high school."

"I didn't—"

He was looking at me from underneath his brow.

"Okay, I did. But you disliked me too."

"I didn't. I admired you."

"That's not what I remember."

"How could you remember anything? We never talked."

Really? I thought about it. I realized he was right. He never had talked to me, except at the prom. But I did plenty of talking to him. And his type. I'd done it through the literary magazine and hundreds of unpublished poems. Whenever I wrote anything back then, I had always imagined him as my audience. "But didn't you consider me your nemesis?"

"Why?"

"On principle. You know, the liberal–conservative thing?"

"Not really. Everyone wants to change the world. I admired you because you were intent on doing it with such beautiful words and such noble gestures. All I could ever do was extol policies and peddle politics."

"I guess I just assumed you hated me." The way I had hated him.

"But didn't you ever wonder why I asked you to dance at the prom?"

"No."

"It never crossed your mind to ask yourself why?"

"Not really. I thought it was a very gallant gesture. Exactly like something you would do. A sort of nod to our antagonistic past and a send-off into the future with no hard feelings. That's what it was, wasn't it?"

Eric bent to look out the window, trying to see the signs of the station we were pulling into. He grabbed my elbow. "This is ours."

We walked up the stairs and out into a night lit with neon signs and traffic lights.

As we waited for the light to change, Eric shuffled his feet. Glanced at his watch. "Would you like to come to my place for dinner?"

"You don't want to cook on Christmas Eve."

"I might."

What else was I going to do? And eating at a hotel on Christmas Eve seemed a little lonely. "Okay. As long as you let me help cook."

"Deal."

After a while, I heard him come into the room and place something on the table. I twisted around so I could see him. "You cooked…what is that?"

Only it turned out to be a shady deal because when we got to Eric's place, the table was already set. For two. With candles. And, if my nose hadn't betrayed me, the food was already prepared.

I followed him into the living room as he turned on some Christmas music.

"This looks prearranged. What would you have done if I had plans for dinner?"

He walked into the kitchen, ignoring me.

I followed him. "What would you have done if I *did* have plans?"

He opened the refrigerator and took out a head of ruffled lettuce. "When have you ever had plans for dinner? Except for Thanksgiving?"

Yeah. Except for Thanksgiving. "But we had a deal that included me helping. Did you leave anything for me to do?"

He retrieved a colander from a cupboard and put it in the sink. "Of course. You can sit in the living room and listen to music."

"Are you washing lettuce? Because I can wash lettuce."

"Not in my house."

"Is this a chivalry thing?"

"It's a guest–host thing. Please. Relax."

I sat on the couch, relaxing to 1950s-style Christmas music and flipping through a *Smithsonian* magazine.

After a while, I heard him come into the room and place something on the table. I twisted around so I could see him. "You cooked…what is that?"

"This?" He held up a plate. "Bread."

"No. I mean whatever's cooking. It smells wonderful."

"It's a brisket."

"A brisket? You cooked one by yourself?"

"It's not very complicated. At least that's what Judy told me. And she was right." He disappeared into the kitchen.

Judy. She and Samantha seemed to have a lot in common. Both were seemingly perfect women in Eric's life who were very often right.

About everything.

Several minutes later, I heard the pop of a cork and Eric placed two flutes of champagne on the coffee table.

"Where did you find champagne?"

"There's a wine store just down the street."

"The one in Hiroo?"

He nodded.

"The one charging a fortune for everything?"

"If you don't ask, then I won't tell."

I felt my eyes narrow and nearly opened my mouth to say something when I realized—just in time—that he hadn't meant to provoke a political reaction. Hadn't meant anything by it at all. So I swallowed what I'd intended to say and held out my glass toward his. "To you."

"And you. And Christmas Eve in Tokyo."

Dinner was perfect. A brisket accompanied by a confetti of diced potatoes with red and green peppers. Salad. Bread.

Eric let me help clear the table, but he kicked me out of the kitchen when I tried to help him clean up. "I have a dishwasher."

"I know. Her name is Allie O'Connor."

"You're cute, but I'm afraid I wouldn't be able to afford your health insurance or retirement. So go sit down and—"

"Relax. Okay. I'm going."

I picked up the magazine again and started reading where I'd left off. He thought I was cute. Was I? Wasn't cute reserved for people under five foot four?

While I was contemplating the definition and connotation of "cute," Eric finished up in the kitchen. He came into the living room, sat down beside me, and placed a package in my lap. "This is for you."

"Really! Wait. Just a minute." I put the package on the couch beside me, found my messenger bag by the door, and pulled a gift from it. Returning to the living room, I handed it to him. "And this is for you."

I opened Eric's gift to discover a guidebook for Japan. It was a slim volume, but heavy with information. I lifted my eyes to meet his. "Thanks."

"I just thought…you didn't have one."

"I didn't. And now I can't get mad at you when you forget yours." I smiled. "Thank you."

"You're welcome. Merry Christmas…Eve."

"Merry Christmas. Now open yours."

He ran a thumbnail under the gift wrapping, separating paper from tape, and uncovered a book. "A Flip Dictionary?"

"It's a reverse dictionary for when you know the meaning of what you want to say, but not the word. Like…" I took the book from him and flipped it open. "Types of Wrenches! Look. They're all right there."

I looked up to find a smile playing with the corners of his mouth.

"You're always asking me for a word that means something, and I just thought…anyway…" I shrugged.

"Thanks. Thank you very much. I'll be the envy of the entire political section." He placed the book on the coffee table and got to his feet. "Do you want dessert?"

"You made dessert?"

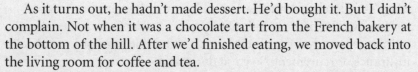

As it turns out, he hadn't made dessert. He'd bought it. But I didn't complain. Not when it was a chocolate tart from the French bakery at the bottom of the hill. After we'd finished eating, we moved back into the living room for coffee and tea.

"So tell me about the adventures of Allie O'Connor. All the episodes I missed between high school and now."

"Well…college was basically a long, extended, drawn-out version of *Survivor*. But I made it. I collected all my work-study money. I won all my scholarships and finally graduated at the top of my class."

"Congratulations."

"Thanks. It felt good for about five minutes, and then I realized I really couldn't write the novel I'd always wanted to write because…well, I also had to eat."

"It happens to the best of us."

"My first job after college was more like *Fear Factor*. Who can do the nastiest jobs and write about the scariest people for the longest period of time without giving up. Or throwing up."

"But you did it."

"I did. Until I could find a job at a bigger paper. Then I felt as if I'd walked into a generic sitcom. Lots of drama, lots of laughs, very little meaning. I wasn't really making a difference with anything I wrote. So I decided it was time to make space for inspiration. *Stripes* was hiring. I figured the worst that could happen was I would write articles for the military. For people who were actually dedicating their lives to something beyond themselves."

"And the best that could happen?"

"I'd be so inspired by the culture that I'd actually end up writing that novel."

"And you have."

"And I have. Such as it is."

"And now your life is like…?"

"I feel as though I've taken up permanent residence on the set of *Lost*. I'm living in an alien environment, at the mercy of nature, with mysterious things happening I just don't understand."

"At least it's an award-winning drama."

"No pain, no gain? No guts, no glory?"

"More like…No stretch, no reach."

It wasn't until later, as I was trying to sleep, that my thoughts returned to our ride on the subway and Eric's question. *Didn't you ever wonder why I asked you to dance at the prom?*

I hadn't ever wondered because I knew what he was like. And I knew what I was like. And in spite of our huge differences, I'd assumed we were the same.

Maybe we weren't.

Why *had* he asked me to dance?

I could remember the song we'd danced to, "Somewhere Out There." I thought it was revealing that he would pick a theme song from an animated movie. And I thought it was a mature gesture for him to make.

I'd gone to prom with a friend, Matt, who was an "artist." It was cooler then to go to the prom with a friend. He had shaggy hair and a scruffy beard. He wore a tuxedo shirt and cummerbund with jeans and Converse high-tops.

I remembered my dress. I had desperately wanted to make a statement—when hadn't I wanted to make a statement?—so I wore a simple straight sheath woven from hemp.

Oh, yes, I did.

It was a smoky-lavender color and floor length. I also wore a wreath of flowers in my hair. I thought I'd looked like nature's princess. When Matt had picked me up, he'd carefully tucked a stray lock of hair behind his ear, squinted, and then nodded at me. He'd said I looked nice.

I don't remember much about the prom, but I do remember seeing Eric across the dance floor, weaving around couples, stopping to shake hands or slap a back now and then. Even then he'd been a politician. I also remember being completely surprised when he showed up at our table. Matt had scowled up at him when Eric asked me to dance. I was so surprised I couldn't think of anything to say. He held out his hand and I just put mine into it. As he walked me to the dance floor, he'd said I looked enchanting.

Enchanting.

A word not usually applied to tall, gangly girls. And "enchanting" was the only word he said to me, if I remembered right. Had I remembered right? I turned over onto my side and slipped my hands underneath my cheek. Had there been anything else about that dance? Anything else at all? Besides the fact Eric actually knew how to dance?

He'd taken my hand in his, placed his other hand at the small of my back, and danced us all the way around the dance floor. It was much more sophisticated than the normal style of slow dancing: Clasping your hands around the guy's neck and dancing in one place by shifting your weight from foot to foot.

At the end of the dance, he'd held my hand just long enough that it made me look into his eyes. They had ranged across my face. And then he had said something else. He'd said "thank you."

So why had he asked me to dance?

What I had assumed then must not have been the right answer after all. So what other reason could there have been? A dare?

No. I'd have known about it long before.

Had he been trying to make Paige jealous?

No. That hadn't been his style.

Had he…he couldn't have liked me?

I felt my lips began to curve. No. I wasn't his type.

Was I?

Was I his type?

That question occupied my thoughts for the greater part of the next day. Contributing, I'm sure, to the various blunders I made at work. Specifically, confusing a photo of a dog wearing a Santa hat for a picture of the Commander of U.S. Forces Japan, a three-star general.

That one brought my concentration to heel.

But I couldn't help remembering the last time I'd kissed someone— Neil—and what a disaster that had turned out to be. So who cared if I was Eric's type or not? Actually, the more appropriate question would be, was he my type?

That was the question.

And the answer was no. Definitely not.

Absolutely not.

Of course not.

Never in a million years.

Even if…even if he were, which he wasn't, everything would be ruined if I kissed him.

So I wouldn't.

That was the deal I'd made with myself. No kissing. Because kissing led to disappointment. And even though Eric had been a good friend, that's still all he was. A friend. And even if he had liked me in high school, that didn't mean he liked me now.

Because I wasn't his type.

At all.

And he wasn't mine.

As I fell asleep that night, a vision of Eric-Buddha appeared. He raised an arm, motioning me closer. I kept saying, "There's something wrong with you." And he kept responding, "No. There's something wrong with you."

I was early to work the next morning. I'd hardly slept at all, and after five it seemed pointless to stay in bed.

I made an extra-strong cup of coffee and took it to work with me. I turned on the office lights and booted up my computer. I finished reading through e-mails and had started back to work on the New Year's traditions article when I heard a noise. Or thought I heard a noise. It was a thump-thump-thump of a sound so low-pitched it was almost just a vibration. It was primeval. A deep, resonating thud. A thud so powerful, my heart started to keep its time.

I placed my hands on the keyboard. Started to type.

Thump. Thump. Thump.

I let my hands splay across the keyboard. Was it the printing equipment?

Thump. Thump. Thump.

It was such a regular rhythm it had to be something mechanical... didn't it?

I willed myself to ignore it and began typing. But the thumping threw off my own rhythm. I decided to investigate and followed my ears into the hall. I had assumed I would end up in the printing room, but I didn't. The noise seemed to be coming from the walls of the building. It wasn't internal, it was external.

Thump. Thump. Thump.

I took the stairs down to the ground floor. It was definitely louder down there. I walked outside, past the protection of the overhang. Still louder.

But where was it coming from?

I looked to my right, over at the gate. The guards were standing side by side at the gatehouse. They were talking to each other, but they were looking down the street, toward my left.

I followed their gaze and then stepped forward toward the line of cars parked along the chain-link fence. At least I was going in the right direction. It was louder over there. I stepped over the ditch separating the parking lot from the walkway around the perimeter, and I saw one of the strangest sights I'd ever seen.

In the middle of Tokyo, in front of a high-end men's shirt store and an elegant lounge, a pair of men, holding huge wooden mallets, were pounding something into a wooden pedestal bowl. Beside them sat two baskets, steaming in the chilly air. They were stripped to the waist, bandanas tied around their foreheads. Surrounding them were a group of men chanting, clad in short kimono coats and what looked like rubber boots.

The two men with mallets worked together, trading off blows. The first one swung the mallet to his shoulder, bent forward, and let it fall. The second one flexed, bent, and went through the same motions in delayed mirror vision. First one, then the other. Not one pause. Not one hesitation. The human machine at work.

Thump, thump. Thump, thump.

Thump, thump. Thump, thump.

A third man crouched next to the pedestal bowl. I saw his hand slip down into the bowl between every swing. Each time I saw it, I held my breath. Both time and distance were minimal between the swinging mallets. Yet, after I had observed for several minutes, I realized there was all the time in the world. All the time needed in a world composed of one bowl, two mallets, and three men. An unbreakable, unstoppable cycle. Six separate elements combined into one ritual.

Watching it was meditative, tranquil, and barbaric.

I turned, went back inside, and started typing again. Later, after everyone had showed up, I found Yuka-san.

"There are some men out there…thumping something."

"This is *mochi*. Today is auspicious day for making *mochi*. It must be made before New Year so it can be eaten in January."

"But what is it?"

"Rice and water. This is…" She made a fist and hit her palm with it repetitively.

"Pounded."

"*Hai.* Until it become soft. And then it is made into shape."

"Why?"

"Eaten in New Year bring good luck and good health. But making *mochi* is Japanese custom which bring luck. This is hard work and need much harmony between worker. Each grain of rice is one soul, but when…" she hit her palm again with her fist, "pounded, this become one million soul."

"They didn't look like they were having fun."

"Making *mochi* is hard work, but it also allow reflection. We reflect on past year. We reflect on nature. On one soul being part of one million."

I went back into the conference room and looked down across the parking lot on the street below. I heard the thumps. And in the vibrations I felt the echo of the past and the unfolding of the future.

I felt one soul becoming part of one million.

*Mutsuki*
*Month of Harmony*

26

*Fall silent, fall hard.*
*Snowflake, your death lends my world*
*a dazzling white grace.*

I WOKE LATE ON NEW YEAR'S DAY AND CONTEMPLATED POSSIBILITIES. I could go to a temple or shrine, just to see what kind of crowds were there. The Japanese seemed secular, but I'd heard they were religious at the right times: birth, marriage, death, and New Year's Day.

I could shop the sales. They were legendary. "Lucky bags" could be bought at any type of retail store for a fraction of the price of the contents. And the contents were all good—no leftovers or factory seconds. The catch was you didn't know what you'd bought until you opened it up. It was the traditional grab bag on a grand Tokyo-sized scale.

I could think about the new year. Not in a resolution sort of way. I'd given those up long ago. But I liked the Japanese idea of beginning a new unit of time. It made sense. Samantha was absent from this first part of the year. And Eric was very present.

Eric.

Maybe I needed to begin again with him. Pretend I'd never known him before. I could start right now. This day. I could even kiss those lips—in six short months—if I wanted to. I could give myself permission to do that.

And I could also stay in bed.

Should I go or should I stay?

I looked toward the window, trying to guess what the weather might be outside.

There were no clues.

And no calls.

I could have called Eric, I suppose, but if he wanted me, I'd decided he was going to have to come and get me. That way, it wouldn't be my decision, would it? Sighing, I turned to my side and burrowed under the covers.

Tokyo's streets began to fill with a slow trickle of people returning from the country on the third of January. By the fifth, everything was back to normal.

And then it snowed.

Snow in Tokyo was a magical fairy dust that softened all the ugly, hard, modern lines of the buildings and froze time. It made the landscapes at once ancient and ageless. Bestowed a touch of grace to a city on the verge of consuming itself.

The snow had fallen overnight. I had gone to bed wrapped in the comfort of darkness and had awoken to an overexposed world of white. And snow was still falling. I could hardly wait to get out in it, pausing only to pull on my coat and holler for my gloves.

They still wouldn't come out from hiding.

Figuring I could get in a quick walk before work, I headed down Gaien-nishi-dori toward Hiroo through thick, dense snow. It crunched under my feet. Dropped in lethal-weight chunks from the wires strung above my head. As I shuddered inside my coat, I passed a group of children on their way to school.

There were boys, ambling along, exchanging pokes. Laughing. One running ahead to wait for the others. Then a different one doing the same. They were wearing navy-colored shorts. Elementary school boys were always in shorts. And they weren't Bermudas. They were mid-thigh length. They had on black hats, cinched to their chins with elastic, and navy blue V-neck cardigans with white shirts underneath. Their socks were pulled up toward their knees. They chattered and played, impervious to the elements. Someone once told me shorts made a boy tough. Built character. Call me a skeptic, but the thought of shorts in the snow just made me feel cold.

Colder.

A group of school girls behind the boys were sporting short skirts. Giggling. Hiding smiles behind cupped hands. For such a modest society, they allowed their girls to wear some awfully skimpy skirts. Even into high school. Even in the dead of winter. Which is why leg warmers have never gone out of style in Japan.

I continued on my pilgrimage, going nowhere, exulting in the season's first snow. Perhaps the only snow Tokyo would receive that winter. I walked about half a mile down the street, trying to place my feet where no one else had, when I happened to look up and straight into Eric's eyes.

I nearly fell into a snowbank.

He was standing there, hands shoved into his pockets, apparently watching me.

"Hi."

"Hi." He moved toward me and crooked an elbow.

I took him up on the offer and slipped my hand around his arm. "I just wanted to…well…"

"It's snow."

"Snow. Yes. And snow*ing*…snow."

An inane conversation for most people, but not for those from the Pacific Northwest. Rain was a constant misery in the winter. Snow was rare…and appealing. It added glimmer to the long, gray days.

We began to walk, arm in arm, continuing toward Hiroo.

Eric glanced down at my hand. "Still haven't found your gloves?"

I shook my head.

"Here." He pulled his off and handed them to me. "Take mine."

"I can't take your gloves."

"Sure you can." He took one back and held it open for me to slip my hand into.

"I am not taking your gloves. It's my own fault if I lost mine. I lose a pair every winter. You know how to keep track of your gloves, so you're the one who deserves to wear them."

"They should be worn by the person with the coldest hands. Let me help you."

"I don't need help. I need logical consequences for my behavior so next time I'll remember where I put my own gloves."

"If you don't need help, then at least let me be a gentleman."

I was about to respond, but then I looked into his eyes and forgot what it was I was going to say. How could his eyes be so blue? Eric would have been referred to in the last century as a strapping young lad. In this snow-chilled air, his cheeks and nose had turned red, his eyebrows had started to frost. And snowflakes had gathered on his eyelashes.

"Will you?"

"Will I what?"

"Let me be a gentleman?"

"Yes." *Fine. Anything.*

"Allie?"

"Hmm?"

"Are you going to?"

"Yes." Dang it, I was going to kiss him. I only had six months left. Who would ever know—or care—if I kissed Eric Larsen early?

He reached out a hand toward my hair but then stopped. "You know... you look like a snow princess."

His words broke the spell. I laughed. "There is nothing princesslike about me."

He squinted. Looked at me. "Maybe not. You're more queenlike. Regal. That's the word, right?"

For me? No. But he was entitled to his opinion. It would have been rude of me to disagree.

"Allow me?" He held up the glove again, and I didn't see any point in resisting. First of all, because I'd decided to start over again with Eric. And second, because he was a gentleman who always seemed to get his way.

But then, I thought of a compromise. "What if we each wore one? And put our other hand in our pockets?" I pulled one off and handed it to him.

"I really don't mind if—"

"I do."

His eyes searched my face, looking longest at my eyes. I could tell the moment he gave up. But right before it, there was also a moment in which he decided something. "No. I insist. I can use my pockets."

I put them on. There was no point in standing in the middle of Tokyo arguing about gloves.

I wiggled into them and found that my fingers couldn't touch the tips. And I thought I had big hands!

He offered me his arm again and I took it. But then, as promised, he dropped his hands into his pockets, and the straightening of his arm had the effect of pulling me closer to his side.

But really, what's not to like about being held close to a man in a snowstorm?

We walked in silence, watching the snow fall for several minutes until we reached the corner at Hiroo Plaza. And suddenly, I didn't want to go back to the barracks. And I didn't want Eric to go home either. "Can I buy you coffee? Tea?"

"No. I have to work."

"Work. Yeah, me too."

"So..." He raised his eyebrows, as if he were waiting for me to do something. Say something.

Like what? *Don't leave me?* That would be a little melodramatic. Maybe I could fall to my knees in tears and wrap my arms around his legs too. "Well...bye." I raised a hand to wave and realized I was still wearing his gloves. I started to take them off.

"No. Please. Keep them."

"I can't keep your gloves."

"I have another pair at my apartment."

"Oh. Well..."

"Really. Please."

I put them back on. "Thanks." I waved. "See you. Thanks for the walk."

"My pleasure."

"Have a good day."

"You too." If I kept walking backward, I knew I was going to end up in a snowdrift. The trouble in flirting with people who don't know how to flirt is they don't flirt back. What did he want me to say? I'll miss you?

I didn't like the walk home. It was cold and I was lonely. The memory of those children in shorts and skirts played through my mind. Being cold made you tough. It built character. It bared a softer nature to the elements.

*Revealing Snow.* That was a good title. On several different levels.

For a book someone else could write.

I pushed my hands into my pockets and shivered all the way to the barracks.

## 27

*Burn old grass, consumed
by flame. Old must pass for new
growth to come again.*

ERIC CALLED ME AT WORK LATER THAT MORNING. "I just wanted to thank
you for the walk."

"It wasn't a big deal. I was just out...walking."

"Well, thanks."

"And?"

"And what?"

"What can I help you with?"

"Nothing."

"Nothing at all? No thank-you notes? No top secret telegrams?"

"No. Just saying thanks. Bye."

He hung up before I could say anything else and left me staring at
the phone. I finally put it back onto the receiver, but it immediately rang
again.

"Allie O'Connor."

"Eric Larsen."

"Eric?"

"If you were invited to a function and wanted to reserve the right to
go, how would you word an RSVP?"

"What?"

"If you were invited—"

"I just asked you if I could help with something and you said no."

"I didn't have anything for you to help me with at the time. I don't
like to mix business with pleasure."

"So..."

"So this is the business call. How would you word it?"

I wasted ten valuable minutes on the phone with Eric concocting gobbledygook I hoped no one would ever give me credit for.

I had just replaced the phone when it rang. Again.

I was afraid to pick it up.

"Hello?"

"Allie. It's Eric—"

"Is this business or pleasure? Because I was making a chart just now. It's entitled 'Billable Hours' and it has your name under 'Client.'"

"Pleasure. Have you ever been to a sumo tournament?"

"Sumo? I've never even watched professional wrestling. Why would I want to watch naked fat guys fight?"

"Because it's a royal and ancient tradition."

"So is golf. And I don't watch that."

"If I pay for your ticket would you go?"

"I don't know."

"I might still be able to get tickets on a mat."

I'd been in Japan long enough to know he probably meant on the ground. "For how much?"

"About a hundred dollars. Give or take."

"A hundred dollars? And we wouldn't even have seats!"

"It's the major championship."

"To determine what? King Sumo?"

"The *yokozuna*. Grand Champion. One retired last year. So this year's a very big deal."

"You're a fan?"

"Yes."

"For how long?"

"A while."

"Is this another childhood thing?"

"We used to go when I was little. Judy has this thing about sumo wrestlers. She thinks they're cute."

"I'll go. But I'm not paying a hundred dollars."

"Fine. I understand."

And I did too. I'd taken Beginning Diplo-speak. "And neither will you on my behalf."

He talked me into it. But at least I'd told him I would pay my own way. I wouldn't have said that, of course, if I'd known it would be thirty dollars. He told me over the phone the next week.

"Thirty dollars? For what?"

"For a seat in the nosebleed section."

"At least there's something to sit on. There *is* something to sit on, isn't there?"

"Just think of it as a cultural experience. You'll thank me later."

"Later when?"

He hung up on me.

When the day arrived, we walked down the hill from Eric's apartment to Azabu-Juban and took the subway to the National Sumo Stadium. Emerging from the station, we joined the crowds walking toward the venue. A festival atmosphere prevailed. Long multicolored vertical pennants were snapping in the wind from flagpoles. Japanese characters flowed down their lengths.

We showed our tickets and were given our choice of English or Japanese programs.

We walked around the broad hall ringing the stadium. Like any sports arena, it was dotted with booths selling souvenirs, food, and drinks. I might have been at a baseball game until we entered the stadium. In the middle of the floor was a two-sided wooden roof suspended over the ring. Huge tassels dangled from each corner.

The sumo ring looked much like a boxing ring, except the floor was light gray and didn't have ropes around the sides. It had low cylindrical bumpers to mark the edges. It wasn't soft-floored, but slope sided. A large white circle occupied the center.

On the floor, surrounding the ring, red padded mats had been set up in rows. They stretched several tiers up into what, in the States, would have been bleacher sections.

We found our seats, shuffling past several people to claim them.

Eric helped me take off my coat. Then he took it from me and folded it up, placing it on the floor next to his. He was wearing a close-fitting roll-neck sweater. Its dark blue color made his eyes seem even brighter.

"Want these?"

"What?" I'd been staring into his eyes and had missed what he'd said.

"Do you want the binoculars?"

"Oh. Sure. Thanks."

I took them and put them up to my eyes, adjusting them to focus on the center of the ring. And then I put them in my lap, waiting for some action on the floor below. "So how does it work?"

"Sumo wrestlers are divided into *higashi* and *nishi*. East and west."

I'd noticed before that *higashi* was used quite a bit in place names around the city. "Why do they do that?"

"For organization."

"No. East and west. Instead of north and south." Japan was long and skinny. Wouldn't it make more sense to divide things north and south instead of east and west?

He shrugged. "Why do you say north and south instead of south and north? Tradition probably."

Tradition most likely.

"Here's how it works. A wrestler joins a stable. He starts at the bottom as a sort of apprentice to a more senior wrestler, and then he works his way up through the ranks."

"How do you lose?"

"When you get pushed out of the ring or touch the floor inside the ring."

"Are there any rules?"

"It's not a brawl. It used to symbolize a human struggle with the *kami* spirits. It's all a ritual, except for the actual match. There are three ways to make your opponent lose. You can pick them up by the belt—"

"And give them a giant wedgie."

He frowned at me.

I smiled at him.

"You can push your opponent. Or you can unbalance him."

"That's it?"

"Pretty much."

I soon discovered it wasn't. A man dressed in a short black kimono and a long gray skirt walked into the ring. Eight sumo wrestlers formed two rows behind him, four wrestlers on each side. They stood there, feet planted, arms held slightly away from their bodies, while the skirted man spoke.

I put the binoculars to my eyes.

Each wrestler had his hair in a slim ponytail. Each was wearing what looked like a Speedo with a wide belt along the top...until they turned around and filed off the stage. What they were actually wearing was a Speedo *thong* with a wide belt along the top. And from those belts hung a sort of skirt of long rigid lengths of cord. When the speaker was done, the wrestlers took a tour of the ring and ambled away.

And then a parade began. There were three men in short kimonos and jodhpurlike leggings holding up large signs outlined with golden fringe as they walked around the ring.

"Those are the prizes to be won during this match." Eric spoke the words into my ear.

I kept my eyes trained on the ring even as a shiver crept up my back. My ears were an especially sensitive part of my body.

*Don't stop talking now.*

I focused on a man in an ornate olive-and-gold brocade-looking robe. He was standing at the center back of the ring. He had a black hat tied underneath his chin and a thick light green cord dangling from his neck. Another thick white cord wound around his waist. White socks peeked out beneath the hem of his robe. In his hand he carried a paper fan.

Two sumo wrestlers approached the ring from different corners.

Then they stepped up onto the ring. They stomped around, bending down, and raised their feet above their heads. Clapped their hands. Stomped some more.

Took a drink.

Threw something over their shoulder.

"Salt. For purification. Sumo used to be spiritual."

The man in green stepped into the ring and took what looked like a whisk broom and swept the floor.

The wrestlers broke off, each moving behind a white line.

"They have to take their position behind the white lines. And then they'll start." His voice might as well have been kneading my shoulders for all the pleasant sensations it was provoking.

The men pushed those dangling cords away from the front of their legs. Crouched. Stared at each other.

Stood up. And walked around.

"Keep watching."

They ambled back to the lines. Pushed the cords away. Crouched. Stared at each other.

Stood up.

They walked around again and then returned to the white lines. Pushed the cords away. Crouched. Crashed!

The match was on.

# 28

*Lone Pine Tree, bend your branches to Wind, sculptress of both body and soul.*

IT STARTED WITH A PRESS OF BODIES, CHEST TO CHEST. A standoff. And then one wrestler abruptly stepped to the side. The other stumbled past. It looked as though he would fall, but then he regained his balance. He grabbed his opponent by the belt and tried to push him out of the ring. Failed. Tensed to try again when his foot slipped, and he was pushed out of the ring himself.

He regained his balance, and then both he and his opponent returned to their starting positions behind the white lines. Bowed. The loser stepped out of the ring and disappeared.

"That's it? No more rounds?"

"That's it."

"But what if...I mean...his foot slipped! It was a fluke. What if he's a better wrestler than that?"

"He probably is. Probably will be at the next tournament."

The winner was given an envelope.

"What's...?"

"His payment. For winning."

Right there? Like that? It seemed just a little indiscreet.

The next two wrestlers appeared for their match. And it went much the same as the first. A lot of ritual. A lot of posturing. And a match that was over in less than twenty seconds. We watched the whole division in near silence. And then I realized I'd been hogging the binoculars.

"I'm sorry!" I held them out to Eric. "I wasn't thinking."

"It's addicting, isn't it?"

It was addicting. It was almost noble. Not a sad, pathetic display of purposely plumped up flesh. Not at all like I'd thought. "They're athletes."

"That's why it's called *wrestling.*"

"I know. I just…I mean…"

"Because they're fat."

"Well…yeah."

"That doesn't mean they can't be athletic."

"I know. But they're so agile. So quick."

"And so interesting that people don't always have to be the way we assume they are, isn't it?"

I thought about that one for a while and then turned to face him. "You're not speaking in general, are you?"

"No."

"So are you speaking about you or about me?"

"Me."

"In what way?"

"In nearly every way you think of me."

That made me sit up straight. "I think very highly of you." More highly than he could possibly know.

He raised an eyebrow.

"I do. Outside of Gina, you're the best friend I've found in Tokyo."

"Exactly." He looked at me with something like a gleam of expectation in his eyes. Then it dimmed and he sighed. "Would you like something to drink?"

I nodded. Slid my knees to the side to let him pass. Tried to follow the trail of our conversation back to its starting point. Assumptions. He had been talking about assumptions. And friendship. And he was right. I had to admit we made a very unlikely pair of friends. Democrat and Republican. Liberal and conservative. An unexpected, but very, very interesting friendship.

*Friends. Not lovers. Friends. Friends, friends, friends.*

He returned about ten minutes later, took a long look into my eyes, and sighed again. He handed me a Coke, sat down next to me, and took a sip from his own.

"Thanks." I took a drink. "You know, you *are* very nice for a Republican."

"And you're very dense for a Democrat."

I nearly choked. Then I sputtered, "I'm trying to be nice to you. I gave you a compliment!"

"A compliment was not what I was after."

"I know. I'm giving it to you for free. Unsolicited. Can't you just say 'thank you'? You're *not* a pompous, arrogant—"

"Ass? That would be you. I'm the elephant, remember?"

"Why does it always have to be about politics with you?"

He took a long hard stare at me. For some reason I had the impression that he was going to lunge. That there was going to be a crash. But then his demeanor relaxed. He began to laugh. He shook his head as he glanced away.

"Care to share?"

"You're really something."

"What kind of something?"

"If I knew, I'd tell you, but I just don't have the words." He looked down at the ring and gestured with his chin. "It's starting again."

I watched the next division of wrestlers parade up onto the ring. Walk around. Fight. Found myself straining forward over my knees as the wrestlers clashed and struggled in the ring. There was a sort of brutal poetry about it. Something fatalistic about a fight determined by only one match. Only one chance. What looked like a battle of epic proportions concluded in just seconds. A fight where a moment's wavering meant defeat.

"What do they feed them to make them so large?"

"Special sumo stew."

I couldn't tell if he was joking.

"They do. Thousands of calories in each serving."

"So they ruin their health in order to do this?"

"They're treated like rock stars. It's not such a bad life."

We watched several more divisions before the final one. When the wrestlers marched on they were all wearing elaborate aprons around their waists. The aprons were embroidered in vivid colors and edged with thick gold fringe.

They made a circle around the ring and then performed a solemn dance.

Then they all left but one.

"This is the *yokuzuna*, the grand champion. To be one, you not only have to have the skill, but you also have to be graceful and dignified."

"Graceful and dignified. They could use some of that on World Wrestling's *Friday Night Smackdown*."

Eric ignored me. "It's up or out for sumo wrestlers. If you don't win your match this week, then you're demoted in the rankings for the next tournament. But once you're a *yokozuna*, you can't lose."

"You mean everyone throws their matches for you?"

"No. You have to maintain a winning record. If you can't perform at your peak, then you voluntarily retire."

Eric stopped speaking as music began to play. The *yokozuna* performed a dance, a demonstration, to music. Holding a long slender bow between his hands, he sunk down, balanced on one foot, lifting the other over his head. Then he rose and balanced on the other, giving an exhibition of flexibility, all the while moving with grace. And strength. A perfect picture of everything I had assumed him not to be.

We stayed until the end and then joined the stream of people flowing down into the depths of the subway. We took it to Azabu-Juban. Eric suggested taking a taxi home. But the night was clear and the air had a pleasant chill in it. I told him I didn't need one.

We walked up through the main street. Smelled a *yakiimo* sweet potato seller before we actually saw him.

"Want one?"

"You buy them?"

"Something else Allie O'Connor has never done?"

I shrugged. There seemed something not quite twenty-first century about buying a sweet potato out of a derelict truck filled with glowing coals. But why not? I'd always wanted to. What could be the harm?

Eric said the words I now recognized for "two" in terms of food items. Because it was something else for nearly everything else.

The man reached into a drum, pulled two out, and wrapped them in paper. Eric handed one to me.

I shifted it between my hands, waiting to take my cues from him. How did a person go about eating a whole sweet potato without a knife and fork?

He inched it up out of the paper and took a bite. Immediately slurped in a mouthful of air. "Hot!"

I plunged my hand into a pocket and felt around for my coin purse. Found it. I looked around for a vending machine and located one just up the street.

I started toward it at a jog. "What do you want?"

"Anything!"

I pushed the potato into my pocket and fed coins into the machine. I glanced at Eric as I pressed a button. I had intended to press the button for a Coke. In my distraction, I pressed a button for something else. Something in a green can.

It rolled out of the machine.

I pulled it out, popped the top, and handed it to Eric.

He took it from me and put it to his mouth. He took a long swallow. And then I saw his face freeze. "What is...?" He held the can up in front of his eyes. His face cleared for an instant. And then he grimaced. "Next time, you'll know that when a can has pictures of an aloe plant, it means it has aloe gel in it."

"Aloe gel?"

He poured the can out into the gutter.

We both watched as glops of...aloe gel...splatted to the ground.

"That's um...well..."

"Interesting?"

"I was thinking more along the lines of gross."

Clutching our sweet potatoes, we walked up the long, steep hill from Azabu-Juban to Hiroo, passing the Austrian, Pakistani, and Argentinean embassies. We crested the hill, across the street from the Tokyo Lawn Tennis Club. As we waited for the light to change I unfastened several snaps on my puffy coat and tried not to pant.

And then I realized I didn't have to wait for the light to change. I was already on the right side of the street for my route to the barracks. "I guess I can go from here. Thanks for the tickets. And—" I held the remains of my potato up in the air, "this."

"Thanks for coming. If I had a car, I'd take you back."

"I can walk. The fresh air's good for the head."

Only it wasn't.

Woven through my dreams that night was an image of Eric-Buddha. He was holding a long slender bow between his hands, balancing first on one foot, then the other. But the vision faded away before he could speak, leaving only an imprint. An impression. The suggestion that he was not at all what I had assumed him to be.

# FEBRUARY | Kisaragi
*Month of Wearing Extra Layers of Clothing*

## 29

*Plum Tree, flowering,*
*show me how I can escape*
*Winter's curse to bloom.*

THE FOLLOWING SUNDAY AFTER CHURCH ON THE SUBWAY HOME, I suddenly remembered I had a suit waiting for me at the New Sanno's dry cleaners. It was only—I rummaged through my bag for the ticket—a month overdue for pick up. It was a consequence of trying to check my car's dipstick at Yokota when I was wearing a dry clean-only suit. I wasn't sure why I'd bothered. Five-dollar cars needed a constant supply of oil. It was a given.

Eric and I got off the subway at Hiroo, let the machines eat our tickets, and then trudged up the stairs. It was raining—still—when we surfaced.

Eric pointed his umbrella toward the sky and popped it open while I looked on in envy. He turned and waited for me to step away from the station's sheltering mouth.

"You didn't bring an umbrella?"

I shook my head. My umbrella was hiding too. I was sure when I discovered my gloves, it would be right there beside them. In fact, most of my accessories seemed to be engaged in an endless game of Sardines.

When Eric tipped his elbow out toward me, I didn't hesitate to grab it. We walked to the New Sanno, skirting puddles as we leaned together into the wind.

Once inside the hotel, it took a couple minutes for the warmth to unfreeze my lips enough to talk. I stood in front of the gas fireplace, trying to coax the heat into my bones. Winter in Tokyo could be sparkling and clear or dreary, drippy gray. Either way, it was numbingly cold.

After a few minutes, I rotated so the fire could warm my backside.

That's when I saw Eric standing in front of a sign advertising the hotel's Valentine's Escoffier Dinner the next Saturday. The New Sanno put on about five Escoffier Dinners each year. They were legendary eight-course dinners with wines.

I waited several more seconds, until I was too hot for comfort, and then moved to join him.

As we stood there, reading about the dinner, my taste buds started to tingle.

Eric glanced at me. "Have you ever been to one?"

"No." There'd never been anyone to go with. All my friends had been too poor. And the dinner was so obviously designed for couples. And, well, I'd never been part of a couple in Tokyo. Except with Neil for a few disastrous weeks. A month. Something like that.

"Want to go?"

"To what? The dinner?"

"Yes. Do you want to go? With me."

I turned to face him and found that, in fact, I did. "I do." What a refreshingly adult idea.

"Okay. Um...great." His head swiveled toward the concierge desk. "I guess I should have asked if there were tickets left. Let me go find out."

I watched as he strode to the desk and talked to the agent. Soon he was pulling out his wallet and surrendering his credit card.

I looked at the sign again. *Sixty-five dollars per person.* I swallowed. Then I reread the menu.

Eric returned while I was trying to decide what sounded best: a panoply of chocolate sorbets or an individual strawberry tartlet served with pistachio ice cream. Happily, I would not have to choose. They both came with dessert!

"Well, we're set."

I tore my eyes from the menu. "Great. Thanks. I'll write you a check."

He gave me the eyeball. "You're not one of those, are you?"

"One of what?"

"One of those women who won't let the guy pay for a date."

Date? Really? "No. I'm not. Forget about the check. I will be happy to allow you to wine and dine me. Thank you, kind, benevolent, and apparently extremely wealthy sir." I fluttered my eyelashes for good measure.

"Aren't you supposed to be picking up dry cleaning?"

"Yeah. Why?"

"Doesn't it close at five?"

I glanced at my watch and then took off for the elevators.

No good! Both of them were on the sixth floor.

I tore down the stairs to the basement and arrived just in time to beg the dry cleaner to keep the door open for me.

A minute later I was climbing the stairs, grasping my suit like a prize.

Eric was sitting in an armchair. He rose when he saw me. "You got it."

"I got it."

"Well…" He smiled at me and gestured toward the door, indicating I should go first. But suddenly, I didn't want to go anywhere. Especially not outside where it was cold and rainy when I didn't have an umbrella.

And I didn't want him to go, either.

"Can I buy you dinner?"

We debated over which of the hotel's restaurants sounded most appealing. One of them was a Japanese teppanyaki place that grilled food in front of you à la Benihana. Another had an American Appleby's feel.

"What sounds good?"

"Truthfully? A grilled cheese sandwich." And maybe some fries.

"Then let's go to Hero's."

"Well…" How could I take him to the deli and buy him a five-dollar sandwich when he'd just bought me a ticket to a sixty-five dollar dinner?

"Allie?"

"What sounds good to you?"

"Truthfully? They have great gyros at Hero's."

We took the elevator down one floor and walked into the deli. It had great neon-lit pictures of superheroes and neon border tubing framing a mirror on the ceiling. I threw my suit over the back of a booth and then went to place our order.

We sat across from each other in the booth and ate as we watched the last half of the movie *Cars* at opposite corners of the room on the restaurant's twin TVs. When we were done, I tried to talk Eric into an ice cream sundae.

"Thanks, but no. I don't really need one."

"Eric, nobody *needs* ice cream. It exists solely in the realm of desire. So do you want one or not?"

"Well..."

"Do you want to split one?"

"Sure."

I went to the cashier and paid for the sundae and then I dragged Eric up to the topping counter.

"Chocolate or caramel?"

"Caramel."

I doused one side of the ice cream in caramel, the other in chocolate.

"Sprinkles or cookie crumbs?"

"Both."

"Cherries?"

"Lots."

I piled them onto his side of the sundae.

When we returned to the table, he picked up a cherry and put it into his mouth. Took it out about two seconds later. The stem was tied.

"Do that again."

He put the cherry down on his spoon and picked up another. He popped it into his mouth and then took it out.

"How do you do that?"

"You want me to explain it to you? I have no idea."

"Did you have to practice?"

"Yes. I bought two whole jars of cherries before I figured it out."

The thought of him going through two jars of cherries trying to learn how to tie a stem was both pathetic and endearing.

"So...why?"

He shrugged. "Why not?"

We hung out, long after the sundae had disappeared, watching CNN and providing our own running commentary about the current state of national politics. And then the image on my television turned to fuzz. It slowly reappeared, but when the picture had cleared, it was showing a basketball game.

I turned and looked over my shoulder, expecting to see a basketball game on that TV screen too, but it was still tuned to CNN.

Eric saw me turn and looked over his shoulder. Realized what had happened. "You could…" He scooted over toward the wall, making room for me.

I slid from my side and moved over to his.

We watched the end of CNN Sunday Morning with our feet propped up on the opposite bench, trading comments. And then, I happened to focus on my watch and realized it was after nine. I bent to look at it more closely. "We've been here for…four hours?"

Eric glanced at his wrist. "Looks like it."

"What time does it close?"

Eric leaned forward to look past me at the cashier. He was sitting on the counter, watching the basketball game. "Not any time soon."

"I should probably go."

"I should too."

Neither of us made a move to go. And then the commercial on TV dissolved into the singular music of CNN's *Headline News.* "I guess I could stay. For a few minutes. Just to see what's happening in the world." Something about seeing news "as it happened" helped lessen the disconnectedness of living life a day and three continents ahead of the average American. I pulled my feet from the bench. "I can let you out. If you need to go."

"No. I'm fine."

I put my feet back and settled in.

It was only a half hour segment and nothing interesting was happening in the world, but we still managed to sit there until ten.

"I really should go." I pulled my feet from the bench again and planted them on the floor. Then I slid from the bench. I reached for my coat, but Eric got there first. He held it for me while I put it on.

I grabbed my suit.

He plucked it from my hand and draped it over his arm.

"I can take it."

"Let's see if it's raining first."

"Even if it is, I can use it as an umbrella."

"You don't want to use it as an umbrella. Not all the way home. I can take it to my place and you can pick it up later."

As we walked from the elevator to the lobby, we could hear rain pelting the roof.

Bad sign. I really did not want to walk home.

If the gift shop had been open, at least I could have bought an umbrella.

"Ready?" He opened his umbrella and then gave me his arm. "How about walking me home? Then you can have the umbrella."

Now that was a thought. A good thought. "Deal."

We walked up the steep hill by the French Embassy. The street was paved with stones, and each one had a circle stamped into it. For decoration? For traction? No matter, under the onslaught of rain, the circles had disappeared, filling and overflowing, leaving the slope trembling with riffles.

We strained forward, bending into the hill, until we reached the top. Then we paused underneath a streetlight, panting. Our breath curled and then mingled in the frigid air. By the time we got to Eric's, my shoes were soaked from overstepping the limits of the umbrella. Frequently.

"Do you want to come up?"

I did.

But I knew I shouldn't.

If I curled up on his couch, I might have stayed. There were times when it was nice to have a girl for a friend. Crashing at my place has been a regular part of Gina's friendship with me. Crashing at Eric's, while convenient, might be misunderstood by someone.

Namely, me.

I liked what we had…whatever it was…something on the friendship side of dating…or the dating side of friendship…and I wasn't sure I wanted it to change. At least not for another five months. Because I knew when I kissed him—and I would—our relationship would be doomed. That's the way it always worked.

Besides, he wasn't what I needed, and I wasn't what he wanted.

30

*Soy Bean, I throw you
far from here. May Evil so
be cast far from me.*

BEING SIGNED UP FOR A FANCY DINNER brought with it one big problem:
I needed something to wear. And I was much too tall to be able to find
anything in Tokyo.

I rummaged through my wardrobe Monday evening after work.
There had to be something in there I could wear besides a pair of chiffon
palazzo pants I'd last worn in the nineties. A pair of glitzy gold sandals
I'd bought the last time I'd dated someone tall. Assorted formal dresses
from college.

I tugged at one and then pulled it from the hanger.

Oh. The bubble-skirted dress from college days.

I put it back.

Maybe I had started at the wrong place. Maybe I should have started
with the shoes. I knew I'd have to wear a pair I already owned because I
truly would not have been able to find anything big enough for my feet
in the city. Not without having to take out a loan. So I was left with a pair
of embroidered Chinese slippers which really were meant to be worn as
slippers or the glitzy sandals.

Eric was tall. I could wear the sandals. I'd have to wear the sandals.

Great—I had shoes!

I could wear…my suit. Shoes could make an outfit. Isn't that what
people always said? I found the suit I'd rescued from the dry cleaner's
the night before and tried it on with the shoes.

210

I stood close to the mirror.

I stood far away from the mirror.

Wherever I stood, I still looked weird. As if I couldn't decide whether I was going to work or going to a disco. I tried out some moves I remembered from high school.

Looked weirder still.

Enough fooling around! It was time for drastic measures. I removed everything from my closet, starting with the clothes on hangers. By the time I'd reached the back corner of the floor, I'd found my gloves, my umbrella, a black pashmina shawl, and a scarf. I also found the length of silk I'd bought in Thailand.

I loved my wardrobe. It was the crowning achievement of my life. Everything matched. I could choose an outfit with my eyes closed and have no worries of embarrassing myself.

I slowly returned everything to the closet, starting with pants. White, then green, then black. I moved on to skirts: from shortest to longest. And then dresses, of which there were two. I ended with shirts. But I debated on the organization. From short-sleeved to long or from white to black? I finally decided on sleeve length.

Which left only my sweaters.

I refolded and reshelved them by color.

And I still had nothing to wear.

But the process had left several odds and ends to figure out what to do with. Like the silk fabric. I opened the tissue paper wrapped around it and remembered, in an instant, why I'd bought it.

It was composed of a dozen different shades between fuchsia and violet and shot through with golden thread. It was not, however, green. Or black. Or white. And since the moment I'd bought it, I had no idea what to do with it. I unfolded it and spread it across my bed. And then I dug out the lumps from underneath it. Gloves. Umbrella. Pashmina.

I loved my pashmina even though I hadn't worn it since it last went into hiding. I shook it out and let it float down to cover the silk. Black over purple. Maybe one day I'd swap my green clothes for purple.

I peeled back the shawl once more and reached for the silk fabric, wishing I could do something with it—make something from it—in the next four days. I could possibly sew a button on it. Or mend a hem, if it had one. Anything else was out of the question. Which was too bad. Wrapping it around my waist, I posed in front of the mirror. It would have made a great skirt. I unwound it and then wrapped it around my chest. It would also have made a great strapless dress.

Hmm.

If I were Molly Ringwald and someone could loan me an old prom dress, then I might just have something. As it was…I tossed it onto the bed and picked up my pashmina instead. I could start wearing it again. It was cold enough. I unbuttoned the suit jacket and put on one of my white shirts, throwing the pashmina over it as a shawl.

Too early nineties.

I tried flipping it over one shoulder, leaving the ends to trail. Too eighties. I tied two ends around my neck and left it to cowl in the front. It looked kind of cool. Less cowboy than I thought it would. If there were only some way to tie it off at my back.

I spread it on the bed and tried folding it different ways. What I needed was a triangle so I could tie the long straight edge in the back. But then I'd still need two ends to tie up at my neck. I folded it on a diagonal into a triangle and held the tips at the top with my chin just to see if it would stretch around my waist.

It did.

And there *were* two ends left up top.

I separated them and tied them behind my neck and then lifted my chin and looked in the mirror.

Very nice!

After taking off the shirt, I played with the folds, trying to arrange them so they wouldn't show off more than they should. If I could just staple them to my shoulders…or maybe…hmm…what if they separated later rather than earlier?

I found a small rubber band in my desk drawer and slipped it down over the two ends until it sat about two inches below my collarbone and then I retied the pashmina around my neck.

That was it! Very sleek. I raised my arms, bent down toward my toes. Yep, everything stayed covered. *That* was the sort of look I wanted for the dinner. Not that I'd wear it.

I didn't have a skirt to match.

But…I eyed the silk again. And then I couldn't resist wrapping it around my waist once more, wishing I'd had it made into a skirt. I looked into the mirror and sighed. It was The Look. The one I wanted.

How hard could it be to make a skirt?

I could just…well…tie it on. I tried tying the two ends together at my hip, but it left a great big knot at my waist and a great big gap at the side. But people wore wrap skirts, right?

Wrapped, not tied. Duh.

I folded the material in half and tried wrapping it around my waist like a cylinder. The ends barely met. I refolded it until I had enough material left to wrap comfortably, but then I had the problem of how to secure it.

A belt!

My skinny glove leather belt was too skinny. The wide leather belt was too casual. And I didn't have a rubber band big enough. But maybe I didn't have to belt it. Maybe a pin would do. I experimented with folding the end on top to the inside and fastening it with a safety pin.

Took a step.

I used more safety pins to secure the top edge to the rest of the material right down to my knee.

Took another step.

Not bad.

I fluffed the pashmina "top" out over the skirt and put on my sandals.

Not bad. Not bad at all.

I just needed to figure out something to do with my hair.

## 31

*Caterpillar, just
when I grew to like your fuzz,
you have sprouted wings.*

By the time Saturday evening rolled around, I was wondering what I'd been thinking when I decided to moonlight as a fashion designer.

Who wore clothes held together by safety pins?

Me…I had. Once. For a whole year, actually, when I was in high school. But that was then. This was an Escoffier Dinner now. Like, right now!

Once I'd figured out the costume earlier in the week, I hadn't thought about it again. Not enough to even think of a replacement for the rubber band holding the pashmina together at my neck.

Round.

I needed something round. And small. Like a…round thing.

If all else failed, maybe I could cut the end off a toilet paper tube and color it black with a Sharpie. Martha Stewart did things like that all the time, right?

I needed a round thing with a hole in the middle. Like a short tube. A tiny cylinder. Or a…ring.

I could use a ring!

A quick search through my jewelry box came up with the perfect one, just thick enough to look as if it belonged. I switched out the rubber band and threaded the ends through the hole.

Okay. Deep breath.

I checked the skirt. Again. Made sure it wasn't falling off or gaping open.

Nope.

I shuffled to the bathroom and started on my hair. I spun it up into a twist and then secured it in the beak of a golden chopstick-looking clip studded with rhinestones. Pulled a few wisps out, hoping I wouldn't spend the evening pushing them back from my face. If I had owned hair spray, I would have used some. As it was, I shook my head a few times to see if anything fell loose. Nope. It looked as though I was done. As I gave my outfit one last check, the thought crossed my mind that someone should invent hair spray for clothes. At least for things masquerading as clothes.

I pulled on my puffy coat and headed out the door for the New Sanno, held together by safety pins, a wish, and a prayer.

I had every intention of being early, but by the time I arrived, it seemed as if everyone else had arrived even earlier. There were no parking spaces left in the garage. So I motored around the surrounding blocks looking for someplace—anyplace—to park. I finally lucked out on my fifth pass down Gaien-nishi-dori, right by Hiroo Plaza. That meant I only had to run the equivalent of three blocks.

I did it. And in record time, considering I was wearing high-heeled sandals.

Eric was standing by the fire in the lobby, facing the front entrance.

I smiled and then tripped on the carpet as I came through the door.

Grace is actually my sister's middle name.

"Are you—"

"I'm fine. I'm sorry to be so late. The parking garage was full."

"They haven't started yet. Can I take your coat?"

Well…frankly…I was afraid to open up my coat. What if something had shifted? What if something had come undone? I unfastened the top snap and tried to look discreetly down at my chest, but the coat was too puffy. It wouldn't give me a view.

"Could you excuse me for just one minute?" I walked as fast as I could down to the bathroom and did the big reveal in there. A few minor adjustments and I was G-rated once more.

Eric watched me as I walked toward him down the hall.

"You look enchanting."

Enchanting, huh? Give him an A+ for consistency. "You look very nice yourself." And he did. He was wearing a black suit and a tie that matched the color of his eyes. Made them glow.

We checked our coats, and then Eric placed his hand just above the small of my back, maneuvering me to enter first into the banquet hall. When we followed the maître d' to our table, he left his hand on my back, as he walked beside me, fixed there with the lightest of touches. It was warm. And it was also proprietary.

And you know what? I liked it.

So far, the new year had provided one big surprise after another. I liked the idea of it being brand new. I could indulge myself with Eric because I was trying to be open-minded. Forgetting everything I knew about him was a little tricky because he had his opinions and they were exactly the opposite and equal of those I called my own. But I could respect him because he held his just as firmly as I held mine. If I didn't understand exactly how he arrived at them, I understood the passion with which he held them.

Once seated, our waiter asked us if we wanted wine to accompany our appetizers.

By all means.

We watched him pour and then held up our glasses and saluted each other after he had gone.

"To a lovely lady."

Lovely. Lovely was just lovely because it could refer to beauty or it could refer to personality or it could refer to anything at all about me. And I couldn't think of a male equivalent. Wasn't that just like a politician? To give away a word for free that required a commitment in return.

His eyes clouded. "I said something wrong."

"No. You said something right." I put on my best Irish accent. "You're a lovely man yourself, Eric Larsen."

We devoured all eight courses of the dinner, talking the whole time. I was fairly up-to-date about the Eric in Tokyo, but I knew nothing about what had happened to him between high school and Japan. I asked him about his work at the State Department in DC. The way I calculated it, he was there right in the middle of Clinton's last term. "So how was that? With peace sprouting up all over the place?"

"What peace?"

"The Dayton Agreement? The Israel–Jordan Peace Treaty?"

"Just because you twist arms and make people sign something doesn't make a lasting agreement. There may have been an absence of fighting in Bosnia, but I don't think there was any peace. And Israel? Clinton's legacy is a disaster."

"He was one of the most charismatic presidents of modern times."

"Yes. I remember. How many scandals involving extramarital affairs took place while he was in office?"

"We all have our foibles."

"Foibles? Please."

"Are you saying you don't have any flaws?"

"No."

"Well, then you shouldn't be casting any stones, should you?"

"But I'm not the president of the United States. And even if I were, I would love my wife enough to protect her reputation by protecting mine. That's one thing I never got about you people. He exploited a *woman*. Women plural. Doesn't that go against everything you believe in?"

Hmm. Well. "They weren't victims. They were willing participants. And lots of powerful men have the same problem. It doesn't reflect on how he did his job."

"You're using the male defense? I find that offensive. And sexist. And I'm a male! It was a misuse of power."

I decided to be the magnanimous one. "You know what? We're never going to agree on any of this. You can't convince me you're right, and I know I can't convince you you're wrong."

"As long as we realize God isn't taking sides."

"Isn't he?"

"Is he?"

"Well…I don't know." I didn't want to officially take the Big Guy off my team's roster, but I wasn't so sure he belonged there in the first place.

"Can we be friends? Just for tonight?"

I looked at him, feeling just a little hurt. "We *are* friends. At least, I thought we were."

"Just—" He stopped himself from speaking. Then he got up from the table and offered me his hand. "Would you care to dance?"

I slipped my hand into his and stood. How was it possible that his eyes glowed brighter in the dark? "Yes."

The band was good. Great, in fact, at nearly every kind of music. We danced to "Wild Thing." I don't know when Eric had picked up his moves, but he had some.

The lead singer started doing a Tarzan yodel lead-in to "Tarzan Boy." We danced along with everyone else, hollering the chorus back to the band. I could relate to that Tarzan Boy, living far away from nowhere in the wilds of Tokyo.

The band switched tempos and played "Let's Call the Whole Thing Off."

I love tomatoes. To-mah-toes.

Eric twirled me across the dance floor. I was getting into it when the song ended and "Groovy Kind of Love" started. And I loved that song.

Eric kept hold of my hand and spun me in close.

I clasped my arms around his neck, and he pulled me near in an embrace.

I was having a great time, playing with the hair at the back of his neck until they played "Next Time I Fall." It hit just a little too close to high school. It all came rushing back: the thrills and the chills of falling in love. I leaned away, just a little bit.

Eric and I were dancing eye to eye, nose to nose.

I sighed and leaned closer, and then we were touching foreheads.

We danced that way for the rest of the song, staring into each other's eyes.

What was I going to do with him?

And what was he going to do with me?

When lead singer began to croon "Kiss on My List," I just shut my eyes. I knew I was a goner because somehow, I knew it would be true. Eric's kiss *would* be on my list of the very best things in life.

Four months, two weeks. And then I'd have to make a choice between a kiss and a friendship.

The next morning, while I was lying in bed thinking about getting up, the phone rang. I picked it up.

"Another word for beautiful."

"Pretty."

"More than beautiful."

"Gorgeous. Enchanting. Bewitching."

"That's everything you were last night." He hung up before I could say anything else.

Slick. That's what politicians were.

Was that fair? Did it count as a compliment if you'd said it about yourself? According to the grin I felt plastered across my face, it must have.

I picked up the phone and dialed his number.

"Eric Larsen."

"Another phrase for thank you."

"Eternally grateful."

"Less than eternally grateful."

"I'll go out with you for lunch."

"I will?"

"Unless you want to be eternally grateful."

We arranged to meet at Roppongi Hills and then go to church together after.

Our second date.

MARCH | *Yayoi*
*Month of Growth*

32

*Petals, fall! Shower*
*me with happiness. This is*
*spring, joy in Tokyo.*

IN MARCH, TV STATIONS STARTED REPORTING THE COMING OF THE
*sakura zensen* or cherry blossom front the same way they reported the
movements of a typhoon. Once the blooming began in the south of the
country it was tracked—with increasing anticipation—as the flowering
spread northward, overwhelming the landscape with beauty and intoxi-
cating the Japanese. Here's how big a deal cherry blossom season was to the
Japanese: Every year, Starbucks produced a new commemorative mug.

Offices planned parties in the parks of Tokyo. One of the best cherry
tree blossom viewing areas was just across from the *Stars and Stripes*
building in Aoyama Cemetery. It always took me by surprise that people
would picnic in a cemetery and be so extraordinarily happy about it. The
atmosphere was festive. Exuberant. Everyone ignoring the real reason
so many cherry trees could be lined up in a row on prime property in
downtown Tokyo.

That year, I had a question I wanted an answer for, so I made a point
of asking Yuka-san. "So when does the *sakura* season in Tokyo officially
start? When all the trees are blooming?"

"When the man whose job it is to watch the tree say it has started."

"There's a man who watches a tree? Which tree?"

"There is Japanese government man. He is weather forecaster. There is
one tree he watches. When he see five or six bloom opening together, then
he announce the season open. This is *kaika,* the first blossom opening.

And he continue each day, maybe several time each day, to count the blossom. When they are eighty percent bloomed, then the season is at the peak. This we call *mankai*."

"Sounds like a great job."

"No. This is very difficult. He must make a report even before he see one bloom. Everything depend on his report. Each office has *hanami*. A party for viewing cherry blossom. And they must plan it according to his prediction. So if he is wrong, if the blossom come too early, then all the party are too late. And if the blossom come too late, then all the party are too early. One year, he is four day too early. This is disaster."

"But that's crazy! You can't control the weather."

"Cherry blossom are very important symbol of Japanese spirit. They do not fade or wither like other flower. At height of beauty, they drop. You see birth, beauty, death. *Sakura* season is end and beginning of Japanese school season. Japanese fiscal season. Everything."

An entire country was run according to the whims of a flower. I guessed I might have heard of stranger things, but I couldn't think of any of them at that moment.

"We will have *hanami* one afternoon here. Like last year. But you must see cherry tree blossom at night. This is most special. Magical."

We did, in fact, have a *hanami* party a week later in Aoyama Cemetery. I had missed the previous year's party due to a deployment. Our *hanami* was a combined party with all the organizations in the building. We planned it several days out, after it became apparent the cherry blossom guy did, in fact, know what he was talking about. Yuka-san went early that morning with several of the pressroom guys to claim a spot and set up tables for food. They found a short path leading into the cemetery, perpendicular to the road, and staked it out. By the time we got there, chips, pretzels, cookies, pies, and a keg of beer had been arranged on the tables.

Ours wasn't the only *hanami* in town. People crowded the sidewalks, laughing and talking as if they weren't walking through a cemetery at all. Farther up, once the gravestones began their spread across the hill, we could see bright blue tarps laid on the ground anywhere and there was room. At the ends of the cemetery paths, at the point where they met the road, food vendors had set up stalls, advertising food, their bright colored banners fluttering in the breeze. They sold *yakitori* sticks, grilled corn on the cob spiked with soy sauce, and copious amounts of beer. And when the wind gusted especially hard, everything was sprinkled with cherry blossoms. Clearly, *hanami* was not a just an office potluck, it was an event.

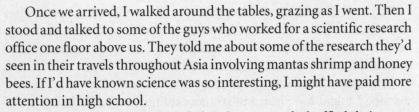

Once we arrived, I walked around the tables, grazing as I went. Then I stood and talked to some of the guys who worked for a scientific research office one floor above us. They told me about some of the research they'd seen in their travels throughout Asia involving mantas shrimp and honey bees. If I'd have known science was so interesting, I might have paid more attention in high school.

Conversation groups expanded and contracted, shuffled their members and regrouped. At one point, Yuka-san came over and took me by the hand. "Come and see real *hanami*."

"This looks real."

She smiled. "It is American *hanami*. Not the same."

"Just a minute." I grabbed a bottle of water to take with me.

We walked up the hill on a sidewalk that paralleled the road. Blue tarps were everywhere. They were all the same size in the same color blue.

"They're all blue."

"Of course they are blue."

"Because…?"

"Because rat do not like blue."

"Really?"

"You did not know this?"

"No."

*Rats Don't Like Blue.* That could be a great title for a post-modern angst-driven book about…nah. I just couldn't get into it.

The tarp parties looked like identical cookie cutouts. At one end of a tarp, people left their shoes in tidy pairs, all lined up in short rows. The rest of the tarp was covered by a crowd of people, sitting on their knees. They were talking, laughing, singing. Drinking. Quite a bit, if the number of overflowing trash cans and overly happy people were any indication. It reminded me of college parties. Same amount of drunk people, same volume of conversation, only much more tidy and organized. *Hanami*, Japanese-style, was frenetic and intense. A hundred separate parties taking place in the same location. An all-out celebration marked by good humor and high spirits. A festival in the center of a city of the dead.

"Isn't this sacrilegious?"

Yuka-san looked puzzled. "To view *sakura?*"

"To have parties in a cemetery. Among the dead."

"No."

"You don't think it's disrespectful?"

"Why would it be? What better place? *Sakura* flower beautiful for one moment and then fall to the ground, dead. Where better to celebrate the cycle of beauty and life than in cemetery?"

"So you're reminding yourself that life is short?"

"We remind ourself to appreciate beauty while it last. To realize that death is part of life. Just because tree flower is in a cemetery does not make them any less a part of the world. Does not make them any less beautiful."

I supposed not. The Japanese had a way of compartmentalizing things— of looking at just one thing at a time—that was admirable, if a bit foreign.

We walked a while longer and then returned to our own party. Yuka-san left shortly afterward to return to the office.

And then Eric appeared. "Hi."

"Hi."

"I came over to the office and no one was there except Yuka-san. She said I'd probably find you here."

I glanced at my watch, amazed to find it was as late as it was. The breeze fingered my hair, let it go, and then sent a shower of petals floating down on top of us.

Eric smiled. Then he reached out and pulled a petal from my hair.

"Cookie? Slice of pie? Beer?" I could do hostess duty when I had to.

"I'll take a beer, but I can get it."

"I'll do it."

I scrounged a cup and poured him a beer. By the time I returned, he was involved in a conversation with Neil. It was interesting to see them standing next to each other. Neil was nice, but he sure wasn't Eric.

I held Eric's beer out to him.

He took it from me. "Thanks." He took a sip, listened to Neil for a few more minutes, and then he turned to me. "Want to go for a walk?"

I looked around, realizing for the first time that half the people had already left. I nodded.

We walked up the way I'd gone with Yuka-san. Most of the party-goers had dispersed. The tarps were gone. They'd taken their songs and laughter down into the subway stations for the long commute home.

The cemetery had fallen silent.

A cool spring breeze spun the air and tickled the hairs on my arms. I shivered.

"Do you want my jacket?" He was already shrugging out of it.

"No. Please. I'm fine."

He didn't listen, settling it across my shoulders instead. I was enveloped in his warmth. In his scent.

We paused at an intersection that split the cemetery in two. Cherry trees stretched in every direction, frothing delicate flowers.

"So."

"So."

"How are you?"

"I am very well, thank you. And you?" I could tell from the twinkle in Eric's eyes that he was mocking me.

"Did they let you go early or did you make a break for it?"

"I finished my work, turned off my computer, and left."

"Mm-hmm. Is your cell phone on?"

He put a hand to my waist and stepped close. He slipped his other hand between me and the suit jacket, and pulled his phone out of an inside pocket. He held it up and turned it off in front of me.

"Well done!" In more ways than one.

He hadn't moved away. "What are you doing for dinner?"

I tried to bring my hand out from beneath the jacket to glance at my watch. He was too close. Regardless, I knew the hilltop store was probably closing. "I have no idea. Cereal, maybe? Macaroni and cheese?"

He leaned his head in the direction of the food stalls and turned me with the pressure of his hand. There were no signs that the vendors were cleaning up for the day, even though the cemetery had emptied. "Let's have dinner here."

"Where here?"

"Here, here." He stepped away from me and held out a hand toward the vendors. An invitation to feast.

"In the cemetery?"

"Why not?"

Was I the only person in Tokyo who still retained some sense of propriety where cemeteries were concerned? I looked over toward the food stalls. The breeze pushed the scent of something wonderful...more wonderful than Cheerios...in my direction. I turned toward Eric and smiled. "Let's do it."

We crossed the street and approached the vendors.

"What do you like?"

I shrugged. "No mystery meats." I'd had some sort of meat on a stick once, some kind of meatball, which squeaked between my teeth when I ate it. No meat should squeak.

"*Yakisoba? Okonomiyaki?*"

*Yakisoba* was always safe. And good. I had no idea what *okono*...whatever was. I stood there wavering between the two booths, ready to eat something I was familiar with but curious about what I'd be missing.

Eric put a hand to my waist and propelled me away from the *yakisoba* stand toward the other one. "Want to share? I'll order one of these and you get *yakisoba*."

Eric ordered in Japanese. Then he pulled me close again and fished a coin purse from his suit jacket pocket.

"This is rather convenient for you, isn't it?"

He shrugged and then grinned. "You were cold. I was just being a gentleman."

He put 600 yen onto a plate. Then he made the shortest of small talk with the vendor as batter was spooned onto a griddle and various vegetables—cabbage, carrots, corn, onions—were sprinkled on top of it as it cooked. The vendor flipped it and then let it cook some more. Then he transferred it to a plate, shook some flakes on top, and put some vermillion-colored shreds of pickled ginger on the side. Looking at Eric, he held up a white bottle.

Eric shook his head.

Held up a brown bottle.

Eric nodded.

The man squirted some sort of sauce over the top and then handed the plate to Eric.

Eric took it with one hand and grabbed two packages of chopsticks with his other.

We walked over to the *yakisoba* booth. It was more my style. Ramen-looking noodles fried with bits of cabbage, carrot, onion, meat, and a tangy sauce.

Eric ordered.

I put a hand on his as it slipped around my waist. I liked the new version of Eric, but I didn't quite know how to handle him. He wasn't normally the flirty type. He was the intense type. "Let me get this one."

"I'll do it. I'm the one who talked you into dinner in a cemetery."

I handed him the coin purse.

He placed some yen on a plate.

The vendor took ingredients from containers circling her hot plate. After frying up a batch of noodles, she transferred it to a clear plastic container. Her hand hovered over a dish of green flakes, and she looked at me.

"Could you tell her no seaweed? But I would like some ginger."

Eric relayed my message.

She placed a mound of ginger on top of the noodles, and then she closed the container and fastened it with a rubber band.

And then we stood there, holding our dinners between our hands.

"Where should we…?"

We looked around for some place to eat. Finally decided to sit on a low wall that didn't appear to be part of anyone's grave. As we ate, a flurry of petals spiralled through the air, like the lazy drift of dandelion fluff borne on the wind. We each ate half of our dinner and then we traded containers. My hair kept blowing over into Eric's face. "I'm sorry!"

"It's fine." He captured it with his hand and rolled it around his fist and used it to turn my chin toward his face. "You know, there's something you and I have never done."

"What's that?" His eyes were so fascinatingly blue I couldn't look away from them.

"We've never kissed."

I couldn't. Didn't want to. Well, I did, but I didn't. I still had four months. I figured the disintegration of our relationship would be much more manageable in the summer than it would be right then. And the truth was, I just didn't want to give him up. "I can't."

"Why not?"

"Is one kiss really worth a friendship?"

"Why does it have to be just one?" The shine in his eyes matched his grin.

I frowned. "Seriously. Why ruin a good thing?"

"Why does it have to be an either-or? Why can't we have both?"

"But what if we kissed and it wasn't any good?"

"I'd be willing to put some time into practicing. I really think we could work it out. How about it?"

He'd captured my eyes with the same ease he'd captured my hair. I couldn't look away. "I don't think it would be...wise...at this point in time."

"Are you saying you don't want to?"

"No. I'm saying I won't."

"But you want to."

"Did I say that?"

"You didn't deny it."

He was too clever for his own good...and I'd learned too many rhetorical tricks from him.

He tilted his head and narrowed his eyes. "You want to, but you won't." He thought about it for a long minute while he searched my eyes. "Fair enough." He relaxed his fist and my hair twirled free. Then he got up and extended his hand. "I'll walk you back."

Yuka-san was right. Nightfall lent the cherry blossoms a whole new dimension. They glowed luminous against the dark backdrop of the sky. It was magical.

We didn't speak until we were at the bottom of the cemetery.

I think it was the darkness that gave me the courage to ask a question that had often been on my mind. "So...did you ever...what did you think of the book?"

"I thought it was good."

"Really?"

"Yes. I thought it was really good. Have you started another one?"

"No. I'm done."

"You should really—"

"I'm done. I did it. For better or worse, I wrote a book. And it's finished."

"Then you should send it out." He leaned over and kissed me on the forehead before he turned and walked into the night.

As I lay in bed, his words echoed through my head. He'd thought it was really good. But what if really good wasn't good enough? What if I wasn't good enough?

I was good enough for journalism. That wasn't the issue. The problem was that I didn't want to be a journalist, I wanted to be a writer…or at least if I did have to be a journalist, I wanted to also be a writer. Lots of journalists also wrote books.

No.

That wasn't it either.

I didn't want to be a writer. I wanted to be a novelist.

And that was the problem.

I didn't know if I was good enough to be a novelist.

If I never tried, if I never sent the book out, then I could blame circumstance. I could still hold on to the dream. Could still say it was only for lack of trying.

If I did try, then the only one I could blame was myself. And then I would not be good enough. And it would only be because I was lacking.

## 33

*Daffodil, waving
in the wind, I wish I were
so very cheerful.*

THE NEXT WEEK, BY FRIDAY, I HAD AN ATTACK OF GUILT. I felt guilty for
not letting Eric kiss me. And I felt guilty for knowing I was planning on
kissing him and ruining everything anyway.

So I invited him to go with me to Nikko.

"Only you'll have to figure out how to buy the tickets. And where to
catch the train. I'll bring the guidebook."

"You know, Allie. I had this great idea. Why don't we go to Nikko this
Saturday? Want me to set everything up? Make all the plans?"

"I knew you'd understand."

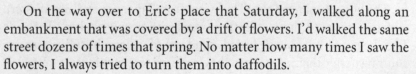

On the way over to Eric's place that Saturday, I walked along an
embankment that was covered by a drift of flowers. I'd walked the same
street dozens of times that spring. No matter how many times I saw the
flowers, I always tried to turn them into daffodils.

They weren't.

They were suggestions of daffodils with long stems and long tapered
foliage. They had butter yellow flowers which nodded from slender stalks.
But they didn't quite appear at the right time of year. They didn't have
quite the right color—they were too pale. And they didn't create quite
the right impression.

In short, they weren't daffodils.

And they always disappointed me.

But that morning I decided to cross the street and look at them. To convince myself to accept them for what they were.

Surprise.

They were, in fact, daffodils. Just not the kind I was used to. They congregated in several clumps of heads per stalk. But they were daffodils, nonetheless.

And in a strange way, it still made me feel disappointed. I could have been enjoying them for the past month, but I'd denied myself the reality of what my eyes had clearly seen.

Eric was ready when I got there, and we hopped on the subway, knowing we had plenty of time to buy tickets and catch our train.

Except we didn't.

By the time we got to the station, the express train to Nikko was sold out. We had to buy tickets for the local, which took twice as long. But we had the whole day and it was springtime, and if we weren't in love, we were definitely in like.

We sat side by side. As we traveled, the countryside became more rural. Broad rice paddies unfurled across the landscape in increasingly larger plots. Densely packed apartment buildings gave way to densely packed houses and then merged into fields. The fields began to undulate, the horizon disappeared, and the terrain evolved into hills. The hills escalated into mountains.

The houses changed too. They went from Japanese-stylized Western with two stories to alpine style traditional with steeply pitched tiled roofs. They began to hide in the broad meadows of valleys, burbling streams running beside them. And then they began to retreat into the forests. We passed through several cities and then we were there.

The Nikko I saw as we left the train station didn't look like an ancient religious center. And it didn't look very picturesque. It did have the attitude of a mountain town: brisk air, timbered buildings, and a curving road leading to the forest ahead.

On the whole, Nikko was both less and more than I expected.

The walk to the temple area was much longer than I'd assumed and much less quaint than I'd hoped. Passing the usual collection of souvenir shops and restaurants, we walked up a long hill before it leveled off at a curve. But at the end, just before a bridge, was a fountain. And a spigot dispensing water from a mountain spring.

We both took a drink. Then another.

I opened my bag and took out the guidebook.

Eric moved closer to me and looked over my shoulder at the page. "There's supposed to be a famous bridge right here."

I eyed the incongruous-looking bridge we were about to cross. "I wonder why it's so famous?"

Eric glanced down at the book. "Red lacquer wooden bridge..."

"Nuh-uh." That bridge was made of sand-colored concrete.

"It says, 'Left of the modern bridge'...?"

Our heads swung upstream, but our eyes were stopped by the draped construction framework straddling the river to our left. On the tarp was printed a colorful life-sized picture of a gracefully arched red lacquer bridge.

"That bridge?" It had to be.

"Maybe we should take a picture. Of the picture."

I gave Eric the book and then posed, an arm crossed in front of me, a finger to my chin as if to say, "Hmm. Something is not right."

We looked at the picture on the tarp for a long moment before turning away and continuing our walk across the bridge and climbing a hill up into the temple area. To our left, below the cobblestone shoulder of the street, a stream trickled back down the slope. Ferns stretched out from the rock wall beside it, waving their fronds. A tree had grown from the wall on the horizontal but had finally set it sights towards the sky. Its leaves rustled in the breeze.

It all looked exactly the way Japan was supposed to. Quiet. Contemplative.

We followed the road around the corner and walked right into a housing development filled with modern but traditional homes. At that point it looked as though we might have Nikko to ourselves. But then we got to the end of the street and looked up to our right. And there, in the distance, above an expanse of concrete steps, loomed a torii gate. And a throng of people were walking up and down the steps.

I sighed.

So much for having Japan all to myself.

We walked up the steps and paused in front of the torii. Carved from massive blocks of granite, the gate was dovetailed at the top and had been pieced together like a giant jigsaw puzzle. We took a few pictures and then reversed our steps and began to walk Cryptomeria Avenue.

Eric glanced at the book. "This stretches twenty miles."

"The trees?"

"Right. There used to be two hundred thousand of them. Now there are only fourteen thousand. It's the world's longest avenue." He shut his book, stopped in the middle of the street, and looked up at the trees.

I did too. It felt as if I were walking in a cathedral. Long slender tree trunks substituted for stone pillars. The arms of the cedar trees replaced arched vaults. The presence of the divine, the soaring of the spirit, the hush of holiness was all there. And more real than in many churches I'd visited. Beside us, a pagoda loomed out of the forest. A silent sentry on the path to holiness.

Desiduous trees reached out from behind the cedars and spread their fingers over the road, weaving a tapestry of leaves in a monochromatic palette of greens. We left the road at Jogyo-do and Hokke-do temples and dipped down to appreciate the fire-red buildings and bright fanciful paintings of flowers underneath the eaves. Bells were hanging from the corners of the steeply pitched roofs. They tinkled in the breeze.

We walked farther on to Taiyuin-byo Temple. Lanterns stood guard outside, silent and lifeless, but just as forbidding as warriors of flesh. Later, as we progressed through the heights of the temple, we glanced off into a valley. Lanterns stood in rows on top of a soft velvet of grass. Proud heads had been softened with moss, their stone helmets spotted with lichens. They looked like warriors turned, in a cruel instant, to stone. Stuck for eternity in the shifting shadows. In suspension between earth and heaven.

At some point, during our fourth temple visit, the colors of paint and the gold leaf used to decorate the temples changed from vivid to lurid. My head felt as though it were being stuffed with fluff and my joints began to ache in places I didn't even have joints.

I made it to one more temple, and then I felt as if I couldn't take another step.

"Are you feeling okay?"

"No."

Eric placed a hand on my forehead. "Do you feel hot?"

"No. I'm freezing."

"Let's go home."

I was all for that, but it was easier said than done.

Eric slipped an arm around my waist, and we walked in the direction of a restaurant we'd seen earlier. He sat me in a chair and then went to talk to the cashier. About fifteen minutes later, a taxi pulled up outside. It took us to the train station.

I curled up on a bench while Eric figured out the train schedule. He helped me onto the train and found our seats. And then he made me lie down with my head on his lap. The last thing I remember was him stroking my hair away from my forehead.

I was deep in the middle of a sound sleep when he woke me up in Tokyo. Bad things began to happen when I opened my eyes. My head hurt, my stomach hurt. Even my elbows hurt.

We shuffled through the station to the taxi stand outside.

I slumped onto a backseat, but then Eric got in beside me and pulled me into an embrace against his shoulder.

"I feel awful." Tears began to dribble down my cheeks, and I didn't have the energy to wipe them away.

"Shh. It's probably just a flu."

"Hurts."

"I know. Close your eyes."

I tried. But everything hurt so badly I couldn't keep them shut.

When we got to the barracks, I used up the rest of my energy digging around for my ID and signing Eric in.

"I can't—"

"I can." He picked me up in his arms and carried me to my room.

"Do you have a key?"

"Pocket."

He got the door open and set me down on the bed.

I moaned and turned over onto my side. Tried to conserve body warmth by huddling in a fetal position.

"Allie? Do you have sweats? Pajamas?"

"Dresser."

I heard him opening and closing drawers. And then I felt his hand on my back. "Can you take your coat off?"

I shook my head.

He dropped the sweats by my head. "You'll be more comfortable in these. Please." I felt him at my feet, taking off my shoes.

"Leave my socks."

I felt the bed depress, and when I opened my eyes, I saw a knee in front of me. "I'm going to help you sit up." Hands pulled me up, underneath my arms. I felt one of my arms, then another, slide out of my jacket. Felt a sweatshirt pressed into my hands. "Put that on for me. Almost done. Then you can sleep."

I pulled it on over my T-shirt. I wished he would just leave me alone.

"Can you stand up? Enough to put some sweatpants on while I make some tea?"

I could try, but I wasn't guaranteeing anything. I unzipped my pants and slid them off. With my protective layer of clothing gone, the room's air hit me like an arctic blast. It was all I could do to pull on the pants before I started shivering.

And once I started I couldn't stop.

I stood there staring at the bed until Eric returned. He peeled back my sheet and helped me into bed. "Do you need anything? Is there anything I can do?"

"Stay."

He stayed for two days.

He helped me to the bathroom, he helped me throw up, and then he helped me back to bed. Many times. Too many times. When I went to sleep, it was with my back against his thigh, his hand on my head. When I woke up, it was to him reading a book, sitting propped against the backboard of the bed.

And on the third day, after I'd smiled at one of his jokes, he went up to the hilltop store and got me something to eat.

"Thanks for taking care of me."

"It was my pleasure."

"It can't have been a pleasure."

"It was. I took notes when you talked in your sleep." He leaned down to kiss my forehead, and then he left me to sleep on my own.

## 34

*Day and Night meet here*
*as equals. In departure,*
*Day strips Night's power.*

IT TOOK ME THE REST OF THE WEEK to feel that I had my legs back under me. Eric phoned me on Saturday. "Any plans for today?"

"Taxes. It'll take me so long, I'll probably be dead before I finish."

"Then vote Republican next time."

"What, so we can let the top ten percent of the country go tax free while the rest of us pay for them?"

"We wouldn't have to if the Democrats hadn't built so many entitlement programs into the budget."

"Like food stamps? Did you know there are soldiers in our military who are on food stamps because you guys don't pay them what they're worth?"

"Actually, I think it's you guys not paying them what they're worth. Anyway, I'm glad to hear you're feeling like yourself again."

I was too. "Thanks again. For everything."

"It was no problem."

"Not even with work?"

"As it turns out, I'm really not that important."

On Monday I drove out to Yokosuka Naval Base to research an article. I liked driving out to Yokosuka. It was farther than Yokota, although it normally took less time because I could drive it all on the expressway. But that morning I spent about half an hour crawling through town, suspended over Tokyo Bay on the Rainbow Bridge. It looked like a white facsimile of the Golden Gate Bridge.

All those cars, all those people, inching along the expressways all day long. It was an expressway to nowhere.

*Express to Nowhere.*

That was a good title. Maybe the protagonist could be a new expat in Tokyo. She could hop in her car one morning, excited to investigate the city, get on the expressway, and never find her way back again. At the end of the book she could reach the top of Rainbow Bridge, look back at the city through her rearview mirror, and see nothing but cars and buildings, stretching out to the horizon while the Odaiba Ferris wheel in carnival colors turned endlessly in front of her.

Hmm.

Lots of symbolism, but too postmodern. Too depressing. Too bleak. I'd probably shoot myself in the head when I was done writing. And besides, I wasn't planning on writing another book.

Once the traffic started moving, I passed myriad cranes for constructing endless building projects. I ducked under Haneda Airport's runway, planes taxiing on top of me. I had no idea how they managed to squeeze a runway into the middle of the city.

I dove into another tunnel, this one decorated with variegated wedges reminiscent of Frank Lloyd Wright. Lots of things in Tokyo were reminiscent of other things but not exactly the same. It was a unique Japanese trait manifesting itself in everything from fashion to food.

As I passed the port, a flotilla of container and transport ships were floating on the steel-colored sea. And an army of cranes, giraffelike with orange-and-white stripes, stood at attention in formation. Past them, the cargo cranes shimmered in the sunlight. These were more graceful cranes with faces like pterodactyls, all angles and sharp planes.

My favorite part of the drive was entering the ivy-draped tunnel that bored through a hill. It gave an illusion of countryside as I drove beneath the city rather than above it. On the other side, rolling hills dense with different shades of green populated the right side of the expressway. On the left, I could see glimpses of city through transparent panels in the wall, but they too were draped with enough ivy that you could pretend to be in the wilderness if you wanted to. I maneuvered off the expressway and dipped down over the lip of a bowl. At the bottom, I met both the bay and Yokosuka. A hint of the Northwest was present in the tangling, tumbling green vines and sparkling water.

I drove onto base and met with the captain I had scheduled to interview.

"Yokosuka just got a huge amount of money in the last budget. What are you planning to do with it?" I always liked to throw an easy pitch first.

"We were definitely pleased. It wasn't on the capital improvement plan, but with a thousand sailors being shifted here, we need it to make accommodations."

"One *thousand* sailors? When?"

"Next year. Of course, that's not common knowledge. No need to repeat it." He winked.

I closed my eyes and sighed. I didn't know whether to slap his forehead or my own. They did that all the time! The commanders couldn't seem to remember that *Stripes* reporters weren't part of the team. We weren't military members. Our articles didn't get censored. The *Stars and Stripes* could print whatever it wanted. And usually, it did.

Whenever I had a premonition that my questions were leading into top secret, classified territory, I usually stopped and came at the topic from a different angle. Because, really, I didn't want to know. It wasn't worth it. Most of the time, it wasn't Deep Throat explosive news anyway. It was just Colonel Big Fat Mouth trying to look important. But what made him feel important made me lose sleep.

Would I write the information up as part of my article or not?

Someone should know who couldn't keep his mouth shut, right? Matters of national security were important, weren't they?

But then, I sort of was a member of the team. And one thousand sailors coming to Yokosuka wasn't the biggest of news. But then, it might cause an international incident if it were reported out of school.

So what was I supposed to do?

Most of the time, it was a dilemma with no good answer. But all of the time, it provided an opportunity to make a commander sweat. And who could pass up one of those?

"You do know, Captain, that I don't have any kind of clearance and that my articles aren't censored and the *Stars and Stripes* can print any news it wants…right?"

"Oh, sure...um...I was just speaking off the record."

Of course he was. And that fixed the whole problem.

See why I didn't belong in this business? I was too nice.

There were strange vibes at the office that week, and they had to do with Samantha's return. Rob, the bureau chief was jubilant. Neil was testy. And I didn't quite know how to react.

My subconscious had been warning me of her imminent arrival for days. The time on my Eric Meter had expired. I was going to have to share him again. Unless, of course, Samantha had changed in the three months she'd been gone. It might have happened.

But I seriously doubted it.

# APRIL

*Uzuki*
*Month of Hare*

## 35

*You swim so lazy*
*in the water, Koi, but I*
*know your dragon's heart.*

ALL OF MY SUSPICIONS WERE CONFIRMED on Wednesday when she arrived at the barracks along with her mountain of luggage. The first thing she did after unpacking was crack open her exam books. She studied late. And her light was still on when I went to bed.

But she woke up screaming in the middle of the night.

Neil was already standing in the hall when I got there. "I don't know... I'm not sure..."

I banged on the door.

The screaming continued.

I tried the handle and it turned.

Samantha was sitting in her bed, clutching her head, rocking back and forth.

I sat down on the bed beside her and touched her arm.

She jumped and turned her head toward me. Tears were streaming down her face.

I pulled her into my arms.

"There was this soldier. He'd been talking to me at the chow hall and then he turned to leave. I didn't even really know him. Had just met him. Then they shelled us. He was there, and then he just...*wasn't*...he was gone."

"Shh."

"He was just gone. He just disappeared." She shuddered and began to weep. "I haven't been able to sleep since then. Could you stay? Just for a little while? Maybe if you were here I could sleep without seeing his face."

I slept in her chair that night.

And the next.

I went with her to meet Eric on Saturday. I assumed they would resume their study sessions, and I wasn't about to let go of a friendship that was mine. But when I saw him give her a hug, and watched them as they studied, I realized something had changed. Samantha was no longer on the prowl. And I knew then that with Eric, there was room enough for both of us.

So I excused myself and left.

I crossed the street to Arisugawa Park and walked around the pond. I found a rock to sit on and tried to figure out exactly what I'd won. And why I was so suddenly afraid.

I was the alpha female. I should have been happy. Triumphant.

But I was scared. Because Eric's eyes kept asking me a question. And I didn't want to answer it. Not right then. Eric wanted something from me I wasn't sure I could give.

Something?

He wanted everything.

And if I gave it to him, then what would I have left?

After church on Sunday, as we were walking to the subway station, Eric surprised me. He led us past the station on an urban hike ending at a vast garden. As we walked around the grounds, I tried to discern a blueprint for Japanese gardens. Tried to figure out how everything seemed to look so natural even when I knew placement was so deliberate. After a while I left off trying to figure it out and began to just enjoy it.

In the course of our walk, we stepped onto a bridge and paused in the middle at the top of the arch, watching carp stir the water. Gold flashed and red streaked with watery blue as sunlight glanced off their scales. They swam wide lazy circles in the stream, tails swaying.

I leaned over the railing to watch them. "Why carp?"

"Here? Or in general?"

"In general. Why is it always carp? In every pond?"

"They're fearsome."

I laughed. "No, really."

"Really." Eric drew a packet of rice crackers from his pocket. He opened it and removed one, broke it in half, and tossed it into the air. The water roiled with fury as the cracker landed in the stream. Mouths gaped open, tails twitched. Fish rolled on top of each other struggling for position. And then, every crumb devoured, peace returned.

Eric rested his elbows against the railing beside me. "Carp symbolize perseverance. Strength and the determination to overcome almost any obstacle. They're like salmon. They swim upstream and jump up waterfalls. They're a symbol of masculinity."

I laughed again. Glanced at Eric. He wasn't laughing.

"They're lazy."

"They're just waiting for an opportunity to be courageous." He looked into my eyes. "They're a symbol of courage and aspiration. In Chinese legend, the ultimate reward for a carp's perseverance is being turned into a dragon."

I looked down at the seemingly indifferent fish, remembering the flash of colors as they lunged for the cracker. Dragons. It wasn't too far off.

But masculinity. Fish equals male? That metaphor would take a while to grab hold of my imagination. A symbol of perseverance? Maybe. More like a symbol of passion. Do or die. I'd have to remember that.

On our way back to the subway station, we passed a small park that had been taken over—in part—by homeless people with their cardboard boxes and plastic crates.

"It always makes me sad."

Eric's eyes turned from the homeless toward me. "What does?"

"The homeless people."

"Homeless? Where? You must be hallucinating. According to official statements, Tokyo doesn't have a homeless problem. They're a figment of your imagination. It's a triumph of mind over reality. If we say they don't exist, then they don't." He sounded almost bitter.

"The Japanese have social programs, don't they?"

Eric shrugged. "They have their culture. The family unit is so strong it should provide a safety net for nearly everybody."

"Well, obviously it doesn't. And then those poor people are left out in the cold. Sometimes, the Japanese bother me."

"They *bother* you?"

"They just seem so…culturally superior."

"They are."

"But they're not."

"How would you know? Because your culture's better? Is it possible to have two culturally superior countries in the world?"

"You're the one who's supposed to be a Republican."

"Well, then start acting like a Democrat."

"I'm just saying that something in their culture isn't working. And when something doesn't work, you fix it, you don't ignore it."

"Maybe they do have programs. And maybe those particular people just don't want help."

"Now *that* is the statement of a true Republican!"

He laughed and hooked an arm around my neck. "And you're just a complete and utter Democrat. Do you need a Band-Aid for your bleeding heart? I might have one in my wallet. You want me to look?"

The next Saturday afternoon, I decided to take another trip to the Oriental Bazaar. My older sister's birthday was coming up, and I was in need of inspiration.

Eric called as I was heading out the door.

"I was thinking…would you like to have dinner tonight? At my place?"

"I'm just on my way to Omotesando."

"Meiji Shrine?"

"I hadn't planned on it. But if…did you want to come?"

We arranged to meet at Meiji Shrine after I'd done my shopping.

Several hours later, I crunched through the pea gravel up to the entrance of the shrine, and standing there, waiting for me, was Eric.

It irritated me that he should be so reliable.

We wound our way through the grounds, past the Treasure House, underneath a cypress torii gate, and approached the main shrine. Stopping at a stone basin, Eric poured water over my hands with a bamboo dipper. I did the same for him. And that got me to thinking.

"Does it…have you ever felt strange visiting shrines? Or temples?"

"Strange how?"

"Like you shouldn't be here."

"Why?"

I shrugged.

"You mean, because it's Shinto and I'm a Christian?"

"Yes."

"No."

"Oh."

"It's not going to rub off on me. Think of the thousands of Japanese tourists who visit cathedrals in Europe. Christianity never appears to rub off on them. I don't come to worship. I come to learn about the culture." He looked at me. "Do you feel strange?"

"No. And the thought crossed my mind that maybe I should. So… thanks."

We walked up and into the main shrine.

There were huge lush sacred trees to the right and left. But even then, in spring, a sudden onslaught of wind brought a downpour of dead, dry leaves. I closed my eyes and heard the pitter-patter of "rain" as leaves were chased across the courtyard first in one direction, then another.

A wedding was taking place, right in the middle of the complex.

It had been turned into a tourist event, with foreigners joining the crowd of family and friends. Everyone was taking pictures. I slowed my walk, viewing the scene between the shoulders of the people in the crowd. I saw the bride in the middle. A pristine doll. The only one without visible emotion. Her face a perfect blank. The groom stood beside her, dressed in a black kimono with white stripes.

I walked slowly, skirting the crowd at the back, keeping my eye on the bride. And then, for a split second, she saw me too.

They posed for ten minutes, the women in the party wearing kimonos and the men wearing black cutaway tuxes with striped pants. Then they dispersed, walking away to the right where a bus and limousine were waiting. The bride paused once more with a woman I assumed to be her mother. They turned around, toward me. And as one last picture was snapped, her eyes again met mine.

The mother helped her daughter into a special chauffeur-driven car with a top section that popped up to fit the bride's hair. Once the bride was seated, the mother pulled out something looking like a clip and the hairdo collapsed. I hoped she'd be happy. In a society with such traditional roles for men and women to play, I hoped that at least they could share a kiss.

Eric found me as the bus and limousine pulled away. We started following them, slipping away from Meiji Shrine, ditching the tourists and losing ourselves in the forest.

Eric took my hand in his.

I gave it a friendly squeeze.

"You know, I've been wondering about your 'want to, but won't' statement. Have you changed your mind?"

"About which?"

"Either."

"No. But be careful what you ask for. I just might. Soon." In about three more months.

As we walked toward the subway station, I pondered on a kiss. The Kiss. The upcoming one starring Eric and myself. Maybe…maybe I could put it off.

I snuck a peek at him.

Maybe not.

He must have read my mood because in plain sight, in the middle of Omotesando, with bicycles ting-a-linging and adolescent Japanese girls giggling, in the isolation of the center of the crowd, he stopped and turned to me.

"Stop doing this."

"Doing what?"

"Stringing me along."

"I am not stringing you along."

"You are. And you're using me as a shield against the greater world. You live in Tokyo. So live. You're a writer. So write. If you want me, then have me, but if you don't, then let me go."

"Why? So you can pursue Sam?"

"Sam? Is that the kind of person you think would interest me?"

"She interests everyone else. And she's perfect for you in every single way."

"Don't prevaricate. Are you interested in me or not?"

Prevaricate. Nice word. "I am "

"Then kiss me."

"I can't."

"Why not?"

"I already told you why. It will ruin everything. Trust me."

"Do you know your way back from here?"

I nodded.

"Good. See you around."

He left me standing right there in the middle of the sidewalk. I turned to watch him go, but he'd already disappeared.

*See you around.* What did that mean? Was he just…gone? Like that? What was it that he wanted me to do? Well, kiss him, obviously, but besides that? What did he think we had going for us?

Friendship?…Okay, we had become pretty good friends.

Shared interests?…Okay, so there were a few.

Mutual attraction?…Okay, so my lips were twitching every time I was around him.

We had everything in common *but* politics. Was that enough to build a relationship on? Were we sure we even wanted a relationship? What kind of future could there be?

I thought about it.

I actually sat down on a curb in Omotesando and thought about nothing but Eric and me. Us. There were so many reasons we were wrong for each other, but I could admit there were other reasons we might be right for each other too. But was that any reason to sacrifice our friendship for a kiss? I didn't want to know that Eric and I wouldn't work. That was the complete and honest truth. I just didn't want to know.

On Monday I called Eric at work, but his answering machine said he was out of the office until further notice.

I called his secretary to find out if he was truly gone.

He was.

He'd suddenly volunteered to go up to Sapporo to sit in for someone at the consulate.

He was *gone* gone. But was it coincidence or had he arranged it? Had he been ordered to Sapporo or had he asked to go?

## 36

*How sweet are all my
sacrifices, poured out to
signal devotion.*

FINE. IF HE WAS GOING TO GO AWAY AND JUST…leave me…then I was
going to go away and leave him.

Ha.

Not, of course, that I was technically leaving him. Because he had left
me first. But still! If he could go to Sapporo, then I could go to…Kyoto.
I could go to Kyoto and see old Japan. I could show him I wasn't hiding
from anything. Or anyone.

I brought up my Internet browser and searched on Kyoto. Tried to
figure out some way to tie the city to the U.S. military.

Then I marched over to Rob's desk.

"I think I should do a story about Kyoto."

He glanced away from his computer to look at me. "Why?"

"Something on the real Japan. The Japan we didn't bomb during
World War II."

"As opposed to the fake Japan?"

"When did we last do a travel story?"

"In the winter. Hokkaido for the Snow Festival."

"So don't you think it's time again?"

"Okay. Sure."

"Sure?"

"Sure. Do it."

"When?"

"Today, tomorrow..."

"Any chance I could take Yuka-san with me?"

"Any chance you're suffering from delusions that you're actually a reporter for the *New York Times?*"

"You never know. Someday, I just might be."

"And by then I'll probably be retired."

I'd gotten permission, I just had to figure out how to get there.

I remembered seeing a travel agency at Hiroo Plaza, so I finished the story I'd been working on and then walked down to the shopping center. I tried to keep myself focused so I wouldn't think about scary things I knew nothing about. Like train schedules, hotels, and the Japanese language. *Deep breaths. Deep breaths. Inhale. Exhale. Inhale. Exhale.*

I loitered in front of the travel agency, waiting for an agent's desk to open up. Then I took another deep breath, went in, and sat down in a chair. I made a promise to myself that I wouldn't leave until I had a train ticket in my hand.

And it would have worked. If the agent had spoken any English at all. Or if I had spoken any Japanese. But neither of us did. So I left and returned to the office, head held high. I would do it. I could do it. The next week, I would be in Kyoto. It would almost be like a vacation. By the time I got back to the office, I figured out a course of action. I code-named it Yuka-san.

"I need to go to Kyoto for a story I'm writing. Is there any way you could tell me how to buy a train ticket?"

"Use A-1 Travel. They have best price. They have an office in Shibuya where you can pick them up."

"But do they speak English?"

"Yes."

I wrote down the phone number she gave me and then wrote it on a second piece of paper and tucked it into my bag. Because if they could help me get to Kyoto—in English—then the whole country was wide open. I could go anywhere I wanted anytime I felt like it.

I called A-1 Travel, bought a ticket for the *shinkansen,* and arranged a hotel room for the next two nights. And then I had trouble sleeping.

In my rational moments, I tried to think of the worst thing that could happen. I could get on the wrong train and end up at the far side of the country and never find my way back. Except that I had a cell phone. If the worst happened, then I would just call the office and they could put a trace on me or talk me back. It might be a little scary for a while, but I would make it. I would survive.

The Day dawned. I was only spending two nights in Kyoto, so I had no need for a suitcase. I stuffed a change of clothes into my messenger bag along with my guidebook and camera.

Once at the station, I found the platform for my train. I noticed the concrete beneath my feet was marked with numbers at regular intervals and figured they must correspond to…something. Train car numbers? Maybe.

I found a number corresponding to the train car number on my ticket and stood in the vicinity. I hoped I'd guessed right. As the departure time approached, several more people joined me. Only they stood in a queue next to a white line that had been painted on the concrete.

I looked down the platform. Other people near other numbers were doing the same thing, so I stepped behind the last person in line.

The futuristic *shinkansen* bullet train finally came and hissed to a halt. When the doors opened, people flooded out. The doors closed.

But weren't we—? I looked at the other lines. No one looked worried.

I tried not to look worried either.

It was really hard.

Several minutes later, the doors opened again. We all filed in. The train seats were marked like airplane seats. I found mine, dropped into it, and then held my breath as the train slid away from the station.

I'd done it.

At least the first part.

All that was left was figuring out when to get off.

It didn't turn out to be too difficult. Not once I realized that approaching destinations were announced on a marquee above the doors connecting train cars. When we arrived in Kyoto, I just followed the crowd off the train and rode an elevator down one floor. Leaving the train platforms behind, I walked out into the train station and felt as though I were going to step off into space. It was an architectural wonder of linear design. Elevators cascaded down each end like waterfalls.

I'd booked a room at a hotel inside the train station. I wasn't quite sure what to expect, but I followed signs for Hotel Granvia and ended up in a four-star establishment. Entering it from the station was like walking into a private club. A discreet doorway slid open to reveal a silent, elegantly appointed hall that twisted and turned past hotel restaurants until it emptied into the lobby.

I checked in without any problems. Visa seemed to be a universal language.

The room was…well, roomy. Surprisingly so. With a sleek bathroom partitioned off with smoked glass. Very nice. I would have liked to have put my feet up and rested for a while. An hour, or the entire day, but I had a story to write.

A story to find.

I grabbed my guidebook and tried to map out some sort of plan.

I decided on the scientific method of visiting the tourist sites with the most stars. Pontocho, Nijo-jo, Sanjusangen-do, Kyomizu-dera, Sannenzaka and Ninenzaka, Gion, Shugaku-in, Daitoku-ji, Kinkaku-ji, Ryoan-ji, Saiho-ji, Katsura, and Byodo-in.

I wrote them all down in my notebook.

Except that…some required reservations.

I crossed Shugaku-in, Saiho-ji, and Katsura off the list.

Then I looked at the guidebook's map to find out where the remaining places were. Pontocho and Gion were districts sitting across the river from each other. Sannenzaka and Ninenzaka were hills. Nijo-jo was a castle. Byodo-in was in a nearby city named Uji.

I didn't want to have to take more trains than I needed to. I crossed Byodo-in off the list.

The rest were all temples. I only had to see…ten things concentrated in about four areas. I could—probably—do that. Or I could stay in the room and write the article based on the guidebook.

No, I couldn't.

Before I could think too much about what I was doing, I shut the guidebook and dropped it into my bag. Then I felt around the inside pockets to make sure my camera, notebook, and wallet were there. I exchanged my glasses for sunglasses, grabbed my key from the top of the TV, and left the room. I rode the elevator to the lobby, strode toward the door, and then thought better of it.

I found a chair, sat down, and pulled out that guidebook.

Where to start?

How to start?

The guidebook map had subway stations marked. And train stations. Japan Rail lines and private train lines. And if it were anything like Tokyo, all three probably needed separate tickets.

Too complicated.

I'd take a taxi…and if I had any problems trying to communicate, I'd just show the driver the guidebook. Point out the name of what I wanted to see.

I took a deep breath.

Okay.

What did I want to see?

It was probably best to start at one end of the city and work my way toward the other. I had a plan. Okay. Time to go. I closed the book and returned it to my bag. Adjusted my sunglasses. Looking around, I watched people—tourists—parade through the lobby. They looked confident. They looked as though they knew what they were doing. Maybe I could just go where they went.

I got to my feet and followed them out the door. Right until they got onto a tourist bus.

Dang it!

If I was going to be brave, I needed to do it then while I still had the courage. I walked over to a taxi and leaned down so the driver could see me. He did and then he pushed a button. The taxi door automatically opened.

I got inside.

The door automatically shut.

"Uh…" My courage failed me. I dug around for the guidebook and hauled it out. I turned to the map. "Uh…Kink-a-kuj-i."

"*Kin-ka-ku-ji? Hai?*"

"Yes…uh…*hai.*"

The driver pulled out into the train station parking lot and then into traffic.

37

*Apricot-scented*
*Air, from where do you come? Which*
*flower is your home?*

I LEANED BACK AGAINST THE SEAT AND WATCHED THE CITY GO BY. It didn't look much different than Tokyo. For all that it had been spared during WW II, it looked modern. I couldn't see what the big deal was about "old Japan."

About fifteen minutes later, the taxi pulled up in front of what was clearly a tourist attraction. Buses filled the parking lot. A queue of taxis lined the driveway.

I thanked the driver and paid him.

He said something in Japanese and then pointed out beyond the windshield, motioning forward with his hand.

I thanked him again. Started off in the direction he had indicated. It turned out to be the ticket booth for Kinkaku-ji, the Golden Pavilion.

I stood in line and consulted the guidebook. Originally built in the fourteenth century, it was rebuilt after having been destroyed by an arsonist in the 1950s. A retirement villa for a priest covered in gold leaf. Hence, the name Golden Pavilion.

I prepared myself for a typical overly ornate example of Asian crafts-manship. I purchased my ticket and followed a tree-shaded path on the heels of the tourist in front of me. And then the path opened out into a garden, which opened out onto a pond. And across the pond, glinting in the sun, its reflection shimmering in the water, was the pavilion.

And it was stunning. Like nothing I'd ever seen.

It was pagoda-like and built of three stories, the top two covered with gold and crowned by a golden phoenix. It was firmly planted in the grounds, placed for appreciation and completely worthy of admiration. I had no desire to touch it, to become a part of it, or even to tour it, had that been a possibility. I just wanted to stand there and look at it.

I took a few pictures.

I walked farther along the wood-rail fence. An outcropping of rock had formed a small island from which had sprouted two pine trees. I walked along until it framed the pavilion, obscuring the shaded right side of the structure. When it looked supra-Japanese, I took a picture. And then another.

As I passed the pavilion, nearing the top of a small hill, I turned back. I saw that a wooden boathouse had been attached to the structure, a narrow rowboat floating beside it. So perhaps the people who lived in gold palaces, who lived perfect lives, had need of something after all.

I wandered the grounds for a few more minutes before leaving the way I'd come.

Next up was Ryoan-ji. According to the map, it looked as if it were nearby. Maybe I could walk. Ignoring the taxis, I went out to the street. Seeing a sign for Ryoan-ji pointing off down an incline, I decided to walk. Why not?

Twenty minutes later, I was asking myself, why?

Why walk when I knew I would be reimbursed for my expenses? Why walk when there was really nothing to see? Why walk, in fact, when it looked as though I was the only one walking? The only person on the tourist circuit taking the long way to the sights.

I walked a few minutes longer. I finally came to the parking lot, found the ticket booth, and paid to go inside. Once in the gates, I stopped for a moment and read through the guidebook, trying to figure out what I supposed to be seeing.

Huh.

Somewhere in front of me was a rock garden that was supposed to be the penultimate experience of Zen Buddhism.

Okay.

And beneath it, a pre-Zen garden that wasn't nearly as disciplined.

The afternoon air had gone hazy. Sunlight filtered through the trees. I walked around another pond. Another boathouse. This one, even more rustic, fit into a cove. Silver-tipped moss covered the ground as if it were a velvet blanket. Moss so thick and so regular it looked cultivated. Could you do that with moss? Grow it on purpose?

I came to the temple. It didn't look like anything spectacular. I removed my shoes and stepped up onto the wooden floor. After exploring it, I emerged into an outdoor room overlooking the rock garden. In front of it—in front of me—was a wooden platform of several tiers. People were sitting, singly and in pairs, just watching the rocks.

Fifteen rocks sat on moss islands, separated from the coarse, raked gravel surrounding them. They were protected from encroaching trees by some sort of clay or stucco wall. It was streaked, from rain and age, and sheltered at the top by a narrow tile roof.

No doubt about it. Everything there was old.

I walked to the edge of the top tier and sat down. I took a few discreet pictures and then put the camera in my bag. And then I sat there for a while staring at the rocks, trying to figure out what they might mean. Because that was the puzzle: What did the rocks symbolize? And what did it all mean?

The rocks looked like islands in the middle of a gravel sea. Raked waves lapped at their mossy shores. But that was too easy an interpretation. Simon and Garfunkel had already figured that out.

Several of the rocks had no moss cushions. They looked adrift in the raked sea, swimming toward a more solid mass. The circles raked around them intersected with the circle raked around a larger outcropping of rock. It made you happy for the rocks that had found each other. Happy they had someone else to sit with for all eternity.

But…maybe it didn't mean anything. Maybe it meant whatever you wanted it to mean. Maybe it was just a big Zen Rorschach test. It was something made out of nothing. Or maybe it was supposed to symbolize the beauty of the unbeautiful. Rocks and gravel were nice, but the garden was awfully monotone. Rather barren. But maybe…

Maybe it was time to go.

I pushed to my feet and padded out through the temple. Found my shoes and walked on. Walked down the steps of a moss-blanketed garden. Appreciated the softness and the curves of trees, bushes, and flowers. Maybe that's what the rock garden was supposed to do. Make you appreciate everything else even more.

I finished my walk around the pond. Took a picture of an arched stone bridge reflected in the water. A glance at my watch told me I had time to visit one more thing, so I decided on Nijo Castle. How hard could that be to say to a taxi driver?

Not very. Because fifteen minutes later, I was there.

The castle was famous for its nightingale floors, they let out a squeak whenever they were walked on, thus foiling assassins and other uninvited guests. The diagram in the guidebook had it all laid out in a zig-zag-zig-zag-zig pattern.

I entered through a massive gate built on large blocks of stone. After paying the admission fee, I walked across an expanse of gravel-strewn courtyards and approached shoji-screened palace walls that supported soaring roofs.

After removing my shoes, I toured the castle, squeaking all the way. The rooms were decorated in Chinese-style paintings. The beginning rooms were ornate, the inner rooms, decreasingly so. Apparently the imperial inner circle could appreciate the subtlety of fine arts in ways the lower classes could not.

As I walked the outer hallway, separated by gossamer-thin shoji dividers, from the outside I could hear footsteps crunching through the gravel, a stream murmuring, birds calling. How had anyone living there ever kept warm in the winter? Or cool in the summer?

I completed the circuit and found my shoes.

After leaving the castle, I decided to enjoy the grounds. There were ponds and more gardens. Those, I liked. But then, why wouldn't I? It had once been an imperial castle. Who wouldn't be impressed by imperial gardens?

A boulder-ringed pond looked doubly fortified in reflection, with trees casting their layers of branches both above and below the illusion. I saw the waterfall I had mistaken for a stream splashing over artfully arranged slabs of stone. Walking farther, I saw another castle on the grounds. It wasn't opened for touring.

I passed a charming roofed entrance to a garden. My pea gravel walkway ended where its flagstone path began. Its wooden-barred gate told me it was off-limits. Apparently, I was welcomed to look all I wanted but forbidden to enter. A firm but polite brush-off. And very Japanese.

I took a picture because it so well symbolized my experience in Japan. I had started to turn away, but then I heard Gina's voice saying, *Why* not *go in? What's stopping you?*

I noticed no lock on the gate. Why not, indeed?

I put a hand to it. Pushed.

Nothing happened.

Pushed again.

It didn't budge.

I looked down and then nearly laughed. The reason it didn't move is because it wasn't really a gate. It looked like a gate, but it wasn't meant to open. A board was nailed across the bottom, sealing both sides together.

Wasted bravery.

At least I'd meant well.

I stood back and looked at the structure again. I began to discern a way around the bamboo-poled side. If I could just slide between the pole and the tree…it was working until my bag got stuck on a branch. I spent five minutes trying to untangle it, praying no one would come along. I bent down, nearly to the ground, to crawl under a bush.

But then, I was in.

I'd made it!

The next ten minutes I spent sneaking around, trying to figure out why it was off-limits. It wasn't that much different from life outside the gate. I turned around and walked the same flagstone path back to the un-gate. I ducked behind a thick stand of bushes when I heard footsteps on the pea gravel outside. Stayed hidden two long minutes to make sure no one else was coming.

Then I pushed my bag out ahead of me and crawled under the bush. Right into the feet of an official-looking Japanese person wearing some sort of uniform. Maybe he was…a gardener? He was standing in front of the fence just watching me.

What would Gina do?

Use the stupid gaijin excuse.

That could work for me too!

I smiled. Got to my feet. Gestured to my bag. "Stuck."

He bowed his head toward me slightly. Straightened. "*Ah…so…*did it get stuck before or after you crawled around the fence?"

I felt my face flush red.

He smiled.

What would Gina do *now?*

I went back to the hotel room, gathered all the pamphlets on the temples and the castle from my bag, and put them on the table. When my stomach started to rumble, I admitted the obvious to myself. Sooner or later, I'd have to find something to eat.

I was not a picky eater. I'd spent a semester abroad my junior year in college. I had no problem ordering odd-looking, unpronounceable food in restaurants from Berlin to Barcelona. I did not, for the record, try haggis in Scotland, but then, who would? I'd covered military exercises in Thailand and Korea, and I'd liked most everything I'd eaten.

Japan, however, had me flummoxed. The Japanese ate foods I'd never seen before. Ate things I'd thought could not *be* eaten. They ate raw many things I'd been told absolutely must be cooked and cooked things I normally liked better raw. Things like radishes and spinach. And so I'd found that my culinary courage had deserted me. I hated watching myself become a baby about food, but I had no power to stop it. I was becoming a type of person I used to have no patience for. I had actually uttered the cliché phrase of The Ugly American Tourist: *Thank God for McDonald's.*

The good news was that I was staying in a hotel at a train station. Train stations always had food vendors and restaurants set up to serve commuters. All I had to do was find one that looked good.

Easier said than done.

The first one I passed specialized in eel. I could tell by the specimens swimming around in the fish tank outside the entrance. No, thank you.

The second was filled with men, and I didn't want to be the only woman in what looked like an after-work watering hole.

The third didn't have any customers. At dinnertime? Not a good sign.

The next was just a counter cut into the wall of the station. It sold bento boxes. It might have been an option except that bento boxes could come with lots of surprises. They looked cute, with different kinds of food portioned out into the small sections, but looks could be deceiving. And after walking around town, I was hungry. Starving.

I decided to head down one level. And I was surprised when that level turned out to contain an entire shopping mall with lots of restaurants. I'd gone from zero options to thirty in less than twenty seconds. I finally decided on a noodle shop, pointed to a picture on the menu that seemed to advertise a noodle combination, and asked for water. I was given a small doll-sized glass of it along with a largish cup of green tea.

When my food came, I received a mound of gray noodles served on top of a matlike coaster. I took my chopsticks and tasted. They were cold. With no sauce. They tasted strong. Like…buckwheat. They weren't bad. Just…surprising. But I could survive on them.

Okay.

The second noodle item was a bowl filled with broth and noodles and…tempura? Maybe. I picked up the bowl with one hand to hold it closer to my mouth. I held my chopsticks in the other hand and quickly shoveled noodles toward my mouth before they could slide back into the broth, just the way I'd seen Eric do. Not bad. Quite good. And it was tempura. A piece of shrimp. A piece of green pepper. And a…sweet potato?

I returned to the hotel and got ready for bed. I thumbed through the guidebook, planning my itinerary for the following day. After that I flipped through the channels on the TV, coming across a sports channel in English. And CNN. I turned the TV off, got into bed, and realized, just before falling asleep, that I'd been on my own in Japan for an entire day.

Take that, Eric Larsen!

## 38

*Grow, Bamboo. Sheltered*
*in the center of the grove,*
*you will grow up straight.*

AFTER MY EXPERIENCE WITH HOTEL RESTAURANTS, I decided to find
my breakfast elsewhere the next morning. I retraced my steps from the
previous evening, intending to eat at a restaurant in the mall, but none
of them were open.

I resurfaced outside, next to the bus depot. Peering in the windows, I
could see a food counter tucked into one corner. I opened the door and
went inside. I stood in line while contemplating my breakfast choices.
I ordered a cup of coffee and pointed to several sweet rolls wrapped in
cellophane.

I returned to the room, opened up the guidebook, and reviewed my
route as I ate.

Daitoku-ji was a temple back near the Golden Pavilion. It had been
hidden in the fold of my map, so I'd missed it. It had a famous garden
like Ryoan-ji, so I figured I could just skip it.

Sannenzaka and Ninenzaka turned out to be hills in an older district of Kyoto beneath Kiyomizu Temple. If I walked from the temple
down to the Gion district, I could see old Japan, the geisha area, and
Pontocho alley in one efficient trip. That just left Sanjusangen-do, one
last temple.

I was impressed with myself!

I finished my coffee, returned the guidebook to my bag, and left
the hotel. I hopped into a taxi and said the magic word, Kiyomizu, and

about twenty minutes later, it deposited me in front of a striking orange gate house.

I climbed a set of steps, heading toward a pagoda-topped structure in the distance. It was a sun-faded shade of vermillion. Tall stone lanterns silently guarded the passage, but the way to the top was barred and the steps had gone mossy with disuse.

I walked past it, climbing a hill instead.

Halfway up, I paused to look behind me, expecting a panoramic view but discovering a massive graveyard instead. Each grave was marked by a tall square-sided stone pillar. The pillars followed the contours of the hills, forming legions of dead flowing from the temple, down through the valley and into town.

I took a picture and then kept climbing, finally reaching the temple. After paying the admission, I walked into the temple itself. It was made of wood, like most temples, but it aligned itself much more closely with the forest surrounding it. It had a lodgelike feel and could have been transplanted to the Northwest without raising any eyebrows. Maybe because its materials hadn't been covered with lacquer and paint. Or maybe because the massive beams supporting the structure were in plain view. The guidebook told me it had been built without a single nail in the seventeenth century.

How does something made of wood, which is so prone to rot and decay, last four hundred years? I had seen castles just as old—older even—in my travels through Europe, but those had been constructed of stone.

I shuffled along the approved circuit. To the side of the main hall was another set of stairs leading up to something at the top of a small hill. Something popular, by the numbers of people coming down its steps. I flipped through the guidebook and determined it was Jishu-jinja shrine, dedicated to matchmaking. You were supposed to find your way between two stones, placed fifty-nine feet apart, with your eyes closed to ensure you would meet your true love. If you didn't succeed, love was very far off. If you needed help to make it…I skimmed the rest of the paragraph and then closed the book. Should I do it? Why not?

At the top, two stones had been embedded in the ground and crowned with a loop of thick rope which dangled paper lightning bolts. The place was teeming with tourists, but in the middle of the crowd, two giggling women were trying to walk between the stones, each with one hand over their eyes and the other outstretched.

I watched them for a moment and contemplated the pitfalls of trying to find love with your eyes closed. But then, I hadn't done much better with my eyes open, had I? Before I could think too hard about it, I walked to the first rock, closed my eyes, and started walking toward the second one.

It was only fifty-nine feet, so I figured I'd need to take at least fifteen steps, maybe twenty. I counted them off in my head. When I reached fifteen, I stooped slightly and held my arms out in front of me, groping for the rock. At twenty-one, just when I was beginning to think I might have missed it, I felt a hand on my arm and heard a feminine voice speak a quiet *sumimasen* in apology for disturbing me. A faint pressure on my arm turned me around and propelled me back several steps. And then a hand on my own guided me to the rock. As soon as I touched it, I opened my eyes and turned to thank my helper, but she had already disappeared into the crowd.

I'd found it, but I hadn't done it on my own. Left to my own devices, I would have walked right on past. So…what did that mean? I stood there and flipped through the guidebook until I found it.

I would find love through the help of a friend.

Shaking my head, I left the hill and continued on my self-guided tour, following a path that curved through the forest and then broke out into a clearing, opposite the temple. There, the vastness of the structure could be appreciated. It projected a full seven stories above the bottom of the hill. The book said the expression "To jump off the stage at Kiyomizu" is the equivalent of "taking the plunge." If you survived, your wish would be granted.

I wasn't sure I had any wishes I valued over my life. Sure, getting a book published would be nice, but there were other things in life that were nice too. Sunsets. Chocolate ice cream. Bananas.

I left the temple complex and walked down through Sannenzaka and Ninenzaka. "Three-year Slope" and "Two-year Slope," respectively, they were really just names for one street that wound down the same hill. But legend said a slip on either one would bring three or two years of bad luck, respectively. My best friend had moved back to Australia and my other…friend…had skipped town. I didn't need any more bad luck than I was drumming up on my own, so I paid careful attention to the flagstones beneath my feet.

As I made my way down the hill, I realized what I was seeing was what I had thought Japan would be. There were rows of narrow two-story houses built of wood and stucco complete with lattice window coverings or gabled windows girded by small wooden balconies. Most of the houses along those streets had a business on the bottom. Wares were displayed on small tables outside, protected from the sun by red paper umbrellas. It was the Japan of my fantasies: a composition in red, black, and white. It was charming and seductive, and I understood in that moment why people fell in love with Japan.

Farther along, I turned into a lane comprised of nothing but a series of wood houses built flush to the side of the street. A car could barely fit between them. Bicycles parked alongside them took up a third of the road. It was neat, tidy, and discreet. It felt like a place to which I wanted to belong, but since I couldn't, didn't dare linger. As I continued, the street became increasingly modern. It ended at Yasaka shrine.

There, low orange fences delineated a stand of trees from the pathway, orange wooden lanterns measuring it out in equal lengths. On the other side of the shrine, I emerged beneath a gate to find myself at the corner of a busy intersection. When I crossed it, I walked into the famed Gion geisha district.

Would I see one?

I felt as if I were walking through a wild animal park, alert for wildlife. I had to remind myself that geisha were normal human beings who happened to work at a job just like normal people.

Were they prostitutes or weren't they?

That's really all I wanted to know as I wandered around the streets in the district. They didn't look at all like I'd imagined. Little more than big city alleys, they featured modern buildings and neon signs blinking at the entrances to clubs.

A taxi swerved to a stop just in front of me. The door opened. A woman, kimono-clad, ducked out of the car. Her hair was elaborately arranged, her face painted white. She was a perfect porcelain doll dressed in all the shades and textures of a flower. She lifted up the skirt of her kimono and shuffled into the building.

The taxi pulled away.

I blinked.

I'd seen one!

I followed the street to its end. It intersected with a noisier, busier street which in turn connected to the main thoroughfare in the area. I turned in the opposite direction, hoping to happen on something more authentic.

Finding a smaller, quieter street, I turned again and old Japan lived— once more—in front of me. There sat more stucco houses with wooden supports dividing space into rectangles and bamboo blinds shading windows from view. It was the kind of country I had been hoping to be a part of.

How could Japan consist of both the old and the new? How could a people who made scenes as charming as those build entire cities out of ugly concrete? How did a national soul that identified so intimately with nature and craved harmony create an environment rife with cacophony and dissonance? How did a people who clung so tightly to tradition embrace the future with such zeal?

And why didn't Japan feel the need to explain it? Any of it?

I had so much wanted to like Japan when I had moved there. But she hadn't given me any reasons to. Hadn't noticed I arrived. Hadn't invited me to participate. Didn't seem to care whether I liked her or not.

What did people like Eric see in Japan? What was it that they found so appealing? I wished I could ask him. I honestly wanted to know so that I could find it appealing too. Because when I left Japan, if I left with relief, if I felt as though I were escaping, then somehow I would have failed. And for me—intrepid reporter and globetrotter extraordinaire— cultural failure was simply not acceptable. Other people went through culture shock. Other people were Ugly Americans. Other people made fun of other cultures.

I did not.

I appreciated them. Valued them. Tried to understand them. All except for the one I was living in. Maybe it was Asia. But that wasn't true, was it? I loved Thailand. Loved Korea. It wasn't Asia. It was Japan.

And it was me.

Something about Japan seemed to bring out the most disappointing aspects in myself, in my personality. Maybe I was culturally incompatible with Japan. Was that possible?

## 39

*Butterfly dances.*
*I follow, hoping for grace.*
*Find myself alone.*

I WALKED BACK TO THE MAIN ROAD that ran through the district and got a latte from Starbucks. Sitting at a stool along the window, I watched the throngs pass by. When I finished, I disassembled the cup. I threw the lid in the non-combustible garbage and threw the cup and my napkin in with the other combustibles. Then I crossed the street and went into the Kyoto Craft Center.

It was a modern store of exposed wooden beams and two airy stories, featuring crafts made from every medium: paper, iron, ceramics, textiles, glass, and wood. There were coasters and fans, lanterns and bowls. I picked out an egg-shaped cat made from papier-mâché for Gina and saw a teacup I thought Eric would appreciate. If he were still speaking to me. I turned it over, looked at the price, and decided not to spend two hundred dollars on it.

But for the second time that day, I wished he were there. As I thought back on the places we'd visited together, the pictures in my mind weren't of temples and ponds. They were of Eric. And my memories weren't of sterile sites and tastes and sounds, they were infused with his presence.

I missed him.

After paying for the cat, I headed down the street toward the Kamo River. Pontocho Alley was supposed to be just across the bridge. The book said it was best appreciated after dark. I hoped I could appreciate it during daylight hours because by dark I planned to be eating dinner underneath the train station.

I crossed the river with the light and then turned right, descended a few stairs, and entered a slender alley filled with shops...which on further examination turned out to be restaurants and bars. Occasionally, I could glimpse the river behind the row of restaurants. And it was right behind them. No back alley to this alley. Step outside a back door, and you were likely to end up swimming.

Two people could hardly walk abreast. There were rectangular sandwich boards or small tables propped outside the establishments. Paper lanterns dangled from low-hanging roofs. Above, blocking the sky, signs waited patiently for nightfall so they could be lit. The alley was crowded, but the restaurants, not so busy. Where were all the people going? They didn't seem to be eating—or drinking—but what else was there to do in the alley? It was wrapped in a mood of lazy anticipation. Everything, everyone, was waiting until dusk.

At the end of the alley, I came out onto a busy street. Looking around, I didn't see any taxis or any evidence of a taxi stand. I only had one thing left to see—one more temple—and then I could concentrate on writing my article about the "soul of Japan." I had planned to leave the temple until the next morning, but I was no nearer understanding Japan. And I couldn't write what I couldn't verbalize.

I pulled out my guidebook.

The map wasn't particularly detailed. It conveniently fit on two pages of my guidebook, but it didn't have any sort of scale. The temple looked close, but then so did just about everything.

I scanned the street again for a taxi.

Nothing.

Should I stay and wait, or should I go?

I peered down the alley and then looked at my watch. It was only two o'clock. What was I going to do if I went back to the hotel? I turned and dove into the alley. I jostled my way through to the end, and then I crossed back over the river and started off toward the temple.

Away from the tourist area, the city became both more modern and more quiet. The frenzy generated by photo-happy tourists was absent. I might have been walking anywhere. I followed the street up and down hills. I walked for nearly thirty minutes before I saw a sign for the temple: Sanjusangen-do.

If I had known any numbers in Japanese, I would have known the name stood for thirty-three. At least that's what the book said. Thirty-three was the exact number of spaces between the temple's pillars, not the number of goddess statues. That would have been one thousand and one. Apparently, Buddha saved the world by disguising himself in thirty-three different roles. The one thousand and one statues pictured him in just one of those roles, as Kannon, the goddess of mercy.

According to the book, the temple was the longest wooden structure in Japan. It was built in 1164, destroyed by fire in 1249, and rebuilt soon thereafter. I assumed it really was more than seven hundred years old. Again, that surprised me, the strength of wood over time.

I puffed up one last hill, turned into the parking lot, and bought a ticket at the visitor's center. Leaving my shoes at the door, I walked through a sort of reception hall and then into the temple along an outer corridor. I turned a corner and found myself standing at one end of the temple's long hall.

It was dim, but there was enough light to reflect off the heads of the one thousand and one statues. They were life-sized, carved from wood, and covered in gold. A large voiceless choir, they had been arranged in long rows on at least five tiers on either side of the long hall. One thousand and one statues, though their eyes were closed, seemed to stare at me. One thousand and one pairs of palms met at mid-chest in a posture of prayer. They were not Japanese featured; they looked more…Indian. And at the center sat one large goddess. One thousand waving arms formed a halo around her.

It was creepy, eerie. But beautiful.

I almost turned around and left. But I didn't. The only way out was through.

At places along the floor, placed in front of the goddesses, were statues of different gods. There were thirty of them. Gods of wind and thunder and other spirits that attended Buddha. They were martial spirits, fierce and intimidating. There were descriptions and designations posted in front of each of them. But some were unknown, simply left unnamed.

Supposed Hindu gods, their identities had been obscured during their relocation to Buddhism.

It reminded me once more of the ties between Hinduism and Buddhism, and it lent an explanation for the surprisingly Indian features of some of Japan's favorite deities. It also left me wondering how a spirit could be important enough to merit a statue without having a name. Or an identity. How could something be worshipped without a reason or a personality?

It seemed an act of desperation. An act of appeasement. It seemed no one there believed in those gods, those spirits, but they didn't want to anger any of them, just in case. Is that what happened when religions collided? Is that where superstitions came from? How much of the Buddhist faith was based on time-shrouded tradition?

And how would it feel to worship other gods? To worship a room filled with them? To be obligated to please a hundred, even a thousand deities? How would it feel to worship in fear, unsure that prayers were heard? With no guarantee that anyone at all was watching? When one hoped for mercy but never expected grace?

What heavy burdens humans give themselves to bear.

I walked on, passing statue after statue. Dozens of them. Hundreds of them. Kannon was the goddess of mercy. Did that suppose a different god for justice? By the time I reached the end of the hall I had passed one thousand and one pairs of eyes.

All of them had been closed.

By the time I reached the hotel, my feet were sore. My shoulder ached from carrying the bag—weighted with a guidebook, camera, and water bottle—for two days in a row. My hair smelled like incense.

I ran a bath, stripped off my clothes, and sank into water up to my neck.

When I closed my eyes, I saw again the heads of a thousand and one goddesses. I saw again the features of the martial statues without identity. I realized that somehow they had been carved in more detail than the faces of the thousand and one well-loved goddesses.

I slipped lower into the water to wet my hair. Felt it go weightless as it floated around my head in a thousand strands, like the thousand arms of mercy.

That night, the floating Eric-Buddha had the features of one of those unknown spirits. And from behind him swayed a thousand arms.

All of them waving at me.

All of them beckoning me forward.

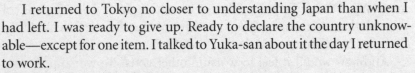

I returned to Tokyo no closer to understanding Japan than when I had left. I was ready to give up. Ready to declare the country unknowable—except for one item. I talked to Yuka-san about it the day I returned to work.

"What, exactly, are geisha?"

"*Gei* is art. Geisha are keeper of the traditional art. They are dancer, musician, talker. They entertain."

"Entertainers?"

"More like your formal meaning of entertaining. They are hostess."

"But it's more than that, isn't it? Don't they have to be pretty... and...?"

"Do you have to be pretty to do a good job?"

"No."

"And neither do they. Their value lie in the quality of what they do."

"But the things they do... Aren't they just glorified prostitutes?"

Her eyebrows rose. "If you sleep with someone you work with, does that make you prostitute?"

"I...well...no..."

"Geisha choose in the same way you choose. She is engaged to entertain. Through conversation, music, and dance."

"Engaged to entertain men."

"Yes."

"So you're saying sometimes she sleeps with clients and sometimes she doesn't? And she gets paid either way? Doesn't that seem...sexist to you? What if the men are already married? Shouldn't their wives be taking care of them?"

"This is not the role of Japanese wife. Japanese wife take care of house and children. Japanese man work."

"But shouldn't his wife be able to meet his needs?"

"Geisha are like…ballet dancer, symphony orchestra, and perfect Japanese woman. They are ideal female. What wife would want to be that? Would you want to be that for your husband?"

No, thank you. I shook my head. "Way too much pressure."

"And so geisha perform this service."

"Of being an ideal."

"*Hai.*"

"And the wives don't mind?"

"It does not matter. Wife has great power in her role."

"But is she happy? If my husband were spending his extra time with some perfect woman, I wouldn't be. And it *is* sexist. The man can go do whatever he wants, and the woman gets to sit at home and wait for him. That doesn't seem fair."

"Japanese marriage is not American marriage. You do not understand the power in tradition. Japanese women have voice. It is just not same voice as you."

"Then explain it to me."

"I cannot. You would not understand it. And you cannot value what you do not understand."

*You cannot value what you do not understand.*

What was I missing?

That afternoon I sat down to write my article about the Real Japan and the lessons I'd learned in Kyoto. I wrote something. I can't remember what. I tried to be profound. I probably failed. I still hadn't figured out Japan. But as I wrote the article, I surrendered. I laid my expectations down and decided to accept her on her own terms, even if understanding only came in kaleidoscope moments that slid away when I looked at them too closely.

It seemed to me Japan was about the relentless search of perfection and the pursuit of fulfillment, gone about by each individual within the culture's constraints. If the siren song of America was "Be who you are," then the anthem of Japan was "Be Japanese. Don't let us down." Was that the power in tradition? Was it like that game where you formed a circle and everyone sat down on the lap behind them at the same time? One person sitting on another person who sat on a third person who sat on a fourth? And if everyone did exactly what they were expected to, then life continued seamlessly according to expectation.

If so, then the soul of Japan was the soul of mankind. It was what happened when work became a metaphor for life. It was an absolute desire to do the best, to be the best, to achieve success. And peace. The soul of Japan manifested itself in a national spirit that recognized beauty in fleeting moments and realized the fate of the nation rested in individual hands, that each step a citizen took rocked the scales of fate.

If all that were true, then perhaps I could identify with the country more than I thought.

## 40

*Do not screech at me,*
*Crow. It will not make you feel*
*better to wake me.*

YUKA-SAN AND I WENT OUT FOR LUNCH that day to her favorite ramen place. I only went when she did because I had never been able to find it by myself. It was only about five blocks behind the office, but it was hidden in the center of a maze of small streets and alleys filled with narrow homes and apartment buildings that all seemed to be made from the same concrete and strung together with the same electrical wires.

Everywhere we looked were strings of carp kites swimming in the wind in anticipation of Boys' Day.

At least that year, thanks to Eric, I knew why carp kites were significant. We passed a house with five carp swimming in tandem, strung on a single pole. The largest on top, smallest at the bottom. They were painted bright colors of red, blue, green, and yellow. They were straining against the wind, looking for all the world like fish swimming upstream, trembling with the effort.

"Why is the top kite different from the others?" It wasn't a carp at all. It was a windsock trailing colorful streamers.

"You know these *koi*, carp, mean courage and overcome every obstacle? These kite represent wish which every parent have for their children. At very top you see two wheel. These are *ya-garuma*. Each spoke of wheel is made from arrow. You hear this sound in the wind?"

I did.

"This is so evil will stay far away. The next one, this is *fuki-nagashi*. Streamer that wind blow. This represent the waterfall that koi must swim up. Next is black carp. This is father. Next is red carp. This is mother. And one for each son. You see this next one?"

I nodded, looking at the next house on the street.

"You see *fuki-nagashi*, then black one, red one, pink one. Pink mean girl. This family is proud of the girl as if she were a boy."

"Because it's bad to be a girl?"

"No. This is because Boy Day is now Children Day. This fifth day of the fifth month is now for all children."

"So…what about Girls' Day?"

"This is still for girl."

Okay then.

Later, back at the office, I thought again about carp. Carp swimming upriver. Strength. Perseverance. Persistence. I liked it. Who in America would ever pray for their child to be like a carp? Carp Child. That could be a title of a B-grade movie. Maybe…*Flying Carp?* No. Too circusy.

*The World According to Carp?*

Too Mel Brooks.

*My Life as a Carp?*

That had some possibilities.

*My Life as a Carp.* It could open with a fish bowl. Some guy feeding his fish.

A guy! This was good. This was new.

He could feed his fish. His goldfish. Because goldfish were carp… weren't they? Weren't they supposed to grow big if they had enough space? I'd have to look it up. So he'd feed his goldfish and he'd have a nice life. A routine life. And then something would happen. He would step out of the routine. His life would become larger. He would grow. And in the end, he would take his fishbowl to a big pond and let his goldfish swim free.

I liked it.

It had a male protagonist. Huge symbolism. And hope. Maybe that was it. If I ever did think about writing another book, maybe it could be that one. Because it could work…as long as carp and goldfish were the same thing.

I brought up my Internet browser and searched on the words

"goldfish" and "carp." And…they weren't the same. Goldfish were a member of the carp family, but they weren't carp.

It wouldn't work. A person might keep a goldfish, but they'd never keep a carp.

Dang.

I saw those kites again in my mind's eye, flicking their tails against an angry gray sky.

Nice try.

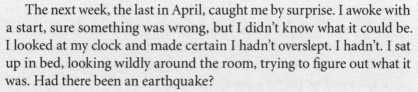

The next week, the last in April, caught me by surprise. I awoke with a start, sure something was wrong, but I didn't know what it could be. I looked at my clock and made certain I hadn't overslept. I hadn't. I sat up in bed, looking wildly around the room, trying to figure out what it was. Had there been an earthquake?

I looked at the pictures on the wall. They were all relatively straight. Couldn't have been an earthquake.

I sat there, listening for anything that would give me a clue. And then I realized I heard absolute silence. That's what it was. That's what was wrong. No noise was coming from the street.

Throwing back my covers, I went to the window and pulled the curtains aside. There weren't any taxis lined up along the cemetery. No cars racing down the street. And that's when I remembered: Tokyo was on holiday. It was Golden Week.

The Japanese had a convenient proliferation of national holidays at the end of April and beginning of May. In fact, they made a holiday up in order to make it even more convenient. First came Showa Day to commemorate the Showa Period, which encompassed World War II, and to contemplate the country's future. Then Constitution Day, and then a day declared a national holiday due to the fact that it fell between Constitution Day and the next holiday, Children's Day. During the right year, when Children's Day fell on a Sunday, then Monday was declared a national holiday too!

Golden Week was synonymous with travel. The reason it was so quiet was that everyone had left the city. Except, of course, for the unlucky Americans. And the Japanese who worked for us. We all still had to work.

I padded into the bathroom and took a shower. Then I ate a bowl of cereal before ambling over to the office. I was already halfway through my midmorning cup of coffee when my cell phone buzzed. It was Eric. "Where are you?"

"Um...at work. Why? Where are you? Are you still 'around'?"

"What?"

"Are you still 'around'? As in 'see you around'?"

"Actually, I'm back."

"Back at work? But your secretary said you'd volunteered to go up to Hokkaido."

"I did. So someone could take emergency leave. And now I'm back."

"But you said...when you left...aren't you supposed to be mad at me?"

"I am mad at you. But I didn't go up to Hokkaido because I was upset with you. It was just a happy coincidence that someone's father died on the same day I...well, it's Showa Day, and I was just hoping we could talk."

"It's Showa Day for the *Japanese*."

"You don't take Japanese holidays?"

"Is that an option? Wait...does that mean the embassy doesn't take U.S. holidays?" Even before I'd finished asking, I'd figured out the answer to my own question. I already knew Eric took U.S. holidays. So what did that mean? Did he...? "Do you get *both* sets of holidays?"

There was silence at the other end of the line.

"Eric? Does the embassy take both U.S. *and* Japanese holidays?"

"Um...yes. So I guess this means that you don't want to go up to Asakusa?"

After the conversation with Eric, I tried to return my attention to the article I was writing, but I couldn't concentrate. My Injustice Meter was pinging. So I tracked down the bureau chief.

"Why don't we get Japanese holidays? The embassy does."

"Did you need to learn Japanese for this job?"

"No."

He took the previous day's edition of *Stripes* from his desk, turned to the editorial page, folded the paper in half, and held it up to my nose. "Read that. Right there." He stabbed at the newspaper. "What does it say?"

"This newspaper is authorized for publication by the Department of Defense for members of the military services overseas."

"Right. And which government did you sign your contract with?"

"The USG."

"Exactly."

"So you don't think it's unfair the embassy takes Japanese holidays and the Department of Defense doesn't?"

"I bet the Defense Attaché office at the embassy does."

I frowned at him.

"I think it sucks, okay? Feel better?"

I smiled at him. "Thank you."

By the time I got back to my desk, Eric was there. He was sitting in my chair, looking so…so…likeable. And I was so…so…mad at him for everything. Hadn't I gone to Kyoto and tramped around the entire city by myself just to prove that if he could leave me, I could leave him? And he hadn't even really left me!

But he was back and I was happy. Happy! I stood right in front of him. Glared. "Are you trying to make me feel happy that you're taking time off or trying to make me feel bad that I can't join you?"

He shrugged. "Tell me how you feel and I'll tell you which it is."

"I feel like…" Frankly, I felt as if I could run away from the office with him and never, ever return.

That was a surprise.

I felt my cheeks flush.

He stood up. Right in front of me. Right in the middle of my very personal space. We were eyeball to eyeball. "There's something I need to ask you. Again."

I was having trouble breathing, but I was able to squeak out, "What?"

"What's going on?"

"With what?"

"With you and me."

"Nothing."

"I think you're lying."

"There is nothing going on."

"Want to try looking me in the eyes and saying that again?"

I crossed my arms, lifted my chin, looked at him, and smiled. "There is nothing going on."

"Nice try. Do you know that when people lie, their pupils dilate? They also dilate when they look at someone they like. So which is it? Are you lying to me about not liking me or do you like me?"

"I can't kiss you."

"Why not?"

"Because I made a promise to myself not to."

"Not to kiss *me?*"

"Not to kiss men. In general."

"But I'm me. In particular."

"I'm sorry. I can't."

"Ever?"

"No. Just for another two months." And two weeks.

"But you want to."

"Yes. No. Listen, if we kiss, then everything will be ruined. That's what always happens. I start out with these great relationships, and then I mess them up. High school. All those boyfriends. That's why! Do you really want to end up like that?"

"Can't you just—"

"And besides, I've never broken a promise to myself before."

"So I'm being punished for some sort of noble self-improvement project?"

"I just don't want to hurt you. I don't want to hurt *us.*"

"You're not even giving us a chance to *be* us."

"I just…I can't…"

"Then your answer is no?"

If I couldn't say yes, then it had to be no, didn't it? "Yes."

"Then my answer is, 'I'm trying to make you feel bad that you can't join me.'"

"What?"

"That's the answer to your question."

My question? Oh. The one about wanting to make me happy or make me feel bad. "Then I wouldn't want to keep you here any longer than necessary. I hope you enjoy your day."

He held his hands out in front of him as if he wanted to grab something. Strangle something. But then he turned on a heel and left.

I sat down in the chair he'd so recently vacated and began typing. I breathed a sigh of relief. I only had two months left. Two months and two weeks. How come he had to be so pushy?

And why, oh why, did I want to be pushed?

## 41

*Wisteria, when*
*you climb a wall, why do you*
*try to pull it down?*

SOMEWHERE ALONG THE LINE, my image of God had begun to assume the shape of the Great Buddha in Kamakura. Still, serene, stolid, waiting. But looming. A God that appeared as if he would overshadow everything. A God that wanted to have everything.

The problem wasn't so much that I didn't believe in God. The problem was that I didn't want him to get too close. I was afraid he'd mess everything up. That he'd crash the party and send everyone home. Not that my life resembled a party. Or that I was having very much fun. Or that I knew for sure he'd do something I didn't want or like.

But *I* wanted to make the decisions. I had plans. *I* wanted to be the one in control.

One thing I liked about the Kamakura Buddha is that he just sat there. If I wanted to see him, I had to go to Kamakura because he wasn't going to grow legs and stalk me in Tokyo. There were limits to his jurisdiction.

But something about his image still bothered me. Something out of kilter. Something wrong. And after I'd dreamed of Eric-Buddha three times in three days, I decided to do something about it. I decided to be brave and go to Kamakura. I also decided to be brave and call Eric.

"Can I borrow your guidebook? I lost mine. Yours. The one you gave me." I'd misplaced it at some point between the train station in Kyoto and the train station in Tokyo.

"Is this Allie O'Connor speaking?"

"Yes. Can I?"

"Are you going somewhere?"

"Back to Kamakura."

"Why?"

"I just...didn't feel like we got to see everything last time."

"I think you'd have to spend about five years living there in order to see everything."

"Please?"

"Sure. Fine. I could...if you want...do you want me to come with you?"

"Would you?"

"Of course. And I'll actually remember the guidebook this time. I promise."

An awkward tension existed in the atmosphere between us on the train to Kamakura, but we both survived. We got off at the station, and Eric fished out his guidebook and pointed to the map. "Do you want to start at this end? Since we didn't see any of it last time?"

I glanced at the guidebook's map. "Where's the Great Buddha?"

He slid a finger across the page to the opposite side of the map. "Here."

"Let's start there."

"I thought you wanted to see something different."

"And something the same."

He looked into my eyes for a long moment. "Okay."

"Thanks."

As we hiked through town, I caught a familiar glimpse of Buddha's head. He didn't look so intimidating from that angle, and I started to think I'd imagined things. That my memory had redrawn him all out of proportion.

We paid our entrance fee, were given brochures, and then walked onto the grounds. And there, in the distance one level above us, was Buddha. And he was exactly as I remembered him. From my vantage point, he was everything I'd remembered. Daunting. Threatening even.

Eric had gone ahead of me a few steps. He pulled his guidebook from his backpack and started reading. But then he stopped and looked up at Buddha. Looked at the page. Then back toward Buddha. A smile played at the edge of his lips. "How would you describe the statue from here?"

I didn't have any hesitation in answering that question. "Looming. Intimidating."

"Let's do an experiment. See if your impression changes as you get closer. Tell me when you start to feel something different."

I stepped closer to him and craned over his shoulder for a look at the book. "What does it say in there?"

He shut it. "I'll tell you after."

"Tell me now."

"No. I want to see if it's true or not."

"What's true?"

"What it says."

"Which is?"

"I'll tell you later. I promise."

"You know, one of these days I'm going to go out and buy my own guidebook. And then you won't be able to act so superior."

"Is that the day you'll be brave enough to travel around Japan by yourself?"

"Excuse me. Who went to Kyoto? Without whom?"

"You. And you should feel proud of yourself." He looked over his shoulder at me. His gaze touched my lips.

I stepped back and looked up at the Buddha.

We walked up the path together, pausing now and then, but nothing about the statue or my feelings toward it changed. When we got to the steps, Eric stopped to take a few pictures.

We climbed a few steps. I paused. Looked up at Buddha.

"Anything?"

"He doesn't seem quite so...I don't know. Something's changing."

He raised his eyebrows. "Wonder what?"

I wrinkled my nose at him and started forward.

I waited until some tourists stepped away from the front of Buddha and then stepped up to take their place. I couldn't get much closer. As I stood there, looking up, I suddenly realized my perceptions of the statue had completely changed. There was no longer anything ominous about him. Whatever I'd seen—or thought I'd seen—had disappeared. He was now comforting. Even peaceful. The serenity of the face had encompassed the statue as a whole.

Eric stood beside me. "Anything different?"

"Yes. It's not intimidating anymore."

He just smiled.

"Give me the book."

He opened it to the Kamakura section and pointed to the paragraph on the Great Buddha. I read it and then returned to the steps. I retraced my steps to the beginning of the path and repeated my approach to Buddha.

Eric just stood by the statue, watching me.

By the time I drew even with him, knowledge had informed my thoughts about the statue. According to the book, the Great Buddha of Kamakura had been crafted to convey a certain principle. His top half had been cast out of proportion to his lower half. Standing far away, at the beginning of the path, he looked top-heavy. He hadn't seemed right because he wasn't. He was out of proportion. But once a worshipper stood at his base, or better, knelt before him, the perspective placed everything in its proper proportion. Created a vision of safety. And peace.

I'd received an incorrect impression of Buddha because I'd stood too far away. No wonder my dreams had assigned Buddha's proportions to God; I'd kept myself far off and hadn't allowed myself to be drawn near. So right there, in front of the Great Buddha, I did. In the quiet space between me and Buddha, I said a prayer to God. It was about my writing and my fear that it wouldn't be enough. Once I'd said it—prayed it—I felt a little less scared, and I could have sworn I heard God answer. I think he said, *It's enough for me.*

And then I knew what I had to do. The very thing I'd been resisting. I'd thought writing the book would be enough to get God off my back, but it hadn't been. I had to start sending it out. But if that's what I had to do...well then, I'd just have to do it. At least that had all been figured out. Buddha as a metaphor for God. The thought made me smile. It might not have been orthodox, but it made sense to me. My problem with the Great Buddha was the same problem I was having with the Great God. But that still didn't explain why Eric had been mixed into the whole metaphor.

Or did it?

Maybe this was the moment of truth. All truth. If I'd stood too far away, then maybe all I had to do was step a little closer.

So I did.

Eric looked into my eyes, questioning, and then he slid an arm around my waist.

I had two months left before I could kiss Eric, but what was two months between friends? If I'd kept myself far off, then maybe all I had to do was allow myself to be drawn near.

So I did.

How much time exists in the space of a kiss? I used to think it was an hour, a week, or a month. Rarely ever had there existed a year. But Eric's kiss offered up an eternity.

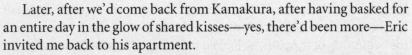

Later, after we'd come back from Kamakura, after having basked for an entire day in the glow of shared kisses—yes, there'd been more—Eric invited me back to his apartment.

"I...um...need to..." My gaze wandered from his eyes to his lips. It lifted to his eyes again when I realized I hadn't finished my sentence. "I need to think."

"About?"

"You."

He smiled into my eyes, leaned over, and placed a whisper of a kiss on my lips. "Then make them happy thoughts."

They were. At least most of them.

That night as I lay in bed, I replayed every single kiss we'd exchanged. I was searching for a flaw, for something that could tell me what was wrong with our relationship. Because there had to be something wrong. There always was.

But if there wasn't, then what did that mean?

I thought about the possibilities. But then I thought of something else. As many people as I'd dated, as many people as I'd kissed, I still didn't know how to do a long-term relationship. And the more I considered it, the more I realized it might just be because I didn't want to. I didn't want to know because, when it came down to it, most of the time long-term was only temporary. So, although I'd trained myself well for the reality of life, I'd just discovered what I really wanted was the fairy tale.

I wanted the happily ever after. And I wanted it with Eric.

# 42

*Catfish, won't you stop*
*swishing your tail? I cannot*
*live on shaking ground.*

THE NEXT DAY, ON THE WAY HOME FROM CHURCH, we decided to walk up to Eric's place through Arisugawa Park. It was too pretty, too mild an evening not to enjoy it. As we walked through the bottom of the park, holding hands, there was a commotion in the center of the lake. A pair of ducks were squawking, kicking up water. There were people walking the paths as we were, others sitting on benches, and still others—those same old men—fishing. Everyone seemed to be intent on enjoying the evening and everyone's attention seemed to be directed at the ducks, but no one was actually looking at them. It only took a moment for me to realize why.

I could feel my neck flush red to my ears. The ducks were...copulating...in broad daylight. All sound, fury, and feathers. And then, mercifully, the drake hopped off the hen and swam back to shore, leaving the female ruffling her wings indignantly. Shaking her tail. Gliding off into deeper waters alone.

I dropped Eric's hand.

Eric cleared his throat.

I shoved my hands into my pockets.

Along the path which bordered the pond, movement resumed. People came to life. Began to talk. Began to fish. Began to breathe. But it seemed Eric and I didn't have anything to say to each other anymore. And just when it seemed silence had been stretched to its absolute limit, Eric asked if we could stop in at National Azabu.

"Of course, yes, by all means." We retraced our steps past the brazen ducks to the park entrance. He said he had to get groceries. I took refuge upstairs in the bookstore. We agreed to meet out in front when we were done.

It took about fifteen minutes for the flush to retreat back down my neck.

When we met up, Eric was clutching shopping bags in both hands, looking at them as if he didn't really know what they were. "Um. I guess... I have to go put these in the fridge."

"Oh. Sure."

We headed up the hill, the park to our left. On the other side of the street. No way was I going in there again. Not with Eric. We both let our eyes trail the ground in front of us. I was puffing by the time we passed the German Embassy and had to catch a breath when we reached the corner.

At his apartment building, we rode the elevator in silence, standing at opposite ends of the walls. Eric opened the door to the apartment and let me enter first. I took off my shoes, waited for him to do the same, and then followed him into the kitchen. I watched as he unloaded his groceries into the refrigerator.

He went to place a carton of eggs in the door, but stopped when he saw a carton already there.

I reached for it, meaning to take it out to throw it away, but it was full. "Um?"

Eric put the new carton there. Took the old one from me and slid it onto a shelf.

He held out a tube of chips to me. "Pringles?"

"No thanks. How much did you pay for those?"

He set them on the counter. "Too much."

"So..."

"Well..."

Eric looked straight at me then. "They were just ducks."

"I know."

"Do I make you uncomfortable?"

"No."

"Are you sure?"

"Yes. Of course. Don't be ridiculous. Why would you make me uncomfortable?" I left the kitchen, went into the dining room, and stood in front of the patio door.

Eric followed me. He unlocked the door and pushed it open. "Want to go out?"

"No. Just looking." I left the door and went to stand in the living room. "I guess…I mean…I'd better go." I took a step, but began to feel lightheaded. I closed my eyes and opened them, trying to make them refocus.

It didn't work. We were having an earthquake.

I grabbed at the couch, but Eric caught my hand and tugged me toward the door frame. I planted my feet as best as I could, trying to determine just how bad it was by how long it was going to last.

It was bad.

The jumbling hadn't stopped and it hadn't gotten any gentler. So the next time he pulled, I followed. He dragged me down once we were under the door frame and then crouched behind me. His body shielded mine as he placed one arm against the door frame and wrapped the other around me.

I clutched his forearm and hung on.

We found out later that it had lasted for two full minutes. And then, as suddenly as it had started, it stopped.

I tried to get up, but Eric had no intention of releasing me. "Are you okay?"

"I'm fine."

"Are you sure?"

"Yes."

While he went to see if the bedrooms had sustained any damage, I checked the living room. One of his vases had fallen, but it hadn't broken. I picked it up and put it back in its place.

I held one of my hands up out in front of me. It was trembling. Earthquakes would do that to a person. It usually took me about a week to get over a major one.

I walked toward the patio. I didn't see any cracks in the cement, so I let myself out. It was probably a stupid thing to do, but I was hoping the fresh air would help. Concentrating on breathing, I saw the moon peek over the trees in Arisugawa Park. I listened to the twilight sounds. There were several taxis parked along the street with their engines running, providing white noise. I wondered if they'd even felt it.

And then something touched me.

I jumped. Nearly screamed.

"Allie. It's just me. It's okay." Eric put a hand out to touch my arm.

I wrapped my arms around myself and nodded, not trusting myself to speak.

He stepped behind me, and placed an arm around my shoulder.

I grabbed his other arm and wrapped it around too.

"The Japanese used to think a giant catfish lived underneath the earth. Whenever he swished his tail, he created an earthquake."

Well, that certainly made the whole thing seem less scary. I tried to smile. That would have made it seem less scary too. "I hate earthquakes. You're going along, minding your own business, thinking maybe Japan isn't so bad after all and then, Wham! It reminds you of everything you hate."

"Well, what do you like?"

"About here? I like the literature. I love haikus. I love Murakami. I like that everyone cares so much about the job they do. I like learning about the odd things. Like the catfish. Or the month of October. Did you know all eight million gods go away for a convention every October?"

I could feel him smile against my hair. "I didn't know that."

After a while, I could feel myself relaxing, feel my heart beating in rhythm with the city. The city at night is filled with blinking red lights. The Japanese obey rules to the letter, so every building over a certain height is considered a flying hazard and marked as such. At night Tokyo is punctuated with thousands of red warning lights. A thousand pairs of eyes, blinking from the wilds of a concrete jungle, making the city at once both modern and primitive. Lending a staccato rhythm to the night.

It reminded me I was at the mercy of forces of nature I could hardly begin to understand, let alone predict. My entire life was built on a thin veneer of fragile substance that could crumble when I least expected it. And when that happened, the only thing I'd be able to count on would be the strong arm of a friend.

Eric kissed me on the temple just before we went inside.

I very nearly turned and kissed him back, but the evening's events had convinced me of something. They'd convinced me it was foolish to sacrifice a friendship for the momentary pleasure of a kiss. Eric's lips might be close to perfect and kissing him was incredible. But ultimately, I'd be left in the same position as that unfortunate hen. Lacking the warmth of companionship, I'd be left to sail out into deep waters alone.

I decided to leave soon after.

When Eric moved to kiss me goodnight, I moved to kiss him on the cheek instead.

But he stopped me. "What is it that you're looking for?"

"What do you mean?"

"When you kiss me, I can tell you're looking for something. What is it? A kiss reveals the relationship. As far as I can tell, there's nothing missing here."

"No. No, no. Kisses are how *I* judge a relationship."

"You think you're the first one to come up with that idea?"

"You do that too?"

"Of course."

What did he mean, *Of course?* He'd been judging me? *He'd* been judging *me!*

"There's nothing wrong with us, Allie."

"Don't you think I don't know that?"

"So what is it?"

"It's everything! And I'm nothing. I'm nothing you need. I'm not... right. I'm not diplomatic, and I don't know people, and I can't do Japan. I'm not even a Republican. I can't do anything for you. I don't think I'm even capable of sustaining a long-term relationship."

"But I don't care who you aren't. I'm in love with who you are."

"You're in love with me?"

"Yes!"

"But—"

"Is this something you want to pursue or not?"

"Are you talking about us?"

"Yes."

"Then does it have to sound like a contract negotiation?"

His face cracked for just an instant. That mask of confidence slid just a little. Just enough to see...what? Impatience? Fear? Self-consciousness? "Could you just tell me? I need to know. Now. For me, it's you. You're the one."

I couldn't breathe. But I was able to squeak out a response. "Capital T, capital O?"

"Allie, this is not about semantics. It's about us. And we're supposed to be together."

"How do you know that?"

"Because I met you again."

"But that doesn't mean anything."

"It does to me. I've always measured other women against you."

"You don't even know me. Who do you think I am?"

"I think you're committed to ideals. I think when you look at the world, you see things no else does. And you have this...this way of conveying them that makes me want to see the world that way too. I think you're one of the most integrated people I know. You don't contradict yourself. I think you're old-fashioned—"

"I'm—"

"—even though you think you aren't."

"I'm not like that! I haven't done anything yet. I'm nothing I wanted to be. I haven't even written a real book."

"Yes, you have. A good one. And you'll write another and another." He said it with such confidence. "I've been in love with you since I first saw you in high school."

"That doesn't mean we're in love now."

"But we are."

"No, we aren't."

"Then prove it to me. Kiss me."

"You don't want me to."

His eyes glinted. "Yes, I do."

"You really don't."

"Why not?"

"Because you're my best friend. And the longer we kiss, the sooner it will be over."

"What if it hasn't even started yet?"

"I'll find a fatal flaw. I always do."

He was getting close. Way too close. And my eyes had no interest in looking at anything but him. I needed space. "Why did you ask me to dance?"

"At the prom?" He stepped back and began to smile. "Do you remember the song?"

"'Somewhere Out There.' And I thought it was very sweet."

"Thank you. But I was thinking of the lyrics, not the mouse movie it came out with."

I started humming the song. Came to the chorus. Stopped.

He picked up the tune, grabbed my hand, and started waltzing us down the hall and into the living room. Started singing it in my ear.

And then it all made sense. All of it. High school. College. My job at *Stars and Stripes*. He was right. It did mean something. And I couldn't think of a reason to fight it anymore. "How did you know this would all work out?"

He stopped dancing.

I held on to him anyway.

And he kept hold of my hand. Only he brought it to his chest and placed it right over his heart. "I didn't. I left it to fate. Destiny. God. I've been waiting—for years—to see if you'd come back into my life."

"The old 'If you love something, set it free…'"

"…if it comes back to you, it's yours."

"…if it doesn't, it never was."

"Exactly."

"That sounds a little mystical for you."

"And why are you so pragmatic?"

I opened my mouth to tell him that I wasn't and he kissed me. And that kiss—the one I finally gave myself to—rocked my world. The entire thing. The past, the present, and the future. Nothing was missing. And everything was in sync.

One afternoon, a month later, Eric walked into the office carrying a letter. He held it out to me with a flourish. "This is for you."

"And it got put in your box? It was sent to the embassy?" I took it from him and read the address. Strange. They'd paired my name with his address. I looked at the return address. I sat down—hard—in my chair.

"Why would a publisher be writing to me? I didn't…I haven't sent anything to this publisher." I hadn't even dared to add them to the list of queries I was slowly sending out.

"Because I sent them your manuscript."

"My…manuscript? The whole thing?"

"Not at first. I sent a query letter, a synopsis, and the first three chapters. Just like they asked for on their website."

I hadn't written a query letter and I hadn't written a synopsis. But that wasn't important. The important thing was that the publisher had received them. "And?"

"They liked it. They asked for the whole thing."

"And?"

"I don't know. You'll have to read the letter."

I looked at it. Drew the envelope between my fingers. It was thin. Very thin. Was that good or bad? I held it out to him. "You open it."

He shook his head. "This one you have to do yourself."

"But what if—"

"You'll never know if you don't open it."

I slid a finger underneath the flap, folded it back, and slid the letter out.

"Dear Ms. O'Connor: We are pleased to inform you that…" I couldn't read anymore because I couldn't see the words. My hands were shaking, and my eyes had sprouted tears.

Eric took it from me. "We are pleased to inform you that your manuscript shows great promise." He read silently for a few moments and then looked up. "They need your street address so they can send a contract."

"A contract. For me."

"For you."

"They liked it."

"It shows great promise."

And then I wasn't crying anymore. I was laughing.

Eric was just standing there, holding the letter and rereading it.

I caught my breath and then stood in front of him, wrapping my arms around his waist.

"Thank you, for this."

He glanced up from the letter into my eyes. "I didn't do anything."

"You believed in me when I couldn't believe in myself. You gave me…. bulletins at church…lunches and dinners…you've given me everything. More than I've deserved."

He dropped the letter onto my desk and put his arms around me. "I just love you."

I was able to murmur "I love you too" right before we kissed.

The best thing about kissing Eric was that it just kept getting better and better. Was it because there were no flaws in our relationship, or was it because the engagement ring on my left hand said we were committed to overcoming any flaws we found? It didn't really matter. We had plenty of time to figure it out.

Isn't it funny how God answers prayers? I'd prayed for a friend who would live nearby, speak English, and would make the coming year more fun than the previous one had been. I knew what I wanted, but God knew what I needed. Left to my own devices, I would have walked right past love. I had needed the help of a friend to find it. And God knew the friend I needed was Eric.

**Aoyama Cemetery**—Located in the Minato ward, this cemetery is Japan's first municipal cemetery.

**Arisugawa Park**—Located in Minato ward in the Hiroo district, the park is named after Prince Taruhito Shinno Arisugawa and hosts the central branch of the Tokyo Metropolitan Library.

**Asahi Shimbun**—A Japanese English-language daily newspaper published in conjunction with the *International Herald Tribune.*

**Asakusa**—A district in the Taito ward famous for the Senso-ji Temple.

**Azabu-Juban**—A district in the Minato ward where many internationals live.

**Banzai**—A cheer.

**Between Day**—Between Day is celebrated on May 4 as a national holiday between Constitution Day and Children's Day. In 2007 it was officially dubbed Greenery Day.

**Children's Day**—Celebrated on May 5, Children's Day signals the official end of Golden Week.

**CODEL**—Congressional delegation.

**Constitution Day**—Constitution Day is celebrated on May 3.

**Daruma**—A wishing doll.

**Domo arigatoo**—"Thank you very much."

**Dori**—Avenue, boulevard.

**Fuki-nagashi**—Streamer.

**Gaijin**—Foreigner.

**Geisha**—A Japanese entertainer professionally trained in dance, music, singing, and conversation.

**Genkan**—A place inside a front door in which to set your shoes before stepping into the house/establishment. This is where outside shoes get exchanged for inside slippers.

**Ginza**—A district with upscale department stores located in Chuo ward.

**Gokiburi**—Cockroach.

**Golden Week**—A period at the end of April and the beginning of May in which there are five national holidays.

**Hai**—"Yes."

**Haiku**—A 17-syllable Japanese poem written in unrhymed verse with five syllables in the first line, seven in the second, and five in the third. Traditionally, the themes revolve around nature.

**Hanami**—Cherry tree blossom viewing.

**Higashi**—East.

**Hiroo**—A district in Minato ward where many internationals live.

**Hokkaido**—The largest prefecture in Japan, Hokkaido is located north of the main island of Honshu and famous for the annual Sapporo Snow Festival.

**Joya-no kane**—New Year's Eve ringing of temple bells.

**Kaika**—Opening of the first cherry flower tree.

**Kakigoori**—Shaved ice.

**Kamakura**—Capital city of the Kamakura shogunate and home to many temples and shrines, located in Kanagawa Prefecture on the Sagami Sea, 25 miles SW of Tokyo.

**Kami**—Objects of worship in the Shinto religion.

**Koban**—A police station.

**Koi**—Carp.

**Kyoto**—The capital city of Kyoto Prefecture and former imperial city, home of 2000 temples and shrines.

**Mankai**—The peak flowering time for cherry tree blossoms.

**Mikan**—A tangerine or clementine-like orange.

**Mochi**—Rice cake.

**Nangajo**—A New Year's card.

**Nikko**—Located in Tochigi Prefecture 87 miles north of Tokyo.

**Nishi**—West.

**Noren**—A partial curtain that is hung from the top of a door frame. If it's long enough, it will have a slit through which a person can push away the sides in order to pass.

**Ochanomizu**—A district located in the Chiyoda ward known for its concentration of musical instrument vendors.

**Okonomiyaki**—A Japanese pancake made from a batter of flour, eggs, water or stock, and cabbage to which is added a variety of other ingredients.

**Omotesando**—A shopping district located in Shibuya ward.

**Onigiri**—A rice ball wrapped in seaweed.

**Onsen**—A hot spring spa.

**O-toshidama**—A New Year's present.

**Roppongi**—A district in Minato ward famous for its nightclubs.

**Sakura**—Cherry tree, cherry tree blossom.

**Sakura zensen**—The cherry tree blossom's front.

**Shimenawa**—A sacred straw rope that keeps away evil spirits and delineates holy spaces or objects from the everyday.

**Shinkansen**—A high-speed bullet train.

**Shoji**—A room divider or door made with *washi* paper and a wooden frame.

**Showa Day**—The official start to Golden Week, Showa Day is celebrated on April 29 to commemorate the Showa period and to contemplate the country's future.

**Soba**—Noodles made from buckwheat flour.

**Sumimasen**—"Please," "I'm sorry," "Forgive me."

**Sumo**—Japanese-style wrestling.

**Tatami**—Woven straw mats traditionally used as flooring.

**Teppanyaki**—A hibachi-style of cuisine.

**Torii**—A Shinto temple gate.

**Toshikoshi**—Long soba noodles eaten on New Year's Eve.

**Udon**—Thick noodles made from wheat flour.

**Ya-garuma**—Wheel-like decoration which sits atop a string of carp kites.

**Yakisoba**—Stir-fried noodles usually mixed with bits of pork and vegetables and garnished with pickled ginger.

**Yokosuka**—United States Naval Base located south of Tokyo in Kanagawa Prefecture on Tokyo Bay.

**Yokota**—United States Air Base located in Fussa City west of Tokyo.

**Yokozuna**—A grand champion sumo wrestler.

**Yukata**—A cotton summer-weight kimono.

## *About the Author*

Siri Mitchell graduated from the University of Washington with a business degree and has worked in all levels of government. As a military spouse, she has lived all over the world, including Paris and Tokyo. With her family, Siri enjoys observing and learning from different cultures. She is fluent in French and is currently mastering the skill of sushi making.

If you are interested in contacting Siri, please check out her website at sirimitchell.com.

HARVEST HOUSE
PUBLISHERS

## What if God has more planned for your life than you do?

Jackie Harrison is a civilian who loves her job at the U.S. Air Force Academy. That is, until she is forced to divide her office into cubicles and share the space with a new history instructor, Lt. Col. Joseph Gallagher. A charmer in a flight suit, Joe wants to explore both Colorado and a growing relationship with his new cubicle mate. The office was bad enough, but Jackie's beside herself when Joe shows up in her home and church, even turning her grandmother's weekly bridge game into poker night!

Jackie goes online to vent, but she eventually finds herself admitting her conflicted feelings about this office neighbor who drives her crazy and makes her heart flutter. But when her blog—The Cubicle Next Door—is featured on TV, everyone begins to read it, including Joe. Will he figure out the anonymous confessions and frustrations are written about him? And how will Jackie ever express her heart offline?

*This tale of limited work space, hidden identity, and cyber confessions is for anyone who has ever longed to be themselves and to find a life beyond cubicle walls.*

HARVEST HOUSE
PUBLISHERS